'One of the most exciting writers to have emerged in Britain for years'   Ian Rankin

'Like all the best crime writers, Mina can make melodramatic events seem credible because her characterisations and settings are so authentic: if she described Alex sprouting wings and flying to Pluto she would make it plausible. There are probably now as many crime writers in Scotland as criminals, but Mina may be the pick of the bunch'   *Daily Telegraph*

'Confirms Mina's place in the premier division ... atmospheric, intense and full of the disturbing flavour of inner-city lowlife'   *Guardian*

'Denise Mina is set to carve a niche for herself as the Crown Princess of Crime'   Val McDermid, *Daily Express*

'This book has passages so powerful that you have to pause in reading it. I'm not ashamed to admit I cried ... Writers like Mina are breaking the mould'   *Scotland on Sunday*

'Funny, raw, compassionate, often brutal ... romps its way to a satisfying conclusion'   *Independent*

'Suffused with telling social commentary and wry humour, while exposing the hypocrisy and passive racism at the heart of modern, intercultural Scotland'   *Times Literary Supplement*

'The plot is unrolled artfully. The writing is lucid, and the minor characters breathe with an almost Dickensian life'

Sunday Times

Denise Mina is the author of nine critically acclaimed novels including *Garnethill*, which won the John Creasey Memorial Prize for best first crime novel. Passionate about all aspects of the genre, she also writes short stories, graphic novels, and is a regular contributor to both TV and radio. Denise lives in Glasgow with her husband and two children. Find out more at www.denisemina.co.uk.

By Denise Mina

Garnethill
Exile
Resolution
Sanctum
The Field of Blood
The Dead Hour
The Last Breath
Still Midnight
The End of the Wasp Season

THE LAST BREATH

Denise Mina

An Orion paperback

First published in Great Britain in 2007
by Bantam Press,
a division of Transworld Publishers
This paperback edition published in 2012
by Orion Books Ltd,
Orion House, 5 Upper St Martin's Lane,
London WC2H 9EA

An Hachette UK company

1 3 5 7 9 10 8 6 4 2

A CIP catalogue record for this book
is available from the British Library.

ISBN 978-1-4091-3526-5

Typeset by Input Data Services Ltd, Bridgwater, Somerset

Printed and bound by CPI Group (UK) Ltd,
Croydon, CR0 4YY

The Orion Publishing Group's policy is to use papers
that are natural, renewable and recyclable products and
made from wood grown in sustainable forests. The logging
and manufacturing processes are expected to conform to
the environmental regulations of the country of origin.

www.orionbooks.co.uk

For Jill and Alan,
Chris and Adrienne,
and, of course, Jonah

Acknowledgements

Many thanks to everyone who has helped me finish this book: to Edith, Marie and Monica for all their help and support, to Odie and Ferg for style tips and keeping me up to date with regurg-chic, to the Consies for the usual, and to Louise, Amy and Sam. Most of all, thanks to Selina Walker, who's a bit of a genius and whose talent and sense of the rhythm of a story always leave me slightly stunned.

Rachel, Henry and Reagan: thank you for my house.

Ellie, Janey, Liza R., Karen D., Jules, Alison K., Becci, Chris C., Benny and Lorraine: I know where you live and you're for it.

And Stevo: I *am* being nice to your ornaments.

I

Naked

1990

Terry Hewitt had never been as afraid as he was now. It was being naked that terrified him. He was stripped of all identifying marks, untraceable, ready for his grave.

Terry had been arrested in Chile, seen a woman necklaced in Soweto, stood on the edge of a riot in Port-au-Prince, but here, lying naked in a shuddering car boot, heading into the dark outskirts of Glasgow, he was paralysed with fear.

Whimpering, his knees tight against his chin, he was aware of how hopelessly exposed he was. He couldn't even cup himself: his hands were bound behind his back, his wrists swelling around the tight binding. The plastic sheet beneath him was scalding his skin. A rough sacking hood over his head restricted his breathing and tiny fibres found their way to the moist back of his throat, making him gag.

The muscles on his neck hurt from the throttle hold that had made him pass out; his eyes ached where blood vessels had burst.

The attack had come from behind as he stood alone and half drunk on his front step.

It had been a good night until then: the celebration of a book deal. The advance from the publisher hardly covered his and Kevin's expenses but a big book of glossy photos and text was expensive to produce. It was Kevin Hatcher's suggestion to cash the entire two hundred cheque and take it to the casino and they had worn their least crumpled suits, worried that they might not be smart enough to get in.

In the event they were overdressed. It was a Thursday night so the other gamblers were serious players wearing minimum swank to get through the door, scuffed leather shoes, jackets that had seen better days. A couple of Chinese women wore faded silk jackets and sat stone-faced, uplit from the tables, their eyes fixed on the dealer's hands at all times, making swift plays. No one celebrated a win with a grin and a cheer the way Kevin and Terry did. Real players met a win with an anxious gesture, a straightening of their chip stack, eyes searching for the next move.

Terry and Kevin were obvious tourists. Terry drank whisky and Coke, Kevin sipped his lemonade. They lost for a while and then showed their lack of courage by stopping after a big win. They were four quid up on the two hundred. They bought a dried-out Havana cigar from the bar, smoked it between them and stayed on, watching the serious players concentrate on the turn of the numbers, willing fate to favour them.

Lying in the boot, Terry now remembered the sounds most vividly: standing shoulder to shoulder with Kevin as the dealers swept chinking piles of chips into black velvet holes, unblinking players clacking their fresh hopes on the baize, the rattling turn of the wheel, the steady rhythm of loss.

Kevin had had several books published already but it was to be Terry's first, the first tangible result he would have of his years of work. It would be something to put on the bookcase, a spine to finger when his confidence and commitment were low, better than a box of yellowing newspaper clippings.

The warm camaraderie of the night had clung to Terry as he stood on the doorstep to his close, swaying slightly and fitting the key. The only warning that anything was amiss was a smell, an unlikely breath, stale, smoky, brushing his left ear. Then the elbow suddenly tight around his neck, pressing on his carotid artery. White bursts of light flashed in his eyes in the seconds it took for him to pass out.

When he came to he was in the boot, bewildered as to who had kidnapped him or why. The first thing he thought of was Kevin – maybe Kevin was playing a mad joke – but Kevin would never, ever have taken Terry's clothes off. Being naked meant it was serious.

Looking for a motive for the attack, he ran through the casino night: he didn't have the money, Kevin had the money. Even if Terry'd had the cash the guy had a car, a big car judging from the size of the boot, and two hundred quid wasn't enough to kill for. He trawled his past for clues. In the last two years he had been in Angola, Liberia, Lebanon, New York, Glasgow. But he was a seasoned journalist, an observer, never participating or intervening, however much he wanted to. No conflict would be changed by taking him out.

But someone was going to take him out. And no one was coming to help him.

Terry remembered a fifteen-year-old prisoner of war, blinking at the scorching midday Angolan sun, a boy with navy-blue skin, his pale brown eyes heavy with terror, exhausted. He had trailed passively along the dusty forest road towards his execution, saving his killers the trouble of cleaning his body from an inconvenient floor. Terry watched him kneel before a gun barrel, eyes darting around behind his executioner, looking for an intervention in the second the bullet left the barrel. Terry had interviewed Holocaust survivors, heard how they had hoped in the cattle trucks, knew they were headed for the death camps but hoped they weren't and so waited.

Assassins depend on that hope, he knew that. Hope was the assassin's accomplice.

He wasn't going to trail down a dusty forest road and kneel passively before a gun barrel. He would forgo hope, face the truth and formulate a plan, find a moment he could exploit.

He took three deep breaths, holding them in to slow his heart rate.

There was no talking in the cabin of the car and no radio or tape was playing. It had to be one man, just the driver who had throttled him. Let it be one man.

He rehearsed the end of the journey: car stops, the lone captor opens the boot and makes Terry climb out, shuts the boot – an open boot on an abandoned car would attract curiosity, might look as if it had broken down and needed help – and leads Terry to where he wants the body to be found. And then the shot.

Terry felt the press at his temple, an indent from the bullet tip, heard the drop of his body to the ground, saw a puff of dry red African dust rise over him. He forced himself to breathe in again, slowing his pulse.

Shutting the boot: that was the moment. It was the only point when his captor's attention would be deflected. If Terry was on his feet he could shuffle backwards, away from the car, so the man would have to move in front of him to reach around to the boot hood. Then, with a bit of distance, Terry could throw his weight against the man's back, shove him or knock him over, land on him, try to really hurt him. He wouldn't be expecting resistance if Terry acted passive, if he cried and tried to bargain.

He thought his way through the graceless climb out on to the ground, felt the cold road beneath his bare feet, the night air on his clammy, damp skin. He wiggled his hips, rehearsing the backwards stagger; he'd act as if he was unsteady from the journey.

Beneath him, the car took a gentle turn on to a new road surface, and the noise from the wheels changed to a crunch. Tarmac, soft from the warm day, with small stones pressed in. They were coming to the end of the journey.

Getting ready, Terry remembered why he wanted to live and immediately saw Paddy Meehan's face. She was luminous, touching her fingertips to her long neck, flushing at a compliment. Since they had known each other, from when they were both in their late teens right up until now, Paddy had been an innocent. She had no idea how beautiful she was. And she was fearless, didn't know all the things there were in the world to be afraid of, all the things he'd seen. Hunger and anger and civil war had passed her by. She worried about her mum and her sisters, fought with her brothers, held a small family together at the expense of everything in her life because she didn't know she could do otherwise. If Terry drifted through the world, belonging nowhere, Paddy was tethered to her small place by connections as deep as her arteries.

He was sliding slowly to the back of the car, the rough road surface articulated through the metal: the car was slowing down. The moment of opening the boot. Three steps at most. No more. Act frightened, cry.

His ear was pressed to the floor and he heard the roar of his own hot blood. He began to sweat.

The car drew softly to the side of the road and stopped. The engine cut out. Through the quiet night Terry heard a whisper of breeze skim the bonnet, the chuckle of a burn.

A ditch. There would be a ditch nearby if there was a burn. That was where he was meant to die.

The driver's door clicked open. A foot hit the gravel at the side of the road, a pause, and then another. He was stiff, perhaps from driving; perhaps he was old. It was good anyway.

Footsteps down the side of the car, not slow but not in a hurry. He might be reluctant, more likely just tired. Feet scrunched into place behind the boot.

Keys chinking, one selected and the scratch of metal into metal. The mechanism clicked.

The boot sprang open, blue-white moonlight filtered through the weave of the sacking to flood Terry's eyes, making him shut them tight. He forced himself to open them again and took a deep breath, feeling the eyes of his captor on his bare back. Act passive.

A cold clammy hand grabbed his upper arm, tugging at him to roll over.

'Look, I'm Terry Hewitt. You've got the wrong man. I'm a journalist.'

'Out.'

Terry curled tighter over his knees. 'Please, for the love of God . . .' He was glad his face was covered: he was never a good liar. 'Don't kill me. You can't. I'm a journalist, for Christ's sake.'

The cold muzzle of a pistol pressed into his neck. 'Get the feck out.'

He sat up unsteadily, banging his head on the inside of the boot, the car swaying slightly beneath his weight. 'Please, please don't do this. My mother . . . she's very old.'

Gun still tight against his jugular, his captor leaned into his face. Terry could smell the breath, still smoky but fresh now, not stale as it had been outside his front door. 'Your mammy and daddy died ten years ago. Get out.'

6

'You know me?'

No answer.

'How do you know me?'

The pistol pressed tighter against the soft skin on his neck. 'Out.'

Disconcerted, Terry shuffled his naked bum around the boot until he was facing out and dropped his feet over the edge to the ground.

'Hurry.'

'Sorry.' Terry sniffed his dry nose. 'I'm sorry. Whatever I've done, I'm sorry.'

'Out.'

Terry kept his face to the man. He knew it was harder to kill someone if they were facing you, breathing on you. Even the most hardened assassin asked his victims to turn away.

One bare foot found the rough stones, then the other and he stood up. Giving a whimper for cover, he staggered, caught his weight, shuffled a step. He was a foot and a half away from the car, he thought, far enough to use his weight against the man's back.

The pistol pressed a kiss into his neck and left.

Gladness and hope flared in his chest. Terry took a deep breath, adrenalin pulsing through him, fingers tingling with excitement. He listened for the shift of the feet, for the step to close the boot.

He didn't feel the muzzle on his temple because it wasn't touching him. He didn't hear the cold metal crack of the pistol shot as it ripped the thick night air and echoed across muddy fields.

Sharp black gravel scattered where his body fell.

The man looked down, saw the eager rush of blood pool under the sacking, watched it seep into the soil.

Judging him dead, he put a foot on Terry's hip and

pushed, rolling the naked body into the ditch by the side of the road.

Terry's corpse splashed into the trickling stream. One meaty arm flailed out to the side, the moonlight catching a silver stretch mark underneath. Fingers flexed, twitched into a loose fist, then flowered gracefully open.

His killer reached for his packet of cigarettes, thought better of it and dropped his hand to his side. He was tired.

The warm summer breeze tickled the tips of the grass on the verge. In the dark field beyond, a small brown bird rose screaming from the ground, circled and flew away towards the yellow lights of a cottage on the distant hillside.

Terry's corpse relaxed in the watery ditch. For the briefest of moments a white thigh dammed the stream, pooling it into a miniature lake, until it found a path across his groin, over his hip and continued its passage to the sea.

Terry Hewitt's corpse began the long melt back into the earth, and the world went on.

2

Safe Home

Paddy took a crouching step from her armchair to the television, pressed the button for STV and sat back down. The adverts were still on. Dub's long skinny body was draped across the length of the settee and he smiled a slow, warm grin.

'This is the best point of the entire fucking week for me. The delicious moment just before the music starts and the half-hour car crash begins.' He slid his hand under his T-shirt, lazily scratching the skin on his belly. She pretended not to look at his flat stomach and the soft cushion of his pectorals. She was having to do that a lot.

'It's getting worse, isn't it?' she said to the TV.

'No.' Dub raised a finger to correct her. It's getting *much* worse.'

They grinned in unison at the screen as the theme tune started, high-pitched, frantic, followed by the flat titles for *George H Burns's Saturday Night Old Time Variety Show.* The graphics were a rip-off of *Monty Python's Flying Circus* but still they were the most original thing about the programme.

A knock on the front door startled them. Dub sat up and looked out into the hall. 'That's not him, is it?'

'Doubt it,' said Paddy, acting casual as she got up. 'Don't turn over though, in case it is.'

She pretended not to care whether it was George Burns, but when she was alone in the big hall she straightened her pyjamas and fluffed her hair up at the sides. She opened the door.

The man in the close was young, fresh-faced behind his John Lennon glasses. His hair was pulled straight back into a ponytail at the nape of his neck, loose, thick. The notepad and poised pen were the real clues.

'Hi, sorry to bother you, I'm Steven Curren—'

Conscious of the loud paint job and messy boxes in the hall, Paddy almost shut the door so they were talking through a two-inch gap. This would be the first of a hundred door stops. She'd better get used to it. 'Who are ye with?'

'*Sunday Mail*,' he said, a little proud. 'When's Callum Ogilvy getting out? Is he coming to stay with you?'

His accent was soft and rounded. Edinburgh or England, Paddy thought, maybe Scottish but educated in England.

'Son,' she whispered for the sake of the neighbours, 'fuck off away from my door.'

'Come on, Miss Meehan, you must know when he's getting released. Where's he staying when he gets out? Is Driver Sean going to pick him up? Is he staying with him?'

He had a grasp of the basic facts but nothing he couldn't have found in old clippings or picked up from office gossip. She waited for him to hit her with something else but he didn't.

'Is that it?'

He shrugged. 'Um, yeah.'

'This is a bullshit door stop,' she said. 'You've got nothing to go on. Do the *Mail* even know you're here?'

'McVie,' he explained, eyes dipping in shame. 'He said I have to try.'

'McVie sent you to my door on a Saturday night?'

'He said to follow up the leads.'

She felt for him. A more practised journalist could have challenged her or made up some fact to goad her into talking. Her own door-stop method had always been to wait until a few journalists had rung the bell and been thrown off the step. Then she'd open her eyes wide and pretend to be a rookie, forced to come here by an evil editor. She'd ask the householder permission to wait on the step for a little while, just so that her editor couldn't sack her. Often they'd side with her against the paper and invite her in. Curren, by contrast, had started combative and then had nothing to back it up. He'd get his face kicked in doing that in Glasgow.

'You're new at this, aren't you?'

'Yeah.' He looked excited.

'New to Glasgow?'

He brightened. 'Been here a week. Just finished my training. "Greatest newspaper city in the world".'

Combative and then suddenly soft; it was the worst possible combination to use when prying into the affairs of very upset people.

'Maybe you should try being more aggressive,' she said, imagining him nursing a black eye in the *Mail* newsroom while explaining where he got the idea from to guffawing colleagues. 'When you get to a door try to push it open, swear at them, do something that'll make them think you're in charge. No one's going to buckle under gentle quizzing.'

Curren nodded earnestly. 'Really?'

'Yeah, Glaswegians really respond to that kind of firm hand.'

Curren hummed at his feet 'OK.' He took a deep breath, steeled himself and demanded, 'When's Ogilvy getting out?'

'Better. Definitely better.'

Confusion flickered on his face and Paddy felt a little bit guilty. In the yellow light of the close he looked young and embarrassed and fed up, while she, content and pyjamaed, still had the taste of oaty biscuits bright in her mouth.

She gave him permission to do what he'd do anyway. 'Listen, just go back and tell your editor I'm a total bitch and you tried really hard.'

Resentment flashed behind his glasses. 'I'll tell McVie he's a fat poof.'

She tutted. Brutal insults were the custom of their profession, but she didn't like McVie's homosexuality used as a slur. 'Nah, don't say that to him, he might get a bit, you know ...' she searched for the word, '... stabby.'

He grinned. Nice teeth. '*Stabby?* Is that an intransitive verb? Only in Glasgow ...'

'Adjective.' She'd never heard of that kind of verb. Even tea boys had degrees these days. 'Well, fuck off anyway.' She shut the door, felt a pang of guilt at her mis-advice and called through the wood, 'Safe home.'

'Thanks,' he answered, his voice muffled. 'By the way, I saw your Misty column about dope. Brilliant.'

Paddy felt vaguely ashamed. She had stolen the argument that no one started a fight in a bar because they'd smoked pot, but that alcohol provided so much tax revenue it couldn't be outlawed.

'Thanks,' she said to the door. 'It was Bill Hicks's line actually. I took it and didn't give him an acknowledgement.'

'Good for you,' replied the door. The kid would go far.

She listened as his foot dropped to the first step, followed the echo of his trail as he walked down two flights and left the close. The outside door slammed behind him.

Lucky her. The biggest crime story in the last twenty years hadn't so much landed in her lap as grown up under her feet. Callum Ogilvy and another small boy had been found guilty of the brutal murder of a toddler nine years ago. At the same time Paddy, a hungry young reporter, was engaged to Callum's cousin, Sean. It was because of Paddy's investigation that the men who goaded the boys to do it were found and charged. Callum and James were done for conspiracy instead of murder and it carried a shorter sentence. Even she didn't know if it was a good idea to release them, but there was no legal basis on which to hold them any longer.

She hadn't met Callum since he went to prison. She knew very little about him, other than the sanitized snippets Sean passed on from his prison visits and the occasional articles about his life there. Sean wanted her to write Callum's big interview when he got out. Working in newspapers for the past six years, he was savvy enough to know that Callum would be hunted down and eventually caught, probably by an unsympathetic journalist who'd print a picture and ruin what little anonymity he had. Most journalists would have bitten Sean's hand off for the opportunity but Paddy had her doubts about writing it: she couldn't guarantee a sympathetic story, and anyway, Callum didn't want to talk to anyone.

She loitered in the hall, looking down at the boxes of Dub's records and a cardboard rack of her work clothes. Unpacking had ground to a halt a month ago and now they only noticed the boxes when they saw them from an unusual angle.

The ceilings were high in the flat. The early Victorians took tenements seriously, built them on a grand scale with servants' quarters and drawing rooms that could accommodate dance parties, and Lansdowne Crescent was one of the oldest tenements in the West End of Glasgow.

It was a student flat before Paddy bought it: the hall was still purple with canary-yellow trim, the detailing on the magnificent cornicing obscured under a century and a half of pasty emulsion. The three bedrooms were painted in colours that would exacerbate a hangover and the kitchen ceiling was so nicotine-stained that it was hard to tell whether it had been painted white or kipper-yellow.

At twenty-seven, this was her first home away from her family and she was still gliding around it like a triumphant child in a longed-for Wendy house.

Back in the living room Dub smirked up at her. Paddy could tell by the crumbs on his T-shirt front that he'd stolen some of her biscuits.

'Who was it?'

'A wee journalist from the *Mail*. Asking about Callum Ogilvy. How's the show this week?'

'Oh, bliss, it's even worse.'

'Can't be.'

They watched as George H. Burns demanded a welcoming round of applause from the audience, his eyes flashing angry as he backed offstage to the wings. The curtain rose on a sweating ventriloquist with a cow-puppet sitting upright on his knee, its impertinent pink udders quivering in the spotlight.

The Saturday Night Old Time Variety Show was arse-clenchingly poor. George H. Burns's compèring style revolved around insulting the audience. He guessed where they were from, told jokes about skinflints from Aberdeen and halfwits from Dundee. His material was obvious, the intervening acts mediocre, the musicians plodding.

'Even the curtains look tired,' said Dub.

The viewing figures were spectacular: every single week the numbers halved. But it wasn't really funny. If Burns's career took a nosedive he'd stop giving Paddy money, even sporadically, and she was stretched tight enough as it was.

Dub had been George's manager when the TV company

approached them and offered the show. He advised Burns not to host it on the grounds that it would be absolutely fucking shit. Burns, greedy and headstrong, sacked the guy who'd brought him to the brink of stardom and replaced him with a manager who wore shiny suits and couldn't talk to a woman without staring at her tits. Now even he knew the show was crap. He was angry, blaming the producer, the writers, the quality of the acts, but the flaw was in the concept: variety theatre needed revival because it was dying, and it was dying because it was patchy and dull. Worse for George, going mainstream had alienated all his comrades on the alternative comedy circuit. Far from being alternative, the circuit was suddenly all there was, apart from guest spots and working men's clubs.

'Mother of God,' muttered Paddy, dropping into her chair. 'Where are they finding these people? Backstage must be like the bus to Lourdes.'

'They're all actual performers. Dinosaurs. Actually, minisaurs. Baby saurs.' He lay there, grinning, his chin folded into his neck, the sole pocket of fat on his entire six-foot-two frame. She'd been flat-sharing with him for two months and saw how much he ate. She'd always hoped that thin people were lying, that they didn't eat giant meals and keep their figures just the same, but Dub ate peanut butter sandwiches before his dinner, snacked on entire packets of biscuits and was still rake-thin. Paddy felt the hefty roll of fat on her middle bulge as she sat down. It was just unfair.

A slow knock echoed out from the deep hall. Paddy sighed as she stood up again. 'Tell him to get lost,' Dub said.

But it didn't sound the same, didn't sound like a journalist's jaunty, faux-friendly beat. 'I've told him to fuck off.' She brushed her hands clean on her pyjama trousers. 'I'm just after telling him that.'

As she stepped back over the boxes the knock was still going, a rhythmic, steady tap on wood, slow and grave. Paddy's heart jolted a warning.

Her hand hesitated on the handle. It could be a lost drunk who'd wandered up the close, or a journalist from a serious paper looking for news of Callum Ogilvy's release date. Or George Burns on a downer. Or Terry fucking Hewitt. God, not Terry, please.

She slipped the safety chain on noisily, hoping it sounded more substantial than it was, and opened the door an inch.

Two unfamiliar police officers, a man and a woman, stood shoulder to shoulder, wearing full uniform and looking grimly back at her.

Paddy slammed the door shut in their faces.

Alone in the hall, her knee buckled. She had shadowed the police often enough to know what a death knock looked like: two uniformed officers, stony-faced, one of them a woman, turning up at an unexpected hour.

When Paddy was on night shift she'd arrived at the door with them, faked sympathy along with them, never once thinking they would come to her. With them, she kept her face straight during the interview and sniggered at the jokes in the car afterwards, laughing at the clothes and the decor, at the family set-up and undercurrents, dead wives found in a boyfriend's bed, car crashes caused by drink, once a husband found dead in a ladies' changing room at a department store, trying on girdles. They laughed, not because any of it was funny, but because it was sad.

Someone close to her had died. They had died violently, or she would have been called by a hospital, and they had died alone, or a family member would have phoned her. It had to be Mary Ann.

'Dub?' Her voice was high and wavering. 'Could ye come out here a minute?'

Dub took his time. When he appeared he stood in the doorway; he was still looking back at the TV. 'What?'

'Two police. Outside. I think something's happened.'

They looked anxiously at the door, trying to read an answer in the lumpy yellow paint.

Dub came over, standing too close, even jumpier than she was. 'Couldn't be a noise complaint? A mistake? The journalist, the wee guy, was he noisy on the way out?'

Paddy pressed her hand to her mouth.

'It could be Mary Ann.'

'Let them in then.' Dub reached over swiftly, slipped the chain off and pulled the door wide.

The male officer was a big shed of a man, fat and broad, blue shadow on both his chins, his chest still heaving from the effort of lumbering up the stairs. The woman was blonde, hair scraped back so tight it looked as if it had been painted on. She was birdlike: a pointy nose, beady eyes, thin lips. Family Liaison. They always sent out a woman from Family to hold the person's hand when they sobbed.

The policewoman attempted a smile but it withered on her lips and she slipped Paddy's eye. She hadn't done many death knocks, hadn't yet developed the cold skill of looking heartbreak in the face.

'Hello.' The portly officer took charge. 'I'm PC Blane and this is WPC Kilburnie. Are you Paddy Meehan?'

They waited for an answer but Paddy was stiff with fright. She couldn't seem to get the air to the bottom of her lungs.

'I know it's you actually.' He half smiled at Paddy. 'I recognize your face from the newspapers.'

Paddy did what she always did when a fan approached her. She bared her teeth politely and mumbled an irrelevant 'thank you'.

Dub moved in front of her. 'Is it Mary Ann?'

Blane blanked his question, stepping over the threshold

and looking exclusively at Paddy. 'Can we come in?'

She backed away, letting the officers shuffle in, trespassing death into her Wendy house.

Neither of them looked at Dub. Usually he was great at taking charge of a situation. He'd done stand-up for many years and was more than capable of demanding the attention of a nightclub full of drunk people but now, strangely, neither officer would acknowledge him.

'He's my friend,' said Paddy, pointing at him.

Blane and Kilburnie glanced warily at each other. Blane cleared his throat. 'Shall we go through?'

Paddy's footsteps felt spongy and unsteady as she stepped across the boxes and walked the length of the hall. She slowed as she reached the living room, stalling, as if she could prolong the unknowing moment indefinitely, but Blane took her elbow, hurrying and supporting her at the same time.

'Please sit down.' He guided Paddy through the door and over to the sofa. She saw Blane clock George Burns on TV, crouching down at the edge of the stage to talk to a busty woman in the audience.

'Burns,' he muttered dismissively, letting the comment write itself.

Burns had been a policeman before he became a comedian. Every copper in Glasgow had a story about him, usually derogatory – how there were ten guys on every squad funnier than him, how they'd done their training with him and he was a prick then too, anecdotes always delivered with a slightly thrilled smile that they knew someone on telly.

Determined to be spoken to, Dub dropped on to the settee right next to Paddy, reaching for her hand, but Kilburnie managed to squeeze her pointy little self into the space between them.

'Tell me,' said Paddy, taking a deep breath and holding it, bracing herself for the blow.

Kilburnie nodded her head to Dub and widened her eyes. 'Maybe it would be better if we spoke to you on your own.'

'*Tell me.*'

'Well ...' She looked uncomfortable. 'I'm afraid we have some rather bad news, Miss Meehan.'

'What's happened?'

'I'm afraid,' Kilburnie continued with the standard speech she had practised in the car, 'we found a body yesterday, in the countryside, near Port Glasgow ...'

Two fat tears raced down Paddy's cheeks. 'Just say it.'

Kilburnie looked down at her lap, patting her knees with both hands, steeling herself. 'Terry Hewitt is dead. A shot to the head, I'm afraid. We would have come sooner only he didn't have any identification on him and we've only just found his flat and been through his effects ...'

Paddy sat up. 'Terry *Hewitt?*'

Disconcerted, Kilburnie glanced at Blane. 'I'm afraid he's dead. I'm very sorry.'

Dub sat forward. 'Terry Hewitt?'

'Single shot to the head.' Kilburnie gave Blane a worried look. 'He's dead, I'm afraid.'

Dub reached across Kilburnie's lap. 'Paddy? Were you seeing him again?'

'No,' she muttered, 'not since ... before. I haven't seen him since Fort William.'

'Why are you telling her this?'

Kilburnie turned to Dub. 'I'm very sorry.'

'What are you saying sorry to me for?'

Kilburnie looked from Dub to Paddy. 'I'm sorry for talking about this in front of your hubby.'

'Oh.' Dub looked at them both, smiling at the suburban phrasing. 'Oh, no. We're just flatmates. We're friends.'

'I'm not married,' said Paddy. 'Is Mary Ann OK?'

'Who is Mary Ann?' asked Kilburnie.

'My sister. She works in a soup kitchen. She's a nun. When you said it was out in the country I thought she'd been abducted. I thought she'd been raped ...' Paddy clamped her hand over her mouth to stop herself talking.

She knew they'd repeat every word of the interview back at the station. A minor provincial celebrity caught off guard wearing ripped pyjamas. There were a lot of pauses in police work, opportunities for gossip. They'd describe the purple and yellow hall, her non-hubby flatmate, how they were watching Burns's show and Paddy was eating biscuits instead of having dinner. They'd tell people about the rip in her pyjama bottoms.

'The thing is ...' Kilburnie tailed off. 'I'm afraid we need you to identify his body.'

'Why me? There must be someone who's seen him more recently than me. I haven't seen Terry for six months.'

'But you were the next of kin on his passport. We found it in his house. That's how we got this address.'

'He had me down at this address?'

'Yes.'

Dub watched the back and forth, interested now that he knew Mary Ann was safe.

'But we just moved in two months ago.' She looked around the living room, at the orange walls, the sparse furniture, carefully chosen from junk shops and auctions. Terry had never been here; she hadn't thought he knew the address.

'So you're not related?'

'No. Terry's parents died years ago. I don't know if he had anyone else. He was a foreign correspondent, travelled, didn't make many friends. I suppose that's why. I'm not completely surprised, to be honest. He wasn't happy.'

Paddy stood up. It occurred to her that she should get to the *Daily News* and file the story of Terry's suicide. It wasn't a great story but the thought of work calmed her. She felt the steel nib pierce her heart, felt her muscles relax, her blood slow. With a notebook in her hand she could walk through fire and feel nothing.

The woman officer stood up to meet her. 'We need you to come and have a look at him, if you would.'

'Just let me get changed.'

As she passed Blane on her way out of the living room he looked down at her and blurted, 'I love your column. I always agree with it. You write things before I'm even thinking them.'

Paddy bared her teeth politely. 'Thank you,' she said.

3

Regal and Bru

Paddy kept her window down. The warm breeze caressed her face, carrying the high-summer smell of dust and rotting vegetables as she followed the red tail-lights of the police car.

Blane and Kilburnie were in the car ahead, sniggering about her purple hall no doubt, passing tasty morsels back and forth about her and George Burns. Everyone would know what Terry's suicide note said by morning. They'd extrapolate every detail: Terry shot himself because of her, she loved Burns and that's why she was watching his show, she'd painted her hall purple and yellow, Dub was a boy-friend or a beard. Rumours of her lesbianism increased in direct proportion to her success. It was intended to belittle her, but she quite liked the suggestion that she was impreg-nable, literally and metaphorically.

A green traffic light switched to orange as the police car passed beneath it. Paddy slowed unnecessarily, stopping before it changed to red. Out of the empty street, a sudden rush of people crossed the road in front of her. She looked back. They were pouring out of the Ramshorn Kirk, a church she'd never even noticed before this year, converted into a theatre for Glasgow's year as European City of Culture.

For a century Glasgow had been a byword for deprivation and knife-wielding teenage gangs but in the past few years the thick coat of black soot had been sandblasted off the old buildings, revealing pale yellow sandstone that glittered in the sun, or blood-orange stone that clashed with blue skies. International theatre companies and artists had started coming to the city, colonizing unlikely venues, old churches, schools, markets and abandoned sheds, places the locals failed to notice every day. Glaswegians no longer felt as defensive of their home, began to look around with renewed interest, like a partner in a stale marriage finding out that their spouse was a heart-throb abroad.

The lights changed to green but Paddy sat still, watching the pedestrians crossing in front of her. They were young for a theatre crowd, smoking now that they could, chatting animatedly about the piece they had just witnessed.

Some of the men cast admiring glances at her car. It was a big white Volvo saloon, a vanity car, bought to show the world of men she moved among that she was doing well and had the readies to buy a big motor. She didn't like it. It handled like a tank and was too big and boxy to park in the handy little spaces she used to manage in her Ford Fiesta. Parking it anywhere slightly rough was to invite a key along the paintwork.

The crowd began to thin and she let the handbrake off, gently nudging forward. Ahead, the police car pulled out slowly, making sure she stayed with them, as if she couldn't find the city morgue herself.

They drove on, turning down the steep winding High Street, once the spine of the city, now a road through plots of dark wasteland. The seven-storey Tollbooth sat on its little traffic island, all that remained of a medieval prison where witches were hanged and the debtors voted in their own mayor.

Glasgow City Mortuary was an unobtrusive single-storey building on the corner of the High Court. Built in red brick, it had windows on either side of a deep doorway like a punched-in nose. The business of the building was conducted below ground, in the white-tiled cellar.

The squad car pulled up right in front, on a double yellow line, so Paddy followed their lead and drew up behind them. Kilburnie and Blane were waiting for her on the pavement, their mood lighter than it had been before, distant and observing. They had been talking about her, she could smell it on their breath.

The mortuary faced Glasgow Green, an ill-lit expanse of grass cut through by the River Clyde, bordered on one side by the damp highrises in the Gorbals and on the other by the crumbling tenements of the Gallowgate. At night it was populated by roving prostitutes and the drunk men who came to fuck them, or rob them. Shadows routinely rose out of the moist night and tried the door of the mortuary. It was assumed they were attracted by the lights or looking for drugs but no one really knew why they came, banging on the oak or scratching at the windows.

The narrow porch was a tight fit for the three of them. Blane's looming bulk swallowed the light. They heard the entry buzzer fizz as he pressed it again.

'You two do a lot of death knocks?' Paddy used the police term to show them she wasn't just a punter off the street.

'Not that often,' said Blane.

'Well, I'm afraid I'm Family Liaison.' Kilburnie smiled sadly and tipped her head to the side, putting Paddy in her place as the bereaved. 'I have to come here quite often, I'm afraid.'

'You're afraid of everything,' said Paddy quietly.

Blane smirked at his shoes. Tell your pals that, Paddy wanted to say: Meehan cracking jokes at the door of the mortuary, coming to view a corpse.

She'd been avoiding thoughts of Terry all the way into town, filling her head with Pete and decorating the new house and how soon she could get into the office to file the story. No amount of anticipating could make her ready for the sight of a dead body. She knew that from experience.

When her father Con died, the family held the nightly rosary around his open coffin. The grey simulacrum of Con Meehan became just that: not the man, but an impostor wearing her daddy's best suit. She clung to her grief, knowing that it was the very last emotion her dad would ever provoke in her.

It was a terrible death: he was fifty-eight, riddled with tumours, but the physical pain was nothing compared to his anger in those last few ragged months. He died scratching at the clod walls of his grave, tearful, never accepting that his time was up. Everyone in the family made of Con's uncharacteristic anger what they needed to: Trisha, his wife, thought it was because of the way things had gone with Paddy and Caroline, because the boys weren't devout. Caroline put his fury down to his long-term unemployment and a lack of counselling. The boys said it was the medication, Mary Ann said pain. But when Paddy looked into his eyes she saw a great roar of regret. Con was a timid man. He had spent his life avoiding conflict, let everyone through the door before him, waiting in a holding position, and then, suddenly, his time was over.

She gave up trying to get her head around the fact of death. She developed the mental trick of pretending that Con had gone away on a long happy trip, that she would see him again one day and everything would be better, he'd be tumour-free, the regret and all the space between them gone. It was later that she realized her mother used exactly the same mental trick but called the destination heaven.

Blane glanced nervously out at the misty Green and cursed under his breath as he pressed the hissing intercom again. Kilburnie looked at Paddy, blank-faced until her training kicked in: her face softened and she reached supportively for Paddy's arm, retreating when she saw the snarl on her face.

Paddy thought she was coming over too hard. 'Did he leave a note?'

Blane looked puzzled. 'Who?'

'Terry. Did he leave a note saying why?'

Blane's jaw dropped in realization. 'No, no, sorry. He didn't do it to himself.'

Kilburnie stole a pinch of Paddy's elbow. 'He was murdered.'

'You're shitting me?'

'Oh yes, definitely. There were tyre marks at the side of the road but no car around and we haven't found the weapon. He was naked and we never found his clothes. He was murdered.'

'Terry was *naked*?'

Blane nodded. 'Stark, bollock naked.'

She knew it had to be murder: even if the gun wasn't missing, Terry wouldn't want to be found naked. He was a bit pudgy, had some fat around his arse, and was ashamed. He wanted the lights off before he would undress in front of her. It was one of the things she'd liked about him. 'But who'd want to kill Terry Hewitt?'

Blane leaned in confidentially. 'They said it looks like an IRA assassination.'

Paddy reeled on her heels. 'Get fucked!'

He nodded, excited, knowing the implications. '"All the hallmarks". That's what they said.'

'No one'd authorize that in Scotland. We're neutral. And Terry had nothing to do with Ireland.'

'Well,' he said, 'I'm sure they'll tell us in the press statement. They usually do that, don't they?'

Kilburnie leaned back, getting between them, pointedly clearing her throat, reminding Blane of the need for discretion. Chastened, he turned back to the door, his shoulder met by Kilburnie's, forming a wall against Paddy. He pressed the buzzer a third time. 'Well, that's what they told us,' he said, defending himself to Kilburnie.

'It can't be.' Paddy addressed their backs. 'He was a journalist. Even the Americans wouldn't stand for that.'

The intercom crackled: 'Yeah?'

Blane leaned in. 'PCs Blane and Kilburnie from Pitt Street. Expected here for an ID.'

The door buzzed and fell open an inch, letting out a jab of sharp lemon. Paddy had visited the city mortuary several times and the smell didn't get any less alarming. She took a deep breath before stepping into the dark hall.

Blane made sure the door was shut tight behind them.

Inside, the lobby was softly lit. A bleary-eyed security guard sat stiffly at the desk, the appointments book in front of him suspiciously flattened. As Blane and Kilburnie showed him their warrant cards and signed in, Paddy moved to the side and spotted the edge of a pillow on his lap.

Blane smiled at the guard, saying his name twice in the course of a bland hello. Police officers liked to say people's names. Made them feel connected. He introduced Paddy but the security guard didn't react to her name. Not a *Daily News* reader.

Blane gave up trying to chat and nodded Kilburnie and Paddy down the corridor to a set of doors with 'Absolutely No Entry' painted on them. Through the doors, after a long landing, narrow stone steps led down into the bowels of the building and a warren of white-tiled corridors.

Kilburnie turned back to Paddy at the bottom of the stairs. 'About the IRA – that's just a canteen rumour.'

Paddy nodded. 'Understood.'

'It shouldn't go in the paper or anything. Could scare people. Cause friction.'

'I'm sure it'll be fine,' said Paddy vaguely, itching to get to the office now.

'Now, this . . .' Kilburnie pointed down the corridor. 'I'm here to support you. Are you sure you're all right?'

'Fine,' said Paddy sharply.

She saw Kilburnie flinch at her coldness. Paddy could have faked a bit of trauma, but that wasn't supposed to be the point. The incessant attempts to prompt her emotions were getting on her tits.

Ahead of them, sheet-plastic abattoir doors glowed yellow from the light behind them and a radio hummed, muffled by the scratched, leathery material. Kilburnie reached out with both hands and pushed them open. The smell hit Paddy's nose like a spiteful slap. Rancid meat and the afterburn of alcohol. She forced herself to take breaths in and out. She'd made herself dizzy in the mortuary once before by not breathing in enough.

The bizarre tableau they walked in on stopped them dead. Kilburnie gasped, afraid again no doubt.

Standing alone against a wall of glinting stainless steel was an elf dressed in green scrubs, face mask hinged off one ear. Her hands hung by her side, turned towards them, like Jesus welcoming sinners in a painting. The wild brown hair was blunt-cut above her shoulders. She smiled stiffly, eyes open a little too wide. She'd heard them coming down the stairs, probably heard the buzzer and the doors. Her welcoming stance had gone stale.

'Hello.' The odd little woman refreshed her smile. She was young, her skin perfect, her figure unformed, as if she was still waiting for puberty to hit.

Blane frowned. 'John about?'

The Mortuary Elf looked Paddy over, smart in a black wraparound work dress and platform orange-suede trainers. 'He's having a kip in the back.'

All three of them considered the possibility that this tiny woman had risen from the Green, broken in for some sick reason and beaten John to death.

She touched a hand to her chest. 'Aoife McGaffry,' she said, her Northern Irish accent thick and warm. 'I'm the new pathologist.'

Blane smiled. 'Oh, I thought you were a nutter. What are you doing here at this time on a Saturday night?'

Aoife stepped back, welcoming them into the big room. 'We're backed up.'

'Old Graham Wilson had a heart attack a week ago,' Blane explained to Paddy. 'They've been storing everyone they can until the new Path started.'

Paddy had never met Graham Wilson but she'd seen him giving evidence at the High Court a couple of times. He was dishevelled, looked as if he'd just been woken up, wore a crumpled three-piece suit and pince-nez.

'Died on the job,' said Aoife. 'Not "on the job" as in mid-coitus,' she corrected herself, 'but "on the job" here.' She pointed at the floor in front of her. 'Again, not in mid-coitus.'

It was supposed to be a joke but Blane flinched.

Aoife McGaffry winced. Police officers might snigger at the nightie someone was wearing when they were told of a loved one's death, they might make jokes about Head and Shoulders at the scene of car crashes, but, apparently, there were bounds of decency and the suggestion that a colleague had died in the course of a necrophiliac orgy wasn't funny. Paddy liked Aoife immediately.

'I'm Paddy Meehan.' She stepped forward and put out her hand.

Aoife smiled at the outstretched hand. 'You wouldn't thank me for shaking it. It'd take ye a week to get the smell out.' She twisted around to look behind her. 'Tend to go a bit ripe if they're left for a week.'

'I'm here to identify someone . . .'

Behind her Blane barked, 'SMR Ref 2372/90,' reading from his notebook.

Aoife listened, dismissed him with a blink and looked at Paddy again, shedding all her awkwardness now she was in her professional role. 'And is this someone close to you?'

'Not really. A friend. He hadn't anyone else.'

'OK.' She nodded. 'Well, I've been here for two days and haven't had the time to dress anyone up. I don't know what kind of state your friend is in but we can do this two ways: I can tidy him up but that'll take time, or I can just bring you to him. How's your constitution?'

Paddy shrugged. It was shite, actually, but she wanted to get to the office and file the story before the final edition went to press. 'Fair to middling.'

Aoife smiled. 'Beckett,' she said, catching the reference. 'Right, come on now you with me and we'll find your friend.'

The police trailed after them as Aoife led Paddy through a small passageway to a big steel door. A gauge on the wall next to it showed the temperature. Paddy had looked at a body here before, a long time ago, as a favour to an old friend.

'Don't you use the drawers any more?'

'Bloody thing conked out ages ago. Heads need banging together in this place.' Using all her slight weight, Aoife yanked the big door open. A gust of frost and alcohol burst into the corridor. Brutal white strip lights flickered awake in the walk-in fridge, casting inky shadows under the sheeted trolley beds. Inside, the fridge was crowded. Aoife had to wiggle sideways between the beds to make her way to the back of the room.

'What number did ye say?' she called back to them.

Blane looked at his notebook again and repeated it.

She checked a couple of toe tags, muttering 'Here we go' to herself when she found Terry. She looked back across the full fridge and sighed a white cloud. 'Hell. We might need to empty the whole place to get him out.'

There were fifteen, eighteen bodies in the place. It would take ten minutes to wheel all the beds out and then they couldn't very well piss off and leave her with the bodies in the corridor.

'Tell you what, I'll come in,' said Paddy, bracing herself and stepping into the cold. She slid between the shrouded shapes, holding her hands high, trying not to touch anything.

'Me too,' said Kilburnie. Family Liaison. Elbow-holder. Empathy in uniform. She followed Paddy's path through the trolleys, keeping close, until they were gathered on the other side of the bed from Aoife, exhaling smog over the cold white sheet.

Paddy looked down. Terry was under there. A Terry-shaped piece of meat. Naked. Rotting. Suddenly, death wasn't a long holiday. It was real.

Aoife McGaffry sensed her tension. 'Was he a relative of yours?'

'No.' Paddy couldn't stop her eyes from mapping the mountains and valleys of the sheet in front of her. 'No, no. We've just known each other for a long time, that's all.'

It wasn't all. They had known each other for eleven

31

years and she thought about him all the time he was away, wondered after him, imagined his absent opinion of her actions. Terry Hewitt had been her touchstone for nearly a decade. He was a marker of how she was doing, a spur to action, a call for decency. She wished he'd never come back to Glasgow.

Aoife was talking. '... pull the sheet back slowly. You're better just looking at him once the sheet's away and not while it comes off. It's easier to look then. And stand back a wee bit, there.'

Dumbly, Paddy took a step away, her bum banging into the trolley behind her. She started, imagined a dead hand grabbing her arse.

'Don't get freaked out, just step back. It's good to have more in your line of vision than just the deceased. Keep perspective. If it gets too much, look up at me. Ready?'

She had her hands on the top end of the sheet. Paddy stared hard at Aoife's face and nodded.

'Right, here we are now.'

Against orders, Paddy watched as Aoife rolled the sheet back, folding it under Terry's chin as if he was a sleeping child. 'You try to have a wee look now.'

At first all Paddy could see was the mess of it. A black hole the size of a fist was at his temple. A tongue, was that a tongue? Purple, swollen, poking out between the bloody lips. He must have been lying on his side after he was shot because tendrils of blood had dried across his face, a black octopus climbing out of the hole above his ear. She couldn't see Terry in all of that. She stole a look at Aoife's shoulder, braced herself, looked at him again through a puff of white breath.

The first thing she recognized was the BCG scar on his upper arm. She had kissed that, stared at it in the gloomy room in Fort William while Terry talked about San

Salvador, knew every fold of the smooth penny, every overlapping freckle. Then she saw that the nose was Terry's nose. It was his double chin. She saw the hair on the back of his neck: black, coarse, gelled, sticky to the touch. She had run her fingertips around that neck, savoured the softness, scratched and kissed it, run the tip of her tongue through the soft precursor hairs, tasted him. Her mouth filled suddenly with salt water.

'Him. It's him.'

Lightness flooded into the top of her head, making her unsteady. Ordering herself to be brave, she raised her eyes to Aoife but her gaze rolled up past the thick brown hair, rushed up the wall and skidded up to the ceiling into a burning strip light.

She hit the floor before realizing she was going down.

II

The light above her was so harsh that Paddy threw her arm over her face and rolled on to her side to get away from it. Aoife was talking a mile away. 'She's fine. No worries. Yez can go about your business now.'

Paddy heard Blane say something. Or was it Kilburnie? Aoife replied and a door clicked shut somewhere.

Keeping her hands over her face, Paddy sat up. She was on a low bed, a leather daybed, covered in a long strip of paper like a gynaecologist's examination couch. She had passed out right in front of policemen while she was wearing a dress. Blane and Kilburnie would have a story to tell now: Burns on the telly, purple hall and herself on the floor, legs akimbo, washday-grey knickers on full show. She cursed to herself and swung her legs over the side of the bed, forcing her eyes open.

They must have carried her in here. It was a small office,

cut off from the rest of the mortuary by wood and glass partitions. Grey box files and papers were stacked on every surface. The cheap chipboard desk had a big white computer sitting on it, the screen blinking a green prompt.

Aoife was watching her from a swivel chair, smoking a cigarette she didn't look old enough to buy.

'Oh, sorry, I'm sorry,' Paddy apologized over and over, trying to think of something else to say. 'I'll go, I'm sorry.' She stood up uncertainly and looked around. 'Where's my coat?'

'Ye haven't a coat.'

'Haven't I?'

'Are ye pregnant or anything?'

Paddy stroked the round of her stomach defensively.

'I didn't mean ... Ye don't look it or anything.' Aoife waved her cigarette up and down Paddy's body. 'Just in case there's something more than shock going on. I'm a doctor, I'm supposed to ask stuff like that.'

Paddy remembered the harrowing moments before she fainted. She covered her face with her hands and groaned Terry's name.

'Your friend,' said Aoife simply.

Paddy looked up. 'Friend.' The word seemed infinitely tender. She felt like crying. 'Who'd shoot him in the head? He was a good guy.' She remembered the hotel room in Fort William. 'Good-ish. A good enough guy.'

Aoife considered her cigarette. 'While you were out of it the police said he'd been shot by the Provos.'

'Terry was nothing to do with the Troubles. He wasn't even interested in that.'

Aoife snorted bitterly and crossed her legs. 'Doesn't take much to cross them bastards. I trained in Belfast. Seen some right messes. Most of them're just thugs with a political justification. Both sides. Wankers.'

34

She sounded like the child she resembled: small, scato-logical, odd. Her ponytail had come undone at the side, probably from yanking Paddy's body off the floor. Her hair was so wiry each strand looked thick and coarse as a horse's tail.

'By God, ye've some head of hair on ye,' said Paddy, letting her Irish phrasing show now they were alone.

Aoife looked at her, sternly at first. Her face broke into a laugh. Paddy laughed along with her.

Aoife pointed to the door. 'Hey, that fat fella says you're a famous person.'

'Aye.' Paddy rubbed her face roughly. 'Couldn't tell ye which one at the minute.'

'Maybe you're Sean Connery.'

'That'd be a turn-up, wouldn't it?' smiled Paddy. 'And me a mother.'

They laughed together again, softly this time. Aoife pointed at her with the tip of her cigarette. 'I'll tell ye this: the Provos never done for your pal.'

'How do you know?'

'Not how they do it. They shoot through the mouth or the back of the head, usually behind the ear, not through the temple. Doing that ye might just shoot someone's eyes off and leave them alive to make a statement.'

'Why do they think it was the Provos then?'

'I suppose assassination by a single shot is pretty rare outside Northern Ireland.'

One of Aoife's lids gave a telltale twitch. She'd given herself away as a Protestant. A Catholic would call the province 'the North of Ireland'. And she'd know where Paddy's own sympathies lay because of her name.

Paddy leaned over and touched her knee. 'Hey, I don't care what you call it.' Aoife smiled weakly. 'You've a strange name though, for an orange bastard.'

35

'Aye. Intermarriage. My da chose the name I think he did it to upset her – they weren't getting on by then anyway.'

'Quick turnaround?'

'Aye, but they stayed together for the sake of the wee one, bless 'em.' She smiled sarcastically.

'I'm sorry.'

'Aye, well.' Aoife took a deep draw on her cigarette. 'D'you and your husband get on?'

'I'm not married.' Paddy stood up and straightened her skirt.

Aoife blinked. 'But ye *were* married?'

Paddy shook her head and looked for her bag. She'd already said she had a child; there was no going back.

When men realized she was a single mother they could be sympathetic, or assume she was a desperate slapper and take it as an invitation to chance their arm. Only women were pitying. Paddy was afraid to look at Aoife. She liked her but knew her background, understood the press of convention in an Irish household and how single mothers were talked about.

'How old's your baby?' Aoife's tiny face was a mask of calm but her mouth curled up at one side.

'Five. He'll be six in a few months.' Paddy picked up her handbag from the floor and made for the door. 'He's called Pete.'

'Oh!' exclaimed Aoife, trying to make up for her disapproving twitch. 'That's a lovely name.'

'Named after an old friend,' said Paddy, letting herself out and shutting the door behind her.

III

The *Daily News* office wasn't far from the mortuary. A committed journalist would have run the three blocks to file her exclusive. Whatever the truth of it, Terry's assassination would make a great, fat, scare-mongering story. The press would embrace it because it suggested they were involved in a noble, life-threatening venture, and the Scottish public would follow it to find out if they were really about to be plunged into a war. She could break the story as an anonymous news item, then quash the rumour furiously in her column on Wednesday and still turn out to be right.

But instead of hurrying to the office, Paddy drove numbly around, taking corners that led her away from the office, slowly circling the city centre and heading down towards the river.

The light above the basement door was sharp and hurt her eyes. It was a dark part of town, a warren of warehouses on the south bank of the slow, cold river, in an area that had once been a bustling commercial centre by the docks. A moist cold seemed to hang over it. When Paddy got out of the car the wet chill hit her face and she huddled in her thin dress as she hurried across the road to the door.

Saturdays were always quiet at the soup kitchen. Everyone who worked there had a different theory as to why: on weekends even the homeless were invited to drinking parties; they got too drunk to make it over on Saturdays; takeaway shops gave out free food when they were closing up and you didn't need to stay sober or mouth prayers to get that handout.

Two men in double coats were sitting at a table near the door, the crumbs from jam rolls and empty bowls of soup lying in front of them. One was asleep, the other blinking hard and looking around, bewildered and innocent as an abandoned child. Nearer the counter a few more men sat at tables, eating. Some of them were respectably dressed in old suits, or clean pressed denims. The Talbot Centre must have been giving away clean clothes.

The steel counter was ablaze with strip lights. Behind it, on scrubbed steel tables out of grab-range, sat trays of buttered rolls with clear red jam dribbling out of them. A large tureen of soup, a plastic slow cooker that plugged into the wall, stood on the counter next to a stack of bowls.

Sister Tansy was alone behind the counter, her mouth perpetually a tightly drawn string bag, eyes despising whatever hove into her line of vision. Sister Tansy wore the long white coat the nuns always wore at the kitchen, a cross between a dinner lady and a doctor. She saw Paddy approaching and her shoulders rose in a silent ripple of fury, eyes glued suddenly to the lentil-crusted soup tureen.

When Paddy had said that Sister Tansy was one dry sherry away from committing a massacre, Mary Ann laughed with a self-censoring hand over her mouth.

'Hi, Sister, is Mary Ann about?'

'No.' She took the lid off the soup and stirred, bringing a cloud of floury green to the surface.

'Hm.' Paddy looked at her insistently. 'I need to see her.'

'Ahe, well, ahe, ahe,' she tittered angrily, 'I really don't think that this is the place for—'

'Paddy.'

Mary Ann was standing behind Sister Tansy, side on to Paddy, smiling over her shoulder at her sister. She wore the white dinner-lady coat, her blonde hair pulled back in a hairnet, her cheeks touched fairy pink from the heat in the kitchen.

'Hiya,' Paddy stared across at her sister, calmed by the sight of her.

'OK?'

'Fine.' She managed a weak smile. 'Just wanted to see ye.'

Sister Tansy stepped between them and did her phoney laugh. 'Ahe, ahe, we are quite busy, *actually*.'

38

Paddy tipped to the side to give Mary Ann one more look. She didn't smile or giggle or give her any prompt, but Mary Ann knew exactly what Paddy would be thinking and her face convulsed into a taut mask of sadness, then panic and then nausea, until she covered it with two hands and scuttled away to have a laugh in the toilets.

'You mustn't come here.' Sister Tansy gave the soup a vicious skirl. 'You've been asked before.'

'Sister, the police came to my door tonight and told me that someone close to me had died. I thought it was Mary Ann at first and got a terrible fright. I just wanted to look at her.'

'That is neither here nor there,' she said, her customary response to any appeal for mercy. Sister Tansy would have said that on hearing about Hiroshima. 'You cannot come in—'

'It was a boyfriend. My ex. He was naked.' Badness made her say it and it felt good. She gave in to the urge and went for triple points. 'They think he was murdered by the IRA.'

Sister Tansy was stunned dumb. Paddy turned and walked away, knowing she was being rude and Mary Ann would pay the price.

Outside, she thought how lucky she was to be able to come and see her sister. Nuns, like priests, rarely got to work near their home parish. More usually they were moved away from their family of origin. The Church said it was so that they could concentrate on their vocation but Paddy saw it as a move to depersonalize them, break the bonds with their own people so that their only loyalty would be to the Church. The Brides of Christ had no family but the Church, who also happened to be their employer. Manager *and* boyfriend. An actress could have sued.

She got back in the car and, before she had time to reflect on what she was doing, she was driving down the empty grey motorway, heading towards where Terry's body had been found.

She pulled out of the middle lane when she saw the slip road for Glasgow airport.

The lobby was empty, all the check-in desks shut and unmanned. A blue-uniformed security guard idled, smoking a cigarette. He nodded guiltily as Paddy came through the automatic doors.

'Havin' a smoke,' he said.

Paddy excused him with a smile.

Behind the counter at the empty newsagent's shop a sleepy middle-aged woman in a blue tabard watched, heavy-eyed and accusing, as Paddy wandered between the chocolate bars and displays of crisps.

She didn't want anything to eat, even though she felt hungry. She kept thinking about the ragged hole in Terry Hewitt's head, at the black spider crawling across his face. A jagged breath caught in her throat and she stood staring into the searing white light of the drinks cooler, blinking back urgent tears, wondering what the hell was wrong with her. She'd identified bodies before, seen horrific injuries, facial injuries, and she had been frightened of Terry; she should be glad he wasn't about to hassle her any more. Aware that she was being watched, she picked up a cold can of Irn-Bru and took it to the counter.

The attendant looked expectantly as Paddy glanced behind her at the cigarettes, asked for a packet of Embassy Regal, dropped three quid on the counter and walked away with her cigarettes and drink, the cold metal of the can burning the skin on her hand.

Back in the car park, Paddy locked the doors and sat, holding the cold can of juice tight, focusing on the chilblain pains in her fingertips. Then she started the car and pulled out, reaching a hundred by the time she hit the motorway.

IV

Scottish summer mornings arrive in the middle of the night. Just after three a.m. the big sky began to lighten, the sun lurking below the horizon like a mugger.

The motorway took a turn on the shoulder of a high hill and Paddy found herself looking out over the wide plain of the Clyde Estuary. The tide was out, baring grey, demi-waved sand with strips of mercury winking in the first rays. Small boats keeled sidelong in the soft mud. Two giant granite hills stuck out of the sand, massive and round as marbles, tiny buildings clinging to them.

The first town she hit was Port Glasgow. A concrete council estate was perched on the hill overlooking the water, panda-eyed windows peering out to sea. On the coast side of the road abandoned warehouses were being colonized by dark, quivering bushes bursting out between the bricks. It was a shipbuilding area and had been hit so badly by the '80s recession that instant coffee had become a form of currency: there was no money to be stolen in the area and the jars, which could be shoplifted with ease, had a set value.

Paddy was crying. She didn't know why, she didn't mean to, but her eyes ached and stung, her face burned, tears were dripping off her chin. It was getting so bad she couldn't see properly.

She pulled into an empty car park, turned the headlights off and sat, staring blindly at the steering wheel, crying still, puzzled and angry at herself. She wound the window down and held her head out, hoping the brisk sea wind would blow the sadness off her. The sun was creeping up behind her, yellow and mockingly cheerful.

A fat, mean-eyed gull swooped threateningly over the car roof and landed next to the car. It stared up at her from the side of its nasty head, snapping its beak hungrily. It was fucking enormous. Paddy dipped her head back in the car and wound the window up. Outside, the gull snapped again, disappointed, and turned his back, spread his broad wings and flew away.

She looked at the passenger seat. Regal and Bru.

Paddy and Terry used to have Embassy Regal cigarettes and Irn-Bru for breakfast when they were young and together. They'd sit on his dirty orange bedsheet and sip their cans, passing one of the stubby fags back and forth and giggling about people in the office. Everyone seemed stupid to them then. The editors and senior journalists were leftovers from an ice age, Helen the librarian was a status-obsessed idiot. They gloried in the belief of their own infallibility and importance. Actually, Paddy didn't believe anything of the kind but she borrowed Terry's certainty. He was handsome in those days, solid, not fat, with dark eyes. He sat with his knees together and played with his ear when he was thinking.

She began to cry again. He was so young and she'd never noticed how lonely he must have been, living in his cheap bedsitter, sharing a bathroom with people he didn't know. To her, trapped by her family, by their history and all their needs, he seemed gloriously free, not alone, not adrift. She thought about how alone he would need to be to have put her down as next of kin when she wouldn't even answer the phone to him.

The car's cigarette lighter glowed red, warming the tip of her nose when she touched the cigarette to it. A nicotine tingle rolled down to her toes and she exhaled at the wind-screen, the smoke flattening into a patty against the glass.

She blinked and saw Terry's head again, his hair, his dear black hair.

She should have spoken to him in Babbity's when she

saw him in the press for the bar. She shouldn't have run away in case he made a scene. She should have gone over to him, apologized for leaving him in Fort William, folded her arms around his perfect head and kissed his face, his eyelids, his mouth and told him he was loved and she loved him. She loved him. Somebody loved him.

An inch of grey ash dropped into her lap and exploded. She brushed it away with a damp hand.

The gull was back, looking at the car as if thinking about taking it on.

'Fuck off,' she muttered, wiping her wet face dry.

It didn't, so she hooted the horn twice, giving it a start but exciting its curiosity as well. It twitched its head at her.

There was something about this area that made her think of *Shadow of Death*, the book she had written about a miscarriage of justice case from the sixties. She'd followed the case all her life because the villain had her name. She became a journalist because the campaign to free him was headed by a hack, and eventually got to know the man she'd followed in the papers and in the press. Patrick Meehan was bitter about his murder conviction. He claimed that the security services framed him for the vicious murder of a pensioner to pay him back for scrabbling under the Iron Curtain to sell secrets about the British prisons where spies were being held. But there was no evidence of a grander conspiracy and she was too well trained to do more than hint at it in the book. Something about Greenock reminded her of him but she couldn't think what it was. Somehow the sea air seemed to relate to him, the screaming gulls, cigarette smoke in a car with the windows wound up. She could see his red skin and the yellowed whites of his eyes, his defensive rounded shoulders. She'd never been down the coast with Meehan; all of their interviews were done in a pub and once in a restaurant but something about this area reminded her of him. She looked inland and then she saw it: a sign for Stranraer.

She sat up straight. Stranraer.

Meehan had no alibi for the night of Rachel Ross's murder. He was casing a tax office in Stranraer, where the ferry terminal to Ireland was. Any IRA man in Scotland would be familiar with this road, with the small side roads, where the heavy traffic ran and where was quiet. This was exactly where they would dump a body if they wanted to.

The possibility startled her. There were so many exiles from the Troubles here, mostly Loyalists but a lot of IRA sympathizers among the Scots Irish Arms were rumoured to be shipped through Glasgow. If the IRA had killed Terry, if the conflict had moved here and Scotland wasn't neutral any more, it would be a bloodbath. And if any journalist of her generation was likely to have discovered the new development it would be Terry Hewitt. His work had that kind of scope.

A single bed back in the early eighties, dirty orange sheets and a blood spot on her knickers, Terry's unpractised hands moving over her body, her own tightness, taking deep breaths, waiting for it to be over.

When he left for South America she helped him take his bags to the London train, smiled and waved from the platform, crying all the way home on the bus. He left her behind to tend her mother and father, to work her way up slowly at the *Daily News*, the calls-car shift, the Women's Page or 'Dab Sheet', to struggle with her book about Patrick Meehan. When she sat in her parents' damp garage pretending to work on the Meehan book, she was secretly rereading his articles about Angola and Central America. She saw him crouched in jungles, sweating under slow fans in tropical hotels, meeting African dictators. When *Shadow of Death* was finally published, she got an address for Terry from his news agency and sent him an invite to the launch. He didn't reply.

In her memory he became slim, tanned and tall, the epitome of a dignified search for truth – until he came back.

She wound the window down and threw the burnt-out fag stub on to the tarmac, not deliberately tormenting the gull-bully, but glad when it pecked at the oily butt and spat it out.

'Fucker.' She lit another cigarette and watched the gull consider its next move. 'Fat, greedy fucking fucker. Arse-hole.'

The Bru was still cold.

Terry didn't drink Bru any more when he got home. Couldn't get it abroad, he said. Lost the taste for it. He preferred Coke. He laughed when she bought him a Tun-nock's tea cake from the canteen.

'I remembered them as bigger,' he said pointedly.

That was unnecessary. Mean of him. She missed that clue. She should never, ever have gone back out with him.

She nodded at the gull. 'I shouldn't have gone to Fort William,' she told it. The fat scavenger blinked back at her.

4

Daily News

I

It was five in the morning but, looking up from the car park, Paddy could see that the *Daily News* building was readying for the day. The long black glass and chrome office building housed a print works downstairs with a glass wall looking into it. A stream of papers flew along the conveyor, print drying, the machine-gun clack-clack of the presses loud in the quiet of the morning. Van drivers gathered by the loading bay, waiting for the bales. Upstairs, on the second floor, the newsroom lights were off at the right-hand side of the room. The Doze Zone. When she worked the night shift they'd kept one part of the big room dark for those who wanted to sleep. Now the staff had been cut so much they only needed to use half the room.

The perpetual decline in *Daily News* sales meant a high turnover of senior editors, each of whom arrived in the job promising to reverse a global market trend and give the proprietors a better return. The easiest way to cut costs was by reducing wages. Paddy had left the *News* for a year. By the time she was poached back from the *Herald* a third of the staff were missing. To be fair, in the glory days of the '60s and '70s the staffing was breathtakingly flabby. Demarcation meant that a driver couldn't load a van and a

46

journalist wasn't allowed to empty a bin. Ancillary jobs were so well paid that they were jealously passed from father to son.

When she started as a copy boy, defying the editors and skiving were considered art forms. Now everyone kept their heads down, aware that they were lucky to have survived each incoming editor's cull, glad to be working in a shrinking market.

Checking her reflection in the rear-view mirror, Paddy saw a face puffy from crying. She could pass it off as tiredness.

'I've just been woken up,' she told herself. 'I was fast asleep and I've just woken up.'

She shivered, still too vulnerable to go in without her work face, without her armour. In another time she had been so inconsequential she could have hanged herself at her desk without exciting comment, but those days were long past. She was a name now, drew a big wage and was female.

Her column had started as part of the *Herald* Dab Sheet, given to her by a sympathetic editor when Pete had double pneumonia. She was glad of it at the time. A column meant she didn't have to leave the hospital ward and could call her copy in from the payphone in the lobby. Her opinions on outside matters were exactly what could have been expected from a mother watching her son struggle to breathe every day. Terror made her angry, ill-considered and blunt. She was so controversial they gave her the whole of page five, a banner byline of her name and a front-page name check. The *News* poached her back to upset their readers.

The column was herself on a bad-tempered rant. She had denounced a perfectly sincere actor who spoke at a political rally in support of a cause he knew nothing about. She once did a whole column about footballers' taste in

47

casual clothes ('Pigs in Knickers'). She was sometimes embarrassed by the stuff she wrote, like a temper-hangover, but the column attracted support from all quarters. She had stumbled on a talent for articulating nationwide annoyances. Her embarrassment was soothed by an exponential rise in her wages and the opportunities it opened up for her. It led to local, then national, radio and on to TV appearances. She did a three-month stint on a Sunday morning TV magazine show, where the lighting made her look extra-fat and mad. People set their alarm clocks to watch it.

She'd wanted to call the column 'Land of Sophistry and Mist', after Byron's observations on the nastiness of the Scots, but the *Herald* editor at the time (from Bristol – lasted five months) said it was pretentious, smacked of a knowledge of literature, and cut it to 'Land of Mist' without consulting her. 'Giving it Misty', to those in the know, meant ignorant tub-thumping.

Fear had been her inspiration but Pete soon recovered. He was prone to chest infections, but no worse than other kids. Although she was now calm and content, once a week she had to dip back into that black lake. The level was getting lower and lower, so she stole: she sought out angry people, milked them for comment, starting fights in the Press Bar to get an angle on any current issue.

She was successful and knew how that would make colleagues talk about her. They speculated unkindly about her sexual behaviour, her income, her home life.

Lauded for her bad-tempered ranting, she feared that she would wake up one morning and find she had morphed into Misty, that she would buy into her public image and actually start to think like that. She had seen it happen to columnists before.

She looked back at the building. Terry Hewitt had stood

outside that door waiting for her once, a hundred years ago, his left foot resting on the wall behind him. He had looked up as she came towards him, a warm smile on his face. He had worn a leather jacket; she was impressed by that.

She had left Fort William in the middle of the night, driving at eighty along back roads to get away from him. His articles told how he had witnessed corruption and brutality, women raped and murdered, children mutilated, whole villages put to the torch. She remembered his article about a fifteen-year-old Angolan boy, shot between the eyes right in front of him. She had been naive to expect him to remain unchanged. Ridiculous.

The work face wasn't going to come. She'd just have to go in anyway or miss the deadline for the late edition. Taking a deep breath, she reached for the door handle and stepped out on to the buckled concrete floor of the car park, locking the car behind her.

Delivery men loitered in the loading bay, looking up as she came towards them. They stopped talking and watched her walk to the staff entrance, their heads following her, moving as one curious animal. She could say hello to one of them, curry for a champion, but she didn't have it in her this morning. She pushed the staff door open and stepped in off the street to the cold stone lobby. As soon as the door shut, one of them would say something derogatory, make a comment about the size of her arse or who she'd gobbled.

She let the door fall shut and then yanked it open again, leaning out into the street, staring straight at them. One of them froze with his mouth open, a chest full of breath, ready to comment.

'Who the fuck are you wankers talking about?' she drawled.

They laughed at her for catching them out.

She slipped back into the lobby before they could retort

and climbed the stairs heavily, pulling herself forward, pausing at the doors to the newsroom. Flattening her dress, she affected a frown. Most states of emotional turmoil could be covered with a growl, she'd found, especially after her father died, when the grief often ambushed her.

She organized her face into a scowl, pushed the double doors open and walked in, keeping her chin high.

The night shift started into action like an automaton during a power surge. They saw it was her and toned it down a bit. Light from computer screens filled the gloomy room, uplighting those sitting at their desks.

Merki Ferris, standing near the door, looked shifty and paranoid. He'd been exiled to the night shift for pissing off Bunty, their current editor. He was a cross-eyed trickster, had guile but no wit, could get into anywhere for an interview but then didn't know what to ask. He was not an attractive man and it was hard to tell in the thin light whether he was smiling or grimacing.

'What are you doing here?' he asked, out of a habit of asking questions.

'Right, Merki?' She slipped past him.

The layout of the room had been changed to fill the gaps. In the old days the noise of typewriters and shouting filled the room, desks were positioned to fit with production needs and everywhere had to be sidled to. Now the slimmed-down news, sports and features areas were further away from each other, circular islands with flat electric typewriters and dirty-white plastic computers that pulsed cadaverous green light into the room. The editors had their own island now, away from the journalists.

Paddy walked across the room to a partitioned office for the senior editors. Outside the door she dipped at the knee to see in through the white venetian blinds behind the glass. Larry Grey-Lips, head of the night shift and king curmudgeon, was at his desk. She opened the door without knocking. Larry froze with a sandwich at his mouth, trying to remember whether Paddy Meehan had the clout to give them shit for not doing relay races from one end of the room to the other. He dropped his hand and looked worried.

'What?'

She picked up a schedule from his desk and pretended to read it. Larry put his sandwich down and leaned back in his chair, balancing carefully on two legs as he stared at her with the same languorous, faintly despising expression he always had. 'Did you wake up and remember someone ye hated?'

'Nope.' She put the schedule down. 'I've got a big news story.'

'You're fucking joking.' He dropped his chair on to all fours. 'For fucksake, we're into feeding time here. Could ye not have come an hour ago?'

She shrugged, looking around the desk. 'Just the way it happened.'

'Spit it out, woman.'

'Um ...' She hesitated, poking around some papers on his desk. 'Terry Hewitt.'

'What about Terry?'

'He's been killed. Murdered.'

Larry didn't speak or move. She stole a look at him. He was frowning at the desk, blinking quickly. He saw her looking at him and coughed for cover.

'Well.' His voice was lower. 'Fuck me.'

Paddy nodded at the desk and bit her cheek. 'I know.'

'No, I mean it.' Larry looked at her. 'Fuck me.'

Each smiled weakly at the papers on Larry's desk, glad of the respite. Quite suddenly the muscles on Paddy's chin convulsed into a tight ball and she lost her breath.

'So.' She found her voice, higher and unsteady. 'They found his body in a ditch. Word is —' she leaned down to whisper to him – '*IRA hit.*'

Larry opened his eyes wide. In nine years at the paper she'd never seen him do that. 'You're fucking joking. *Here?*'

'I know . . .'

'The Provos are killing people in Scotland?'

'Well, one anyway. "All the hallmarks of an IRA hit," said a source within the Strathclyde Police Force. The body was found out near Greenock.' He didn't seem to realize the significance so she spelled it out. 'Off the road to Stranraer, where the ferry runs to Belfast.'

'So was Terry just getting off the boat? Had he been in Ireland?'

'Dunno. He was found stripped naked in a ditch, single shot to the head.'

'Jesus Christ, this is huge.' Larry turned to his computer screen to see who was on. 'Merki—'

'No.' Paddy put a firm hand on his desk. 'I'll write it. No byline, but I'll do it.' Merki was a skilled hack and he'd want to know how Paddy had found out about Terry. If he caught a whiff of her personal involvement he'd tell Larry and they'd have her writing an emotive first-person account about identifying the body. They always wanted that, especially from female reporters.

Larry leaned back in his chair, picking bits of sandwich out of a molar and appraising her suspiciously. There was a time when no one in the press would volunteer to do a job without a byline. Even now it was still the custom to feign reluctance.

'What could you possibly have against Merki?'

'Nothing, just I know Terry. Knew Terry. By the time I've briefed him I could have written it.'

Larry hesitated.

'OK.' She threw her hands up. 'Get Merki. Better than that: you do it. I'll fuck off home to my bed.'

'Can you bang it out in five minutes? We're due to set in ten.'

'No bother. When did you last see him?'

'Friday. He was drinking in Babbity's. He had a book deal, was showing the cheque around to everyone. Two hundred quid.'

'Not much, is it? I got more than that for *Shadow of Death* and no one bought it.'

'Yeah, Terry's was a picture book, not much text. Expensive to produce.'

'What sort of picture book?'

'Photos of people. Americans. Published by the Scotia Press, who the fuck are they?' Larry looked around his desktop, bewildered. 'It's definitely *our* Terry? Are they certain? It couldn't be a mistake?'

For a second they looked one another in the eye, a clear moment of sadness and shock and loss. They had both known Terry Hewitt for a decade, since his parents' death in a car crash, through his early promise and his trips abroad, had both taken private pride in his triumphs, and, knowing him again more recently, had seen him bloated and scouring for work. Paddy bit her cheek hard, crunching through a nipple of hard skin at the corner of her mouth. She could taste blood.

'Larry,' she growled, 'just ... don't look at me. I need to hold it together until I get out of this fucking place.'

Larry nodded sadly. She turned to the door and raised her chin again.

'You're fat and everyone hates you,' said Larry to her back, reminding her who she was supposed to be.

'Thanks, Larry.'

II

Paddy felt as if she was vibrating with the need to sleep. She watched her hand tremble as she opened the car door. The cul-de-sac was bare of cars, the neighbouring house boarded up. Thick summer grass was growing wildly in the gardens, lush weeds flourishing through cracks in the pavement. The house next to the Meehans' had stood empty since Mr Beattie went into a nursing home. The roof sagged too, looking close to collapse.

She had grown up on the Eastfield Star, a small estate of council houses built for a mining community in the wilds between Cambuslang and Rutherglen. The houses were small and low, cottages with flats in them or larger for big families like her own.

The streets radiated off a central roundabout and had once been a nice area of good families. They should still have been. The houses were a little damp and the windows small but the basic stock was good. As the older residents died, they were replaced with less salubrious tenants who cluttered up their gardens with crap and had loud fights in the street. A drug dealer was rumoured to live in one of the houses near the main road, but Paddy suspected that they were just young and prone to partying. If she made more money she'd move her mother out of there.

She lifted the rusted wire hanger holding her mother's garden gate shut and stepped down the narrow path. The garage where she had imagined Terry off on his travels was just to her left, damp green lichen growing over the small high windows. She thought about going in there for a moment, just to look at all the damp boxes and the chair she used to sit in, but knew she'd start crying and might not be able to stop. It was the tiredness. And the shock. It had been a shock seeing an old friend dead. Seeing anyone with a hole in their head was a shock.

She fitted the key in the lock and opened it as quietly as possible. Her mother's house smelled perpetually of dampness and baking, a scent that, to her, conveyed certainty and stability. The smell hadn't changed a ripple since her father died. It was as if he'd never given off a smell.

She dipped her finger in the holy water font hanging by the front door and crossed herself. Her mother liked to see her doing it. Although she had made it clear that she wasn't going to church and didn't want Pete baptized, her mother took the holy water habit as a sign that one day she might return to the bosom of the chapel, confess her sins to a gnarled old arse of a priest and accept that she was, indeed, a bad girl who made the baby Jesus cry. Paddy let her think it. That she wasn't even prepared to take communion and had had a child out of wedlock was hard enough for her mother.

Paddy's post was propped on the window sill. She flicked through it: credit card offers, flyers for catalogues, a couple of requests for money from charities, and one flimsy white envelope, coffee-stained in the upper corner, with her name and an approximation of the address. She put her finger under the flap and ripped it open.

A single sheet of creamy paper and handwritten words:
Now offering 50k for Callum O. exclusive.
Ring me,
Johnny Mac.

She stroked the figure with her fingertip and then crumpled the note in her fist, squeezing it tight, as if the words could be wrung from it, shoved it into her pocket and climbed the stairs. She could sleep soon, catch a few hours before mass.

She stopped at the top step, listening. No one was awake yet. Alone in the quiet of the morning, she sensed more than heard the breathing behind the doors. Ahead of her was her parents' old room. She could hear Trisha's faint nasal whistle. To Paddy's left was her old bedroom. BC and Pete now shared it every Saturday night, taking the single beds she and Mary Ann had left behind. Paddy fitted her hand on the worn wooden egg handle, turned it silently and opened the door just enough to slip her head round and look in.

Pete was curled up, brown blankets and a lip of white sheet curved around the line of his little body, lying so still that she had to watch his chest to be sure he was breathing.

She relaxed, letting her burning eyes droop half shut as she leaned her cheek against the edge of the bedroom door.

She forgot about Terry and Aoife and John Mac's letter. She forgot about her job and Burns and Callum Ogilvy. She forgot everything in the world but the essential, glorious fact of her son: safe, nearby and breathing in and out.

5

Callum

It was a gentle tap at the door, two beats, and then the guard walked on to the next cell door, his knuckle drumming the same call on the steel followed by his steps again, another two-beat call. His signal. It was Haversham.

Callum jack-knifed upright in his bed, sweat prickling at his temples. Haversham didn't often work the isolation block but when he did he always did his knuckled call, telling them he was there. He didn't need to bang on the door any more or whisper abuse through the tray slit. All it took for them to get the message was a tap. *I am here*, it said, *I can see you.*

Haversham was on when a prisoner in the isolation block cut himself and bled to death. There were rumours that he had watched the prisoner through the Judas hole and seen him die, not raising the alarm until it was too late.

The footsteps were heading back up the corridor, coming towards him, tapping two doors down. When Callum got out the world would be full of Havershams. *A mob'll find ye. The papers will tell them where you are. Rip ye to ribbons and no one'll blame them.*

A mind can only hold one thought at a time.

Callum peered across the early morning gloom and reread

the graffiti scars on the wall. *I fuck Harry. JS+B. John Harrison is a supergass*, the missing '*r*' floating above the last word, angrily scored deeper into the plaster than the rest of the letters. Other than that, the carving was meticulously done: the 's's perfectly curved, not just straight lines joined together to form a Hellenic 's'. Fuelled by resentment and the desire to tell the world what he knew, the writer had worked into the rock-hard plaster, past the five layers of deep green paint. The green was faded below, like time, like memory, lighter and lighter. Callum's own message went all the way through, gouged through to the brick. He had curved his letters too.

It was an old prison. Victorian. The isolation cells were small and even nastier than the main block, Mr Wallace told him. Callum'd never been in the main block himself. For the full three years he'd been in the adult prison they'd kept him here because *This place is full of nutters*, Mr Stritcher told him, *of nutters who'd like to make their name killing you. Hurting you. Men with nothing going for them*, he said, as if Callum had something going for him. He was famous and that was something. Not a good thing but something.

Haversham was outside his door, looking in at him. Callum could hear his breath, razored with spite, hitting the metal, a slow hiss through sharp teeth.

Leaving us, are ye? Think that wean's mother won't find ye? Cunt. Think ye can walk out of here and live a life?

Callum got out of bed and stood facing away from the door, his trembling hands balled into fists. Don't listen. Don't react. It'll go on longer if you react.

A mind can only hold one thought at a time.

When he left here he would walk from his cell, through his door and turn left. Down the corridor, past three cell doors, green and chipped, to the exit. Eleven steps.

They'd shout goodbye to him as he passed, the men behind the chipped green doors. Hughie, C3, had raped a girl, a really young girl, but seemed nice enough when you met him. Tam in C2 had killed his wife, which wouldn't put him on protection normally because the main block was full of guys who'd done that, but she was just about to have a baby and it had been in the papers. And the last cell, C1, a quiet man who wanked all night, groaning animal noises but never speaking when the window warriors shouted at him to shut the fuck up. He wouldn't say goodbye. Mr Wallace said he wasn't well and shouldn't be here. C1 might be James for all Callum knew. James with a different name. They'd been keeping them apart throughout their nine-year sentence, but maybe it didn't matter now, if James was mental. There weren't that many places to keep the two of them.

The papers'll find you, in your new house. Tell everyone.

Past the cell doors. Eleven steps. Through the big door that opened inwards, out to the corridor where the officers on watch sat and read the paper. Smells from the kitchens came through the wall, smells so strong you could lick them from the air. The softness of sponge, sulphurous egg, the warmth of mince, onions. They ended last year's riot with onions. The officers got the guys down from the roof by frying onions at the bottom of the stairs and fanning the smell up to them. Sometimes the corridor smelled of burning.

Cunt.

Everything smelled the same when it was burning.

You baby-murdering cunt.

Twenty-six steps, along the kitchen-smelling corridor to the big grey metal outside door and out into the yard, the bright grey sky above him. He could feel his irises ache at the sharp slap of light as the door opened. He would have

59

that sky above him all the time soon, his eyes straining to cope with the painful brightness of it.

Ogilvy? They're already looking for ye, they'll find ye, take pictures, print them.

The bright sky above the yard and the wind coming off the sea. Even with the thirty-foot wall around the prison the salty wind managed to sneak in, skirling around the corners of the yard, sweeping leaves into tidy little heaps against the wall. The sea was just over the wall and the air had a bitter salty tang that stung chapped lips. Standing at the door to the yard the wind was only at head height, blustering the top of his head but not touching the face, an unseen hand ruffling his hair.

Ogilvy. Ogilvy. They're offering big money.

More than anything else, he had missed being touched. Sometimes he hesitated by his cell door after exercise to make them reach for him, the press of a hand on the back, on the arm, a soft cuff across the back of the head. Some prisoners were beaten by screws for doing things wrong but Callum was a sheep, followed gently wherever they led him, and they knew what to expect. He never had the guts to give them cause, but he understood the urge to defy them, to get beaten, just for the touch.

Your pal James, he lost an eye last year.

Lies. Haversham lied all the time.

In the infirmary up in the Big House. Came out of isolation for a bad leg and some cunt got him with a pencil.

James. Callum saw his eyes smouldering in the dark, the cold night wind cutting between them and the baby in the grass. The story had been told so many times, to him, by him, with him, by police when they questioned him, by the social workers, by the psychiatrists who came and went, by the papers. So many tellings, he couldn't remember which was true any more.

James was my only friend. The man took us there in the van, with the baby. We battered him with stones and strangled him until he died and then we stuck sticks up his bum because I'm a pervert, eh? I'm a fucking filthy pervert. I probably think about it when I'm alone, masturbate and think about it.

James was my only friend. In the van, I was glad we were picking on the baby because we weren't picking on me. James strangled him and the baby messed himself. I ran up the hill and James did things to him. We hit him with stones before he died. Hitting is nothing. Hitting means nothing. Prisoners hit you, parents hit you, screws hit you. What's wrong is for me to hit you. I don't think about it when I masturbate. I see women, bits of women, tits and cunts, disjointed pictures from magazines. It doesn't take much. I was scared before the night, sometimes, but since the night I've never stopped being scared.

I thought James was my friend but he wasn't. I take full responsibility for what happened. The baby was crying and James held his throat to make him stop. We fiddled about with the body to make it look like someone else. I am sorry for the family, for the baby's mother and family. I am sorry for what I have done. I will try to live a good life in the future. My dream is to work in a factory and live within a loving family structure.

Everyone liked the last version best but ten years later all the different versions of the night had become as true as each other.

When he remembered it, when he was alone, all he recalled were James's black eyes smouldering as they stood over the tiny body crumpled in the wet grass, of the cold wind on his face as he stood on the verge looking back at the van, and behind him James making noises, sniggering, pulling things around to suit himself.

When he remembered it now, Callum stood on the blustery verge and looked at the grass in front of him. It was trampled deep into the mud from the feet of all the people who had been there, the psychiatrists, the social workers, the guards who asked questions kindly and then sold the story to the newspapers, other prisoners who'd ask about it, sly, interested in details they shouldn't be asking about.

Cunt.

Haversham was getting tired of Callum's back. He tapped the door again, making his point, and shuffled off to taunt Hughie.

Callum carried on his walk. From the door he stepped into the yard, straight across the yard to the guard block, around the concrete path at the side, staying off the grass. That would take thirty steps, maybe thirty-something. He had never been that way before. Along the grass to the door out. They would have to wait at the door until it buzzed open. The guards wouldn't have keys for that door in case they were taken hostage. Security zones. Inside the door it would be warm, they'd have the heating on high for the guards. There would be a waiting room probably. Plastic chairs probably. Posters maybe. And beyond that an unknowable number of steps to the main doors. Through one. Locked behind him. Next door and out, out to the eye-aching brightness and the unbridled wind salting him. Out, out into a world full of Havershams.

No one would come with him through the final door. He would be unsupervised for the first time since he was ten. He didn't know what he would do.

He looked back at the messages on the grey wall.

Supergass.

Callum's own message was finished. Took him months. He curved all four 's's, gave curvy tails to the 'g's and 'y', spelled it right. It was finished now. He could leave now. Callum's own message:

Everything smells the same when it's burning.

6

Bang Bang

With his soft Dublin accent, fine, long face and green eyes, Father Andrew was an Irish mother's dream. He was fresh from seminary when he came to St Columbkille's. Eager to make the Good News accessible to young people, he made everyone use his first name, introduced guitars to mass, made self-conscious teenagers mutter inaudible bidding prayers. The parish was elderly and didn't like the unfamiliar. They revolted, complaining to the Monsignor, and soon Father Andrew's radical reforms were curtailed to occasional mentions of already-out-of-date pop stars in his sermons and wearing a cassock with a rainbow embroidered on the back. Paddy saw defeat in him nowadays. She'd have felt for him more if he gave fewer sermons about the evils of unmarried, working mothers, homosexuality and sex before marriage.

Opening his arms, he raised his eyes to the giant plaster Jesus dangling over the altar. 'Go in peace, to love and serve the Lord.'

The organist launched into the opening bars of 'How Great Thou Art' and Paddy found herself singing along in the strange, strangled falsetto she only ever used in chapel.

Pete giggled at her side and she nudged his head with her elbow.

Before the altar, the priest and altar boys formed an orderly group, processing down the central aisle, gathering the congregation in their wake. Pete ducked out of the pew as the procession came past, desperate to be near the chubby greasy-haired altar boy who was his hero: BC, named for his grandfather. None of the family could bear to say his name since Con senior died. Baby Con's name had changed as suddenly as the family dynamic.

Because the boys stayed at Trisha's on Saturday nights it would have been difficult for Paddy to insist Pete didn't go to mass. As well as avoiding conflict with her mother she had a superstitious fear that organized religion might hold some romance for Pete in the future if she didn't cram it halfway down his throat as a child. He wasn't baptized and hated the dreary rigmarole of mass, but he still wanted to be an altar boy like his cousin. He wanted to be everything like his cousin. He shuffled ahead of her in the aisle, ducking between clustered families to get closer, keeping his adoring eyes on BC's back.

Paddy held on to his shoulder, following him through the throng, afraid of losing him.

Ahead of them, standing between the doors, Father Andrew was holding an old woman's hand, steering her by the wrist out of the door, dismissing her with a blessing. His eyes were on Paddy, willing her to him. He had already developed the faintly despising attitude to his parishioners that many older priests had. They were as cynical as strippers, some of them.

Beyond the doors and Father Andrew, Paddy could see Sean Ogilvy out in the warm sunshine. Sean Ogilvy, teetering on his tiptoes to look back in for her, dressed in his Sunday suit, his dark hair receding from his face.

65

Father Andrew reached across the throng and grabbed Paddy's hand as she came past, reeling her in through the crowd. 'My dear Lord, what's this I'm reading about in your headline today?'

'Oh, well.' She broke eye contact and tried to move on, to Sean.

'Please, God, it's not true.'

But Father Andrew had a firm hold of her hand. 'Please, God.' He looked imploringly at her. 'Please, please, God.' Then added, as he always did, 'I'll pray for you, Patricia.' He ruffled Pete's hair. 'And you, son.'

If Pete hadn't been with her she'd have kicked Father Andrew's shin and passed it off as a mistake. Instead she dipped her eyes. 'And I'll pray for you, Father.'

At the top of the steps Pete wriggled out from under her hand and ran over to Sean's four kids. They were younger than him and therefore not as interesting as BC, but he could boss them and they loved him, especially now that he'd moved across the city and they didn't see him all the time. Mary, the oldest, and Patrick hung on his arms, gurgling with delight at his presence.

Around the women a puddle of children gathered, dazed from the boredom of mass, holding on to their mothers' legs, staring at each other or trying to eat stones from the ground.

Sean took Paddy's elbow and pulled her aside. He looked grim.

'Tomorrow morning, OK?' he whispered.

'*Tomorrow?*'

He rolled his eyes. 'Don't tell me you can't come.'

'No, no,' she said, shaking her head, 'I can come, I can come. Just didn't think it would be so soon. There was a journalist up at my door last night asking about his release. He asked if he was going to stay with you.'

'*Shite.*' Sean looked around to see if he'd been heard uttering a curse word in the chapel yard. 'I need you there, you know everyone, you'll be able to spot them in the car park. I don't know all the faces, you know?'

Elaine was looking at them so Paddy gave her a wave. Elaine was holding baby Mona on her hip and had Cabrini strapped tightly into a stroller. She was standing with another mother, equally laden. Elaine had qualified as a hairdresser and always managed to keep herself looking good. She had a short brown bob at the moment, a break from her usual blonde hair. Paddy envied her slim frame, especially after four pregnancies, but she was so decent and straightforward that no one who knew her could fail to like her. She waved back to Paddy, the tight muscle in her jaw cutting sharply across her cheek.

'Seany, you don't have to do this.'

He looked at Paddy's chin, his hand still clamped over his mouth. It was going to happen. He had volunteered to assuage his conscience and now it was actually happening. Callum Ogilvy, the notorious child-killer, was coming to live in his tiny house with himself, Elaine and their four children.

'I do need to,' he said, sharply. 'That's the thing, I do need to do this. He won't get out otherwise. But we'll both be in deep shit if the *News* management hear about it and we don't give them the story. *You* don't need to do it.'

'I do. It'll be something selfless to tell my son one day. *I pass up a chance.*'

Sean smiled at her. He hadn't driven her anywhere for a long time and they both missed it.

'Elaine knows it's tomorrow, does she?'

'Of course she does.'

Together they looked over at Elaine, who bumped the baby up her hip and ground her teeth. She sensed their eyes on her and looked back at them, suddenly rocking the buggy back and forth. Cabrini's arms shot up in surprise. Paddy sensed that Elaine was trying to comfort herself, not Cabrini.

'And she's all right about it, is she?'

'She's fine.' He didn't sound very convincing.

'Fucking hell, Sean, you were lucky when you married that woman. I wouldn't have done it.'

Sean looked at his wife and nodded. 'I know that,' he said, 'I know.' He didn't sound very convincing.

'Terry Hewitt was murdered,' Paddy blurted, surprised again to find herself tearful. 'I had to look at the body, they said it was the Provos.'

'Hewitt? That fat guy you chucked me for?'

'I didn't – oh, for fucksake, let's not get back into that.'

Her words choked her and Sean softened. 'Sorry.' He pulled her out of the crowd to the side of the chapel and the shadows. 'Was he investigating something in the Six Counties then? I thought he did Africa.'

'No, he was killed in Scotland. Out on the road to Stranraer.'

He stepped away from her. 'The Provos'd never do that. Not a journalist. Not *here*.'

'Well, that's what the police said.'

'Phff, what do they know? Our boys'd never do that.'

'Come on, Sean, don't be naive, they're kneecapping teenagers for selling hash.'

'They're maintaining order.' Sean still believed the Easter Uprising was a week ago, that the Troubles were about goodies and baddies, and that an Irish Catholic with a gun could have nothing but God and the good of mankind on his mind. He was a season-ticket holder for Celtic and went to the Tower Bar on Sunday afternoons to sing rebel songs with all the other armchair revolutionaries. 'The RUC can't be trusted to police those areas . . .'

'Shut the fuck up. It's just – it's the last thing I need right now with Callum getting out. You wouldn't believe the pressure I'm under.' She felt the note in her pocket. 'The *Express* offered fifty thousand pounds for an exclusive. Maybe Callum should do one interview? Maybe that would get them off his back. Give him a bit of money to get going.'

'He doesn't want to,' said Sean. 'I think he should but he doesn't want to.'

Elaine was waving Sean over to her. He dropped his foot down one of the steps and turned back. 'I'll pick you up at six.'

'Six a.m.?'

He wrinkled his nose. 'I know. Sorry about Terry. I know you liked him.'

'It's a bit more complicated than that, but thanks.'

11

Condensation streaked the window on to the messy back garden. The grass was two foot tall, almost obscuring a rusting twin-tub, gathering around the trunk of the tree at the far end.

The babble from the radio and the crackle of the frying pan drowned out the noise of the two boys at the table. BC was breaking his fast and Pete was having a second bowl of cornflakes so that he didn't feel left out. Caroline sat across from them, ignoring everyone, reading a magazine about hairdos. Five places were set at the table that used to hold seven. She couldn't remember how all of them used to fit in here.

Trisha broke three eggs into the frying pan. 'And was this the boy who used to phone here all the time?'

'Aye. Terry. You met him once. 'Member he came here with his pal's van to take my old desk out of the garage? Dark hair, a wee bit fat.'

Trisha kept her voice low so the boys wouldn't hear. 'And what was that boy to you?'

'Just a friend.'

'Why did he call all the time then?'

'Dunno. Well, he'd been abroad and didn't really have any pals when he came back. He was lonely, maybe.'

Trisha gave the frying pan an angry little shake.

'Why did they ask you to go and see his body then?'

Paddy shrugged, trying to be casual about it, but one of her shoulders got stuck up around her ears and betrayed her. 'I just knew him from way back. We started at the paper at the same time.'

Behind them the boys were squabbling over the free toy from the cereal box. Without looking, Trisha called over her shoulder, 'It's BC's shot, son. You got it the last time.'

'But *that*'s the one I want.' Pete crossed his arms tight and scowled, a tiny despot planning a coup. 'I'm the one that likes dinosaurs.'

BC waggled the cheap toy at Pete, taunting him. Paddy and Trisha smiled at the frying pan, keeping their faces from the boys.

'Give it to him,' Caroline ordered her son, always quick to take a side against him.

'Shots each,' said Trisha, 'or I'll keep the toy for myself.'

Using the wooden spatula, Trisha splashed hot fat over the top of the eggs and dropped her voice again. 'I mean, the boy surely had some family.'

'Terry had no one,' said Paddy, adding, by way of explanation, 'He was a Protestant.'

Trisha smirked: it was a old country joke about non-Catholics, designed to appeal to Trisha's prejudices, about how Protestants neglected to breed like rats and didn't all live on top of each other. 'You've got me down as a right old greenhorn, don't ye?'

'Ma, I've got you down as class on a stick. 'Member the time you dressed the pig up in a tuxedo?'

Trisha smiled into the pan, corrected herself and gave Paddy a reproachful look. She had taken to widowhood with a wizened vigour and was prone to tutting at anything resembling good fun or high jinks. Without the timidly tempering cynicism of her husband she was more devout now, and since Mary Ann had taken her vows she wouldn't hear a word against the Church. It left a chasm between them.

The eggs were done, the potato scones and bacon browned, so Paddy picked up the plates and poured the hot water warming them into the sink, dried them with a tea towel and held them out to her mother.

'Terry put me down on his passport as his next of kin. That's why they came to me.'

'And the police said the Provos killed him?'

'Yeah. "All the hallmarks", they said.'

'God help us,' muttered Trisha, her voice little more than a breath now, shielding it from the boys. 'God help us if that's true.'

She glanced fearfully at the table and fixed on Pete. 'Maybe you should think about giving him his daddy's name,' she said, still believing that young Catholic men could be arrested for having a name that sounded Irish.

'I don't think even the Met are rounding up five-year-olds, Ma. Terry was just a friend.'

Trisha didn't look at her as she dished the breakfast on to the plates and put the pan back on the cooker, clenching her jaw to silence herself.

'Honest.'

They stood, stiff, Trisha looking at the plates in Paddy's hand and Paddy looking down at her mother. Not long ago Paddy would have been looking her straight in the eye but Trisha was shrinking. Now she could see the top of her head, the grey roots under the gravy brown, loose hairs creeping out from the Elizabeth Taylor set she had done every Monday at Mrs Tolliver's house.

Trisha wouldn't catch her eye because she suspected that Paddy had slept with Terry. Since Pete was born her mother had suspected Paddy of sleeping with every man she mentioned and her disapproval wasn't just an intergenerational values clash: she believed that Paddy would go to hell for her sins, that the rest of the family would spend eternity in heaven, staring at an empty chair if they didn't nag and disapprove and vilify her enough.

Compared to her mother Paddy had put it about, but not by much. She'd developed the habit of denying everything.

The boys were fighting again, this time about who was reading the cereal packet.

BC laughed joylessly. 'You can't even read yet.'

'I can so read.'

'Ye can't read. Read it to me then, go on.'

'I can so read!'

'Go on then, read it out, if ye can read.'

Without looking up, Caroline told BC to shut up.

Trisha tipped her head to the table, telling Paddy to put the plates down, and then followed the turn of her head, swinging towards the table without looking at her. She poured two cups of tea from the steel teapot, setting one in front of Paddy's place.

The boys had reached an impasse. BC was elaborately reading the back of the cereal packet and rubbing his cheek with the plastic dinosaur, a faded smile on his chubby face – just enough to upset Pete, not enough to get into trouble.

He sighed contentedly, as if to say that everything he had ever dreamed of was here: the toy, the reading of the cereal packet, everything. Pete had his arms crossed up near his nose, was about to hide his face in his arms and curl over the table and cry.

'Son.' Paddy touched his arm. 'You can choose what we're doing this morning.'

Too late, she realized what he was bound to say.

Pete looked at her hopefully. 'Really? I can choose?'

Anything but not that, she wanted to say, we're not doing that. But if she forbade him she'd have to explain why and telling a five-year-old that her friend had been shot in the head was beyond her.

'Yeah. Go ahead.'

To her right Trisha tutted under her breath. She didn't approve of doing things children liked. She thought it would ruin them.

Pete's tiny tight fists rose from the nest of his arms. 'Lazerdrome!'

'OK, pal.'

Pete threw his head back and silently mouthed a big hurray, observing Trisha's rule about not shouting in the house.

'Ruined,' muttered Trish through a mouthful of egg and bacon.

III

Throbbing music filled the dark room, disguising the shriek of trainers on the rubber floor and squeals of excitement. Paddy was crouching on one of the wooden walkways, keeping her body behind the partition so that she couldn't be shot from the ground.

The memory of Terry's BCG stabbed at her throat.

Somehow her relationship with Terry was getting confused with the seagull in Greenock: a big ugly threat that wanted something from her that she didn't have.

She heard a scream and turned to look down the dark walkway. Through the smog of dried ice she could just make out a strip of tiny coloured lights, red through to yellow. There was a child down there and they'd just been shot.

Every person in the room had a pack strapped to their front and back, little light sensors on it to pick up the beam of the bulky laser guns they all carried. Shoot someone and their pack went off for thirty seconds and you got points. Her job here was to lose by a higher margin than Pete and be good about it, to show him it didn't matter. She had thought it might freak her out after seeing Terry, being here among excited children shooting each other, but it was just an electronic version of tig.

Pete was down there somewhere, on the floor, chasing other kids or hiding, sneaking along a wall, the pack too big for him really, banging off his thighs when he raised his legs to run or climb a ladder.

They came here all the time and Pete always played the same game. He liked to run around as much as possible, fodder for the bigger kids who lay in wait in the good vantage points. She loved it that he was reckless but if he had played cautiously she would have cherished that too.

Her pack vibrated and gave off a little wind-down tune. She turned to see a smug boy of BC's age standing behind her. 'Looserrr,' he drawled.

She tutted and stood up straight, knowing her pack was off and she couldn't be shot again for a while. 'Oh dear,' she said, being good about it, 'I'm rubbish at this.'

But her assassin wasn't listening. He sauntered past her towards another set of lights twinkling in the dark, shot his laser gun at the target and she heard a pack sighing the death jingle. She recognized Pete's groan in the dark. 'Looserrr.'

'Is that you?'

He walked over to her. 'I'm getting shot all the time,' he whined.

'Everyone gets out sometimes.'

He dropped his head and his shoulders sagged with disappointment. Together they looked over the top of the walkway at the scurrying figures below. Somewhere a pack sang sadly in the darkness. 'Looserr.'

'I don't think that boy's very nice,' she said, but Pete was watching the floor and didn't answer.

Sweat beaded his face. He pushed the hair back from his forehead, the sweat making his fringe stand up in a spiky tiara.

'This is a good laugh, eh?'

'Aye.'

She wanted to reach out and kiss him but contented herself with touching his shoulder with her fingertips.

Paddy had been ambivalent all the way through her pregnancy. She was unsure about her fitness to be a mother, whether she could love the baby, whether she should have had an abortion and waited for the right man. But she didn't believe in the right man, didn't think she'd ever want to get married and thought Pete might be her only chance to have a child.

From the moment he was born she knew she'd done the right thing. His fingers, his toes, the wrinkled promise of his testicles, every detail was hypnotic. It was like living with a pop star she had a crush on. For the first year she had a compulsive need to kiss him. Being in another room, even waking to his screams in the burning-eyed middle of the night, her heart rate rose at the thought of seeing him. The rest of life was nothing but a hollow interval until he was there again.

Her intensity worried her. She could only imagine how hard Pete would have to fight to shake her hand from his shoulder. She'd have done it for him but she didn't know how.

Standing next to her now, he raised himself on tiptoes, looked out over the ridge and turned back to her smiling. 'Hey, Mum, guess what?'

'What?'

Grinning, he raised the barrel of his laser gun and shot her in the chest. 'You're hit again.' Both their packs had come back on and she hadn't noticed.

'Ya wee bissom!'

He laughed and ran away.

'Hey,' she called after him in the dark, 'I'm not feeding you for two days.'

'My dad'll feed me,' he called back.

IV

George Burns knocked on the front door like a hungry bailiff with a short temper. He didn't even bother with a hello when Paddy opened it but swept into the hall, tutted at the boxes still scattered on the floor and looked around for Pete.

'Hi, Sandra.' Paddy held the door open further and invited his wife into the flat.

Sandra was blonde, tall, and so thin she could have opened letters with her chin. Her rigorous grooming routine verged on manic and always made Paddy think of unhappy zoo animals that lick the same spot over and over until they go bald.

'Paddy.' Sandra dipped at the knee, making herself smaller, an apologetic smile twitching at the corner of her lipsticked mouth.

'Come on in.' Paddy took her warmly by the elbow and brought her into the flat. 'Did you have a nice weekend in Paris?'

Sandra's eyes skittered around the floor. 'Nice. Good weather. Lovely hotel room—' She stopped abruptly, pressing her lips tight together, as if the words were fighting behind her lips. Paddy could imagine what the words were: he's furious, get me out of here, I'm hungry all the time.

Paddy regretted having a baby to Burns. He was a nightmare to negotiate with and wasn't a particularly warm father. Keeping her options open, she'd tried to muddy the father issue but Pete had popped out a perfect model of his dad: thick black hair, wide green eyes and the telltale dimple on his chin. And there was Burns at visiting time, the clay and the mould. When Pete was hospitalized with pneumonia Burns visited once a week and brought the four-year-old bunches of flowers.

'Where is he?' Burns was already brisk and impatient to get away. He usually saved it until he was bringing Pete back.

'He's just getting his new Transformer.' Paddy spoke slowly, calmingly. 'He wants to show it to you.'

'Is Dub in?'

'Naw, I haven't seen him today.'

'Tell him I was asking for him.'

Pete arrived then at the door to his bedroom, already wary, sensing the atmosphere among the adults. Dumbly, he thrust the blue-and-red plastic robot out at them.

'Show your dad what it does, though.'

Without a word, Pete pulled a robot head here, clicked the legs that way and held the truck out for inspection. A brittle silence descended on the hall.

'Wow,' Paddy tried to prompt Sandra and Burns, 'that is *amazing*.'

Neither of them said anything. Sandra shifted her weight uncomfortably.

'Isn't it?' Paddy said to Burns, a vague threat in her expression.

Sandra looked at the floor again and Burns gave Paddy a furtive smile. 'Great, yeah. A real breakthrough in toy-making.'

Paddy could have hit him. 'We watched your show the other night.' From the corner of her eye she saw Sandra bridle. 'That was breakthrough, too.'

The effect was immediate. Burns snapped at Pete, 'Where's your coat?' Pete ran back into his room and came out with his blue-and-white tracksuit top. 'You can't wear that, we're going to lunch with a television producer. We're going to a nice restaurant. You need to wear something smart.'

It was too much for Pete. His mouth turned down at the corners and he started to bubble. 'I don't wanna . . .'

Paddy rushed across the floor to him, glad of an excuse to hold him. 'Aw, son.'

Behind her Burns sighed, 'For God's sake, you shouldn't baby him like that. He's got to learn that he needs to dress smartly sometimes. It's not a big deal.'

But Paddy had her boy in her arms, her fingers in his hair and he was holding on to her tightly. 'I'm just guessing here, but I don't think Pete's upset because you want him to wear a different coat. It's the way you said it. Am I right, pal?' She pulled Pete's damp face away from her neck and made him look at her. 'Am I right?'

Pete nodded sadly.

'You treat him like a baby.'

'He's only just nearly six.' Paddy brushed his hair back from his face and kissed him. 'He's a big boy but even big boys are still babies to their mums.' She held his chin and smiled as warmly as she could. 'You can change your coat, can't ye, darlin'? And have a nice night with your daddy. He'll take ye to school tomorrow and I'll pick ye up after.'

Pete looked longingly over her shoulder to his bedroom as Burns muttered 'fucksake' to himself.

Paddy stood with her nose touching the cold window, looking down to the big black Merc parked next to the private central garden. The perfectly waxed boot glinted yellow sunlight as Burns dropped the overnight bag in and shut it. Sandra folded herself into the front passenger seat and Burns opened a back door for Pete, watching as he clambered in on all fours. He slammed it shut with a great sweep of his arm, took a step towards the driver's door and stopped. He checked across the roof of the car to see if the wife was out of sight, which she was, then he looked up to the window, at Paddy.

He flashed her a flirtatious smile. She didn't respond. He smiled again and, using his thumb and pinkie finger, made a telephone gesture to his ear. Paddy paused for effect and then made a slow, laborious wanking gesture back.

Burns stood on the pavement and laughed his arse off.

7

Babbity Bowsters

I

Had it not been sunny, the lane would have looked like a film set for a Jack the Ripper movie: cobbled street, a high brick warehouse with tiny barred windows on one side, a huge black wooden shed and, plonked between industrial giants, a pretty Georgian merchant's house with a hand-painted wooden sign outside: 'Babbity Bowster'.

A Babbity Bowster, Paddy had been informed, was always the last dance played at a ceilidh. It was a partners' dance, designed specifically for courting couples to stake a claim in each other at the end of an evening. The name of the pub couldn't have been more apt, given the manner in which the press used it.

Babbity's was the favoured hangout for most of the names and senior management in the Scottish press. It was close to the *News* offices and the Press Bar, a homeland for newspaper men all over the city, but Babbity's was expensive, which stopped the grunts from coming in. The usual characters who hung around in journalists' bars were filtered out by the prices too: petty thieves and city gossips were left behind in the old place. Here the familiars were all high-ranking city officials, politicians and businessmen, beguiled by the shabby glamour of the press. Upstairs in the restaurant deals were done, high-paying columns doled out, talent poached and arguments resolved over the scattered remains of the cheese board.

Designed by Robert Adams, the merchant's house had three perfectly proportioned storeys topped with a jaunty pediment and a doorway framed by flattened Doric columns. It had languished in the city centre for two hundred years, served as a storehouse, a fishmonger's and finally lain empty for twenty years until an enterprising French hotelier renovated it. Inside, the decor was understated Scottish bothy, no tartan or glassy-eyed stag heads but whitewashed plaster, slate floors and black-framed photos of crofters and forgotten fishermen. The bar had a vast malt whisky selection and took pride in its Scottish beer. The restaurant menu offered herring in oatmeal, old-fashioned cuts of ham and beef, and the sort of seafood that Scotland usually exported straight to France or Spain. A Scottish hotelier would have done it up as a French restaurant.

The early drinkers were in, stoically working their way through the late Sunday afternoon, alone or in twos, keeping company for the necessity of hiding their lonely look. The smell of warm ham and leeks hung softly in the smoky air.

Paddy felt their eyes on her as she clattered across the slate floor, her high heels announcing her arrival as effectively as gunfire. Merki waved to her from a corner, his black hair looking almost impossibly greasy today. She waved back and heard a voice from the bar:

'S that bitch doing here?'

She turned back, found the voice coming from a long strip of bitterness hunched over a pint of stout. 'Evening, Keck.'

Keck sat up and sipped his drink at her, not deigning to

answer. Time had not been kind to him: his face looked like a coin purse that had been kicking around an octogenarian's handbag since the end of the war. They stared at each other until he turned away. Keck was a sports writer, a good sports writer, and would have done better if he hadn't been handicapped by his personality. Whenever anyone got the chance they made him redundant. He had a long, clear stretch of bar for four feet on either side.

Paddy looked at the back of his neck, hesitating, thinking she should have gone over and commiserated with him about Terry: they had all been young together and should have been friends. But Keck would know Terry was dead already; it had been in every paper and on the TV news.

It was then that she saw another pair of eyes, not looking directly at her but watching in the mirror behind the bar, angry fearful eyes, narrowed and peering at her between the optics. Detective Chief Inspector Alec Knox knew her and she knew him: a sallow-skinned man who took bribes from gangsters, initiated and pulled investigations to suit his own purposes. She'd been watching him for years, knew he was dangerous, but could never get a shred of evidence on him. The police officers below him were too cowed, he'd avoided crossing other journalists and no editor would back her investigations. Knox never did anything headline-worthy: no ostentatious displays of wealth or attending boxing matches with cigar-smoking hitmen. In desperation she even tried disseminating rumours about him through Press Bar gossip, but for some reason it didn't take.

She stepped around the corner to look him in the eye. Knox was sitting with a leader writer from the *Scotsman*, an ex-academic evangelist for devolution. Knox's eyes widened as she looked back at him. He was glad she had seen him, knew he was connected to important people.

She nodded at him. 'Knox.'

'Meehan,' he said but Paddy had turned away, climbing the stairs, hearing the leader writer quizzing Knox about where he knew Paddy Meehan from.

The restaurant was even emptier than the bar but smokier. A non-press couple were in for a nice meal, their eyes locked on each other. Nearby, in front of the curtained wall leading to the offices upstairs, was a table of four Rottweilers in suits. Known as the SS, they were reporters for the *Scottish Standard*. By the back wall, three pals from the *Daily Mail* were smoking, drooping over their dinners after a day-long binge. It was quiet but there were enough people to see her there and put the word out. As soon as Keck heard she was meeting George McVie, the story was as good as delivered back to the *Daily News*.

A lithe young waitress saw her standing at the empty reception desk and walked over, stepping on her tiptoes like a dancer. The *Standard* reporters laughed loudly behind her and she flinched. New girl, Paddy guessed, first shift. She was in for a night of it. She led Paddy to a table for two over by a window and brought her a glass of water.

The *Standard* table was warming up, looking around at the other tables for someone to fight with. They were a new gang; the *Standard*'s London management had noticed that the Scots had a ravenous appetite for newspapers and revamped the Scottish edition of the paper, putting in more local stories and adding 'Scottish' to the title. They recruited the two biggest arseholes in the Scottish trade to run it: Jinksie and Macintosh had worked at the *News* and *Express* respectively. Neither had shone and no one quite understood why they'd been given the top jobs. The *Standard* managers had seen something in both men that everyone else had missed: they were petty to the verge of obsession. No personal foible was too unimportant to be printed, no story too distasteful, no individual too tragic to be exploited. Sales soared.

Paddy had been sitting at the table just long enough to read the menu twice and think up a couple of good retorts to Keck's snub when George McVie made a dramatic entrance, bouncing the outside door off the wall.

He paused, drawing all eyes to him, scowling back at the faces in the room. Nature, time and his temperament had conspired to perfect McVie's glower. His face and posture fitted around misery as neatly as cellophane over a cup. The drunken *Mail* journalists gave him a whoop and a couple of handclaps, really just to wind up the *Standard* table. McVie wilfully misinterpreted the greeting as congratulations for a great issue: that morning's *Mail on Sunday* had exposed a High Court judge for being gay and cruising for rent boys in Edinburgh. They had been investigating the story for months, a rare occurrence now, and McVie could rightfully take a bit of credit for lending the resources to it. The applause died while his hand was raised in modest triumph, leaving him to right himself to the hisses and boos of the *Standard* table. One of the *Standard* reporters cupped his mouth and shouted, 'Poof.'

McVie stood by the door looking as if he'd walked in with no trousers on. Paddy stood up and called him over. The wit shouted 'Poof' at her as well and got a round of applause from the table even though the comment was neither apposite nor particularly insulting.

'You lot are wanted back at the office,' she said, quietly and, she thought, with great dignity. 'Someone somewhere's just taken their underpants off.'

The *Mail* boys erupted into forced laughter and bread-throwing at the *Standard* table. The romantic couple broke off looking at each other, glancing around, realizing suddenly that they were not on a pleasure cruise but on a pirate ship. The waitress stood at the side of the room, nervously chewing the cuff of her shirt sleeve.

McVie sloped across the room to Paddy. He kissed her hand in a way that made the meet look staged, which it was.

'That'll do,' she muttered. 'Sit down, for fucksake.'

He dropped his shoulders and his perfectly tailored suit jacket slid down his arms and into his hands. He draped it carefully over the back of the chair, flashing the electric-blue silk lining as he whispered, 'Can I go home now?'

'Probably. Thanks for this.'

He settled in the seat in front of her. Meeting the editor of a rival paper would suggest to anyone who heard about it that Paddy was about to be poached to do a column for them. Having dinner with him would suggest he was offering more money than the *Daily News*. The *News* editor, Bunty, had only been in the job for a year but his sales were steadily falling. He wasn't giving anyone a raise but might if he thought his beloved Misty was about to move.

'You're paying though, right?' he said.

McVie was as rich as God now, could have paid the bill for everyone in the place and not even noticed the dent in his bank account, but he had to pretend he was getting something out of the meeting. Otherwise he'd just be doing Paddy a favour and that was tantamount to an admission of friendship. 'Where's that wee bastard of yours tonight, then?'

'Off with his dad.'

'Talentless prick. That show of his is an affront to humanity.'

The waitress skipped over to them but her smile died when she saw McVie's face. 'Get me a big gin 'n' tonic. Just tickle it with the tonic.' He jabbed her in the stomach with the menu. 'Haggis and neeps and hurry up.'

He glared at Paddy, prompting her to order. She chose the ham haugh in sherry sauce and the waitress withdrew, glad to get away.

Paddy tutted at him. 'You're laying it on a bit thick, aren't ye?'

'Am I?' He took out his cigarettes and lit one, flicking the packet across the table at her as an offering. It always took McVie a while to calm down after he left his work. He wasn't a natural leader, was a loner by inclination but maintained control of his staff with displays of temper a two-year-old would have thought vulgar. He tried to give her a friendly smile. 'Better?'

'No. Ye look as if a rival just had an anal prolapse.'

He sucked a hiss between his front teeth, as close to a genuine laugh as he did these days. McVie had a better side: away from work he was a very slightly different man. He gave Pete age-inappropriate presents, but presents none the less. He loaned Paddy his cottage on Skye for a holiday after Pete got out of hospital because he was still on oxygen and they couldn't go far. It was full of dodgy wiring and gay pornography.

'Come on,' said Paddy, 'I've had a bit of a grim weekend. I could do without this.'

'Terry?'

She nodded. 'Terry.'

'Sad,' he said and meant it.

Paddy frowned at her plate. 'Yeah. Sad.'

In a little cheering display of bonhomie, McVie shook his napkin jauntily at his side, pulled it across his lap, took the end of his cream silk tie, tucked it loosely into his shirt pocket and touched the cutlery on his place setting with his fingertips, a concert pianist greeting the keys. He sighed and looked up at her.

'God, I'm hungry.'

'You sent a child to my door last night,' she said.

'That young man said you're a bitch.'

'Did he?'

'Yes.'

'He grilled me pretty hard.'

McVie hissed at his place mat. 'What can I say? When the boy gets the scent there's no stopping him.'

The *Mail* journalists shouted at the waitress for more wine. One of them was humming, drumming his fingers on the table edge, trying to remember a song from his youth. They were on the jagged verge of singing.

'Tell me about Terry,' said McVie.

'God. It was awful. I had to go and look at the body, say it was him for sure. He was shot in the fucking head. His face was all over the place.'

The waitress brought his gin and tonic over and he took it from her hand, acknowledging her only by waving his free hand to dismiss her. She hesitated in surprise and Paddy smiled a weak apology. She backed off.

McVie sipped his drink. 'He was working for me, freelance.'

'Who? Terry?'

'Yeah, on nothing stories, local bullshit. Waiting for a war commission from London. We'll organize the memorial service. Will you speak?'

'God, no.' She couldn't speak about him. Everyone there would know she'd chucked him. 'The police said it was the Provos.'

McVie sipped. 'My source in the police said it wasn't.'

'Bit of a coincidence though, his body being found out on the Stranraer road.'

'Why's that significant?'

'The ferry for Belfast leaves from Stranraer. Anyone who travels to Ireland regularly would be familiar with it, know the cut-offs, where's busy, where's quiet. It suggests it was an Irishman who killed him.'

'Well, I heard it was a mugging or something.'

'A robbery?'

'Aye.'

'Was he missing anything?'

'They never found his clothes and his wallet.'

She looked at him. 'Bit elaborate for a mugging, isn't it? The guy could afford a gun and a car; he's hardly going to kill someone for their trousers.'

She knew that McVie was just playing her for clues: the other newspapers would want the *Daily News* to be wrong about the Provos because they had blown the other papers off the stands.

'Your contact wouldn't happen to be Knox, would it?' she asked McVie.

'Christ, don't start that shit again.'

'He *is* bent.'

'I don't give a fuck. No one gives a fuck except you and him.' He stubbed out his half-smoked cigarette messily, chasing the scarlet tip around the ashtray. 'Terry was involved in a lot of things. When he started out he didn't mind the danger, but I think he got to like it.'

'I suppose. Who *wants* to be a war reporter?'

'Yeah, exactly. Ambitious young men who don't know any better and old men with a death wish.'

The *Mail* journalist had remembered his song and was giving it his all. His head was tipped back, eyes shut tight as he murdered Neil Young's 'Heart Of Gold'. It probably sounded better in his head.

'Right, Meehan, come on: Callum Ogilvy. When's he getting out?'

'No one knows, do they?'

He was looking at her, a smile somewhere in his eyes. 'You do,' he said quietly.

'No, I don't.'

The waitress brought them some bread and individually wrapped butter portions, fresh from the freezer.

'But you do.'

'George, I don't know when he's getting out, I promise.'

'Swear on the life of your child.'

She grinned at him. He knew she was lying, everyone knew she was lying about Callum Ogilvy, but McVie could read her better than most.

'How are ye, George?'

He hissed at the feeble detour, and took out another cigarette. She tried again. 'How's that nice young man of yours?'

He sucked his teeth, lit the cigarette and blew thick smoke across the table. It hit her place mat, lifting off it like a morning mist rising from a lake.

'Meehan, we've got guys camped outside the prison. We can wait for ever. You tell Callum Ogilvy this: we'll pay top whack for an exclusive. With pictures. Someone's getting it and he might as well make a few quid off it. Set him up in his new life.'

'Johnny Mac from the *Times* offered him 50K and he doesn't want it.'

'Unless you're keeping it for yourself, exclusive on the cheap, family connections and all that.' He gave her a sly look. Callum and Sean Ogilvy weren't members of her family. People forgot that she had been engaged to Sean and that he wasn't her cousin. She herself forgot sometimes.

'George, what does your man think about you outing gay men in your paper?'

McVie's face tightened. 'The judge was picking up teenage junkie prostitutes and fucking them in his car.'

'Still,' she sipped her mineral water, 'it was a bit of a gay bash.'

He excused himself with a wave of his cigarette. 'Sells papers. That's the business we're in.'

The *Standard* guys were sniggering at the waitress, who was trying to lift the plates from their table. 'Aren't you frightened those bastards'll out you?'

'No,' said McVie, but he looked worried.

McVie had left his wife seven years ago and had gradually come out to the industry. Under the unspoken rules of engagement his sexuality had never been mentioned in the press, even when he took over the Scottish *Mail on Sunday* and became a name, but the *Standard*'s spite knew no bounds.

'If they decide to out you it'll be ugly.'

McVie wriggled as if he had a cockroach between his shoulder blades. 'Shut up about that.' He took a slice of bread from the basket and then a butter portion, cracking it back and forth in the paper to thaw it. 'What did Hatcher say about Terry?'

As luck would have it, the butter was frozen solid and McVie didn't notice the moment's pause before she spoke. '*Kevin* Hatcher?' she said as if she was correcting him.

'Mmm.'

'Nothing much.'

'He must have said something. He left Terry outside the casino.'

Paddy took a slice of bread too, pulled the soft guts out of it and chewed, 'Just, you know ...' She took a guess. 'They lost money.'

McVie unwrapped the butter portion and put it on his bread, trying to spread it with his knife. The butter gathered the soft bread to it, pulling the slice into lumps.

'So,' said Paddy casually, 'Kevin was the last person to see Terry? Where is he now, the *Express*?'

McVie looked angrily at the mauled slice of bread. 'Free-lance. Got his own agency.' He picked the bread up, used both hands to form it roughly into a ball and threw it towards the startled waitress, who was taking a pudding order from the romantic couple. The ball of bread hit the curtains and dropped to the floor. He didn't need to raise his voice: everyone was looking at him already. 'I want butter that isn't frozen fucking solid.'

The couple looked appalled. The *Standard* boys cheered, because they always cheered bullies, and the *Mail* clapped half-heartedly because he was their boss.

'You're an arsehole.'

He sat back and sucked his cigarette. 'When's Ogilvy getting out?'

'Shut the fuck up.'

The waitress brought the plates of haggis and ham over, apologizing for the butter and explaining that the chef had forgotten to take it out earlier but as soon as it was softened she'd bring it right over. McVie grunted an answer. She backed off as soon as she dared, hurrying away to hide in the kitchen.

'Meehan, this is my one night off,' he said when she'd left. 'I'm doing you a favour.'

Paddy made him look at her. 'George, you know you've barely looked me in the eye since you got here. Ye were never very nice to start with, but for Christsake, are ye in there?'

Resting his elbow on the table, McVie poked his fork at her, his scowl lifting. 'I'm in here, aye.'

'Good. Remember, you don't have to be an arsehole to be an editor. It helps, but you don't need to be. Remember Farquarson? He was decent.'

'Yeah, and where's he now?'

As far as she knew, their old editor was enjoying a leisurely retirement in Devon, but that wasn't what George meant. 'Every editor gets the bump some time. It wasn't because he retained a sliver of humanity.'

'Come on. Give me something. I'll look like an arsehole if I come away with nothing.'

She pretended to think about it. 'Ogilvy is getting out, you're right about that.'

'When?'

'In a while.'

McVie tried to read her face. 'Two weeks, that's what everyone thinks.'

'They're wrong.'

'Three weeks?'

Paddy wobbled her head from side to side and sliced into the soft pink ham.

'Three weeks?'

She tipped her head encouragingly.

'Three weeks then.'

She looked up at him. 'I didn't say that.'

'No, that's right.' McVie nodded and smiled at his plate. 'You didn't. Thanks.'

II

The night shift were absent from the newsroom, most of them out on assignments or hiding in different secret places around the building. Larry was in his office listening to the radio. She kept her coat on and lifted the phone book from the secretaries' desk, flicking through the residential numbers for 'H'.

'What are you doing?'

She started and looked up and to find Merki standing at

the side of the desk, peering at the listings. 'Christ, what are you sidling about after?'

Merki stared hungrily at the phone book. 'Looking for something?'

Paddy pursed her lips at him.

Merki licked the side of his mouth, trying to think of another move. 'The Provos say it wasn't them.'

'They told you that, did they?'

'Naw.' He craned his neck, trying to read the page upside down. 'They didn't claim responsibility. They have a code word they use to admit responsibility and they haven't done it yet.'

'Well, maybe they're all away on training this weekend.'

His eyes were fixed on the phone book listings. '"H"?'

'How soon do they make the phone call?'

'Usually before the body's even found. It's been twenty-four hours now and nothing.'

She stared at him, blank and still, until he sloped off towards the coffee cupboard, glancing backwards at the phone book, wondering.

Paddy found Kevin Hatcher's name. His address was listed as Battlefield on the South Side.

She looked up to the coffee room and saw Merki's shoulder. He was waiting in there, ready to come out and check the phone book after her. She could phone Sinn Fein and ask if they'd heard anything about Terry but they'd have to deny all knowledge of IRA activities: the only reason they were legally allowed to exist was that they claimed to be separate from the IRA. She looked up the contacts book on the secretaries' table and called the *Irish Republican News*.

The call was eventually answered by a bored copy taker.

'Sorry, not copy, I want to talk to a reporter.'

'Is it a story?'

'Yeah,' she said. Well, it kind of was. She'd be lucky to

get a journalist who could be bothered to help her.

A news reporter caught the call and asked her what the fuck she wanted in a thick brogue. She lowered her voice and tried to sound terribly senior.

'Paddy Meehan here, from the *Scottish Daily News*. Big story over here: suspected execution of a journalist by a soldier of the IRA. Any word on it?'

He covered the phone with his hand. She couldn't hear any talking at the other end. He might have put the receiver down and walked away, for all she knew. Suddenly he came back on and surprised her. 'We've heard nothing.'

'Would you have?'

'Aye, yeah, usually. No press release, nothing. Here, hang on.' He covered the phone again but she could hear talking in the background this time. 'Right? 'K. No, right ye are.' He came back on. 'Getting it in now. Not them.'

'They're denying it?'

'Official,' he said. 'Any jobs over there?'

'Some. What's your name?'

'Poraig Seaniag.'

She wrote it on an invisible bit of paper with an invisible pen, just to get the right effect to her voice. 'Poraig, you're a doll.'

'If you need anything done on the story I could do with a byline.'

She'd never heard of anything so pushy: an informant asking for a name check as the author of an article. 'It's not necessarily an article, to be honest. We were close. I just want to know what happened to him.'

'Oh. Was he family?'

'Kind of.' She let the conversation trail away, adding in a sniff for flavour.

'OK, sorry. Well, keep an eye out for my name.'

'Will do.'

She tutted indignantly at the receiver after she'd hung up.

Merki was still hiding behind the door to the coffee room, she could see his feet shuffling. He'd come running over the moment she left, look for notes jotted on a pad, try to find the page she'd been checking out in the phone book. Spitefully, she opened the phone book at the 'p's, running her hand down the spine to flatten it before she shut it and put it back on the shelf.

8

The Darkness in Fort William

I

Kevin Hatcher moved like an old man, his actions stiff and slow. He wasn't old though. He actually looked younger than Paddy remembered him being six years ago when she last saw him up close, but he was a drinker then. His hair was blond, lighter now that his life didn't consist of staggering from bar to bar, and he had a tan. Through the thin denim of his worn shirt she could tell that he exercised and had developed broad shoulders and solid arms.

When she called ahead he didn't ask her why she wanted to come over, even though it was eight o'clock on a Sunday night. He opened the door to her, mumbled 'hello' as he took her coat, dropped it carelessly on to a chair in the hall and pointed her into the living room. He was still shocked, she could see that.

The flat was on the top floor of a red sandstone tenement, nice but fantastically messy and cave-like, definitely a bachelor's house. They passed the kitchen door and she caught a whiff of sour mop. She suspected that a woman had lived here at one point: framed pictures were hung with care and there was a degree of order under the blanket of mess. Two sofas faced each other in the living room, there was a carpet under there somewhere but the flat was layered with dust and clutter, dirty mugs, prints of photographs, mysterious bits of kit and wrappers from motorway cuisine. Tripods of various sizes were propped in the doorway. A lone chair had been placed right in the middle of the living-room floor, directly in front of the television.

As he followed her in he told her that he'd gone out to buy milk at noon and seen the *Daily News* headline several times before he recognized the photo of Terry.

'That was an old picture,' he said, pushing a clutter of magazines to one side of the settee so that Paddy could sit down.

'Yeah,' she said, 'from before he went away.'

He stood in front of Paddy, looking at the floor, clasping and unclasping his hands as if trying to cast his memory back and recall where these interactions went next. At last he remembered. 'Tea?'

'I'm fine. Are you OK?'

Kevin shook his head.

'Sit down.' She patted the settee next to her. 'What have you been doing all day?'

He shuffled over to the settee, waved a hand helplessly over the jacket and cup sitting on it, trying to magic them away. Finally he picked them up, put them on the floor, sat down and wrapped his arms around his waist. He'd called the police and spent a few hours with them, reiterating the events of the night in the casino.

Kevin's work was everywhere. The coffee table held several open boxes of slide negatives and large black port-folios sat against the wall or lay open on the floor. The photographs were wonderfully crisp street portraits, each of them brimming with narrative: a fishmonger with blood on his overalls smoking a cigarette, three jolly men in leather aprons outside a Brutalist abattoir, a fat man in sports gear on a bleak winter hillside, his reflective sunglasses showing the hordes of tourists trailing up a steep path. She wanted to compliment Kevin on them but thought it would sound frivolous.

Kevin was nodding rhythmically at his feet and looked at her suddenly. 'He really loved you.'

She shivered.

'I don't mean that you should have loved him back, just – you know – he did.'

'Kevin, Terry hadn't spent any time with me for years. I don't know who he was in love with but he didn't know me anymore.'

'Do people change?' he said, as if it was news to him. 'Bigger houses, kids and money, it's all just garnish, isn't it?'

She liked his phrasing. 'You're pretty smart for a snapper.'

He flashed a polite smile. 'Did you see his body?'

Paddy nodded. 'They came to my house and took me to ID him.' She could see that he wanted to ask about it but couldn't bring himself to. 'They said it would have been fast. They shot him from behind so he wouldn't even have seen them coming, might not have known it was about to happen.'

He knew she was lying, she could tell. He nodded for a bit, his eyes skittering around the floor as he gnawed a cuticle.

'I heard you were with him earlier that night.'

'Yeah, we went to the casino. We're writing a book together. Were. It was a short text to accompany the pictures. They gave us a shit advance to finish it so we went out to spend it all in one night. Casino's the only place you could do that really.'

'What, on drink?'

'No, gambling. I don't drink any more.'

She'd heard that Kevin had got sober. He had disappeared for a while back in the mid-eighties; everyone had assumed he was dead but then he had reappeared, working for himself. She had only seen him across dark banqueting halls, jogging up to various stages to accept prizes for his work.

He was looking at her out of the corner of his eye. 'I recognizc you from telly but did you used to work at the *Daily News?*'

She nodded. 'I'm back there again now.'

'Did we work together?'

'Yeah, for about four years,' she said, adding, 'I was just a copy girl,' to excuse the fact that he didn't recognize her.

He shifted uncomfortably on the chair arm, straddling it. 'When I was there I was a bit ... unconscious. Sorry. Sabbatical from reality.'

'I remember you getting redundancy and disappearing. We were running a book on how long it'd take for you to kill yourself.'

He smirked. He didn't look bad for a dead man. 'I'd have taken short odds on that myself.'

'Did you manage to spend the advance?'

Kevin looked up at a framed poster on the wall. An Edwardian portrait of a woman in a large red hat. Red and green, like Christmas. He sighed a 'no'. 'We came out four quid up. Just as well, wasn't it? I'll have to give it back now. Terry hadn't nearly finished the writing.' He glanced at her shoes. 'What happened between you two in Fort William?'

She wanted to get up and leave. Instead she said, 'I got a note from him last month, came in the post to work. He said he was sorry.'

'What was he sorry for?'

They were looking at each other, less than a foot apart. If she was ever going to speak about Fort William it would be now. 'People do change, Kevin. He changed. He wasn't who he used to be. He was more soft before, you know?'

She looked to Kevin to absolve her for not loving his dead friend.

They both watched as he turned his toe to her. He spoke softly. 'He'd been about.'

'He'd seen things,' she added sadly.

'He had. I think Angola was pretty heavy.'

'Yeah?'

He shut his eyes and nodded once. 'Yeah.'

They left it at that. She didn't need to go into the details or explain that Terry frightened her so much she couldn't bear to talk to him.

It was in the dark hotel room in Fort William. They'd been out for a meal: it was lovely, she hardly remembered where, just Terry's eyes smiling and him taking her hand in the street as they walked back to the hotel. They started kissing in the lift, the first touch after eight years of thinking about each other. In the privacy of the room he was older, more considered and mature. Paddy didn't get distracted by the wallpaper or noises in the hall or work worries. They spoke to each other, making requests, laughing when he couldn't get his trousers off over his shoe. They ended up on the floor because the bed was covered in stupid little cushions.

But at the end, as he came, Terry forgot himself. He held on to her hair, digging his nails into her scalp, and banged her head hard off the floor five times, too many times to be a mistake. Far too many.

He apologized briefly and fell asleep while she lay beneath him, shocked and silent. His breathing became regular, the heat from his skin burning where it touched her. She disentangled herself, grabbed her clothes and ran, speeding all the way back to Glasgow.

She couldn't articulate why it bothered her so much. Perhaps it hinted at him secretly despising her. But really it was the casualness of his apology. He'd done that before, it had the feel of a habit. He'd done it many times to many women and not one of them was in a position to tell him to fuck off and never do that to her again.

She was ashamed and embarrassed for him. She didn't want to tell anyone and Kevin was too graceful to press her for details. She wished she'd got to know him before now. Terry had so much not to talk about, and she could see now why he had liked Kevin so much.

'So what was your book going to be about?'

Kevin stretched his legs out in front of him. 'Street portraits. Scots living in New York and London. It was just an excuse to go to New York together, really.'

'So he did the interviews?'

'No, he did the pictures and I did the text, that's what was unusual about the book.' She looked at him and found him almost smiling at her. 'Joke.'

'It was a very funny joke,' she said flatly, making him really smile this time. 'Do you think the book had anything to do with him being murdered?'

'Nah,' he said with certainty. 'Like the police said today, if it did I'd be dead too, wouldn't I? I think it was something to do with somewhere he worked. Maybe he saw some incriminating things, executions, money deals . . .' He ran out of vacuous ideas and shrugged an apology. 'I'm a photographer,' he said, as if that explained his confusion about international affairs.

'How far did you get with the book?'

'Only a couple of mock-up pages for the project proposal.' He stood up and left the room, coming back with an A3 folder. He unfurled the elastic band around it and sat two huge pages next to each other, a beautifully crisp photograph on one page and a small paragraph next to it. The picture was of an American street scene. It could have been anywhere: boxy clapboard houses with settees on porches, a big electric-blue sky framing the scene. Stars and Stripes flags were hung in dirty windows or drooping on flagpoles, big cars parked in a broad patchwork concrete street, and in the foreground a woman of eighty, arms crossed, grinning, the folds in her skin deep enough to lose change in, her dentured teeth a wall of perfect white.

The caption read 'Senga – Kilmarnock / New Jersey'. The facing paragraph of text told the woman's history, how she came to be in the US and why she stayed. Paddy smiled at the text. Terry was smart: it wasn't what a reader would have expected. Senga drew no false comparisons between the two places, stated no preference. She came to visit her sister and married an Italian shopkeeper. She fell in love with his shoes and the way he mixed her drink. Her sister had cancer in her leg but still danced. It was very much Terry's writing style. He always came at a story from a unique angle, edited out the obvious and left the story to resolve itself in the reader's mind. She stroked the picture of Senga with an open palm but Kevin pulled her hand away.

'Sorry,' he said, 'it's ... the photographic paper doesn't like that.'

'Sorry.'

Kevin looked tearful suddenly and turned the page for her. 'Bob – Govan / Long Island'. Bob smiled on an unspoiled seashore, his shirt sleeves rolled up to show his forearm tattoo of a fey King Billy on a rearing horse.

Kevin pointed at the tattoo, a Loyalist commemoration of the defeat of the Irish Catholics by William of Orange. 'That's an invitation to fight in Glasgow. Over there people just think he likes horses. Reinvention. That's what the whole book's about really.'

'I'll buy a copy when this comes out.'

'It won't come out now.'

'Couldn't someone just use Terry's notes?'

'Nah. He was the reason it was getting published. He knew the woman who owns Scotia Press and all of the promotion was going to be on the back of his world travels.' Kevin nodded. 'He bought your book.'

She was surprised. 'The Patrick Meehan book?'

'Yeah, *Shadow of Death*. He got me to send it to him in Beirut.'

She hadn't known then that Terry even remembered her. She stumbled across his articles about the Lebanon while she was in hospital having Pete. Terry'd had a rare, bizarre dinner with a Hezbollah leader and wrote about the new constitution, about the hardship of the ordinary people and the raw beauty of the landscape. Until Pete, Terry's world was everything she thought she wanted, brim full of glory and history, shining a light into shadowy corners. And then Pete was born – a happy, trouble-free baby, thriving from the moment he arrived, surrounded by family and friends and cousins. She felt detached when she read the series of articles but she was heading out into the quiet waters of motherhood, drifting off from the shore, alone in the boat. She was glad Terry was out there, protecting people by telling the truth, but her own life was more immediate and all-consuming.

As she felt the weight of the pages on her knees and looked into Kevin's shocked eyes, she realized that she had been furious with Terry because, in the dark of Fort William, he had killed her most fondly held delusion: that someone somewhere was making a difference.

11

She was alone in the house. Dub was up in Perth with two of his acts and Pete was at Burns's, leaving her with just the radio for company, sitting at her desk, trying to think of an opinion to beat to death with a thousand short words. She'd left the lights off in the rest of the house to help focus her attention, leaving just the angle-poise shining on her blank sheet of paper, but the darkness was making her feel exhausted.

Out in the street she could hear a steady rumble of cars on the Great Western Road, the distant gurgle of the river, the chat of occasional passers-by coming back from the pub.

The hard part of a Misty column was getting a start. Once she found her hook it was like skidding on oil. She loved it, and rarely got edited beyond her punctuation, which was poor. The difficult part was deciding what to rant about.

Whole areas of comment were closed to her because she was female: emotional first-person accounts about anything, stories about children, all things domestic. If she touched on those issues she wouldn't be taken seriously and would end up right back in the Dab Sheet ghetto. And Callum Ogilvy. If she mentioned him, favourably or otherwise, she'd leave herself open to being outed as a friend of his family. She was amazed no one had mentioned the fact in print yet.

The Rats. Under Milk Wood. After just nine minutes at the desk she had already reached the point where she was testing her eyesight by reading the spines of books twenty feet away across the study.

Fat is a Feminist Issue. Fifteen years of unsuccessful self-denial had made her no slimmer and bloody miserable. She read *Fat is a Feminist Issue* and felt a wash of relief at the suggestion that she give up dieting. Actually, the book was far more complex, laying out a series of exercises for dealing with a fraught relationship with food, mirror work that involved standing naked and looking at yourself, sometimes jumping, but she didn't do those things. She just let herself eat and it was a joy. She put on half a stone and plateau'd there, the fattest she had ever been and the most content. She still felt flashes of disgust when her backside jiggled as she ran up steps or her stomach folded into a perfect round cushion when she sat down, still resented not being able to buy clothes she liked because she couldn't get them over her head, but the pleasure of unbridled eating more than made up for it.

She looked at the box files high up on her shelves. The old yellowed clippings of all of Terry's articles were stored up there. When she still had high hopes for their relationship she had meant to show them to him one day, to get them down and let him see how she had followed his every move, how much he'd always meant to her. She could get them down now and look through his articles from Liberia, see if there was anything in them, any tangles with the government that could explain his death. But Kevin was wrong. Liberia was an internal conflict. They were getting so much money from the CIA they'd never risk killing a journalist and alienating their American bankers.

The polite rap at the door was a welcome interruption. She stood up and walked lightly to the door, expecting a kindly neighbour or an evangelist or an Ogilvy-hunting journalist at worst.

He was short, sandy-haired, wore a neat pale blue jumper over a white T-shirt, beige slacks and steel-rimmed square glasses. She immediately assumed he was a local with a petition about the parking.

She opened her mouth to say hello, but the look in his eyes stopped her. The eyes were cold, emotionally flat. The suburban neatness was a cover, the staypress crease down the front of his trousers suddenly a knife edge.

'Paddy Meehan?' He was Irish. He spoke quickly and

quietly; she couldn't tell whether the accent was North or South.

'Sorry?'

'Are you Paddy Meehan?'

The sensation began between her shoulder blades, a hot tremble, exacerbated by her tiredness no doubt, but spread to her arms, her neck, her throat. She cast her mind back into the flat, mapping Pete's empty bed, the knives in the kitchen drawer, the dagger-shaped letter opener on the desk.

He smiled coldly, a cheerful snake. 'Can ye not remember who ye are?' His breath was acid with the smell of stale cigarette smoke.

'Ah, she's not in just now,' said Paddy. 'I'm just trying to work out when she will be in.'

The smile widened but didn't deepen. 'It's you. I recognize ye. Seen ye on telly.'

She smiled back, more convincingly than him, she hoped. 'Are you a fan?'

'No, no, no.' He dropped his head to his chest, thrusting his hands into his pockets, and didn't seem to feel the need to elaborate.

'So . . .?'

He smirked at his shoes. The dim yellow light in the close glinted off the lenses of his spectacles. 'You phoned about Terry? Said you were his family? Can I come in?' He shuffled towards the door without giving her the chance to answer, took the step and slid into the hallway, shutting the door after himself.

The lights were still off in the house. The anglepoise in her study pooled light by the doorway, darkening the rest of the hall. They were standing close.

'What's your name?'

He smiled again, cold-eyed. His hands slithered out of

his pockets and he raised them in a shrug. 'You phoned about Terry. Said you were family.'

She thought of Pete and felt a flash of hot anger and reached over to the front door, swinging it open so that it banged loudly off the wall, denting the plaster behind it.

Steven Curren was stepping on to the landing. He stopped and looked at them, startled. 'Oh,' he said, 'Sorry. McVie made me come back again.'

Paddy grabbed his forearm and pulled him in. 'Steven! Come in!'

Snake Eyes was looking from one to the other but put his hand out to Steven. 'How are ye?' he said. 'Nice to meet ye.'

'Hi.' Steven was young and well brought up. He shook the guy's hand and introduced himself, said he was from the *Mail on Sunday* and didn't really want to be here but his editor had sent him out again. He'd just started in the job.

'I'm sorry,' Paddy smiled at Snake Eyes, 'I forget your name.

His eyes flickered to the left, signalling a lie. 'Michael Collins,' he said and let Steven's hand fall.

Steven didn't recognize the pseudonym but Paddy shuddered. The Republican hero was remembered for many things, for successfully conducting the war that threw the Brits out of Ireland, for signing a peace treaty that authorized partition, for dying in the brutal civil war that followed. What always stuck in Paddy's mind was Collins's time as director of intelligence for the IRA, when he formed the Twelve Apostles, an assassination squad who targeted British agents. On the first Bloody Sunday, in 1920, fourteen agents were either shot or had their throats slit in one night.

'How could I forget?' she said seriously, telling him she understood. 'So you were just leaving?'

'No,' smiled Michael Collins, 'you were just going to make me tea.'

They looked at each other. If he had a gun she would be no safer with him just outside the door than inside. There were knives in the kitchen drawer. 'Of course.'

The kitchen was big enough to have a table with four chairs in it but not to move comfortably around. Steven and Michael sat down as she filled the kettle, shuffling sideways around the table, brushing their backs as she reached for teabags and sugar. Into the taut silence Steven rambled about Glasgow and how he came to be here and how it was the greatest place for a journalist to begin his career because the competition was so fierce, you see? Best training ground in the world. They trained you to be really aggressive, really proactive, to really find your own stories. He left a pause but no one filled it. He missed his friends from uni, of course, it was a bit isolating, coming up here on his own, but still, lots of advantages.

Collins gave nothing away. He listened to answers politely, and all the while his hands sat flattened on the table top, unnaturally still.

He wasn't flustered by Steven's presence; it was a complication, not a bar. He might kill both of them, she realized suddenly as she picked the cups out of the cupboard. She needed to get to the phone. She flicked the kettle on, sat the cups on the table and got the milk out of the fridge.

'Biscuits?'

Steven said yes, he'd love a biscuit, he hadn't had his tea yet and Paddy slipped out of the room.

She stepped into the study, the calm site of work. The debris of her uneventful Misty night lay on the table, the letter from Johnny Mac propped on the typewriter, the empty packet of crisps she'd had from Dub's food cupboard. The time felt like a treat in hindsight. Steven was still rambling behind her but, she realized too late, his voice was carrying out to the hall, coming towards her, following the back of the man who was creeping after her. She lunged for the phone.

'I only want to talk to you.'

She clutched the receiver to her chest and spun to look at him. The dagger-shaped letter opener was on the right side of the desk, she could see the tip of it in the shadow of the typewriter.

'Honestly.' He stepped towards her, a creep, a liar, a true Apostle. 'Just a talk.'

She was sweating, wanted to step back from the smell of his sour breath but hardly dared move. 'What about?'

He looked around the dark room, at the pine bookcases, at her old desk, the leatherette top scarred along the edge with fag burns from before it was hers, at the letter from Johnny Mac propped on the typewriter. 'Terry Hewitt, he wasn't one of ours.'

'So I've heard.'

'That was a separate thing,' he said and corrected himself. 'Nothing to do with us.'

'*Separate* thing?'

He blinked slowly, thinking his way through the implications before he spoke. 'Someone else's thing. Not ours.'

Still shielding her breastbone with the phone, she chanced a step towards the desk, her hand resting by the typewriter, inches from the dagger. 'Do you know what that *thing* was?'

'So, are you Terry's family? A cousin?'

'Ex-girlfriend. Terry had no family.'

He tipped his head back, showing her his throat, and laughed joylessly.

Behind him she could see Steven Curren at the kitchen table, bending sideways out of his chair to see them. Collins composed himself. 'Lovely cornicing. My father was a plasterer. Later he ran a chip shop.'

'Who killed Terry?'

A smile slithered across his face. 'Goodbye.' He stepped backwards out of the room. She didn't hear him walk across the hall but the door opened and shut quietly. Steven smiled at her from the kitchen. 'Is he off then?'

Paddy dropped the phone and looked out into the dark hallway. Gone. She looked in the hall cupboard, checked Dub's room. He lived a curiously spartan life. His books and precious collection of rare comedy albums were kept in cardboard boxes that he used variously as a bedside table, a desk and a lamp stand. She looked under the bed, and then skipped into Pete's room. He was gone.

Steven was calling to her from the kitchen. 'The kettle's boiled. Shall I make the tea? D'you want one?'

Paddy stood in the dark bedroom. The room door had been open when Collins passed it. A pile of fresh boy's clothes was folded neatly and sitting on the end of the little bed, a box of plastic trucks visible under the bed.

Collins knew she had a child. He knew where she lived, what she looked like and he knew she had a child.

III

She heard his footsteps in the hall at two forty in the morning, rolled on to her back, an arm over her burning eyes, listening carefully to the rhythm and the distance, unable to shake her body awake enough to sit up.

Tiptoeing across the wooden floorboards, trying not to make a noise, he went to the kitchen, then to the bathroom, and finally into his own room. He hadn't seen Pete's door lying open or he would have come in to her.

She summoned the energy to throw the duvet off with a

hand, paused and sat up, swinging her legs over the edge of the bed, keeping her raw eyes shut.

She felt for her dressing gown at the end of the bed, pulled it on and stood up unsteadily, staggering over to the door and out into the hall.

Dub had only just climbed into bed. He looked up at her, standing by the door, her hair a tangled mess, her head tipped back so that she didn't have to open her eyes properly.

A sensual, sleepy smile bloomed on his face. 'Hello, gorgeous.'

She staggered over to the bed, dropped her dressing gown on the floor and found her way under the covers, wrapping herself around his warm naked body.

'Pete . . .' he said.

'Still at Burns's.'

Dub kissed her hair, pushing it back from her face, the tender smell of sweat and cigarette smoke from his night engulfing her.

His hand slid down her bare hip, the backs of his fingers nestling in the warm soft comma at the top of her thigh. He pressed his forehead to hers, their eyelashes touching at the tips.

'You're the nicest landlady I've ever had.'

'Wake me up when you've had your fun,' she said and met his smile.

9

Family Unit

Paddy put her hand on the bonnet of a silver estate car that looked vaguely familiar, feeling for warmth. She'd been halfway round the car park, had felt so much cold metal that her fingers were numb and she couldn't really tell if the engine had been running recently. She didn't care if other journalists were here, hiding and waiting for Callum. She didn't care about Callum at all or whether Bunty found out she was up here at the gates of the prison, planning to come home with no story, just doing her duty as the only person Sean knew who would be any kind of support.

She pulled her coat collar up. It was always colder at the coast. The chill came from the vicious North Sea and the glassy granite, locals said, from the cold hard stone under the rich black sod.

The thirty-foot-high wall was blackened and bleak. The roof of the main building was just visible, peering over it, the small barred windows like the eyes of a malnourished child. She knew this car park well, even though she'd never been here before.

One of the biggest scenes in *Shadow of Death* was set here but she'd been heavily pregnant as she finished it and had used file photos from the *News* library and showed them to

Patrick Meehan on the pretext that a lot had changed at the prison since his day, could he just tell her what was different. Meehan was smart, not especially personable but he was fly. No real changes, he said, pretty much the same as it was on the day of release. He had a prisoner's talent for spotting weaknesses in others. He knew she couldn't be bothered going up there. He forgot, of course, that the railway to the quarry had been dismantled and several outbuildings had been added. He only remembered at the book launch.

No one else noticed the flaws in her retelling. The press were too interested in their role in his release, looking for themselves in bit parts. The public simply weren't interested. Paddy's book was the seventh written about the case and tastes in true crime had moved on from local miscarriages of justice to sex murderers and serial killers.

The day Patrick Meehan got his royal pardon a grey mist rolled in from a threatening sea, bringing the sky so low over the heads of the waiting pressmen that they cowered in their cars, expecting a deluge of rain. The *Express* had the deal sewn up: they paid Meehan tens of thousands for an exclusive, no one knew quite how much, and even years later he wouldn't disclose the exact sum. Back then, before the details of a footballer's sex life were considered a leader, the papers made stars of gangsters and murderers and Meehan was the ideal story. He was a gentleman criminal, a peterman of the old school, and wrongly convicted of a vicious attack on an elderly couple. He had been protesting his innocence for seven long years, had appeal after appeal knocked back by the judges while the real killers touted their story to the newspapers. The campaign for his release began in the papers, so everyone who'd ever written an article about him felt that they owned a little bit of him and his story.

Naive about the value of the man, the prison service gave all the details of his release in an official statement so the mob outside the gates that morning could have constituted a Parliament of the fourth estate. It was the wait that caused the trouble.

Had they released him first thing in the morning, at seven fifteen, just as the night shift went off and the day officers came on, those who arrived overnight wouldn't have had time to plan their moves. As it was, the gate opened at ten thirty and Meehan stepped out of the small door punched into the big metal gates, straight into the hot hands of the waiting press. A riot broke out.

The *Express* grabbed him by the arms and threw a jumper over his head so that no one else could get pictures. Jostled and battered by the crowd, he was bundled into the back of a car where his wife was waiting to be reunited and interviewed with him. They locked the car doors, shouting at him to get down on the floor. Meehan complied, lying flat, his face obscured by a grey jersey. The *Express* men jumped into the front seats of the car and started the engine as the crowd closed in around their bonnet. Excited that they had managed to pull it off and thrilled at the envy on their rivals' faces, they drove into the crowd a little too fast, rolling over a snapper's toes and causing a senior journalist from the *Mail* to fall awkwardly and bang his face on the car park surface.

Outraged that the *Express* men were looking so smug and had damaged a couple of them, the rest of the press didn't stand by and watch the car roll out on to the main road. They leaped into their own cars and gave chase. Meehan told Paddy that he saw a guy on a Triumph motorbike coming up the side and the *Express* driver shouted at him to get down, it was a snapper, cover yourself and get down. He was pulling the jumper over his head when he saw the

Triumph veer too close to the side of their car, get a fright, overcorrect and swing out, crashing into a ditch. Paddy knew the guy; he'd shattered his ankle, still walked with a limp and swore that the car had bumped him.

The *Express* car and its pursuers roared down uneven back roads to a field and, still covered with a jumper, Meehan was made to run blind to a waiting helicopter. God, they had budgets in those days, but not a lot of access to weather forecasts: almost as soon as it took off the chopper was forced down in a field by the heavy mist, and they had to hitch a lift to the hotel they'd booked for the interview. Luckily for them, they didn't meet anyone on the way and secured their exclusive.

Telling her about it afterwards, Meehan managed to imply strongly that everyone was at fault but himself, that his advance hadn't been as much as everyone said and that he somehow had a right to sell his story exclusively to a newspaper. A bloody farce, he said of it, but he was always angry about everything, and the details of the day got lost in the list of his other complaints.

That was how motivated other journalists were and Callum Ogilvy was just as big a story as Meehan. Journalists from all over Britain had contacted Sean and sent letters to Callum, offering money and the chance to tell his story. They suggested he could blame it all on James. Callum told them he didn't want the money and he didn't want to talk. They offered more: higher rates and a picture with his eyes blacked out. He didn't want it. He wrote back to some of them, always saying the same polite thing in a childish scrawl: he wanted to live within a loving family unit and to work in a factory. One of the papers printed the reply under the banner 'Our Letter from a Murderer'.

Paddy did a second tour of the car park. No one was hiding, as far as she could see, but they would only find out for sure when Callum came out of the gate. She made her way back to the *News* car.

Sean was eating his sandwiches, laboriously peeling back the top slice and extracting a limp lettuce leaf with a pinched thumb and forefinger, holding it up as if it was a dead slug, cursing Elaine under his breath.

Paddy watched as he dropped the leaf out of the car window. 'She worries because of your folks.'

'They died young because they'd a hard life.'

She looked out of her own window at the big grey sky. 'I think you've forfeited the right ever to slag that woman off again, after what she's doing for you.'

'It's not that big a deal.'

'She's got four kids.'

Sean closed his eyes patiently. 'They wouldn't be letting him out if he hadn't changed.'

Paddy didn't answer. The prison authorities were letting Callum out because they couldn't keep him in. A sudden gust of wind buffeted the side of the car, rocking them slightly. Sean reassembled the sandwich and held it up, glaring at it spitefully. 'Turkey ham. What is that anyway?'

Paddy considered the sandwich. 'It's turkey made to taste like ham.'

'Why couldn't she just get ham?'

'It's cheaper than ham. It's better for you.'

'I don't want stuff that's better for me.' His brow darkened.

She pulled herself upright. 'You want to make your own fucking sarnies then. A guy came to my door last night. Creepy guy who stank of fags and was something to do with the IRA.'

'What did he want?'

'Dunno. Called himself Michael Collins.'

'Maybe that's his name? Lots of people are called that.'

'No.' She looked out of the window and bit her nail. 'I think he was trying to scare me.'

'Why would he do that?'

'Dunno.'

The car phone trilled abruptly, making them both start and laugh at how jumpy they were. Sean picked up, straightening the mangled coil of flex.

'Aye? No, I'm at the Makro for my missus. I'll get Beefy on to it.' He looked at Paddy. 'Yeah, I'll see her later. OK, I'll pass it on.'

He hung up, holding the flex away as he sat the phone carefully back on its cradle. 'A lawyer rang the work for you.'

'A lawyer?' She immediately thought of Burns and the child support. What about?'

'Terry Hewitt. His lawyer. You've to ring back.'

She might have to arrange his funeral, maybe being his next of kin gave her the obligation. But the police wouldn't be releasing the body until they got someone for it so it couldn't be that. Terry might have left a note. She hoped to fuck he hadn't. It would mean she was his last thought and she found that unbearably intimate, definitive, as if he was carving himself into her life for ever. She could refuse to read it. She could refuse to arrange his funeral, but the rest of the press would think she was a skank if she did that.

'Can I call the office from your phone?'

'No, they'll know we're together. The car phone makes a weird crackle when they pick it up.'

A red Vauxhall was cruising slowly towards them, checking carefully through the cars, looking for a space. Paddy and Sean slid down in their seats as it approached, checking out the driver. It was no one they knew. Finding a space near the compound fence, he parked, gathered his things and when he stepped out they saw that he was wearing a prison officer's uniform. He strolled past them, checking his wallet for something.

'Nah,' Paddy whispered at the dashboard. 'A hack wouldn't be here on his own.'

'The photographer might be in the car,' said Sean. 'I'll go and have a look.'

He waited until the prison officer was skirting the wall and climbed out of the warm car, blanching and staggering at the unexpected wind. Walking casually over to the Vauxhall, he glanced in at the cabin, shaking his head to himself when he found nothing there.

She saw a man carrying a plastic bag of shopping at the far end of the long grey wall, heading towards them. Shift change maybe.

Sean came back to the car but stopped outside, looking away from the prison, taking the air and stretching his legs, his hair flattened to his head by the wind.

The man with the shopping bag was cutting across the car park, coming towards them. A grey bomber jacket, too short at the cuffs, a sweatshirt with 'Wrangler' written on it, a crease across the front where it had been folded in the packet, brand new, and dark blue denims, creased across at the knee. It was a strange look, all new clothes, like a costume.

Paddy recognized the hair first. Black and wavy, a little long over the ears. And then his face: heavy black eyebrows, a broad nose, grey skin, features more square than she remembered them. His jaw was solid, muscular from the habit of being clenched tightly. What she didn't recognize was his height and the width of his shoulders: he was six two at least and built like a dray horse.

It was Callum Ogilvy.

She leaned over and threw open the driver's door, catching Sean on the thigh.

'It's him, it's him, it's him.'

'All right,' he said, jumpy because she was. 'Calm down.'
And he turned to meet his cousin.

11

Fifty-three steps so far, another eight to get to the side of
the car, nine maybe. The distances between cars, sky and
ground were too far, everything spaced out so much that
there was nothing to cling to. In nine years he hadn't been
further than twenty feet from a wall; even the exercise yard
was narrow. The wind that had ruffled his hair when he was
inside walls now skirled unkindly around his face, jagged,
sharp. Here it was unbridled, unstoppable. He felt he might
blow out to sea at the next gust, drown, salt water flooding
his sorrowful lungs while people watched from the shore,
happy to see him go. *And who could blame them.*

His toe hit a break in the concrete and he stopped, the
plastic bag containing everything he owned slapping against
his leg. Dizzy suddenly, he stood still, staring at the ground,
calculating whether it would be less painful to move again
or just wait here to die. The muscles on his arms and legs
were so taut that he was twitching.

The mind can only hold one conscious thought at a time.

Fifty-three steps so far, fifty-four, fifty-five. He looked
up and saw Sean at the side of the car, his cousin, his family.
A woman was with him. He'd said there would be a woman
with him. A friend of the family. Their family.

The woman had seen him now, he could tell by the way
she moved in her seat, sitting up tall, straining to catch a
glimpse when he lost them behind a car. She reached over
and opened the driver's door, talking to Sean, keeping her
eyes on Callum.

Sean looked up.

119

Fifty-eight, fifty-nine. They stared straight at him. Not the way screws looked: screws saw you, looked away and then looked back again, thinking about you and what a bad person you were, muttering to each other. Killed a baby. Quiet. Weirdo. But Sean and the woman looked straight at him, their expectations drawing him in like a tractor beam.

Sean turned to meet him, the vicious wind blowing his hair flat. He looked small outside the visitors' room.

Sean's face was open and his arms rose from his sides in greeting. He was smiling hard but his eyes were full of reservations.

Callum didn't know what to do. He stood stiff while Sean put his arms around his shoulders and hugged him. He was smaller than Callum, not as wide. When Callum tried to respond he twitched a big nod, accidentally butting the side of Sean's face. Touch. Sean's arms were tight around him, his cheek brushed Callum's briefly and the warmth stung his skin.

When Sean let go, Callum wanted to grab on to him, make him do it again but the woman was beside him, hands rising, expecting a hug as well. A woman. Callum blushed at the thought that her tits might press into his chest like when he masturbated, that he might hold her low on her waist. Ashamed, he cast his eyes downwards and, she saw what he was thinking. She extended a hand.

Nice to see you again.

He looked at her. Big arse on her and a coldness in her eyes like the nurse in the infirmary. He knew her, remembered a cold room a long time ago, before the dark night, ripped wallpaper hanging off walls, and feeling ashamed that everything in the house was dirty. Ashamed of his mother, drinking. Clean people sitting around, wondering when they could leave.

'You were at my dad's funeral.'

'I was.' She looked kinder then. 'And I met you in hospital, Callum, d'ye remember? Your wrists were bandaged.'

He didn't want to remember that time. It was after the night in the grass, before the trial, and no one had ever talked to him about it. It was a time that belonged only to him, his footprints were alone through that. The grass from that time was up to his chest. When he went there in his head he felt it suck the breath from his lungs.

He found himself looking at the prison. It was OK now he was next to a car. The big grey wall blocked the view of the sea. For the first time he felt glad to be out of prison.

Let's get in out of this wind.

Sean smiled up at him, hopeful, nervous. He held the door open for him, and dipped down to look at Callum after he got in.

I'm awful glad to see you out, pal. Come on, we'll go home.

The car had a phone in it and room for his legs. He hadn't been in a car for nine years, not since the dark night. It was always vans after that, prison vans, police vans. The last time he was in a car his feet hardly touched the floor.

The woman got into the front passenger seat, Sean in the driver's. Sean started the engine and they rolled slowly out of the car park.

Callum was watching them, looking at the sides of their faces. Sean opened his mouth a couple of times before they hit the main road, as if he was going to say something but decided not to. The woman was looking out of the window, her elbow resting on the sill, her hand over her mouth. She didn't look happy. When they got to the junction she turned to Sean.

That went well, anyway.

Sean nodded and looked to the left for cars coming down the road.

'What went well?' Callum couldn't quite believe he'd said it so casual and normal.

'Well, to be honest,' she turned to look at him, 'we thought there might be other journalists in the car park. Hiding, you know, waiting for you.'

'Why?' He'd done it again, normal, real.

'They'd be looking for a photo of you. It could be worth a lot of money so there's going to be a bit of a competition. You should be ready for that in the coming weeks. I don't think there's any way of stopping them from getting close to you. Most of them have guessed you'll be at Sean's house so they'll probably stake that out. You should be careful who you talk to.'

She ran out of breath and looked away for a moment. But Callum hadn't been listening to her. He was still back at the first thing she'd said.

'*Other* journalists?'

The woman shut her eyes, blinking too long, shuttering him out. She cleared her throat. 'Um, aye. Other journalists.' She looked at Sean but he shrugged a shoulder. 'I'm a journalist. Don't you remember, we spoke in the hospital?'

She was Paddy. He had met her before.

'You have a SON,' he said, too loud at the end.

She turned her head quickly towards him, angry.

'PETER.'

She looked furious and turned away.

He swung his head at the window. They were travelling down a wide road, few cars on it, flat fields on either side, a tractor in one of them, a long way away. Sean's eyes were reflected in the rear-view mirror, narrow, hiding something. The skin on his cheek twitched.

Callum looked back at the prison, a speck now on the horizon. Panic rose in his chest. Sean had brought a journalist with him. Was that normal? Was he taking money? Act normal. Behave normal.

My wife made sandwiches.

Still keeping his eyes on the road, Sean leaned over the back of the car seat and showed him a plastic box with bread and an apple in it. Callum lifted it and found a can of fizzy juice on the floor under his feet.

He pulled the tab on the tin of juice and drank it in two gulps, to show that he was grateful, to fill his mouth, stop him shouting or saying anything that would make them turn round and drive him back.

He opened the box, ate the sandwiches, sitting with the empties on his lap, not knowing what else they wanted him to do.

Sean had brought a journalist with him. *And who could blame him.* Callum supposed there had to be something in it for Sean but he hadn't expected this. Maybe he should have known, maybe it was obvious. It wasn't enough just to be family: he'd had a family before and nothing was for nothing, not for him. For children in story books, maybe, but not for him, not for him.

I want to live in a loving family unit

He was shouting, bits of the dry sandwich scattering on his knees.

The woman spun to look at Callum and found him crying, a trickle of red-juice saliva at the side of his mouth. Alarmed, she looked at Sean.

MY DREAM IS TO WORK IN A FACTORY

His loud voice rang around the hollow inside of the car.

Sean didn't look at him. He slowed the car, gently easing over to the side of the road and pulling on the handbrake.

He was going to put Callum out, make him get out and leave him there for shouting in the car. *And who could blame him.*

He'd freeze because of the wind and no walls, moving would be so hard he'd have to wait there until he died. His heart was hammering in his chest. He could feel his pulse on his cheeks, on his nose, in his eyes.

The woman wasn't looking at him any more. She had her hand over her mouth again, was turned away from him, looking out of the car at the side where he would be left.

Sean undid his seat belt and turned, taking Callum's hand in one of his and stroking it with the other. 'Pal,' he said as Callum gasped for breath, 'we're going home, where it's warm. Together. Look at me.'

Callum forced his eyes from the woman's neck to Sean's face. He was nodding slowly, like he wanted Callum to nod back. 'OK? Are you going to be OK?'

Callum nodded. Sean stroked his hand again. 'It's natural to feel this scared, OK? Perfectly normal.' He let go of his hand and turned, pulled the belt back on and restarted the car, checked to look out of the side window for a car coming and then pulled back out into the road.

They were going home. Where it was warm.

A journalist. The woman's dark hair pulled up on top of her head, exposing the soft skin on the back of her neck. The necks he saw as the protected prisoners were crocodiled to work or the canteen were always leathered or spotty. Gold chains dangled from her ears, swaying with the motion of the car, never touching her neck.

Exhausted, Callum sat back on the seat, slowed his breathing and reminded himself of the one thing he knew for certain: everything smells the same when it's burning.

10

Bunty and the Monkey

I

Sean stopped the car at Glasgow Cross under the railway bridge. 'This do you?' he whispered.

Paddy looked back at Callum, sleeping in the back. He seemed to have grown during the drive, filling most of the back seat as his hands fell to the side and his knees relaxed and spread out. Although asleep he remained upright, ready for an attack, like a bear.

Sean whispered again and nodded towards her door. 'Can't drop you any closer in case we're seen.'

Paddy looked from Callum to Sean. Not wanting to wake him, she made a horrified face at Sean. 'How does he know about Pete?'

'I must have mentioned it.'

She hissed at him, '*I don't want him knowing about Pete. I don't want him knowing anything about him, understand?*'

Sean said nothing but tipped his head at her, his eyes liquid disappointment.

'Peter's your son. He's five.'

They both turned sharply to look at the bear in the back. Callum hadn't moved, hadn't twitched or stretched or done any of the normal things people do when they wake up. He had opened his eyes so that the white showed all round the iris, and was staring at her like an accusing corpse.

She nodded, breathless, wondering whether he had ever been asleep at all. 'Yes.'

He sat up, clenching and unclenching his hands. 'Why don't you want me to know about him?'

Sean was watching her. There was nothing he could do to save her from the situation but Paddy sensed that even if there was he probably wouldn't anyway.

'I, um, my son . . .'

'Pete,' Callum reminded her.

'Yes, my son Pete has been ill . . .' She couldn't think of a single plausible excuse. 'He's been ill . . .'

'So you don't want me to know about him?'

He was sitting forward now, his face just inches from hers. His eyes were quite brown, chocolate, the lashes long and thick, but they were open a fraction too wide, a threat in them. What do you think of me?'

She looked back at Sean but he was examining the crumbling rubber seal around his window, flicking it with a finger. 'Dunno.'

'I'm not interested in your son.' Callum leaned forward. 'Wonder what I think of you?'

As if sensing an impending explosion, Sean snapped, '*Sit back.*'

At once Callum threw himself back in his seat, sliding into the corner behind him.

Sean turned round to face Callum. 'You're only out four hours and already you're threatening people.'

'I *never.*'

'You did so.' He looked at Paddy, angry at her too but trying not to let it show. 'Apologize.'

Callum cowered, eyes flickering from one to the other as he kneaded his hands on his lap. 'Sorry,' he muttered. 'Sorry.'

'I'm overprotective of my son,' she said, quietly. 'Callum,

I don't know you, I don't know what you're like but you just got out of prison for hurting a boy – what would I think?'

'Sorry.'

'No, I'm sorry.' She reached across to him, touching his knee with her fingertips.

Callum looked at Sean, found him looking away out of, the window. He looked back at Paddy and moved his leg a fraction, towards her and away, towards her and away, so that her fingertips were brushing his knee. She whipped her hand back as he slid down the seat; if she hadn't her hand would have been on his thigh. He was smiling.

Her mouth was open in shock but Sean was oblivious. Callum had checked that Sean wasn't watching before he did it. He knew it was wrong.

'You creepy wee prick,' she shouted, throwing the door open and stepping out into the street.

'Oi, wait.' Sean leaned over to look at her. 'What the hell happened there?'

'Ask your fucking cousin.'

She stormed off up the road, her feet warmed by the hot pavement, her face flushed with panic and disgust, desperate to get away, not quite believing that a nineteen-year-old murderer had just tried to get her to feel him up.

She turned to look back at the car and saw Sean pulling out slowly and joining the line of traffic heading down the Gallowgate to the river. God help Elaine, trying to sleep under the same roof as him. Paddy wouldn't sit next to him on a bus.

II

She walked up through the busy Cross, ducking across the road at the lights, aware that her shoulders were aching from tension. She had to hand one thing to Callum: he was wise to refuse an interview. She hoped for his sake that when the first photo was taken of him, he wouldn't know. She could only imagine how mad he'd look otherwise. It was worth it, taking the money from Burns. Humiliating, but worth it to move Pete away from Rutherglen, where Callum would be staying.

As she walked up the road she could see busy shadows at the window of the Press Bar and hear a rumble of noise coming from inside. The presses were still, a dry dust rising from the car park opposite the *News* building.

Paddy took the stairs, feeling relieved to be back where the fights were familiar and playful, back among her pack. She thought more calmly about Callum. He was nineteen. How many women would he have met in his adult life? Two? Three? Still, the parole board shouldn't have released him, even if they'd run out of legal justifications to keep him in.

Upstairs, a crowd, back from an early lunch and full of patter and drink, had gathered inside the newsroom doors. As she pushed through, they greeted her warmly; a sub-ed put his arm around her shoulders and gave her a couple of hearty squeezes.

News of Paddy coming in in the middle of the night to write the copy about Terry had got around and everyone was assuming she'd done it out of decency and fellow feeling. Even being greeted on the basis of a misunderstanding felt warm and welcome. She wanted to turn to someone and tell them that she'd just met the most famous criminal in Scotland, and he was a car crash waiting to happen. But she didn't. She stood with them, smiling sadly as they talked about Terry, letting the sub-ed squeeze her shoulder again, drop his hand and try for the waist before she pulled away, saying she needed to get something out of her pigeonhole.

'I have that trouble all the time,' said someone and everybody laughed.

She turned to the guy nearest her, a short bald veteran. 'Who's our Home Secretary?'

'Billy, over there.'

Billy Over-There had his coat on and was smoking a cigarette with such robotic precision he was almost certainly very, very drunk.

'Billy, who can I talk to about the IRA?'

Billy's eyes weren't focusing properly. He blinked at her several times before rolling his mouth around a name: 'Brian Donaldson.'

'Short, dirty blond hair, specs?'

He shook his head. 'Five eleven, brown crew cut, fat, no specs.'

'Where could I get hold of him?'

'Shammy's.'

She hesitated. 'Are you drawling "Sammy's" or saying "Shammy's"?'

Billy Over-There took an elaborate draw on his cigarette as he considered the question. A finger of ash tumbled down the front of his coat. 'The shecond one.'

Paddy left him to his smoke and returned to the group. 'Is there a pub called Shammy's?'

A sports desk guy raised his arms triumphantly and shouted yes to jeers from everyone else. Shammy's was short for the Shamrock, a Celtic pub over in the Gallowgate. Glasgow had three football teams: Catholic Celtic, Protestant Rangers and Partick Thistle, for supporters who eschewed sectarianism and liked their football tinged with disappointment and hardship.

Paddy found the number in the phone book and asked the barman for Brian Donaldson. He asked who was calling, as if that was any kind of a security check, and Paddy wondered at the wisdom of it as she told him the truth. If journalists were being targeted maybe she should have used a pseudonym. But it was too late. Donaldson came to the phone.

'Wha'?' His voice was smoky and warm.

'Ah, Mr Donaldson, I wonder if you can help me: a man came to see me at my home last night. He said he spoke for your organization and wanted to tell me that Terry Hewitt's death was nothing to do with you—'

'Neither it was.'

'He was quite threatening. Can you tell me if it's deliberate policy to target members of the press?'

'It is not. I'm sorry if you were troubled. Who was it?'

'He said his name was Michael Collins.'

Donaldson laughed softly at the other end.

'I know,' she said, 'daft, I know it's not his name. He's wee, fair hair, wore steel-rimmed glasses and a blue jersey.'

'Right? OK, right.' She could tell by his voice that he knew who she was talking about. 'I'll, ah, ask around and see what I can do. Sorry, Miss Meehan, if you got a fright or wha'.'

He hung up.

Paddy made her way over to the pigeonholes.

The stack of wooden shelves was divided up into small squares, each with a name underneath. Those who had been at the paper since the sixties had their names picked out in italic calligraphy, while those who had joined in the seventies had a sticker with their name printed on it. Recent recruits had blue tickertape with their name punched out in white. Originally the most lowly members of staff were given the lowest shelves and moved up as they got promoted. As the staffing got more bloated, pigeonholes became scarce and everyone tended to hang on to the first one they were assigned. It was a mark of honour to be a senior member of staff with a pigeonhole near the ground.

Paddy's hadn't been claimed while she was away and her shelf was one of the lowest. She crouched down on her hunkers, not a very dignified stance but better than bending over and baring her arse to the room. Inside she found some flyers for union meetings. A talk by the new chair of the NUJ, Richards, who had been at the *News*. A blank sponsored walk form. And a yellow note from one of the secretaries, a number, time of the call 9.15, McBride's Solicitors and Notaries, ask for Mr Fitzpatrick re Terry Hewitt.

'Miss Meehan?'

She looked up to find Bunty's sidekick standing formally in front of her. He had arrived at the *News* with Bunty, like a bonded servant. People called him 'Bunty's Monkey' behind his back but never knew what to say to his face. He hadn't introduced himself or clarified his position to anyone but he moved and talked like a henchman, always gliding sideways, easing people around his master, human lubricant, making things run smoothly.

'Bunty would like to see you for a moment.'

Bunty, the paper's editor, had arrived from an Edinburgh daily a year ago. He had promised the *Daily News* owners an economic miracle but after all the redundancies and reshuffling the paper was still leaking profit. Bunty wasn't a happy man.

The walk across the floor of the newsroom felt very long. Paddy had time to panic about having been seen with Callum, about Sean losing his job and herself ending up with no job or home and Burns laughing at her as he drove away from her mother's house with Pete on visitation days. She was very tired, she realized. The weekend had been less than restful.

The glass cubicle Larry Grey-Lips inhabited at night had the lights on inside and the blinds drawn down. The

Monkey waved her towards the door with the grace of a butler. She knocked on the glass and opened the door quickly, keeping the advantage.

Bunty sat at a small corner of the big table, pencil in hand, shading in a big doodle. He was a small bald man and as such didn't like to be seen doing small bald things. He stood up, cheeks flushed defensively, and covered the sheet with his hand. The Monkey slipped into the room behind Paddy and tiptoed up the table to his handler's side.

'Hello, Patricia.' Bunty covered his annoyance with a flash of teeth. 'Shut the door, would you?'

She clicked it shut and took a seat in front of the desk. It was a surprisingly large room and housed the big table Bunty used for smaller meetings: the full news ed meetings were held downstairs. Despite the table being a good six feet long, the Monkey and Bunty were taking up barely three foot of one side and looked across at Paddy in unison, smiling, mock-friendly.

Bunty made a pyramid of his fingers. He looked like a man with the shadow of professional death hanging over his shoulder, which he was. Sales of the *Daily News* were in a steady decline, and advertising was plummeting as more and more of the big spenders were going over to the *Standard*. The *Daily News* wasn't making a loss but they weren't turning a great profit either and the board of directors had been through four of the five stages of economic grief already: hope, disappointment, blame and fury. The next stage, Paddy knew, was goodbye Bunty.

'You'll be pleased to hear that Terry Hewitt's obituary is going in tomorrow. It's a full half-page.'

As usual, Bunty had misheard all the office gossip and thought she was Terry's girlfriend. Paddy thanked him anyway. 'That's good of you. He started here, same time as me.'

'So I read. Shocking business.' Bunty looked over at the Monkey. 'It could bring the Irish Troubles over here.'

Everyone knew that twenty hours ago but Monkey took his henchman's duties seriously and nodded as if he was just finding out.

'So. Yes. *Oui*, as it were.' Bunty chewed the inside of his mouth and scribbled hard on the sheet, a vicious doodle. '*Alors*. I heard a rumour about you.'

'There are a lot of rumours about me. I started many of them myself.'

He smiled courteously at her attempted joke. 'I heard you were in Babbity's last night with McVie and you haven't handed in this week's Misty. Anything I should know?'

She tried to look non-committal.

'We'd hate for there to be any misunderstanding.' He looked to Monkey, who nodded and smiled, and Bunty turned back to her. 'We value you *tremendously*.' He strained over the word, closing his eyes. 'Just *tremendously*.' They looked at her expectantly.

'Good,' she said.

'Are you happy here?' Bunty waved across his desk, leaving his fingers wide as an opener for her to say something. Monkey copied his facial expression, as if he'd posed the question himself.

'I asked you for more money two months ago and I'm still waiting for an answer.'

Bunty leaned over the desk, narrowing his eyes at her. 'Have you been offered more money elsewhere?'

She stared back at him. She could lie. 'I want more money and to investigate Terry's death.'

Bunty smiled and shook his head. 'It's a long time since you did a news story. We can't assign stories to placate people. It might be too big.'

'But I want it.' Paddy thought she sounded like Pete.

Bunty sighed at his doodle: a lot of regal looping lines angrily shaded in with pencil. A potentate foiled. 'You know,' he sighed, 'McVie takes people on and buries them, d'you know that? Gets everyone on short-term contracts and dumps them.'

It was a scurrilous lie.

He scratched in another loop with his pencil as the Monkey watched her for a reaction. 'I think, Bunty,' she said carefully, 'that you must have been a fucking good journalist.'

Bunty looked up and smiled wide at her. His yellow teeth were gappy, the gums receding. She suddenly, inexplicably, liked him enormously.

He straightened his face. 'OK, we'll give you the money but you're not getting the story.'

'But I've—'

'NO!' His hand was up and that was that. 'If you want it you'll have to do it in your own time. I'll put someone else on it too. You beat them to it, all well and good.'

'Who?'

'Merki.'

She snorted. 'Merki?'

'Merki. Get out.'

Merki was good at finding leads. He could get into a house but people didn't take to him, no one wanted to talk to him because he was funny-looking. It would be a walk-over and she was getting the raise. She stood up quickly and put one knee on the table, clambering across the highly polished wood on all fours and, before the Monkey could intervene to stop her, she planted a wet, noisy kiss on Bunty's bald head. The skin was smooth and papery.

He laughed, embarrassed, brushing the kiss off coyly as she climbed down off the table and pulled her skirt straight.

'Long live the King,' she said, making her way to the door.

The Monkey called after her. 'We'll have your copy today?'

'I'll phone it in to Larry tonight,' she called back.

III

She used a phone on Features and called Terry Hewitt's solicitors. First the receptionist had to put her through to his secretary, then his secretary wouldn't put her through to the lawyer, then she tried to get Paddy to agree to an appointment two weeks hence.

Paddy said that was a real shame because she wrote for the *Scottish Daily News* and she'd been hoping to speak to him about doing a series profiling prominent lawyers.

The secretary hesitated. Paddy assumed she was a little awestruck. She was feeling smug and cosy, tricking a slippery lawyer into an early appointment with the promise of an ego rub, when the secretary said, 'But he's only twenty-three.'

'Ah.' Her feeling of superiority evaporated. 'Well, you know, up-and-coming lawyers, the future and all that ...'

Thirty seconds later she was talking to the squeaky-voiced boy and he agreed to see her in half an hour. She thought he sounded a little breathless.

IV

By day Blythswood Square was an elegant square of Georgian town houses, now offices, set around a private garden. The kerbs were high to the road, the step steep to accommodate descent from a carriage. At night the square became the working route of roving prostitutes, bare-legged girls with poor hair and prominent bosoms, faces dripping rank misery, ready to be peered at and pawed.

McBride's Solicitors was in one of the older houses but the impression of elegance was lost at the door, where a cheap black punch-hole board was hanging with the names of the resident companies picked out in white plastic lettering. McBride, Solicitors and Notaries, were on the very top floor.

Paddy was panting and damp by the time she reached the sixth flight of stairs, leading to what had once been the servants' quarters, shallow and sagging wooden steps worn in the middle, the banister sticky from trailing sweaty fingers. She caught her breath on the top step, embarrassed, as she always was when she lost her breath, to be a fat woman, sweating.

McBride's office was a fading brown nod to the seventies. A motherly receptionist was dressed accordingly, in a brown skirt and matching jersey with a modest rope of pearls at her throat. The fittings in the reception area looked as old as she was: the phone was two-tone brown, the appointments book a battered black-leather puff of paper.

She was impressed when Paddy introduced herself, clutched her neck and said she was a big fan.

'Thanks,' said Paddy and looked for somewhere to sit.

'No, no, go through. Mr Fitzpatrick's waiting for you.' She pointed to a flush dark-wood door.

Inside, a chubby teenager in a suit was standing stiffly by his desk. Mr Fitzpatrick was not only pleased to see her but seemed to have had a shave just before she got there. As she stepped forward to shake his hand she could smell soap and see that the skin on his cheeks was glossy smooth, a small nick at his ear still oozing white blood cells. He fussed her into a chair.

'I don't know how you could even have heard of me. Did someone give you my name?'

She bit the bullet and admitted the ruse: she needed to

find out about Terry and couldn't get an appointment for two weeks so she'd fibbed. His disappointment was palpable.

'But I phoned my mum.'

Paddy cringed in sympathy. 'I thought you were older,' she said. 'I thought I was playing a trick on a smug big lawyer who couldn't be arsed seeing me. I'm really sorry.'

'What'll I tell my mum?'

'Can't you tell her it didn't come off? That's what I always tell mine.'

'She'll call the paper.'

'You could say the article is about left-wing lawyers so we had to leave you out?'

He considered it for a moment. 'Yes, that might work.'

'Tell her it was for the *Star* or some paper she won't see. Or the *Daily Mail*.' She didn't want to be presumptuous, but guessed his mother wouldn't take the *Daily Star*.

Having resolved his angst over his mother's disappointment Mr Fitzpatrick turned to the matter of Terry, far more kindly than she would have done in the circumstances.

He took out a file and opened it. Terry had left her everything: there was a car, an old model, worth a couple of hundred pounds, all his papers and books, some clothes and the house.

'Which house?'

'Eriskay House.' He peered at his notes. 'A two-bedroomed house with three acres of land in Kilmarnock. It's an old house of the family's. I don't know what sort of condition it's in but it must be pretty good: we've already had an objection lodged by Mr Hewitt's cousin, a Miss Wendy Hewitt.'

'What does that mean?'

'It means that she's challenging the validity of the will. In short, we can't execute.'

Paddy shifted uncomfortably. A house. She didn't want anything to do with Terry, didn't think she could stay in a house he'd lived in or owned, but it was, after all, a house. Not one that Burns paid for either. And it had land around it for Pete to play in.

'Could I sell it to her?'

'No. You need to own it before you can sell it. You don't own it at the moment.'

'Well, who does own it?'

'Mr Hewitt's estate owns it.'

'So . . .?'

'Mm.' Fitzpatrick looked at his notes again. 'So we'll have to wait to see what happens.'

'How long could that take?'

He blew his lips out. 'Months? A year? Longer?'

Paddy glanced at her watch. It was five past three and Pete got out of school at half past. She had to get a parking space near the gates or he'd try to cross the road himself. The lollipop lady sometimes hid behind a tree for a cigarette and the road was busy.

'OK.' She stood up. 'Fuck it. Let me know what happens.'

'There are these papers . . .' He waved his hand towards a folder on the table. It was brown, made of soft cardboard, fraying all round the edges. She could see that it was stuffed with well-thumbed sheets of notes, yellowed newspaper clippings folded over on themselves, a bit of a magazine. Her name was written on the outside cover, 'Paddy', in a blue felt pen, the pigment faded into a yellowed green. If Fitzpatrick had been trying to lure her into a cave full of tigers, he could have done worse than leave the folder at the mouth. Paddy could feel herself salivating. 'Where did it come from?'

'He left it with me, in the safe.'

'When?'

'A year ago.'

It might be nothing to do with his murder. Her interest blunted, she looked at him, but Fitzpatrick was working a move. He licked his bottom lip, looking back at her with a steady, distracted eye.

'What's in it?'

'I couldn't say.' He almost smiled.

She pressed him further. 'Can I look at what's in it?'

'No. I could give it to you now, to take away, but you'd need to sign off the claim to the house.'

He waited. She waited. His eyes slid to the side. With every second thudding past, the realization dawned on Fitzpatrick that she wasn't that hungry for the folder.

She cleared her throat. 'You know Wendy Hewitt then, do you?'

His eyelids contracted momentarily, widening. 'Not personally, no.'

'Do you represent her professionally?'

'No,' he said, too quickly.

She suddenly didn't give a shit any more. She stood up. 'Fuck this, I'm off.'

Fitzpatrick stood up to meet her. 'But his effects, you need to clear out his flat.'

'What?'

'His effects. The landlord wants the flat emptied or he'll have the house cleared . . .'

'Well, that's your responsibility, surely?'

'It's a tiny amount of stuff. Rubbish. You could bin it.'

Paddy had the impression that he'd had a first scan of the belongings and thought it was all worthless. But he wouldn't know, and whatever it was, it was stuff Merki wasn't being offered.

She thought of sitting in the house tonight with Pete playing in his bedroom, listening always for Michael

Collins's soft knock at the door. 'OK,' she said. 'Where is it?'

'Partick.' He opened the top drawer of his desk and pulled out a set of keys on a round of dirty string with a paper tag. '40 Lawrence Street. Here are the keys.'

Paddy snatched them from his hand. 'This is your job, Fitzpatrick. I know it is. Don't think I don't know.'

11

Terry's Effects

The gardens set the street apart. Old trees flourished in the small front gardens, high as the blocks themselves, roots escaping the gardens and bursting up through the pavements like fingers through warm butter. Some of the front gardens were chaotically overgrown, one was gravelled, but the one in front of Terry's close door was a picture book of giant flowers, bushes heavy with vibrant red and blue and yellow. A sun-bleached deckchair sat under a gnarled old tree, a book lying face down by its side. The gardens were fenced in with functional black railings, replacements for the wrought-iron rails melted down as part of the war effort.

Pete looked out of the car window at the deckchair. 'Why do we need to come here?'

'I need to sort through a friend's things,' said Paddy, reluctant to get out of the car. She was afraid of what she might find in Terry's flat, afraid he might have photos of her, have written her one last desperate lovelorn missive and not had time to post it.

'Why?'

Dub raised an eyebrow at her from the passenger seat.

'Just promised I would, that's all.'

141

Pete looked out of the window again. 'Has the friend gone away?'

'Yeah.'

Whatever questions Terry's flat threw up, they couldn't be more complicated than the ones in the car. Paddy opened the door and stepped out into the warm street. The high summer sun lifted the soft smell of cut grass and blossom into the air. Beyond the block, cars hurried by on the busy road, but Lawrence Street was sleepy, the warm air trapped in the shallow valley of flats.

Terry's flat was in a classically proportioned, pedimented block of low blond sandstone. Golden summer sun picked out the dirt on the windows and the shabbiness of the cheap curtains. One of the windows on the second floor had a big dangerous crack across a pane, mended on the inside with masking tape.

The car door next to Paddy opened but she stopped it with a firm hand. 'What have I told ye? Always get out on the pavement side.'

Pete mumbled an apology and bumped his bottom along the seat to the other door.

Dub was standing next to her. 'Do you get to keep all this stuff?'

'I don't really know. I think so. I get to keep it until the will's overturned anyway.'

'Might be worth a few quid. Might be jewellery.'

'Yeah, Terry was always mad for his big gold chains, wasn't he?'

'Well,' said Dub, reluctant to be wrong, 'I saw him wearing a ruby tiara and matching sandshoes once.'

'Oh, yeah.' She smiled away from him. 'I remember them. High heels?'

'High heels and a sketch of the Last Supper picked out on the toe. Judas was cross-eyed.'

'A lovely shoe.'

'Two lovely shoes.' Dub nudged her supportively. She turned to look at him and found him smiling at his feet. He was a full foot taller than her, handsome in an odd way. They had been friends for years, since before she ever spoke to Terry Hewitt, and sometimes, like today, she felt so fond of him she wanted to grab him and kiss him. She looked away. 'Right, let's do this.'

Pete waited dutifully on the pavement until Paddy walked over and took his hand, leading him along the street and up the path between the two sets of railings to Terry's front door. She fitted the key and let them into the close.

It was dark and smelled of damp chalk. A marble-patterned rubberized floor was stained with greasy puddles. As they climbed the wide circular stairs to the top floor, Paddy trailed her hand along the curved oak handrail. Cobwebs hung between the cast-iron banisters.

The front door to the flat was unpainted plywood with a single lock, the tang of newly seasoned wood still hanging off it. On the door frame, peeling Sellotape bordered a list of six names written in biro block capitals. The doormat was filthy. They could hear the squawk of a television inside.

Dub curled his lip. 'It's a bedsit. Why was he still living in bedsits?'

Paddy shrugged and put her arm around Pete's shoulders. 'He always did. I don't know why. The lawyer said he had a house. Should we knock or just go in?'

Dub shrugged. 'Knock, probably.'

'I'll knock,' said Pete and gave the door a loud, rude thump with the base of his fist.

'Pete! You don't knock on a door like that—'

Steps preceded the flinging open of the door. A man in a stripy T-shirt opened the door, wiping floured hands on a tea towel tucked into the waistband of his trousers. He looked expectantly at them.

'Sorry about the banging.' Paddy nodded at Pete. 'A bit eager.'

'What can I do for you?'

'Um, well, you know about Terry? I'm here to get his things.'

The man wasn't really listening though; he was smiling at Dub's trousers. They were made out of ticking, blue and green with a white stripe, like the covering on an old-fashioned mattress.

'I recognize those kegs. You're Dub McKenzie. I used to see you compering at Blackfriars Comedy Club all the time.'

'Right? Do I know you?'

'Nah.' The man shook his head. 'Nah, nah, nah, just a punter. I heard you were managing George Burns.'

'Was, yeah.'

'Did you fall out and tell him to do the *Variety Show*?'

Dub smirked. 'I told him *not* to do it and then he sacked me.'

'God, it's shit.'

'Isn't it, though?'

They grinned at each other for a moment until Pete's patience ran out and he pushed at the door.

'Pete, don't,' said Paddy, wishing she could open her mouth without getting him into trouble.

'Ah, come in, wee man.'

The guy opened the door and let Pete in. Seven doors led off the hallway, all of them shut tight apart from the kitchen, which was straight ahead. A red tartan carpet had been laid over a number of other fitted carpets and stood two inches off the ground. A ripped paper shade hung from a flaking ceiling. The warm smell of bacon floated out to greet them.

'Bacon sarnie?' asked Dub.

'Just, eh' – the guy looked embarrassed – 'knocking up a quiche.'

'Can ye do that? I thought they were sterile.'

The guy mouthed a drum roll/cymbal clash and the two men smiled.

'Which room's Terry's?'

He pointed to the door next to the kitchen. It was sealed with a padlock small enough to fit on a suitcase. The key to it was on the string Fitzpatrick had given her, flimsy as paper. She fitted it in the lock and opened the door into a large room.

Two long windows at one end looked straight across the street into facing flats. The sun was shining in through them, filtered and softened by the dirty filigree on the glass. The floorboards were painted black, chipped and dusty.

Terry had pulled the wallpaper off. Small scraps were still clustered by the skirting board and powdery residue covered the walls. The paint underneath had been a dark green but it was chipped and faded, a South American wall. She could imagine markets being held in front of it, executions taking place against it, children idling at its foot.

Terry had been camping more than living there. His bed was a bare mattress with dirty crumpled sheets, his duvet coverless and grey. The room was too big for his meagre belongings: a silver trunk sat by the near wall, an old ghetto blaster nearby. Next to the mattress sat a large blue duffle bag, already packed with his clothes. Paddy recognized it: he'd had that bag when she saw him off on the train to London eight years ago. Lined up along the bottom of one wall were novels, Penguin Classics mostly, the paper yellowed and battered from being lovingly read.

'I'm really sorry about Terry,' said the quiche-maker. 'He was only here a month or two, I didn't really know him. Nice guy though.'

In the empty expanse of dusty black floorboards she could see footsteps picked out in the dust, a cleared muddle in the middle of the room and steps leading away and back from it.

'People have been in here,' said Paddy, pointing at the disturbances in the dust.

'Police.' The quiche-maker had followed them into the room. 'They went through everything. They were fucking obnoxious too, made us all leave the house for the night while they did it. As far as I can see they took nothing but his passport. And a journalist. Cross-eyed and rude as fuck.'

'Merki,' nodded Paddy. Did he take anything?'

'No. Brought a bottle of whisky, put it on the table and asked us about Terry for an hour, then put the bottle back in his pocket and fucked off.'

Dub laughed but Paddy didn't. 'Why did he live like this?' she said aloud. 'He owned a big house in Kilmarnock.'

'Oh, was that true then?' The quiche-maker was surprised. 'I kind of thought that was bullshit.'

'There isn't really that much here, is there?'

'There might have been more but we were broken into last week. That's why we've got the new door. The other one was made of paper. This one's sturdy new cardboard.' He laughed at his joke, unperturbed that no one else was joining in.

Paddy traced the pattern of the dust, looking for disturbances. A flat empty space by the trunk looked cleaner than the rest. 'Did they take something from there?'

The quiche-maker looked from her to the space. 'No, Terry moved it. He had a portfolio there. He moved it after we got broken into.'

'Where to?'

He gestured for her to follow him out to the hall and led the way into the kitchen.

The room was moist and smelled gorgeous. A table was scattered with flour, a dusted work strip where he had been kneading the pastry. On one of the two gas cookers sitting side by side was a frying pan, with strips of prosciutto cooling in it. The cookers were fed by a gas pipe that hung loose from the ceiling. Under the window a precariously sloped unit housed the sink. Odd cupboards and a red-and-white larder from the fifties were lined up along the near wall.

In Victorian times the kitchen was the servants' arena. It was customary to build a small wall recess for the maid to sleep in, soaking up the heat from the ever-warm cast-iron range. In bad modernizations the recess was walled in and converted into a cupboard or sometimes a windowless kitchen if it was large, but here it was being used as a communal area. A grubby settee faced away from the kitchen towards a boxy old television twittering in the corner. Above the television, hovering seven feet in the air, was a giant cupboard with sliding plywood doors.

'It's a good wee attic thingummy but you'll need a ladder to get up there,' he said. 'Terry put stuff in the back in case we were burgled again.'

Paddy looked around. 'Is there a ladder?'

'Aye, aye, we've got one.' He disappeared off into one of the rooms and came back with a rickety paint-splattered wooden ladder. 'Chris is painting his room.' He set it open and pushed it up against the door of the cupboard.

He expected Paddy to climb up but she pointed out that

she didn't know what they were looking for. Reluctantly, the quiche-maker climbed the ladder himself. With great difficulty, he bumped the sliding door to the side. The cupboard was deep and black dark, at just the wrong angle to the strip light.

He reached into the black hole, pulling down a tent and poles, two sleeping bags tightly rolled in sleeves, and a cardboard box of dusty Christmas decorations, handing them down to Dub who set them on the floor. Next came three black binbags of bedding, old duvets and pillows. The quiche-maker then climbed off the top rung of the ladder, kneeling into the cupboard, his feet sticking out as he felt towards the back.

They heard a long sliding noise and he stepped carefully back on to the ladder, his knees grey with dust, screwing up his face as if he might sneeze. He was holding a large, square yew box. Although it was dusty the wood was still gorgeously yellow and leopard-spotted, the edges perfectly dovetailed. A flat brass hook on the front held it shut. He handed it down to Paddy, who flicked the hook from the eye and opened it.

Inside were photographs, mostly old, of family members. One near the top looked like it might be Terry's parents, a couple with their arms around each other standing under an apple tree in high summer. The colours had faded to orange and yellow, the white-framed edges worn from being held. Scratched in thin biro on the back it said 'Sheila and Donald '76'. Creepily, the mother looked a bit like her.

Dub looked over her shoulder, sighed on to her neck. 'I'm not saying it.'

'Me neither.'

'Hang on.' The quiche-maker reached further in. 'There's this.'

He climbed out again, dragging a large black portfolio,

A3 size, just like the one Kevin had shown Paddy on Sunday night. The quiche-maker looked puzzled. 'Didn't want to lose it, I suppose.'

'It's a book Terry was writing,' said Paddy. 'He'd already been paid for it.' She reached up and took it off him. 'Thanks so much. It's really kind of ye.'

'No bother,' he said, taking the camping equipment back from Dub and chucking it into the black hole. 'My pastry needs to rest anyway.'

He dragged the reluctant door back across the hole and climbed down the ladder, brushing his hands clean.

'We'll empty Terry's room and get out of your way.'

'If you could leave the keys for the next person.' He wrestled the ladder shut and put it over his shoulder. 'There's binbags in that cupboard on the wall there if you want something to put the stuff in.'

Back in the room Pete set up a little play camp by the window, taking marbles out of his pocket and chipping at them, chatting to himself, playing the audience to his own moves. 'Wow, good one. Close, very close, wee man. Superb.'

Dub grinned at Paddy as he shook a black binbag open and dropped the Penguin Classics into it. 'What's in the portfolio? Why did he hide it so carefully?'

'Dunno,' she said quietly. 'Could be just because it's work. Could be he knew whoever'd broken in was after it.'

Dub put the binbag down, said hang on and left her to it. She found a suitcase full of papers hidden in the trunk, Terry's own clippings mostly.

'The guy out there says Terry's room wasn't the focus of the break-in. They nicked a bike and a penny collection, so it doesn't look like a master burglar.'

'Maybe Terry was just paranoid about it because it was his work. He'd never had a book published, had he?'

'No.'

'You know how different that feels. It might have really mattered to him.'

'Maybe.'

She went back to stripping the bed. When she raised the duvet up to fold it into a binbag, his smell enveloped her face. She poked it into the bag, shoving it in angrily, promising herself that she'd dump it in a skip on the way home.

They made a tidy pile of binbags in the middle of the floor, filled the trunk and shut it, put the duffle bag by the door. Quiche-maker said they could leave the mattress. The next person might use it.

They were ready to go.

'Come on,' said Dub, 'Mary Ann'll be there soon.'

Paddy gave Pete the portfolio to carry while she and Dub managed everything else in two trips up and down the stairs.

At the last they stood in the doorway to the huge dusty room. The sun was low and the lights were out in Lawrence Street. When they switched off the bare bulb, the big room was lit by the windows of the facing flats.

Across the street a family had gathered to watch their television set under the window, sitting in a line along a settee as if they were looking straight into Terry's room. In another window a woman dusted a pristine front room, lifting doilies and straightening antimacassars. In another, an elderly woman looked out of the window into the street, watching for someone.

Paddy could smell Terry in the dust, could see him sitting on his bed drinking a cup of coffee and contemplating his day. He looked small and alone as she imagined him there, a speck, helpless as a dust mote floating gently away on invisible currents.

Dub cupped her elbow. 'You're not just shocked, pet. You're really sad about this, aren't you?'

Ambushed, Paddy drew a deep wavering breath. 'I don't even know why.'

'Maybe it's really about your dad.'

'Aye, maybe,' she said, 'maybe.' But she knew it wasn't.

12

The Secret Language of Soup

I

It didn't look very nice. The pasta had cooked too long and was soft and cloudy at the edges. Paddy dropped the contents of the sauce jar on it and stirred the pot. It still didn't look very nice, but she knew she'd eat it. She put the lid on and took some ready-grated Parmesan out of the cupboard, setting the cardboard tub on the table.

Dub looked up from the free local paper, chewing his pen seriously. '"Man's best friend", three letters?'

She shrugged. 'Jesus?'

She took plates and glasses out of the cupboard and set the table for four. Here, among the steamed-up windows, in the peaceful pocket of the house with all the workaday reminders of routine and pending chores, the threat of Callum Ogilvy and the horror of Terry's death seemed faintly ludicrous.

She stood over the basket of fresh ironing on top of the washing machine, looking at the creases Dub had carefully worked into her office clothes and Pete's spare uniform, telling herself not to think about it, just for the evening, until Mary Ann left. They saw little enough of each other and it was a shame to waste a whole evening on distractions.

The doorbell rang out a soft chime and Dub tried to

stand up but banged his knees on the underside of the table. Paddy and Pete met in the hall, rushing for the door, a little throb of excitement in Paddy's throat too. She let him get it.

Mary Ann was standing outside the front door, dressed in a plain blue button-down dress and carrying a plastic bag with a heavy tub in it, her blonde ringlets newly and brutally cropped. She smiled wide, stepping into the hall, touching her head self-consciously. Pete wanted to touch it so she bent down to let him.

'Oh dear.' Paddy slipped her arm through her sister's and tutted. 'That is one terrible haircut. But you're still prettier than me. It's damnable.'

They came into the kitchen and found Dub standing proudly over the pot of hot pasta on the table as if he'd made it. He took the plastic bag Mary Ann offered him and pulled out a clear Tupperware box, setting it on the edge of the table. It was soup, yellow from the lentils, flecked with green peas and white chunks of potato. The lid wasn't fitted on properly and a floury dribble had dried down the side. Pete pressed his nose against the box, trying to see through it.

'Soup,' said Mary Ann.

Paddy recognized the cut of the potatoes, the particular yellow tone Trisha got from soaking the dried split peas for two nights instead of one. She took it from Dub, disguising her irritation. 'Did she come into the mission to give you this?'

'No.' Mary Ann touched her hair again. 'I was home.'

Soup was Trisha's secret language. Trisha's soup meant love and home; it meant a mother managing on a poor income, passing on good nutrition to the children; it meant concern. If Trisha's life had been a musical she would have ended up with all three daughters living a hundred yards from her, raising a dozen well-behaved children between them and gathering every morning to make soup together, to her recipe. As it was, her eldest daughter was divorced and living miserably with her; Mary Ann was a nun, which was good, but made soup from a sack of dried ingredients, which was terrible; and her youngest bought overpriced soup from delicatessens. Sending soup was a reproach to a daughter who couldn't be trusted to look after herself or feed her illegitimate son properly.

Paddy took it and put it in the fridge. 'We'll have this later. We'll have it tomorrow.'

Dub sat back down in his seat. 'Or we'll leave it in the fridge until it gets smelly and then chuck it down the toilet.'

Pete giggled because Dub had said toilet.

Mary Ann was shocked at the suggestion, frowning at her empty plate. Paddy sat down next to her, keen to change the subject. 'What were you doing home anyway?'

Dub dropped a lump of overcooked red pasta on to Mary Ann's plate. She looked down at it, the fusilli swirls reluctantly letting go of each other, tumbling down to the cold plate. Usually Mary Ann giggled at everything – a dog running past, a pencil dropped, an incongruous turn of phrase, anything could set her off – but tonight she wasn't giggling. Tonight she looked down at her dinner settling on the plate and sighed like a grown-up.

Dub and Paddy looked at each other.

Paddy sat down next to her and took her hand. 'What?'

Mary Ann shook her head as if she was trying to dismiss an unpleasant thought.

'Is Mum ill?'

'No.' She picked up her fork and prodded at her food.

'Are you ill?'

'No.'

An uncomfortable silence settled over the table. It was

Dub's favourite dinner and he ate as quickly as he could. He shovelled the food into his mouth, washed it down with a pint glass of apple juice and then excused himself, taking Pete with him, leaving Paddy and Mary Ann alone, side by side at the table. Exiled to the living room, the men put the television on loudly, letting them know they weren't listening.

'So?'

Mary Ann hadn't eaten much. She moved the food around slowly, chasing a swirl halfway round the plate and leaving it there. She put her fork down. 'Don't want it.'

If a plate of stewed puppy had been served to her she would probably eat it, out of piety and gratitude. Paddy realized with a start that she hadn't prayed over the dinner before she began eating either.

'Mary Ann, what is going on?'

Mary Ann didn't move. She sat still, staring at the food as tears dropped on to the table, and then she turned to look at her sister.

'I'm in love. With a man. He loves me.'

'Who?'

'Father Andrew.'

'At St Columbkille's?'

She nodded unhappily, touched her mauled hair again with her fingertips, and cried. Paddy touched it: it was as soft as a baby's. 'Did they do this to you because of that?'

But Mary Ann was crying so hard, she couldn't speak. Paddy dabbed her cheeks with a sheet of kitchen roll they were using for napkins but it did no good. The tears weren't about to dry. She wanted to ask a hundred questions, tell her that Father Andrew was a creep, that she should never have been a nun in the first place, but those were things she wanted to say, not things Mary Ann needed to hear.

'Did you tell Mum?'

Mary Ann touched her head again.

'Did you tell your Mother Superior?'

She mouthed 'no' and carried on crying.

Paddy didn't know what to do. She dried her sister's face again, squeezed her hand for a while and then dried her face once more. 'D'ye want some soup?'

Mary Ann spluttered a laugh through the veil of wet, finally catching her breath in short, painful gasps. She used her own napkin to dab at her face.

'Do the two of you have any kind of plan?'

Mary Ann folded the kitchen roll into a neat square and blew her nose, wiping it hard, dragging her nose to the side as if she was punching herself in slow motion. She couldn't look at Paddy. 'We don't talk . . .'

Paddy was shocked. Father fucking Andrew, two years out of seminary, forcing his will on the parish and touching Mary Ann in ways she had no defence against. Paddy wanted to jump in the car and go over to the parish house and beat the living shit out of him. She wouldn't, for Mary Ann's sake, but it was exactly what their brothers would do if they found out.

'Don't tell Mum.' It wasn't much by way of comfort but it was the best she could come up with.

Mary Ann started crying again, not from the pressure of love this time, Paddy thought, but foreseeing all the pain and shame she'd bring to the family.

She took her sister's wet face in her hands. 'Listen, Mary Ann, listen, you can't hurt Mum more than we have. Trisha's strong, she's really strong. Caroline's divorced, Pete's a bastard, the boys don't even go to mass any more.' Somehow, adding Mary Ann's love affair to the list of their mother's wounds wasn't helping to calm her down. 'I've got some cigarettes. Will we smoke a cigarette?'

Paddy got up, pulled the packet out of her handbag, brought over an ashtray and lit one, handing it to her sister. Sometimes, when they were younger and Sean smoked around them a lot, the girls would share a cigarette. Mary Ann didn't inhale but liked holding it, touching it to her lips like a movie star, flinching when a stray tendril of smoke got up her nose.

Now, she took the little cigarette, going cross-eyed as she held it to her mouth, and inhaled the longest draw Paddy had ever seen. Half the fag was gone. She held the smoke in her lungs, her chest barrelled out and she exhaled expertly over Paddy's head.

The sisters looked at each other. Paddy was astonished. For the first time in their lives Mary Ann wasn't playing the giggling little girl. She was a woman now.

Holding her eye, Mary Ann put the filter to her lips and sucked again, drawing the remaining life out of the cigarette, leaving it a grey crumbling shell. She held the smoke in her chest for an unfeasibly long time and then blew it out to the side, pausing at the end, turning to her sister and blowing two perfect smoke rings at her, raising her eyebrows to emphasize her point.

Paddy started laughing and couldn't stop. Blindly, she slapped the table, knocking her plate to the floor, her fork bouncing off a chair and clattering on to the tiles.

The phone rang out and she looked up, expecting to see Mary Ann's face split in a silent howl, but Mary Ann wasn't laughing. She bit her top lip and stabbed at the ashtray with the cigarette, her eyebrows rising and lowering in a silent argument.

McVie didn't bother with hello. 'Memorial service, Thursday. Big deal. Ten a.m. at the cathedral. You're speaking.'

'No, I'm not.'

'Everyone'll be there.'

'Everyone *who*?'

'Everyone.' She heard him ruffle a sheet of paper. 'Have you seen Merki's article?'

She turned to the wall. 'Merki's got a byline?'

'Go and get tomorrow's edition of the *News*. They've found the gun.'

She hung up.

Mary Ann had helped herself to another cigarette and held her head in her hands, the contaminating smoke curling up to the pulley of Pete's clothes drying above her head.

'Put that fag out,' Paddy said firmly. 'We're going for a drive.'

II

It felt strange bringing Mary Ann to the *News* building. Just sitting in the car with her felt like a bizarre clash of the two distinct halves of her life. Paddy didn't really know who to be: Mary Ann's giggly wee sister or the braying harridan she was for work. It would have felt more odd if Mary Ann had been acting like Mary Ann but she was quiet, worried, fretting. She kept touching her hair, looking for a strand long enough to lose her fingers in. The cut was so bad it looked as if her hair had been singed off.

'Wait here,' said Paddy, opening the door. The absurd thought occurred to her that Mary Ann might slip out and disappear for ever in the dark of the car park. She swung her handbag on to her sister's lap. 'Get a cigarette out of there and smoke it. I'll be two seconds.'

The delivery men were working hard, swinging bales of papers along a line into the vans, their rhythm interrupted by the sight of Paddy Meehan walking out of the dark night to take a copy from a burst bale that had been discarded to the side.

It was front page, with Merki's name on it and a picture of the ditch Terry had been found in, strung along with police tape. A small inset photograph showed Terry as a young man, grinning cheesily at the photographer. She could see from the collar that he had his leather jacket on, the one with the red shoulder pads. She turned, walking back to the car, stroking the picture tenderly with her index finger, inadvertently smearing the damp ink and staining her hand.

The burning red tip of the cigarette flared in the wind-screen as Paddy walked towards the car. She hardly knew this Mary Ann. She hadn't yet taken her final vows so leaving the convent would be slightly less of a wrench, if that was what she wanted. But Father Andrew had. Paddy could well imagine the courtship, the looks and Mary Ann's blushes, the stolen moments in chilly convent corridors, a brush of the hand, a longing look, and Father Andrew's pasty arse as he pumped his cock into her sister.

She opened the door and fell into the driver's seat, snatching the cigarette out of Mary Ann's hand and throwing it on to the dirt floor of the car park. 'Right, you. I need to know some things: how long has this been going on?'

From the habit of complying with barked orders Mary Ann told her: nearly a year. They'd met when he came to say a special mass for the missions. They saw each other in secret. He didn't want to leave the priesthood.

'Do you want to leave the convent?'

Mary Ann said she didn't know.

'You can come and stay with me.'

Mary Ann didn't answer and although Paddy would never say, she was a little offended. She flattened the newspaper out over the steering wheel and flicked on the cabin light.

Mary Ann muttered by her side, 'Got any more fags?'

Paddy nodded at her bag.

'Finished,' said Mary Ann.

'We'll stop in a minute and get some.'

Merki was back on form, no doubt about it. In perfect house style he reported that the police had found the gun used to shoot Terence Hewitt in the head, execution-style. Contrary to previous reports it wasn't an IRA gun and they were now certain that the murder wasn't anything to do with the Troubles in Northern Ireland. The gun had been found near the scene of the crime, and police ballistics had confirmed a match with the bullet used to kill Terence. They were now looking for a lone gunman and robbery was the suspected motive. The report was headlined as an exclusive.

'What's this?' Mary Ann was trying to read it over her shoulder.

'In a leap and a bound he was free,' said Paddy. 'The guy who wrote this hasn't had his name on an article for ten months. He's ambitious though. An unscrupulous source could get him to write that the Queen was a man if he thought it would get his career out of the toilet.'

She folded the paper in half and threw it on to the back seat.

III

Mary Ann cried in the car as they sat outside the convent, smoking in the dark. She tried to talk to Paddy but her feelings came out as a jumble of unconnected half-sentences, absent verbs and missing nouns making a non-sense of a painful but familiar story of thwarted love. Paddy didn't want to question her or make her clarify what she was saying; she did want to know the details but flinched from prying. At the same time, she suddenly felt she had her sister back, a woman who was the same age as her, instead of a childbride of Christ who believed in miracles and fairy stories.

Paddy watched as she walked off to the convent gate, pressing the illuminated doorbell and giving her a last longing look as she waited for the answer. Mary Ann looked so pretty suddenly, with the ivy on the convent walls curling up around the door to frame her, her short blonde hair lit from behind by the light on the buzzer; even the plain dress with its dowdy shirt collar and nasty buttons looked nice.

The door opened and the convent swallowed her once again.

Paddy drove away down the hill towards the West End. Stopped at a light, she imagined Mary Ann coming to stay with her, leaving the crushing grey conformity of the Church, and a flare of burning exultation exploded in her chest.

She threw her head back and screamed her sister's name.

IV

She left the radio off, the television off and the door to her study open so that she could hear any noise at all outside the front door. Michael Collins wouldn't come back, she knew he wouldn't, not tonight anyway, although her instinct to scan the horizon for tigers had been strong since Pete was born. Every sharp corner, every fast car was a potential assailant. It made her police him and nag and put anything dangerous up high, and now write an inflammatory column about the Troubles with one ear to the door.

They'd left all of Terry's things in the hall, keeping them separate in case the lawyer asked for them back. She'd moved the silver trunk behind the front door so that anyone breaking in would need to push it along the floor before they could get in. Even so, she'd sleep with her door open tonight.

Having finished her column, she got it down to within five words of the word count so the editors didn't have the scope to chew it up too much, and lifted the phone to call it in. The male copy taker took her column down for her, clarifying a couple of lines, correcting her punctuation once with a polite question. When she was finished she thanked him, pretended she did remember him from Father Richards's leaving do years ago, and hung up.

She should clean up the kitchen and get Pete's gym kit ready so she didn't have too much to do when she woke up in six hours' time. She stopped for breath in the dark hallway, listening for the rhythm of Pete's breathing but getting Dub's narrow whistle instead. Terry's portfolio was leaning against the wall with the yew box at its foot. She picked them up and took them into the kitchen.

Putting them both on the table, she went to Dub's food cupboard and took out the giant jar of peanut butter, scooping a spoonful out and sticking it in her mouth before she could think about it, rolling her tongue around the spoon, savouring the salty sweetness, promising herself that she wouldn't have another. Except one. She rolled the spoon around the inside of the jar, getting a gravity-defying spoonful and eating the top off it so it didn't spill while she was fitting the lid back on.

She sat down. Terry's box was lovely, well crafted and made from thick flawless wood. She opened the lid. It was lined with lilac velvet, faded over time to a crisp brown. Most of the photos were of Terry, as a baby, as a toddler in a garden, Terry at Pete's age standing proud and stiff in a brand new school uniform, Terry as a chubby teen with his hair over his eyes, drinking Coke and laughing. The photos stopped abruptly when he got to seventeen, when his parents died. There were photos of his parents and some older ones, black and white, of an old lady grinning by a large oak mantelpiece, of his parents' wedding. His mother had a bob and a shy smile. At the bottom of the box were small nameless mementos: a newspaper cutting about a school play with Terry's name underlined, a cat collar with a flattened tin bell on it, a tiny piece of green ribbon holding two matching wedding bands together, his and hers.

His parents had died in a car crash. She kissed the dusty strip of ribbon and felt sad, whether for them or for him she didn't know. If she'd been honest she might have admitted it was for him.

These were his most important family memories, she realized, which meant that the worn brown folder Fitzpatrick had in his office had something altogether different in it.

She dropped the pictures back in the box, shut it and wiped the lid with her hand, setting it gently on the chair next to her, and turned to the portfolio.

It was black, greying because of the dust from the high-up cupboard in the flat, an exact copy of Kevin's portfolio. Maybe they had bought them together. Terry always liked stationery. He used Moleskine notepads when he travelled – they'd found a box of the battered notebooks in the suitcase in the trunk.

She unfurled the elastic strap and opened the portfolio, slipping the sheets of photographic paper out of the cupped side and setting them flat on the table. A small Moleskine pad was tucked in at the back. Flicking through it, she read Terry's jittery shorthand and realized that these were notes of the interviews of all the photo subjects, numbered up to forty, dated variously over a month last year. She looked back at the pictures. Senga – New Jersey. Billy – Long

Island. The others were without the accompanying text, just bare photos, but they each had Kevin's touch. Brilliant crisp light, sharp colours and a person in the foreground, smiling or not, beautiful or not, all relaxed, all honest and open-faced.

There was one black face, a woman with an aristocratic African profile, standing on the sunny side of a long narrow street of red-brick tenements in New York with fire escapes snaking up them. Quartz specks in the tarmac glittered in the sun. Her smile was crooked, as if she was trying to hide her teeth, and her hair was pulled up into waspish yellow and black braids that swirled around her head.

Whoever the woman was, Paddy assumed she'd made a happy transition to the States. There were so few black people in Scotland that the two black Glaswegians she knew of were minor celebrities. One was an academic from the West Indies who taught at Glasgow University and had married a fellow linguist. Another, younger man worked as a sound engineer for Scottish Opera and drank in the Chip. Kevin's woman looked African and Paddy assumed she had been adopted by a well-meaning Scottish couple and escaped as soon as possible. She looked very young to be an expatriate.

Paddy was looking at the photo when her eye caught a detail in the background. If the picture had been smaller or the image less sharply defined by the slanted light in the street she wouldn't have noticed it.

Michael Collins had been thinner then. He was two hundred yards behind the woman, leaning over the roof of a big green car. He wore a thin peach summer shirt, his trousers sitting slack on his hips, the sunlight flashing off his glasses. Collins wasn't looking at the camera. In fact, if Kevin had been quick, he wouldn't even have been aware that a photographer was taking a picture down the street at all. As he leaned over the roof of the car his mouth was open in a laugh, hair cropped tight to his head. Across, at the roadside passenger door, was another man, a fat man in a dark suit, his face obscured as he twisted and reached for the door handle.

Paddy sat back and downed the wine, elated. She had a photo of him. It was him in New York and some time ago, but it was a photo of him none the less, captured in a mundane moment, giving a friend a lift.

She checked Terry's notebook for names, looking for any with an African flavour: Morag, Alison, Barney, Tim, none of them fitted with the black woman. But if she had been adopted, her parents might have given her a Scottish name The Scots had colonized half of Africa on behalf of the Empire. For all she knew, Morag could be a common Ethiopian name.

She thought of Terry again, sitting in a bar, sweating, drunk, his arm around a hungry young girl, and shivered, shaking the thought away.

Kevin Hatcher would know who the woman was, where the picture was taken, maybe even the name of the man in the background or some information Paddy could use to trace him and protect herself and Pete. But it was one o'clock in the morning and it would be rude to phone.

Instead, she packed Pete's gym kit and loaded the dishwasher. Instead, she washed her face, brushed her teeth. Instead, she went to bed feeling pleased that she had something to go on, a picture of Michael Collins.

She should have grabbed Pete and run.

13

Yeah

His neighbours were having a party. Back in his drinking days Kevin had been at many Monday night parties himself and knew how joyless they were. They were after-closing-time affairs, dragging through to the cold, damp morning, full of melancholy drinkers chasing a cheap carry-out, banding together solely to consume. He remembered ten-hour nights when conversation was an irksome incidental. Badly coordinated women, who had lost their looks to wine and late nights, doing sexy dancing together while dead-eyed men looked on. Music was mortar to plug the silences. He never wanted to go back there. But tonight the occasional howl and whoop through the wall, the guitar music and the grim hubbub sounded warm and friendly.

The pain in his arm and chin were seeping away and, held still as he was, he could feel the certainty that everything was going to be fine pulse through his body.

His stomach disagreed. It convulsed, once, twice, and the grip on his chin tightened.

'Don't fucking spew. You spew you swallow, understand?'

He was holding Kevin's mouth shut, a hard hand pressed tightly under his chin.

It was dark in the room. He'd left the lights off when he

dragged Kevin in here and threw him into the armchair. The curtains were open. They were always open: Kevin didn't mind people across the road looking in if they could be bothered. He could see out now, a couple with their backs to him watching telly in a soft light. A dark room. A man washing his hands at a kitchen sink.

The man had been kneeling on Kevin's forearm for what felt like hours. He had lost the feeling in his fingers, in his wrist, and his elbow was pressed tight against the leather but it didn't seem to hurt now. Nothing seemed to hurt now. Even his teeth, even his jaw which the man had levered open with a chisel before he put the little paper packages into the back of his throat and forced the water in, making him swallow.

Kevin looked up at the steel-rimmed glasses, the orange street lights from below reflected on the square lenses, and sensed that, of the two of them, his assailant was feeling worse than he was. The man was desperate and afraid. Sweating.

'Spew and you swallow.'

Kevin's mood had turned as quickly as a loose feather in a high wind. He knew everything would be OK, whereas a moment ago he had felt helpless and trapped.

The heat came first, a burning heat to his face and chest. A veil of sweat slid across his eyes and the music next door was matched and overtaken by his own heartbeat thudding, faster and faster, pushing through his face. He couldn't see.

Suddenly, his every muscle tightened to its fullest extent and he stood up, the small man sliding off his lap like a napkin. The man grabbed Kevin's ankles but was powerless against the buzz of strength flooding through Kevin's every sinew.

Smiling, a ray of all-powerful light himself, Kevin lifted his foot and stamped on his assailant's hand. He heard the man cry out, curl into a ball at his feet, half under the coffee table, but Kevin didn't care. It was wonderful not to care. He stamped again, missing him this time but it didn't matter. He turned to the room. Light was bursting from every surface. The door. He should go to the door and get out.

He took three steps, a colossus striding forth, the cool night air caressing his hot skin, his chest leading the way, his heart bursting forward, pushing him out to the close where it would be even colder, even better. He imagined his face pressed tight against the cold of the bare stone, absorbing the delicious tingling chill. One of the drunken neighbours shouted 'yeah' and Kevin turned back at the living-room doorway, shouting back, his voice touching theirs through the wall.

Yeah.

An absolute communion of voices. Perfect. Something small was scrabbling at his feet, something grabbing, scratching, pulling at his legs, tugging him.

White light, cool light, flooded spontaneously out of the wall at him, glorious, thrilling. He shut his eyes for one second but forgot to open them again.

He was on the floor, on his side, his arm curled into a tight ball under his chin, his whole left side throbbing to the music. His face was wet.

In the sky above him a foot stepped over his head, a body moved and a sole hovered above his face. Two orange squares of vicious brightness glinted down at him.

Kevin shut his eyes again.

A voice through a wall called to him, tugging him back to grimy rooms, to sticky settees and black Monday night parties full of the dead.

Yeah.

14

Sleek Rats

Callum was exhausted. His room was small and dark and warm, warmer than any room he'd been in for a long time. Although it was summer they had the heating on and he couldn't have the sheet over him without getting clammy. But the tiredness was partly because he hadn't been alone for over nine hours. He didn't think he would miss being alone so much.

It was a tiny room, half the size of the smallest cell he'd lived in. The single bed took up most of the floor and faced a bookshelf and a white plastic wardrobe with one door missing. He had to walk sideways to get round to the window.

Two of the kids had slept in here. Their bunk beds had been moved to the end of Sean and Elaine's bed. The yellow wallpaper had bits of stickers on it, half a spaceship, a lion's mane and legs, the face missing. In the corner Elaine had tried to wash off a scribble of black felt pen.

The window in Callum's room looked out over the street. It's better this way, said Elaine over dinner, because now the kids won't get woken up with the noise of cars in the street. Better this way. As if she was trying to convince herself. She was slim for a mum of four, brown hair, shiny.

When she bent forward at dinner her shirt fell open a bit and he saw her bra. Nearly jumped her there and then.

They'd lied about him to the kids. The oldest girl, Mary, told him while they were out of the room getting the wee ones bathed. *You've been away in Birmingham,* she said. *You've got a lot of problems.* She was tiny, hands so small they didn't cover his palm. Everything she did was cute. When she spilled milk all over the floor it was cute. She smiled at him a lot, set an example to the others. The toddler, Cabrini, liked him too but the atmosphere was still tense. Elaine was nervous and Sean never took his eyes from him.

Who could blame them.

Callum sat up in the bed and dropped his feet to the floor, holding the curtain away from the wall with one finger, watching the cars speed past outside, craving the fresh cold radiating from the glass. A woman passed by, head down, jeans too tight for her, showing off all her lumps and bumps. He thought about masturbating to get to sleep but someone might come in and find him.

It was so warm, the curtains, the carpet and the heating on. He was used to walls breathing cold, to pulling the prison blankets around himself to stave off the chill. He didn't know if he could stay in this heat; he could hardly draw a breath in it.

It was dark outside. Across the road, on the step of a close mouth, he saw something move and thought it was a rat. A couple of rats. But they were shiny, caught the orange street light, sleek. Feet. A pair of feet hiding in the dark doorway, shuffling to keep warm. Someone was watching the street.

Sweat prickled at the nape of Callum's neck. His fingers began to tremble, making the curtain quiver. He dropped his hand but stayed where he was, trapped, tearful, panicked and alone.

He sat there all night, sleeping in small nervous bursts, his head lolling against the wall, craving the cold from outside the cluttered little flat.

15

The Sound of Music

I

The morning was bright as Paddy led Pete around the corner. The street was swarming with small children in red T-shirts and grey skirts or trousers, ready for the new school year. The children came from a poor catchment area and the uniform was minimal.

It was an old-fashioned primary school, the playground railed off from the street and the building arranged in a tall U around it. The two entrances were at opposite ends of the yard and carved into the stone above them were 'Girls' and 'Boys'.

Pete stopped dead. 'Mum! Gym kit!'

Paddy touched his backpack. 'In here.'

He did a comedy phew, rolling his head in a figure of eight, showing the small hairs on the back of his neck, like Terry's. She considered picking him up and running back to the car. Phone the school. Plead a cold. She could give in to her fears every day and keep him under her bed until he was eighteen.

A young man in a black tracksuit stepped out in front of them, crossing the road to the railings, pressing his face through, looking for a kid.

In the yard a blonde teacher, Miss MacDonald, was

marshalling the children into groups of their own year in preparation for the line-up and roll call they took before the kids went into the school building. Out on the street parents were lined up along the railings, staring into the yard at their children who were showing off their latest toys, making alliances for the fresh day or chasing each other within the limited parameters of the group Miss Mac-Donald had put them in.

Suddenly, Pete slipped Paddy's hand and bolted into the road. She leaped, grabbing his shoulder with a talon hand, spinning him so hard he almost fell to one knee.

'Mum!' He looked up at her, mouth hanging open in shock.

She saw herself, grabbing him to assuage her insecurity, keeping him from his life. Flattening his hair with her hand, she avoided his eye. 'What have I told you about running into the road?'

'You hurt me.' He looked at her, demanding that she look back.

She busied herself straightening the straps on his backpack. 'Just . . . be careful.'

He hit her hand away. 'I *am* being careful.'

'I'm sorry. I got a fright when you ran out. Sorry.' Apologizing to a child – her mother would hate that. Never apologize and never explain, Trisha would say, which was all right for her: everything she did was explained by the Church or by teachers in the Catholic school. Paddy wanted Pete to grow up being able to question authority, but it was a lot more work than telling him to shut up and do what he was told.

'Sorry.'

Pete nodded and looked over at his friends, his face lightening in delight, her offence forgotten.

'Come on.' She took his hand and led him over the road.

He ran into the yard, straight into Miss MacDonald who ordered him over to another group, away from his friends. Paddy followed him in.

'Miss MacDonald? Could you keep an eye on Peter today?'

'Is he ill?'

'No.' She didn't want to sound paranoid. 'You know Peter's father and I aren't together?'

Miss MacDonald touched the tiny gold crucifix around her neck and mugged sorrow, as if everyone had tried but failed to keep them together.

'We're in dispute about access,' she said, sounding stern when sad would have done better. 'I'm concerned Peter's dad might try to come and take him out of school today. Could you keep an eye on him?'

'Of course.'

'He might not come himself. He might send a friend to get Peter.'

'We'll keep an eye on him.' She turned to a child who was wandering around between groups, ending the conversation.

'Don't let him leave with anyone but me, is what I mean.'

But Miss MacDonald was out of earshot.

Paddy shuffled out of the yard and stood outside with the other mums, holding on to the railings with both hands, fighting a familiar knot of terror with phrases that didn't mean anything: he's fine, you're worrying too much, it's normal to be afraid, you have to stop this.

A loud rankling bell ripped through the cheerful sounds from the children, bouncing off the sides of the building. Late parents hurried their children along the road and shoved them roughly through the gates. Miss MacDonald waited for the last few stragglers and pulled the gates closed, shutting them with a latch.

Paddy watched as Pete was put in line, hoping for one last wave from him, but he was talking to his friends.

She walked sadly back to the car, thinking about Michael Collins and how terrifying being a mother was. There was no need to be so scared: she had a photo of Collins now, she could show it to people, get an ID.

She unlocked the car door and climbed in, rolled down all the windows and lit a cigarette.

Parents were dispersing in the street. Women walked in ones and twos, those with cars pulled out slowly, all a little dazed at the sudden calm after the rush of the morning, looking forward to the next six hours until home time.

The one-way system in the small back streets channelled Paddy up to the lights on Hyndland Road. She stopped for red and shut her eyes, thinking through what she had to do today. Find Collins's real name. Kevin Hatcher should be up now. She'd call him and ask him about the picture.

A car behind her hooted its horn. Glancing in the mirror she saw a mum she recognized from the school, a pretty woman whose son had a stammer. The woman smiled, pointed at the green light up ahead and the empty road ahead of her. Paddy held her hand up in apology and took the handbrake off. She glanced to the side, looking for oncoming cars, pulling out into the road.

She was focused on the distance, that was why she didn't see him at first. He was in the corner of her vision, a small blurred head, leaning casually on the bus stop. The silver zip on his black tracksuit caught the sun, glinting like sun-kissed water, and made her look at him.

It was the young man from outside the school, the childless man who crossed in front of her and Pete and watched through the railings. He was standing, body casual but the expression on his face curiously intense, staring straight in at her. Under the black tracksuit she could see a flash of green and white. He was wearing a Celtic top.

Unnerved and jittery, she pushed hard on the accelerator, shot straight across the road and into the mouth of a lane, throwing the door open as she pulled the handbrake on, jumping out and looking back.

A bus was between her and the young man but she ran across the road anyway, bolting around the back of it.

She reached the corner no more than five seconds after she'd seen him, but he was gone.

II

The tenements in Kevin's street were five storeys high and in an area so aspiring that every single flat had at least one car. Paddy toured the street twice, looking for a space to stop.

One of the corners looked marginally less illegal than the others and she parked carefully, her car bonnet sticking out into the street. She'd only be ten minutes. Kevin probably wasn't in anyway and, if he was, all he had to give her was three lines of information. She wasn't going to take a cup of tea if he offered. She'd get a name, call the police and go straight back to Pete's school and pull him out of his class.

Kevin's close was nicer than she remembered. She'd only seen it in the dark and the dusty forty-watt bulbs didn't do justice to the green wall tiles. The neighbours had put plants out on the landing and they flourished in the south-facing light coming in through big wire-meshed windows.

Kevin's door was firmly shut. She rang the bell and waited for a polite length of time before knocking. She could hear the sound of her knuckle raps echo around the empty hall. He wasn't in. Considering the trouble Michael Collins had taken to frighten her, he might have freaked Kevin out too.

She took a notepad from her pocket and scribbled her

number on the back with her name and a request that he call her. She was holding the letter box open to slip it in when she heard the sound of music.

Bending down, she peered through the letter box. She couldn't see anything: on the other side of the door was a two-sided brush, the bristles coming up and down to meet in the middle, a device designed to stop draughts and nosey people from doing exactly what she was trying to do: looking into the flat. She tried pushing the bristles apart with her fingers but the letter box was too deep and she couldn't reach. There was definitely music coming from in there, from the living room, she thought.

Kneeling down on the rough doormat, she used her pen and one of her house keys to hold the bristles slightly apart. She could just see in but not much. She put her mouth to the opening.

'Kevin? Are you in?'

He could be sleeping in the living room, using the music to block out morning noises and sounds from the street. She could see the rug on the floor, the foot of a tripod, the chair where he had put her coat on Sunday night.

Shuffling sideways on her knees like a pilgrim, she changed her point of entry: the living-room door was open, sunlight pooled on a discarded trainer lying on its side, the worn sole towards her. The music was coming from there, the cheerful overture to *Marriage of Figaro*. It sounded like the radio was on.

She was just about to withdraw her eye, to pull back and shout in again, when she saw the toe of the trainer twitch. The trainer had an ankle attached to it.

16

Negative Negatives

I

The police broke the door down and Paddy followed the paramedics into the flat.

Kevin was in the living room, limp, lying on his left side, his cheek sitting in a pool of dry, chalky saliva. Behind him, bright yellow sunlight flooded the living room, casting a grey shadow over his face. His eyes were open a little, a slice of white. They looked as dry as the saliva under his cheek. His right hand was clamped at his breastbone, the hand clawed tight. He'd had a stroke, they said, almost certainly.

Paddy's voice was a strangled whisper. 'He's thirty-five. How could he have a stroke?'

The paramedic pointed to the coffee table in the living room. The boxes of negatives had all been moved. It looked strange because it was the only clear surface in the house. Sitting on the smoked-glass surface was a single line of white powder. 'Cocaine.'

'Will he be all right?'

'He'll be fine,' the paramedic said, avoiding her eye.

'You'll be OK, Kevin,' she said, raising her voice and sounding more frightened than she meant to. 'Don't worry. They've said you'll be OK.'

Paddy stood in the cosy mess of the hall and watched as

the ambulance men took Kevin's vital signs and declared him not dead, yet. One of them touched his fingertips to the chalky mess under his cheek, rubbing it between his fingers. It was gritty, he said; definitely an overdose. They asked if he was a habitual drug user and she said she didn't really know but didn't think so: he didn't even drink any more. They nodded as if that was exactly what they expected her to say. One of them seemed to be trembling, which alarmed her.

Two police officers stood in the door of the bedroom, talking quietly. Their summer shirts were so starched they looked like blue cardboard. Start of the shift.

Kevin's hall wasn't used to having five people in it. They had to pick their steps. He had dropped things as he came home, ran out to meet people, staggered home after a good night out with pals. She looked around, imagined him seeing it and vowing to tidy it on quiet Sundays but having warm lie-ins instead, lingering over his breakfast, listening to the radio or reading a book.

She looked back at him. His left arm was beneath him, the soft inside of his forearm facing upwards. It was blue. A huge blue-and-green bruise covered the skin, deep, a memory of trauma. He hadn't had it when she saw him on Sunday.

She stepped forward. 'That bruise on his arm.' She pointed it out to the ambulance men. 'Could he have done that when he fell?'

One of them shrugged, irritated that she had drawn their attention away from their work. 'Suppose.'

She tried to imagine a fall that would occasion a bad blow on the inner forearm. And then she noticed it: a matching bruise under his chin. It wasn't obvious because of the sharp light behind him. A U-shaped bruise, a grip on either side of his chin, holding him tight.

'Excuse me.' She reached forward and touched the ambulance man's shoulder. 'Are you sure it's a stroke?'

He shook her hand off, angry at being distracted. 'Aye, it is. It just is, look at his hand.'

She stepped around Kevin's feet to get a better look and the ambulance man sighed and glanced back at the police officers. 'Can ye . . .?'

A noise came from deep inside Kevin, a gurgle that seemed to emanate from his stomach. A small bubble of wet formed at his lips and burst.

He was dying. She knew he was dying. One of the officers saw Paddy reel backwards and grabbed her under the arm, turning her away. He took her out to the cold dark close and encouraged her to catch her breath.

'Is he dead?'

'He's going to be fine. The paramedics say he's going to be fine.'

'He's dead, isn't he?'

'No, he's fine.'

'He's dead.'

He sat Paddy on the neighbour's front step and told her to bend over and put her head between her legs. She couldn't quite hear him so he held her head down, cupping it as if she was being guided into a police car. She had a pencil skirt on and her cheeks were pressed tight against her knees. Staring at her orange suede trainers, the cold stone numbing her bum, she didn't want to see any more, couldn't bear the thought of looking up. She thought of Terry, how sad he would be, and thinking about that reminded her of Kevin showing her the photos on Sunday night. He said no one was after him. He said it was nothing to do with the book.

She watched as they lifted him carefully on to the stretcher, one side limp, the other tight as a traction band. His left knee was almost up to his chin, his clawed hand in the way. The walls slid sideways and she dropped her head to her knees again.

Paddy had been to the site of a hundred car crashes and fatal accidents but the bodies in the bags weren't people she knew, the blood was a faceless stranger's blood, the weight of sorrow someone else's.

She eased herself upright. The police officer was in front of her, looking into the house, stepping from foot to foot, his hands fiddling with his belt. He was young and excited to have a job that didn't involve hassling truants in the park or chasing junkies out of Woolworths.

Kevin looked smaller on his side. Paddy watched as the paramedics lifted the stretcher slowly, carried it through the door and negotiated the turn of the stairs. She saw Kevin's blond hair darkened and crusty, a white residue over it.

The older officer was standing in front of her, nodding as his walkie-talkie crackled instructions at him. He signed off and hung it on his belt, turning formally to Paddy.

'We'd like to ask you about how you came to be here and what you know about—' He thumbed back to the hallway.

'Kevin.'

He nodded gravely. 'About Kevin.'

She looked back into the hallway. The sun had moved, the tip of it touching the crusty saliva mess.

Kevin wouldn't take cocaine. If he'd been taking it she would have known. She'd seen him drinking when he worked at the *News* and he was a compulsive, mental drunk. Men had gone to their graves swearing they'd chuck it if they got as bad as Kevin. She had once seen him have an alcoholic seizure in the office, then sit for a while with a cup of tea before going out drinking again in the afternoon. Men like that didn't take an occasional line, not like Dub did sometimes. Someone had made him take it.

Collins. She could see him stand by while Kevin vomited

on the floor, watching calmly as a stroke curled him up like a dead leaf.

'Look, I need to go but take it from me, Kevin didn't do drugs,' she told the older officer. 'The bruises on his arm and chin – didn't you see them?'

He looked at her. 'Not really.'

'I think Kevin was killed by the same guy who murdered Terry Hewitt.'

'Terry . . .?'

'Hewitt. The guy found shot dead on the Greenock road? The journalist?'

Terry's death had been blanketed over the papers, over the television and radio news, but neither of the officers seemed to know what she was talking about. Not the sharpest pencils in the box.

The younger officer sensed her disapproval. 'Oh, I think I heard something about that,' he said, nodding at his colleague.

'How do you know it's to do with that?' The older officer leaned in, as if half expecting Paddy to confess to the killings herself.

'Oh, for Christ's sake,' she said impatiently, 'just call it in. Ask for the team investigating Terry Hewitt's murder. They'll know what I'm talking about.'

The older man pulled himself up to his full height, nostrils aflare, and she realized that her sniping tone had been a bad mistake. He might be an idiot but, in common with all police officers, he didn't want to be spoken to with anything but fawning respect.

'I will decide what we do and don't call in, and I'll thank you to watch your language when you speak to me.'

She apologized, said it was the shock, and tried to explain how she needed to look through the portfolio of photographs Kevin had taken for the book.

The younger officer glanced at his mentor, nodding so much she guessed he wasn't listening. The older officer seemed to understand this time but didn't take notes or react. When she had finished he told her to wait here and went downstairs, presumably to call it in and ask a senior officer who the hell Terry Hewitt was and what the fuck he should do now.

The younger man stayed with her in the close. Paddy knew they were keeping her with them, intending to take her in for questioning, which would mean a two-hour wait, a short conversation and then another two-hour wait before someone decided she could go. She could leg it but the squad car would probably be just outside the close. Even if she ran, both officers looked fit enough to outrun her. Actually, her mother could probably outrun her. She wasn't very fit.

'So you knew this guy?'

'We worked together.'

'In papers?'

'You a secretary then?'

'No, I'm a journalist.'

He grinned, not maliciously. 'So you make things up for a living?'

'Kind of.'

He smirked a little and looked away, leaned over the banister, looking for signs of his partner. When he found none he stepped into Kevin's flat, shrugging and smiling like a naughty schoolboy. He beckoned Paddy to come too.

'Let's look for the photos,' he said, showing he had been listening after all.

She stood in the hall watching him in the bedroom, stepping over a tidal wave of dirty clothes stacked against a chest of drawers. She turned away, looking back into the living room. The line of cocaine on the coffee table was wrong. She tipped her head at it: if Kevin had cleared a space to chop a line he would have put the boxes of negatives on the floor under the table, which was the only empty space that was big enough. She glanced around at the settee, under the television, by the chair. The boxes were gone.

'There should be boxes of negatives somewhere near the table, they were on the table . . .'

The nosey officer was smiling out at her, standing beyond the rumpled bed, triumphantly holding a big black portfolio that Paddy recognized from her last visit. He put it on the bed.

'Wait, wait,' she said. 'If Kevin's attacker picked it up his prints'll be on it.'

He shrugged, slipped the elastic band off its shoulder, flipped it open, dragging his greasy fingertips down the cover with a recklessness that Paddy couldn't quite believe. She realized that he wasn't a considered liberal or a genius working undercover. He was an idiot who didn't believe her fantastical story that Kevin and Terry had been killed by someone Kevin had photographed. Quiet people always fooled her.

He lifted the photos, one after the other, looking at them and at her, waiting for her to say stop, there he is, but the black woman's picture wasn't in the portfolio.

'Well, it was there,' she said, 'and the negatives have gone.'

He replied with his customary smirk.

Echoing footsteps heralded the return of the older officer. Panting lightly, he rolled his eyes at the stairs and caught his breath enough to order the other officer to secure the flat. They shut the door, fixing the lock to stop it blowing open in a draught but not much more.

'Listen,' Paddy told their backs, 'I really have to go. I'll give you my number if you need to call me.'

'You're coming with us, Miss Meehan,' the older officer said with relish. 'DI Garrett wants to talk to you in Peel Street.'

Outside, Paddy could see that they hadn't had any trouble finding a parking space for their squad car. They had stopped it in the middle of the two lines of cars and got out, and now it was jammed between the other cars in the street. The officer who had pawed the portfolio could only open the back door halfway for her.

'But I've got my own car,' she protested.

'No,' his friend said, 'you can't drive your own car to the station.' He didn't want her driving in on her own in case she took a wrong turn and pissed off, presumably. Nor would he agree to his partner accompanying her while he drove the squad car.

'Corroboration,' she said, letting him know that she understood. If she suddenly confessed that she'd attacked Kevin they wouldn't be able to use it in court without a second officer hearing it too. He didn't answer her. 'So I'm a suspect?'

'He had a stroke.'

'If I'm a suspect you should caution me.'

But he wasn't willing to arrest her, or let her go.

'Can I get something out of the boot of my car?'

They glanced at each other and said no.

'It's another portfolio like the one upstairs, but it's got the picture I was telling you about.' She handed them the keys. 'You get it.'

Together, they walked down to the corner and found her car parked precariously on the turn of the kerb.

'This is illegal. You can't park here. You'll get towed.'

It might have been the shock, or the worry, or just the officers' cold officiousness, but Paddy found herself trembling with annoyance.

'Look, I was worried about Kevin and just stopped the car to run up and chap the door, OK? I didn't think I'd be in there for a full fucking hour and a half, havering about.'

But they were unmoved. 'You'll still have to move it. What if a fire engine needs to come along here?'

'The ambulance got in OK.'

'Fire engine's wider.'

They saw her look back accusingly at the squad car. They'd blocked the entire street.

'We can do that,' the younger officer said smugly, 'because we're on police business. But you'll need to move yours.'

'Where to? There isn't anywhere.'

'Put it down there at the turning circle.'

She threw her hands up. 'Right,' she said loudly, 'fine, I'll fucking move it.'

They gave her the keys and she climbed in, shut the door and started the engine. She threw her Volvo into first, mouthed 'fuck ye' at the officers and sped off, heading straight for the main road.

It would take them fifteen minutes to get out of the narrow gully of cars they'd jammed themselves in.

II

The West End was the student quarter of the city and every second shop, whether a dry cleaner's or a newsagent's, had a photocopier in it.

She stopped at a newsagent's near her house and opened the boot, sorting through the portfolio, pulling the photo of the black woman out and rolling it into a cylinder, before shutting the boot and going in.

A hand-scribbled sign on the door said that only two schoolkids were allowed in at one time. When she got inside she could see why: she was in a shoplifter's paradise. Crisps and sweeties were stored in boxes near the door, the magazines were in a blind corner by the exit and they even had cheap toys piled up on a shelf at elbow height to a child. The woman behind the counter sat up nervously as she came in, as if expecting a fresh assault.

Paddy could tell by the concentric circle of dirt around the copy button that the photocopier had been used a lot. She made three black-and-white copies, moving the picture around to get Collins's face in the centre of the frame, then made an extra enlarged one and a colour picture that didn't come out very well. There wasn't a lot of colour in the background anyway but Collins's shirt came out an irradiated pink that bled into his neck.

She was looking at it, worrying about the quality, when her eye was caught by a shadow in the cabin of the car. A rainbow of shadow in the passenger seat: the driving wheel. She realized suddenly that Americans must drive on the other side of the road, the car was left-hand drive. Collins wasn't the driver. He was just the passenger: the fat man was driving him somewhere.

She paid the woman behind the counter and bought a giant chocolate bar and another packet of Embassy Regal, justifying the fags with the thought that if she wasn't going to drink with Brian Donaldson, she'd better have at least one vice and overplay it. Guys like that never trusted the abstinent.

17

Love Was an Accident

I

The Shammy was certain of its clientele, that much was clear. The barman was all but wearing a buckle hat and hollering begorra.

They sold Guinness on tap, two kinds of lager, Irish whiskey and Tayto-brand crisps. Everything that wasn't smeared yellow with cigarette tar was green, even the seats. Wizened paper shamrocks were strung along the back of the bar, a souvenir of a St Patrick's Day past, although what the noble-born stoic would have made of the filthy bar was anyone's guess.

Along three walls a high shelf held memorabilia of a less benign kind. A brass armour shell had a blackened commemoration band around the bottom. Dusty flags of several Irish counties, Mayo, Galway and Cork, were propped up in among tankards. A plastic replica gun and a small, very badly executed model of an H block from the Maze prison made out of painted cardboard, with tiny men sitting on one of the roofs, were placed near the front.

The centrepiece of the bar was a brass engraving of Bobby Sands mounted on a block of wood, his eyes not quite matching, his long over-the-ears seventies hairdo just as misplaced on his square farmboy's face as it had been in real life.

The smog of cigarette smoke made Paddy want to light up herself, if only to mask the smell. She took out her packet and pulled out a cigarette, lighting it with a match, inhaling half-heartedly and thinking she probably looked shifty.

A row of men sitting at the bar turned to stare as she approached. She had thrown on clothes this morning, but she still felt wildly overdressed. They were all wearing T-shirts or sweatshirts under black leather jackets and denims that hung under their beer bellies. She nodded at them.

'Howareye?' she said, running the words together as the Irish did, meaning to be friendly.

Someone snorted cynically. She took a covering drag of her cigarette and felt foolish, stepping towards the rail. The barman was resting a half-poured pint of Guinness under the taps, patiently waiting for it to settle.

'Ah, hello, I'm looking for a guy called Brian?'

'No one called Brian here,' he said. Scottish with an Irish twang, an affectation members of her own family used sometimes.

'I spoke to him the other day. I have some photos of the gentleman he was telling me about.'

He looked her up and down. 'And you are . . .? Detective Constable . . .? Detective Inspector . . .?'

Paddy held her hands out indignantly. 'Do the polis take fat birds now? I'm five foot four, for fuck-sake.'

He shook his head and flicked the Guinness tap back on. 'No one named Brian in here, love.'

'Well, when No-one-named-Brian gets here, tell him Paddy Meehan was in looking for him and I've got the photos to show him. He knows where I work.'

Wood screeched against stone as one of the line-up pushed his stool back, stepped off and squared up to her.

Paddy guessed he would have been the pride of the pack once. Now, fat had gathered around his middle, and his round paunch, starting below two well-formed breasts, was vivid under his cheap white T-shirt. His black leather jacket was elasticated at the waist, drawing in where he spread out, showing off what would once have been fine legs. He stepped into the light and she saw that a tidy slice was missing from the top half of his ear.

Paddy half expected him to chase her to the door but, instead, he picked his pint up and flicked his index finger at her, beckoning her to follow him She stubbed her cigarette out in a nearby ashtray and walked after him to the back of the bar.

The booth was set at ninety degrees from the room so no one could see into it from the floor. It was dark, dimly lit with a yellowed wall light, the heat from the bulb burning a brown oval on the plastic shade. The benches were worn wood, the table marked with water rings and cigarette burns. He slid along a seat, his paunch pressing against the fixed table, and nestled in the corner, resting one leg along the bench, motioning for her to sit opposite him.

'Nice of you to come in person.' His tongue slicked up the corner of his mouth like a sleepy lion. She knew his voice immediately Brian Donaldson.

She took out her cigarettes and lit one, offered them to Donaldson but he refused, tipping his glass at her as if one weakness was enough. He was in his mid-forties and handsome beyond the scars. A square jaw, blue eyes and the manner of a man in charge. His face had wrinkled into the memory of a smile, tide marks around the eyes and mouth.

'Kevin Hatcher's dead.' She didn't want to tell him Kevin was injured. They might go to the hospital and finish the job.

He shook his head. 'Who's this?'

'Kevin Hatcher,' she repeated. 'Hatcher and Terry Hewitt were working together on a book, about expats in New York.'

'Irish expats?'

'Scottish. They took photos of people, street portraits, and Terry wrote a little bit of text to go with them. A coffee-table book. A light thing really, an excuse so that they could go off on a trip to New York together.' She imagined Kevin and Terry eating peanuts on the plane, giggling together, and found herself tearful. 'Two good guys. Now they're both dead. I told you about the guy who came to my house? Michael Collins. Very threatening, said he spoke for your people.'

'He doesn't.'

'You said you didn't know him.'

'Neither I do, but I know who speaks for us.'

'I think you knew who I was talking about when I described him before, but I wanted to show you this.' She unrolled the photocopies. 'I found him in the background of one of the portraits.'

Donaldson peered down at the grainy enlargement, flattened it and looked again.

Collins was laughing in perfect profile, and his glasses were perched on his nose.

'Is this the whole photo?'

'No, it's an enlargement. That's why it's so grainy.'

'I was going to say, it's not a very good photo of anyone.'

He sifted slowly through the other pictures.

Collins wasn't as distinct in them – she wouldn't have recognized him herself if his face hadn't been emblazoned on her mind – but Donaldson didn't seem to be looking at him anyway. She watched him examine the street, the buildings on either side, the fat man by the driver's door, the car licence plate, the slice of the black woman's face at the edge of the photocopy.

Going back to the enlargement, he looked through all the pictures, one by one, stone-faced. He pushed them across the table to her.

'Do you know him?'

'Never seen him before.' His tone was studiously flat, his eyes steady and expressionless.

'Yes you have.' She rolled the pictures up into a tight cylinder. 'I'm not researching a story, Donaldson, if that's what you're worried about.'

'Journalists are always researching a story. They don't wonder what time it is without researching a story.'

'This isn't about a story.' She tapped the rolled-up sheets. 'This cunt sent someone to my son's school this morning. He's been to my fucking house. I need to know what kind of threat he is.'

Donaldson's expression didn't waver. 'We've all lost family.'

'You bastard.'

He blinked, lifted his glass and swallowed three-quarters of a pint of Guinness, watching her over the rim. Placing his glass on the table, he did a clean sweep of his top lip with his tongue. Never once did his gaze waver. He was waiting for her to speak.

'If violence is a gamble . . .' she said carefully, 'if it's about who has the higher stake, remember that I'm talking about my son here.'

Donaldson stared through her, his fingertips turning the rim of the empty glass as white scum slid slowly down the inside.

'Do you hear me, Donaldson?'

'I can hear ye fine, girlie.'

She pointed across the table with the rolled-up sheets,

leaned across at him and poked him hard in his soft chest. 'Tell your friend this and mark it well: neither you, nor he, nor the entire mustered armies of thugs who've hijacked the history of the Fenian Brotherhood of Ireland want to get between me and my young.'

Donaldson looked down at where she had prodded him and slowly raised his eyebrows in amusement, as if a threat from her was a joke.

Paddy could feel herself getting hot and angry; never a safe combination.

'Donaldson, for all I care you may be the King of the fucking Maze, you may have cut your own ear off in a bet – you might just be that fucking hard – but if there's a whisper of a threat to my wean, I will find you and I will ruin you.'

She sat back and caught her breath, hoping she frightened him a little bit.

Donaldson smiled. 'Miss Meehan, d'ye not think every wumman who's ever lost a child thinks that? We're all fighting for our children, they're why we're fighting.'

She stood up and leaned across the table, her nose an inch from his. 'I'm not talking about the struggle. I'm talking about you. I'll ruin you.'

He laughed a puff of grainy Guinness at her. 'Are ye trying to threaten me?'

She sat back down and looked at him. A total miscalculation. He hadn't flinched, hadn't even bothered to keep his poker face on. In fact, he looked a little bored, as if he'd heard a hundred threats of bloody violence and ruin.

She sighed and looked out of the booth. 'I was trying to, but it doesn't seem to be taking.'

Donaldson chuckled to himself, shaking his tits at her, his neck folding over into two round rolls.

She held the sheets up. 'I will find out who this guy is.'

He swatted her adamance away with a flick of his wrist. 'Aye, ye maybe will. Ye maybe will.'

'Have you thought about the effect these killings are going to have on your organization? Killing teenagers in Ulster is one thing—'

'We *don't* kill Ulster teenagers.' For a flash his nose wrinkled, mouth turning up at the corner, shoulder rising as if he couldn't bear the accusation.

'Charles Love,' she said, referring to a sixteen-year-old Catholic boy accidentally killed earlier in the year by a remote control IRA bomb intended for soldiers.

'Love was an accident.' Donaldson narrowed his eyes. 'Seamus Duffy wasn't: the RUC shot him dead last year. He was fifteen.' He shrugged. 'We could go on and on.'

'Killing journalists on neutral soil is going to undermine everything you've worked for. Even your Americans won't fund this sort of thing.'

'We are *not* killing journalists on neutral soil.'

'Does that mean Scotland's part of the civil war now?'

'No.'

'So you don't count Kevin and Terry as journalists? Why? They weren't anything else. I've known Terry since he was a teenager and he would never work for British Intelligence.'

'You'd be surprised who's working for British Intelligence.' It was an aside, a sad note to self more than a statement. Looking for a consolation drink, Donaldson tipped his pint glass a fraction, remembered it was empty and set it straight.

'You're wrong,' Paddy told him. 'Two nights ago Kevin said there was no one after him. He thought Terry had been killed by someone he met in Liberia, for Christsake. If you're justifying this by saying they were part of some big espionage plot, you're wrong.'

Donaldson leaned over the table at her and spoke slowly.

'We are not involved in this, officially, unofficially or in any of the grey areas in between. We didn't do it. We wouldn't do it. It wasn't us.'

'As far as you know,' she said flatly, implying that he was nothing but a foot soldier.

'No.' He spoke slowly. 'From on high. Not us. No way, in no capacity, under no circumstances.'

She sat back and looked at him. Donaldson was scruffy, fat and smelled of Guinness, but he did have the assured demeanour of a man with power. She might need to speak to him again.

'I'm sorry for threatening ye, Mr Donaldson.' She put her papers in her bag and noticed that his eyes followed them. 'But I'm desperate.'

'It's OK.' He nodded softly at the table in front of him. 'I understand. A mother's love's a blessing.'

'No matter where you roam,' she said, filling in the next line of the hokey old Irish song she'd been hearing all her life.

He gave her the end of the chorus. 'You'll never miss a mother's love 'til she's buried beneath the clay.'

They smiled, each seeing the frightened Catholic child in the other.

'An anthem for emotional blackmail. Have ye kids yourself, Mr Donaldson?'

'A son,' he said, and something seemed to snap shut in his eyes. 'He died. On remand in Long Kesh.'

'Oh. God. I'm so sorry.'

Donaldson sighed down at the dirty table top in front of him. 'Aye,' he said. 'Me too.'

II

The summer street was blinding compared to the dark bar. Paddy walked along the busy pavement, stepping out on to the road to skirt around a lorry making a delivery of carpet rolls to a shop. She chewed her tongue to clear away the nasty taste of the cigarettes, thought about Kevin lying on the stretcher, wondering whether his parents were alive and whether she should phone them and let them know he was in hospital.

She didn't look back along the street. She didn't see the young man in the black tracksuit who had followed her from the bar, watching her as she stopped at her car, memorizing her number plate.

She drove aimlessly around the busy city centre, thinking about Collins and Donaldson, hardly paying attention to the pedestrians dodging out in front of her. After a close shave with a small woman carrying heavy shopping bags, Paddy had a future flash of herself explaining to a policeman that she had run away from two officers at a serious assault, mowed down an innocent shopper, but didn't mean any harm.

She pulled into a car park at the foot of the huge glass-tent shopping mall, found a space and stopped.

Women in thin summer clothes flitted past, dragging reluctant children after them. A bigger car park sat between her and the flea market next to the river, the sharp sun glinting brutally off the bonnets and roofs. She took a breath, thought about lighting a cigarette but couldn't face it.

She could be completely wrong about Collins. She didn't have any evidence that the man watching the school was anything to do with him, or that he had hurt Terry. He had come to her door and asked about Terry, but that was all she knew for certain. Other than that, it was just a gut suspicion and she was off form anyway. Terry and Kevin might have known him, he could have been a strange pal of theirs, journalists often had contacts who appeared unlikely as friends, people they were working for stories. She'd had contacts herself when she was doing news, creeps and weirdos who'd scare you out of an alley if you met them on a dark night. Half the Press Bar was like that.

A skinny man brushed past her car, his plastic bag sweeping noisily over the bonnet, bringing her back into the bright day.

Kevin was in a hospital somewhere and she had no idea if he was alive or dead.

III

Standing outside the Albert Hospital, she smoked a cigarette she didn't want and puzzled it over. It was unusual, to say the very least. The best she could come up with to explain the fact that Kevin Hatcher wasn't registered in any of the four major hospitals with a casualty department in Glasgow was that they had misspelled his name on the registration form. But she had spent half a year doing the hospital rounds every night in the calls car and knew that they were meticulous when anyone came in. She had clearly told the officers who Kevin was and his name was on all the mail on the hall table.

She had called in to all four hospitals, flashed her NUJ card, told them she was from the *News*. No Hatcher, Catcher or Thatcher was registered anywhere.

18

Making Heroes of Butchers

Noise moved strangely in the busy morgue. The tiled walls shattered and amplified sound so that drills, metallic clangs and strange muted calls ricocheted down corridors, distorting and warping, masking everyday sources and turning them into growls from monsters, saws through skulls.

Through the effort of not ingesting the smell, Paddy found herself breathless by the time she reached Aoife's office.

The door was open but the chair was empty. A lone cigarette smouldered in an ashtray, the sour tang a welcome interruption to the vivid yowl of disinfectant.

The office was a mess. Storage boxes of papers and files took up most of the floor space. A stack of brown files on the desk threatened to spill on the floor.

'I was surprised when the desk said you were here.' Aoife McGaffry was standing behind her. 'Kind of thought I'd offended ye, to be honest.'

She was smiling, genuinely pleased to see her, and Paddy felt a pang of guilt. She had been offended. Now everyone was a potential source of information.

'Auch, it takes a lot more than that to offend me.'

Aoife bought it and looked relieved. 'Well, come on in anyway.'

She gestured into the office with a roll of address labels in her hand and they shuffled in and shut the door after themselves. A saw started up some distance away, a high whine, and Aoife saw Paddy wince. She hid a smile and held up the roll. 'I need to go through all the files and change the serial numbers. They've been put in out of sequence.'

'Does that matter?'

'Does if it comes to court.'

'What are you doing this for? Shouldn't you have an assistant?'

'I have got one, somewhere, but she never comes in to work and the managers don't seem to care. I was wondering if she's the Provost's daughter or something.'

'Oh yeah, the City Council is a lazy bastard's dream employer. Both my brothers worked for the Parks Department. Spent their days hiding behind trees.'

'Aye, well, it's weird moving somewhere new. All the unofficial regulations and rules. I think I've offended half of Glasgow and I've barely been here a week. It's a personal best, even for me.'

Aoife took the desk chair and offered Paddy the examination bed to sit on. Box files were propped all along it and rather than move them and get comfortable she perched her bum on the edge.

'So . . .' Aoife looked at the files on her desk, patting her work space with both hands, remembering where everything was. 'What can I do for ye?'

Paddy nodded at the files. 'Sorry for interrupting.'

'No, you're fine.' Aoife turned to give her her full attention. 'I never really said it the other night: I'm awful sorry about your friend. It was a rotten thing to happen.'

'Brutal,' said Paddy. She took a breath. 'I came to see you because you did your training in Belfast.'

Aoife gave her a wary look. 'You're not thinking of writing an article, are ye? I don't know what it's like here, but back home we're not allowed to be interviewed.'

'No, not an interview.' She didn't quite know how to phrase it. 'A friend of Terry's had a stroke this morning. He was only thirty or so. I found him.' She looked away, her mind back in the messy hall, seeing the dried chalky saliva. 'They said he'd taken coke and given himself a stroke, but I don't honestly believe he'd use drugs.'

'A lot of users are secretive, you wouldn't necessarily know if he was using drugs.'

'No, it looked staged.' Paddy felt certain now when she thought about it. 'There was a line of cocaine out on the table, I think it was cocaine—'

'If it was a line and it was white it probably was. Speed's the only other thing people snort and that's kind of yellow.'

'Thing is, Kevin drank for years. He was a wild man in the drink, famously wild. He drank everywhere, from first light to home time. And then he stopped a few years ago. If he was taking drugs everyone would know. He wouldn't hide it. He'd be mad with it.'

Aoife nodded. 'Right? But there was a line out on the table?'

'Yeah,' Paddy conceded, 'and he'd vomited chalky powder in his saliva. I know it looks as if he'd—'

'Wait.' Aoife had a hand up. 'He'd vomited white powder and there was a line for snorting on the table?'

Paddy hesitated. 'Aye, I know it looks as if he was using but an ambulance took him away and he wasn't admitted to any of the casualty departments—'

Aoife stopped her dead. 'Who knows we've met?'

Paddy shrugged. 'Anyone could know. The officers would have gossiped about Saturday night. Believe me about Kevin, it looks obvious but he—'

Aoife interrupted her again. 'It doesn't look obvious. It looks odd.' She stood up, suddenly, inexplicably angry. '*Odd*. Come you now with me.'

She grabbed a brown leather handbag off the floor by the strap, swinging it over her head and shouting out of the door into the corridor. 'I'm going out for lunch. Don't yous be tickling them in there.'

Paddy followed her out into the corridor and saw a man's head looking back at her from the walk-in fridge. He shot her a smile and a thumbs-up.

'Follow me,' said Aoife, marching off down the corridor.

II

He stood in Lansdowne Crescent, hands tucked tightly into the pockets on his tracksuit trousers, taking in the general feel of the place. It was right next to a busy road but the houses were wrapped around a private garden, which seemed to absorb the noise. The old buildings faced each other with a quiet dignity. He had been up west loads of times, to Clatty Pat's nightclub, choking with fanny on a Monday, but you wouldn't really notice this place, not unless you were looking, not unless you'd got someone's address from the phone book and come here deliberately.

The fat bird was two up, top flat. No security on the close door.

A big arch ran under the building, for carriages in the olden days, leading to a deserted back yard of overgrown gardens with tumbledown walls separating it from the lane. It would be dark at night.

The north bank of the Clyde was a godforsaken place. Paddy had gravitated here during smoky moments of self-pity and despondency. It was fly-blown, paved over with cracked and stained concrete, and there was a sheer drop to the grey swirl of the water. There weren't even very many seats.

Thin bushes separated it from the busy road, empty gold cans of super-lager strewn at their feet. The sun though, the warm days and softness of the air, attracted a smattering of office workers there for their lunch.

They sat on the edge of a concrete box of bushes and Aoife offered her half her sandwich, a large baguette stuffed with enough egg mayonnaise to fill a skip. Someone in the office ran out with the lunchtime orders, she explained; it was all they'd had left with egg in it.

'Why would they even sell food this big?' She looked at it, puzzled. 'It would do a coach party.'

'Yeah.' Paddy had eaten one of them herself once, and then had some biscuits. 'So why did you say the thing with Kevin looked odd?'

Aoife took a bite and munched it into one corner of her mouth. 'You see, a line is for snorting, inhaling. Vomiting cocaine means you've swallowed it. No one does both.'

'Do people swallow it?'

'Sometimes. Wrap it in a Rizla and swallow, just as effective but takes longer and it's harder to pace yourself. But doing both is playing Russian roulette. It's a hard enough balance to achieve through one method of inges-tion.'

Paddy chewed a mouthful of creamy egg filling, enjoying Aoife's accent, the hard nasal 'r's and short vowels. 'How could he disappear? Does that mean he wasn't admitted to hospital at all? His hand was all curled up at the side.' She mimicked Kevin's claw hand. 'Could he have recovered before they got to hospital and gone to his parents or something?'

Aoife looked shifty. 'Don't think so. He may not have made it to hospital. He may have … you know … *passed on*.' When Aoife spoke again her voice was low. 'They don't trust me.'

Paddy looked at her, 'Who?'

'*Them*. Upstairs. Graham Wilson was in with the bricks, one of the boys, they could trust him. That'll be why your friend has disappeared: they knew I'd find traces in his nostrils and stomach and blurt it.'

'Who though?'

The hard sun glinted on the water as two businessmen walked past, giggling and swinging their briefcases.

'Will we whistle after them lads there?' said Aoife, her mood lifting suddenly when she changed the subject.

'Yeah, go on,' Paddy dared her.

Aoife turned back to them and shouted under her breath, 'Hey, you fellas: wheet whoow!'

They laughed to themselves, watching the businessmen retreat down the river.

'God, it's been a hell of a morning,' said Paddy, and told Aoife about Collins coming to her house and the man watching her son's school.

'This guy's Northern Irish, ye say?'

'I've got a photo of him.' She opened her bag and took out the photocopies. 'You might know him.'

'Aye, he's probably my cousin or something, 'cause you know, Ireland's only twelve foot across.' Aoife looked at the enlargement of Collins and smiled. 'You're having a laugh.'

Paddy was bewildered. 'Am I?'

They looked at each other, both searching for a clue.

'You know him,' prompted Aoife.

'Do I?'

'Don't ye?'

Paddy shook her head.

'He's famous, like you.' She could see Paddy didn't know what she was talking about. 'Martin McBree. He's a major highheadjan in the IRA. Don't you work in the papers?'

'Yeah, but I don't know who this guy is.'

'Martin McBree?' she said again, as if that would clear it up. 'The photo holding the guy on Bloody Sunday?'

'Never heard of him, sorry.'

'He was over in New York last year, ambassadorial duties, restructuring the Noraid funding people. It was on the nine o'clock news at home. He shook them up pretty badly. Brought in a whole new management team and got rid of the old guard. Those old fellas'd send them nothing but guns and psychos. The Republicans are shifting their position, moving towards a negotiated settlement. What they want now is to put a raft of peace-seekers into positions of power.'

'So McBree's a good guy?'

Aoife nodded that she thought so. Paddy thought back to Sunday night and McBree in her hallway. She could have had it all wrong, really. It was just a gut reaction to the guy: he was there with an agenda, she gathered that much, but it didn't mean he was violent.

She was pleased to have been so wrong.

They had both done as much damage to the baguette as they could so they abandoned it on the wall and Paddy got out her cigarettes. Aoife took one from her.

'He's made a wild lot of enemies.'

'McBree? Surely everyone wants peace?'

'Ye'd think, wouldn't ye? That's the trouble with armed struggle. Even if it starts out very noble with good men putting their higher feelings aside it's always going to be a magnet for thugs and sadists. There's always going to be a faction who don't want it to end, you know?' Aoife stretched out her papery white legs, catching the sun. 'Pathology is the sharp end. We see it all.' She squinted at her cigarette. 'My old boss at home, he dealt with the Shankill Butchers' victims. You ever hear of them?'

'No.'

She took another draw and held it in. 'They charged them with nineteen, but really there were about thirty murders. The Shankill Butchers were a gang of men, twelve or so of them, Protestant loyalists. They got hold of a black taxi cab, drove around at closing time. Whoever hailed them got killed. They wanted Catholics but sometimes got their own side. They weren't that fussy. What does that tell ye about the depth of their political convictions?'

Paddy tried to affect concern, but to her it was just a story about faceless men killing other faceless men. 'It was an excuse?'

Aoife looked over at groups of workmen sunbathing their lunch break away, stripped to the waist across the glimmering water. 'One fella, Thomas Madden, wee quiet man, forty-eight, unmarried, a security guard. They hung him up by his feet for six hours. One hundred and forty-seven stab wounds. Chipping away at him for hours.' She flicked her wrist. 'All the work of the same hand, ye can tell that from the shape of the wounds. They put the time of death at about four a.m. Later, when they found him and saw where he'd been killed, they found a witness, a woman who'd been coming past around four. She was walking home after a party, she said, and heard a man's voice. She thought someone was wild with the drink. He was shouting, "Kill me, kill me."' Aoife flattened her hand to her chest wearily. 'I don't know why that hurts me so much.'

Paddy held her hand up. 'That's enough for me, actually.'

'Aye well, there's my point: in peacetime the Butchers would just be sadistic serial killers, but to some people they're folk heroes. And they're the people the peace-seekers have to go through. Both sides have their share of bastards. Any one of them can single-handedly break a ceasefire and keep the fight going. That's who they need to weed out if there's to be any hope.'

'And McBree's doing the weeding?'

'So I've heard.'

Paddy leaned back on her elbows, letting the sun warm her face. 'When you said they don't trust you, who were you talking about?'

Aoife shrugged as if it was a silly question. 'The bosses.'

'Why would the bosses want to hide how Kevin died?'

Aoife prodded Paddy in the shoulder. 'That's your job.'

IV

Helen, the chief librarian, was busy giving a junior member of staff a bollocking. She looked down her nose through her red plastic glasses.

'Tell him that the reason we need one or two keywords is so that an idiot like you doesn't end up with a truckload of envelopes to lose on the way up the stairs.'

The copy boy was a teenager, his skinny legs hardly filling the smart trousers his mum had ironed for him. He was looking at the red beads on Helen's glasses chain, trying to give the impression of looking at her without having the courage to actually do it.

'The next time they give you a clippings request, take them this form.' Helen held up a small yellow sheet with three questions on it. 'Get them to fill it out. That way you won't waste my time and yours.'

Paddy leaned over the copy boy's shoulder and pointed

at Helen. 'She used to give me grief all the time too.'

He turned, afraid at first and then grateful at her comradely tone. Helen wasn't pleased. She scowled after the junior as he shuffled out of the office and gave Paddy a cold smile. They were friends sometimes, when Helen forgot about office politics and power games, which was about once a year, usually when her heart had been broken by yet another separated or divorced man. She was on an earnest hunt for love.

Paddy had met a few of Helen's dates when she bumped into her in bistros around the West End. Red-faced businessmen in expensive suits, mostly. She wondered Helen could eat looking at some of them, much less sleep with them. But although Helen was handsome she was a nippy cow and Paddy supposed that brought her trade value down a lot.

She glared through her glasses at Paddy. 'I don't appreciate you speaking to me in that manner in front of a junior member of staff.'

'Yeah, OK.' Paddy was looking back into the library, at the big table where women with scissors used to cannibalize endless copies of each edition, cutting out stories and filing them in small brown envelopes under subject headings. Nowadays it was all done electronically: the copy was typed into computers to be set and sent to the print room downstairs, and a disk of the articles went to a company with expertise in these things. Helen was alone in the library, general of a dispersed army, and it had made her more unpleasant.

'OK: Brian Donaldson.' Paddy smacked her lips and leaned across the desk. 'Martin McBree. Independent and joint.'

Helen sucked her teeth at Paddy to show that she wasn't happy, turned and went down to the clippings drum to call up the search. She punched in the names to the panel, the metal drum churned and clanked and slits opened up along its body. She lifted the envelopes out and slapped her hand with them, thinking for a moment. She looked at Paddy, a smug thought shimmering across her face, came back to the desk and stamped them.

'These cross-ref for IRA and Northern Ireland.' Helen handed her the envelopes, trying not to smile. 'Did you see Merki's copy last night? Contradicts your IRA theory a bit, doesn't it?'

Paddy nodded politely. 'Yes. I'm a fool, Helen,' and she walked out of the room.

In the corridor she looked at the dates stamped on the front of the clippings envelopes. No one had had either of them out for over eight months. Merki wasn't following the same trail because he was convinced the IRA weren't involved.

She ran upstairs to the newsroom, clutching the envelopes and pulling her narrow skirt up to her thighs so she could move faster.

v

She found a space on a desk in a quiet corner and opened the first envelope that came to hand.

Martin McBree was IRA royalty. His career was outlined in two separate full-page profiles. He joined the organization when he was little more than a boy, pledging his loyalty three years before the Troubles began in the North, in the balmy days when IRA was said to stand for 'I Ran Away'. He came through as part of the generation of Northern Irish Republicans who ousted the old guard when the Troubles began, turning the IRA into a significant paramilitary force.

On the second Bloody Sunday, British soldiers, unprovoked, had fired upon a peaceful civil rights march and killed thirteen unarmed civilians. McBree had been in the crowd that day and a photographer captured him in a moment of such tender glory that the image was published in newspapers all over the world. He was carrying another man, one arm under his shoulders, the other under his knees, leaning backwards to counter the weight. He was small, only five foot seven or so, but he must have been all muscle and sinew. The man had an open chest wound, was probably dead already. He had a black coat on and the photo was in black and white, but there was no mistaking the thick black blood on his chest, running down his arm and dripping from his limp hand. McBree's pale shoes were splattered with blood. It was a good picture but what made it famous was the wild-eyed priest standing in front of them, holding up a white hankie in surrender, begging safe passage through the government snipers.

Paddy read down: the dead man was a plumber. He had four sons and a daughter. He was thirty-one.

She looked at the picture more closely. McBree didn't look frightened. His jaw was clenched tight at the strain of the weight he was carrying. Here was a man used to blood. Here was a man who could face a hard task without flinching.

She found his name in an article about the first round of hunger strikes: he had been imprisoned many times for arms offences and was the prisoner representative at the Maze for a year. Talks broke down when he left.

More recently he had been arrested and released for travelling on a false passport. He was on his way back from the Lebanon. She checked the dates, counting back to Pete's spell in hospital. Terry had been reporting from Beirut at the same time.

Later clippings reported that McBree admitted to attending a training camp in the Lebanon, and they cited off-the-record speculation that he had been training both PLO and ETA guerrillas in hand-to-hand combat.

McBree was pictured in New York, a stolen snapshot of him at an airport. Just as Aoife had said, he was sent there with a mandate to restructure Noraid, ostensibly to make it more efficient but actually to shift power to a new raft of soldiers. He was ruthless in taking power away from the factions supporting the armed struggle and giving it to those who wanted a negotiated settlement. McBree's hand-to-hand combat training must have come in useful, Paddy thought. His wife and two children had stayed home in Ireland while he was gone and a bomb had gone off near his house. Police suspected infighting in the Republican movement.

He had been in her house. She thought back to the blunt letter opener, imagined herself trying to stab him and realized how lucky she had been. Sweating lightly, she sat back and saw Bunty's Monkey watching her, his arms crossed, looking smug.

The Donaldson clippings told her little of interest: he was pictured at a couple of press conferences, looking slimmer, less debauched. His son had died in the Maze and Donaldson himself was forced out of Northern Ireland after a turf war.

The joint clippings filled out his story: his son, David Donaldson, had been stabbed to death aged nineteen by a junior member of a Loyalist paramilitary group just two days after he was brought in on remand. The assassin had been given an amnesty under Martin McBree's orders, only to be found with his throat cut the day after his release. Rumour had it that McBree averted a gang war to give his group leverage with the prison authorities, and to afford the Donaldson family the courtesy of killing the assassin themselves.

Donaldson owed McBree. He would have phoned him the minute she left the Shammy, reiterating every detail of what she had said, telling him that her son's safety was her only concern.

She sat back and thought about what Aoife had said: McBree was a good guy but only compared to the likes of the Shankill Butchers.

19

Callum in the Street

I

Maggie, the social worker assigned to his case, came in the morning and sat with Callum in the living room. She asked him questions about how he felt and he guessed the right answers: scared about the press, ashamed of his offences, happy to be free. She waited long after they had run out of things to say to each other, drank a cup of tea Elaine gave her and then said she'd come back next week, same time.

Elaine avoided him. She spent most of her time in the kitchen. It was two in the afternoon and she was no longer strained but nippy now, sniping at the two babies, waking them when they fell asleep, trying to make them sleep when they were awake.

Callum hadn't moved from the sofa since watching *Count Duckula* with the kids before school, because no one had told him to and he didn't want to just wander around the place. He went to the toilet a couple of times, accepted a cheese sandwich from Elaine and a cup of tea when Maggie came, and watched the television all day while the toddler came in and out. Sometimes she approached him, curious, pawing at his trouser leg, but she always went away. He didn't know how to play with her.

Finally Elaine came back into the living room.

'Right.' She had her purse open and was looking through it. 'Here's two quid. Could you go three doors up and get me four pints of milk and a loaf?'

Callum looked around. She couldn't mean the toddler. 'Me?'

'Aye. Save me going.' She held the notes out to him and he took them. They looked at each other. She went into the hall and came back with his coat. 'Just out the door and to the left, three doors down.'

He stood in the close and looked across the road to the door where he had seen the rat-feet hiding. He could see straight through to the dirt in the back yard, to the bin shed and next to it a big puddle with two small children crouched on its shore, playing. Women bustled past the close mouth, hurrying down the street, summer tops and jeans. Old women wore overcoats.

He stepped out of the close, one, head down, keeping close to the wall, two three four five steps, slipping along to the left until he came to a shop door with stickers advertising cigarettes and bananas. Nineteen steps outside, alone, and nothing bad had happened.

The door jingled as he opened it. A small Asian man looked up from the counter and then looked away again. Callum hurried over to hide behind the shelves, struggling to catch his breath. Twenty-six steps outside and nothing had happened. No one had looked at him twice. No one had recognized him. Maybe he wasn't as famous as Mr Stritcher said he was.

The radio was on in the shop, a jagged song with an insistent fast beat that the cheery DJ announced was by somebody Hammer. Callum liked it. He played another one, a slower song with long notes and a sad way about it.

Callum stood still, staring at the bread and the boxes of cakes, and listened to the end. Wonderful. A mind can only hold one thought at a time and his mind now was full of beautiful music. He could feel the beat on his face, the stirring, sweeping notes through his chest. He wanted to dance, to sway and move his feet.

'Ay, you there, are ye going to buy something?'

The shopkeeper was talking to him. Callum stepped around the stand and looked at the man. He was tiny really, wore a turban and that made him look bigger, but he was less than five foot four and skinny, comical. 'Eh?'

'Are you going to buy something or just stand there?' The man was so small and so angry. He wouldn't have lasted a minute in prison. Men that slight couldn't get that angry in prison unless they had a knife or a minder, and then, Callum realized, even if they had a really big argument it wouldn't come to blows. That was why he was so angry, because it was safe to be angry. He poked his finger at Callum rudely.

'Yeah, son, I can see the top of your head over those shelves there. What you doing standing so long? You're not stealing from me, eh?'

Callum held his jacket open to show he had nothing, hadn't hidden a loaf in there. 'I was listening to the radio. Forgot what I was doing.'

'Aye, yeah, you like those tunes nowadays, bang bang bang? You like them, you young ones, at your discos. Load of old rubbish, man, garbage.'

The tiny old man and Callum smiled at each other. *You young ones*. I am young.

'What you come in for anyway, eh?'

'Milk.'

'Over there at the back.' He waved Callum towards a fridge with a glass door. Cartons of green and blue were stacked up on top of each other.

'I don't know which one to get.'

'Who is it for? For you?'

'No, a baby.'

'Blue.'

Callum put it on the counter and held out the two pound notes. 'And a loaf, please.'

'You get that off the shelf. White, brown?'

They gave you a choice of white or brown in prison but they tasted the same. He thought he remembered the cheese sandwich being white.

'White, I think.'

The old man punched the price into the till and charged him one twenty. He gave him his change. 'Where you from?'

'Just moved near here.'

'Good,' he said, still sounding angry, but half smiling as well. 'You be a good customer to me, yes? Don't give your money to those bastards in supermarket.'

'OK,' smiled Callum, taking the change from him. 'OK.'

Outside he smiled all the way along the road, swinging the loaf by the neck, thinking about the music he had heard and the funny man. He was at the close mouth before he realized he hadn't been counting.

Smiling, he turned back to the street and saw the leather shoes. They were parked in the close, same as they had been the night before. Brown, sleek, a pattern punched out on the toe. The bloke looked up. A young one, like himself. Long blond hair pulled back from his face, glasses, wearing a red-checked coat, watching down the road the way Callum had just come.

The children who had been playing in the puddle in the back court pushed past the shoes. He let them through, smiling, touching the top of a head, and looked down the street again. He must have watched Callum coming out of the shop. Must have watched him swinging the loaf, off guard, smiling about the funny shopkeeper.

Callum leaned his back against the close wall.

They were coming for him.

Pete had finally settled in bed after only six trips back into the living room to ask for water, a bit of bread because he was hungry, a cuddle after a particularly badly feigned nightmare, the horror of which dissipated as soon as Dub smiled at him.

Paddy and Dub were alone in the living room, sloped at either end of the settee, and Paddy told him about Kevin and the police. He agreed with her: there was no way Kevin Hatcher had been quietly taking drugs while living a relatively normal life. Could it have been his first time, though? Dub'd heard of people dying the first time they took an E and maybe it could happen with cocaine. They both considered it and decided that Aoife was right: no one swallowed and snorted at the same time.

Paddy was tired, worried about Mary Ann and frightened for Kevin: she'd phoned the casualty wards again in the early evening, when the night shift receptionists who knew her would be on. There was still no trace of him.

Dub knew what would cheer her up: he put on an old tape of *Evil Dead II*. They already knew it by heart. They'd watched it a hundred times and knew all the jokes already but it was still comforting.

Bruce Campbell had sawn halfway through his own wrist when she suddenly thought about Fitzpatrick and the folder.

'I've been left a house,' she said, and told Dub about the folder with her name on it. He laughed at her.

'That's ridiculous, he can't make you choose between a folder and a house. It's a will, not a quiz show. Go back and ask him what the fuck he's on about. Better yet, get another lawyer to look into it.'

Paddy nodded, watching the tape. A woman in a bad mask was menacing the hero. Dub stretched out on the settee, his foot making contact with her leg. He flinched, withdrew from the electric touch until she smiled at him and wrapped her hand around his toes, pulling his foot on to her lap and holding it.

They watched the TV, both smiling, as the Deadites came to claim the world of men.

20

Rat Shoes

I

Paddy stood by the doors for a moment, clutching the envelopes from the clippings library. The morning newsroom was empty. Everyone was packed into Bunty's cubicle for the editorial conference. Admin staff and the dregs and strays were rattling around and, although it was almost two hours after his shift had finished, Merki was still there, strutting, pleased with himself, offering cigarettes and prompting people to acknowledge his article the day before.

Just then Bunty's door opened and the conference emptied out into the newsroom, eds and subs spilling out to the desks, journalists heading purposefully for the doors or phones to follow up the stories they had been assigned.

Merki trotted over to a desk and claimed his place at the keyboard, notebook propped up against the monitor, fag packet and lighter at his elbow, ready to bang out a story. She made her way over to him, standing shoulder to shoulder with him. She was a full head taller, and she wasn't tall.

'Merki, where did you get that story, about the gun?'

Without turning to her, he scratched his neck. 'That would be telling, wouldn't it?'

'Yeah, because none of the other papers ran it or picked

up on it, which made me think, you know, single source, known only to you. If anyone was confirming it they would have run it too. Did you cross-check it with anyone?'

Merki grinned. 'You're jealous of me and my success.'

They stood together and laughed. Merki was pretty funny: he had a face like a bag of spanners, worked nights and she made four times his salary for eight hundred words a week.

Paddy looked over his left shoulder and the Monkey appeared, scowling when he spotted her. She stepped away as he waved her over to Bunty's door. She held up a finger to the Monkey and picked up a phone, dialled 9 again for an outside line and rang directory enquiries, covering her mouth so Merki wouldn't hear her asking for the number of Scotia Press. The area code was deep in the heart of the West End.

The woman answered as if she'd been expecting her call. 'Yah?'

'Ah, hello, this is Paddy Meehan from the *Scottish Daily News* here. I wondered if I might come over later and talk to you about Terry Hewitt?'

Reluctantly, the woman gave her the address, told her not to come in the next three hours and to ring the bell firmly. Paddy thanked her and hung up.

The Monkey wasn't smiling as she approached. He held the already open door to Bunty's office and bowed as she passed on the way in.

Bunty was sitting with his elbows on the desk, his index fingers steepled against his mouth. He looked up at her. She had never seen him quite as white before.

'Sit.'

Paddy shut the door behind her, leaving the Monkey outside, and took the nearest chair. The table was ten foot long, they were sitting at either end and it still felt too close.

Bunty sat forward. 'Callum Ogilvy. Is he *out*?'

He left the name hanging in the air between them. It wasn't clear whether it was an accusation, a story suggestion or a reproach. She could bluff it, tell him an outright lie, but big lies rarely went well for her. The porous paper on the clippings envelopes was suddenly damp from her damp hands. She put them on the table.

'Bunty—'

He had her column copy on the desk in front of him. 'And this flimsy crap is all you bring me.' His voice rose suddenly, his words tumbling over each other in their hurry to get out. 'Where's the bite in this? Say it was the Provos or say it wasn't. And Misty doesn't use semicolons. What the fucking bloody hell am I paying you for?' He wasn't a habitual user of bad language, didn't understand the rhythm of it, and it sounded desperate. 'At the prison: you were *seen*.'

'Look, there's been another attack.' She was matching his speed, talking louder than she normally would. 'Kevin Hatcher, our old pictures editor. I saw Merki's article but just because they found a gun doesn't mean it's confirmed either way. Someone threatened me at my house. My son—' God, she was personalizing it, making it emotional. She hadn't meant to. 'They threatened me, at my house.'

But Bunty had barely heard her. 'You were outside the prison. It's all over Glasgow. Everyone knows. I look like a bloody fool.'

'But this other story, it's going to be huge, boss. When Terry and Kevin were in New York– There's an IRA guy, McBree.'

'*I could lose my job.*'

His voice was so loud she felt the glass walls on the cubicle shudder and a silence fell in the newsroom outside.

A red flush rose up his cheeks and his eyes seemed to deepen in their sockets.

Paddy's mouth opened, her brain disengaged, and to her astonishment she said, 'I visited Ogilvy. I'm working him.'

'For me or for McVie?'

'For you, boss, of course for you.'

Bunty's red fog ebbed and subsided. His lips reappeared at his mouth. He blinked at the desk. Outside, the noise of the newsroom resumed.

'He's not out?'

'Ah.' The second she said Callum was no longer in custody a scrum of journalists would form outside Sean's house. She took an educated guess that they hadn't asked the prison service about Callum's whereabouts and covered her back. 'Not to my knowledge.'

'Bring me six hundred words on your visit to Ogilvy in the next two hours or I'll sack you and tell every single person in this business why. Out.'

'OK.' She stood up, wondering what the fuck she had said that for. She'd even called him boss. She hadn't called an editor boss in five years.

The Monkey must have been listening to the entire conversation because he opened the door from outside for her to leave. Paddy picked up her envelopes and walked out.

The Monkey pointed her over to a small space at a computer on the features island. 'You can use that desk there.'

People wandering around the room watched her, as she walked uncertainly over to the desk and sat down, setting her clippings envelopes in a tidy pile.

The Monkey was watching her too so she reached forward and switched on the computer. The monitor gave a green yawn and flickered to a DOS prompt.

She couldn't write up a fictitious visit to Callum. It was

checkable; other journalists would look at the prison visitors' book and see her name wasn't in it. If she wrote the truth about the release, Sean would never forgive her – she had accompanied him as a friend, not a reporter. I have a life, she reminded herself, beyond my job: I have a life. Callum was volatile, living in Sean's house with his children and his wife, and he didn't want to be written about. If he saw her name on an article he'd be sure to blame Sean.

The Monkey was watching so she directed the DOS prompt to take her into a word-processing package.

II

Callum stepped out of the close into the street, watching the feet opposite from the corner of his eye, and turned to the right, heading up the street in the opposite direction from the way he had gone this morning. He resisted the urge to look back at the man, to see where he was watching. He'd find out soon enough.

He walked on, head up, staying calm, not drawing the man's eye, until he had passed a garage forecourt and an old kirk and come to a bend in the road. Only then did he cross the street to the right side, the side the man was on.

Callum didn't know this area but he took an educated guess and skirted around the block, looking for ways into the back court and the flooded midden. It was a red-sandstone quadrangle of tenements, old style, not cleaned up like a lot of the buildings he had seen on the drive in. Black soot still coated the stone, thickest against the top floors. The glittering red stone showed on the ground floor, where the rain had run it off. It was tenements as he remembered them, Glasgow as he knew it as a child: black and forbidding.

He found an open close mouth and looked through.

There was the bin shed, there the puddle where the children had been playing this morning. The man would be around the corner, standing in a close that ran at a ninety-degree angle to this one, looking out into the street. And he'd be bored now, thinking about other things, his guard down.

Callum's mouth felt dry as he flattened himself against the inside wall and looked out into the back court. Bright sunlight sliced the yard in half, glinting off the puddle and the upended skeleton of a pram. Swarms of midges hung in the air. It was a school day, but the children would be coming home soon. Elaine had taken the babies off in the pram, setting off early, she said, to pick up messages before she went to get the kids from school. She wouldn't even know he'd slipped out of the house but he had only fifteen minutes until the back court was overrun with children.

He looked up. Windows were open all round the square, kitchen windows. He could see taps in front of one window, a clothes pulley on a ceiling. Somewhere a radio crackled an old show tune.

He stepped out onto the dirt floor, tiptoeing, keeping against the wall and in the shadows, and crept around to the close door.

There he was, Rat Shoes, standing fifteen feet away from him, leaning on the close mouth, tipping his head back to drain a can of Coke as he watched the street. Callum could see his own bedroom window, the curtain pulled up at the corner where he had kept watch over the street all night.

A man walked past on the other side of the road and Rat Shoes followed him with his eyes. Callum used his toes to slip his shoes off his feet, leaving them where they fell. His stockinged feet absorbed the bitter chill from the concrete beneath him. It was cold here, damp; the sun hadn't touched here.

He took a step forward, testing, seeing how alert the guy

was. Luckily the guy was looking out into a bright street and Callum was coming from the shadows. He took another step and then another but still Rat Shoes looked out into the road, shaking his can of Coke to see if it was finished, finding a small splash and tipping his head back again.

Callum was three foot behind him and the guy didn't know. He had a ponytail, glasses, he was taller than Callum and his clothes looked expensive, a nice red-checked jacket open to a red T-shirt, baggy jeans, rat shoes.

In prison, in the first prison he ever went to, the opportunities for fighting were kept to an absolute minimum. No one was allowed to be alone with anyone else for any length of time. All the cells were single cells, because the inmates were all so young the authorities didn't want them sharing, in case they'd fuck each other or kill each other or get gay or something, he didn't know. But fights broke out just the same, people fell out, met guys from rival gangs. It all went on just the same but everything, from the shouting of abuse to the physical fighting, had to happen in tiny slivers. Sudden wars were won while queuing for food. A wee guy died once in a three-minute library call. They had to develop techniques for it. They called it 'a sudden'. A sudden war, a sudden marking of a young man's face, a sudden rape, a sudden kill.

Callum brought his hands together, making a fist of them, and raised them over the guy's head. He opened his mouth to take a silent deep breath and brought his fists down.

A sudden punch carried all his weight on to Steven Curren's temple, swinging back so that the force made him fall into the dark of the close, swinging sideways so that his head ricocheted backwards on a diagonal, smashing off the close wall and leaving a trail of blood as he slid to the floor.

Callum put his hands under Steven's arms and dragged

him back so that his feet weren't trailing out into the street. He reached into his jacket and took his wallet, not because he wanted it, just to cover himself, and backed off down the dark passageway.

He skipped across the yard, grabbing his own shoes, keeping in the dark, and stopped when he got to the close he had come in through. He ripped the Velcro open on the wallet and took out the notes, twenty quid, leaving the rest in place and dumping it in the dark.

As he stepped out of the close into the sunshine he felt elated. Fingering the notes in his pocket, he made his way back to Sean's house, slipping back in the front door he had left open and taking his place on the corner of the bed. He lifted the edge of the curtain, smiling, panting as he looked out to the bright street.

Three children wearing their school uniform and eating sweeties came up to the dark close and found him. They stood staring down at him, prodded him with a foot while one of them ran across the road. A woman came and then the police. Steven Curren stirred and stood up, holding his head where he had hit it on the close wall. He felt for his wallet. Behind Callum, out in the hall, the door opened to the flat and the house was suddenly flooded with the cries and calls of children.

Callum stood up, looking for a sense of satisfaction inside himself. He didn't feel it. He fingered the notes again and felt stupid, sorry for the three kids who'd found the guy in the close, sorry that they'd seen the blood on the wall.

He went out to see his family.

21

In Conversation with a Fridge

I

A shadow fell over Paddy's desk and she looked up, expecting to see the Monkey.

The officers who had been at Kevin's flat yesterday were standing at her elbow.

'Miss Meehan, you'll come with us.'

'Oh, hello!' She jolted to her feet. 'Hello!'

They were very annoyed. The old one grabbed her arm, squeezing tighter than he needed to, his lip curling as he yanked her away from her desk. Instinctively she pulled her arm back. 'Calm down, I'm coming with you. I'm pleased to see you.'

'Like fuck,' muttered the young one, yanking her free arm up behind her back with needless force. But they weren't worried she'd run again, they were just annoyed that she ran the first time.

Two sports guys stepped forward, gentlemen to their bones. 'Oi, leave the lady alone.'

'This is nothing to do with you.' The younger one was very angry and she guessed that they'd been given an earful by their superiors for letting her slip their grasp.

The sports reporters were usually fairly mellow, but they were fond of a fight. Whether she liked it or not, Paddy was part of their gang and an insult to one was an insult to all. They took a police officer each and stood in front of them. '*Get your fucking hands off her.*'

Paddy raised her voice to a volume she usually reserved for warning Pete about fire and oncoming cars: 'STOP. RIGHT. NOW.'

The few people in the newsroom who weren't watching stopped still and stared. Bunty appeared at the door of his office. A copy boy looked in from the stairwell.

'These officers and I are going to leave now, without incident. Am I making myself ABUNDANTLY clear?'

The sports boys nodded dumbly. The police officers almost apologized. Even Bunty looked as if he'd been caught stealing apples. She'd yet to meet a man who was immune to her angry mum voice.

Paddy picked up the cuttings envelopes, putting them in her bag. She stood up and smiled at the sports guys. 'Thank you.'

Flanked by the police officers, she swept through the newsroom to the doors feeling very important, carrying every pair of eyes in the room with her. Inadvertently, the officers pushed a door each, holding them open for her like footmen. She turned back to the room and spoke to Bunty.

'I'm going to be a wee bit late with that copy. Sorry.'

As the door swung shut behind her, the newsroom erupted into an excitable round of applause. Everyone loved a renegade.

The policemen took the stairs in single file, one before her, one behind. She felt rather grand, knowing she'd be on the front page tomorrow and the copy would cast her in a favourable light.

The illusion of glamour lasted until they got outside, when the officers took an arm each and shoved her roughly towards the squad car at the kerb. Someone must have called down to the Press Bar because a photographer came flying out, loading a fresh roll of film into his camera and snapping away at them.

She looked up and found the population of the newsroom lined up at the window, waving to her, grinning down as if she was heading off on a royal tour.

The rest of the Press Bar emptied into the road. Journalists and editors, hangers-on and specialists all lined the street, still clutching their pints and cigarettes, toasting her and cheering.

She grinned back at them, then stopped abruptly.

The young man looked sheepish, standing behind the gathering crowd as if he had been caught out, keeping his head down, hoping not to be seen. His jacket was open but she could see the black collar and the silver zip of his tracksuit and the neck of his Celtic top underneath.

The officer started the car and pulled away, easing down the busy street to another smattering of applause. As they turned the corner she looked back and saw the man in the black tracksuit slip away in the opposite direction.

Paddy cleared her throat and sat forward. 'Did you get into trouble because I ran away?'

'Sit back and put your belt on.'

Every single car on the road gave way to them, let them cut in, slowed down when they noticed the squad car. She watched the driver, saw the expectation of deference and how angry he got when a driver didn't let them in, noticed how he muttered under his breath that they must be blind.

'You're not arresting me, are you?'

They didn't answer.

'How's Kevin? Is he OK? Where is he? I went looking for him yesterday and couldn't find a trace of him.'

She looked at the back of their heads, at their shoulders. Neither of them cringed or twitched, they weren't withholding anything: they didn't know how Kevin was.

'They haven't told you, have they?'

Seen in the rear-view mirror, the driver's eyes were heavy. 'Shut the fuck up,' he said.

So she did.

III

Squad cars lined the street in front of a modest red-brick office block, built in the thirties, all long lines and big windows. The cantilevered slab over the door had been updated, clad in raw steel and extended so that it covered the entire pavement. Picked out in confident blue letters, the building declared itself to be Strathclyde Police Headquarters. The overall effect wasn't friendly. It was a public space annexed by the big boys.

They found a parking place in the street, and straightened their uniforms as they got out and came round to her door. They glanced up at the building and Paddy thought they looked intimidated, two constables from the South Side bringing her to their unseen masters. They grabbed her as she got out, holding her elbows too tight, pinching the bones, nasty little bullies as they huckled her towards the glass doors on behalf of their bosses.

'You really don't need to hold me this tight,' she said, as they pushed the doors open and brought her into reception.

They weren't in a police station, Paddy could see that straight away. Reception looked like a corporation's. There were no holding cells here and the public had little reason to drop in, so leather seats lined the wood-panelled hall, a pretty receptionist looked up attentively, and the phones on her desk weren't nailed down the way they were in other cop shops.

'I'm not going to run again,' Paddy told the older officer.

He shot her a dirty look. 'Be quiet.'

The younger officer came over, settled on her other side and they waited. She'd have to speak to Sean and tell him they'd been seen picking Callum up. It wouldn't be as bad for him as it was for her, she thought. He was only a driver for the *News* and was Callum's cousin. Sacking someone for not reporting a member of their own family was too Maoist, even for panicky Bunty.

She looked up the slatted wooden stairs. Whoever had sent them to get her was up there, reading about Terry, or Kevin, or her. She'd come back from this with a story about Kevin Hatcher, squeeze something out of the person questioning her and feed it to Bunty to appease him. Whatever Merki was writing, he was still a hundred miles behind her.

'I think I'm being followed,' she said to the chinless officer next to her, 'by a wee guy in a tracksuit. I'd suspect the police, but he's wearing a Celtic shirt and I know you're all Prods.'

He wasn't listening though; he was looking past her to the stairs. He stood up, raising an eyebrow.

Paddy turned to see a frumpy woman in a cheap business suit coming down towards them, nodding once at the officer. She spoke as she took Paddy by the upper arm, urged her to her feet and marched her to the lift. 'Miss Meehan, I'm DI Sharon Garrett. Can you come with me, please.'

It wasn't a question.

Paddy looked at their watered reflection in the steel

elevator doors. She was flanked by Garrett and the young officer, the older guy standing behind them, allowing himself a smile. She looked very small in among them, her clothes crumpled. She could smell the smoke off herself.

The empty lift arrived and they got in, Garrett pressed the button for the fifth floor and the door slid shut.

'Do you want to question me about Kevin? Is this whole thing about Kevin or are you factoring in Terry as well? I've got a photo of the guy I was telling you about.'

No one spoke.

'How is Kevin? Did you see his bruises?'

Garrett shifted her weight to her other foot.

'I was thinking, why would he have a line out to sniff if he was swallowing cocaine? And stuff was missing from his house, boxes of negatives. Did they tell you that?'

The doors opened out on to a long, quiet corridor of partitioned offices. At the far end a man in blue overalls was buffing the green lino floor with a humming machine. The corridor was very quiet.

As Garrett led them to the end, Paddy could see that all of the offices were empty. Windows on to the corridor looked into dark rooms, straight through to the windows. They passed the cleaner, stepped over the flex of his humming buffer and went into a disused office. The shelves were empty, the desk clear. Someone had worked here once though: pale oblongs where posters and wall charts had hung marked the wall. It smelled of dust.

Garrett sat Paddy down and moved about behind her, pulling down the blinds on to the corridor, adding gloom to the office's many other crimes. Then she sat down behind the desk, facing Paddy, blinking every ten seconds, leaving the two officers to stand by the door.

In the corridor outside, the floor buffer bumped gently

off a skirting board, the hum missing a beat before continuing its journey.

Paddy had been interviewed by the police before, but this didn't feel like a police interview. It felt like an ambush.

'Sorry' – the wooden chair creaked beneath her as she leaned forward – 'who are you again?'

'DI Garrett.'

'You're a policewoman?'

'Police *officer*.'

'Aren't you a woman? Sorry. The skirt made me think, you know . . .' Garrett continued blinking to schedule. 'You prefer "officer"?'

'It's customary.'

'What do you prefer though?'

'Whatever is customary.' Garrett didn't display a flicker of emotion. It was like talking to a fridge. No one at personnel would be tempted to strong-arm Garrett into Family Liaison.

'Hm.' Paddy sat back. 'This empty office, away from everyone, waiting. We are waiting, aren't we? For someone. Someone more senior than you.'

Garrett wasn't unattractive but she had gone to a lot of trouble not to make the best of herself: shoulder pads emphasized her square body, the skirt didn't fit her and her haircut was boxy, the blonde streaks fooling no one. She didn't have a smear of make-up on.

'Miss Meehan, why were you at Kevin Hatcher's flat yesterday morning?'

Paddy told her the truth, aware that the stuffy office was isolated from the rest of the station; no one passed in the corridor outside, the lift didn't ting as it reached their floor.

Garrett asked pointless questions, things she already knew the answer to, about Paddy's claims regarding an Irishman who had come to her house, descriptions of the man who had been at her son's school yesterday. She didn't seem to be coaxing information out of Paddy but rather keeping her busy.

She made Paddy go over the details of finding Kevin, of going to his house on Sunday night, but cut her off whenever Paddy mentioned the Lebanon or the IRA. She didn't even want her talking about the missing photograph from the portfolio so Paddy pushed it, starting to answer a question innocuously and then veering off to speak about the Irishman, naming him as McBree, mapping Garrett's reaction when she said it. McBree. The name made her blink out of sequence.

'So you went there yesterday morning expecting Kevin Hatcher to—'

'Would a police officer ever wear a Celtic top?'

'Just answer the question—'

'McBree. He's an important man in the IRA, very, very high up. International profile. Why does that not interest you?'

No one spoke.

'My family are Irish and my mum thinks the police'll arrest you for being in possession of a potato. Why am I getting no interest in this guy? If I told you one of the Guildford Four had done it, would you pull them in? A big man in the IRA is in the city and that's of no interest to you? What, because you already know?'

Before Garrett had the chance not to answer, the door behind the officers opened and Garrett sat up, her face warming. 'Afternoon, sir.'

Knox was standing in the doorway, face pinched, shoulders square, ready to make his mark. He turned to the officers behind him. 'Wait in the corridor.'

Suddenly sweating, Paddy stood up. 'I'm leaving.'

He smiled calmly. 'You can't.'

'I'm not under arrest.'

'I want to talk to you.'

Knox shut the door slowly, listening for the secure click of the mechanism, and turned back to the room. As he sauntered over to Garrett's seat she backed out of his space, standing subserviently at the side. He sat down, looked out of the window and back at her, overplaying his insouciance.

Paddy took out a cigarette, lit it and blew the smoke at him.

'No one will believe you,' he said coldly.

'That you brought me to a deserted part of the building to menace me?'

His eyes flickered in Garrett's direction. 'About Hewitt,' he said casually.

Paddy uncrossed her legs. 'Terry's murder.'

'The officers told me what you said this morning. You're wrong. The IRA have denied responsibility. The gun has been found and traced to a drugs murder in Easterhouse last year. We have evidence that it was nothing to do with the IRA.'

She took another draw on her cigarette, listening to the hum of the buffer slowing to a dying whine. She could hear the plug being snapped out of the wall. The lift tinged and she heard the doors slide shut after the cleaner. They were alone on the floor.

'Why am I here?'

What little colour there was in Knox's face drained away. He craned towards her, the skin so tight she could see the hammering of the pulse in his neck. 'You're here because you ran away yesterday morning. You should have come straight here as the officers requested. It makes police officers suspicious when someone they want to question runs away.'

'If it was such a big deal why didn't they come to my

house last night? Everyone knows where I live. The police found me easily enough on Saturday night. And by the way, where is Kevin? I spoke to all four casualty departments yesterday and couldn't find him registered as a patient.'

'Kevin Hatcher is dead.'

He watched her face, taking a clinical interest in her reaction as the news sank in.

'When? When did he die?'

Knox cleared his throat, tipping his head back to Garrett. She stepped forward and spoke, her voice softer than before. 'Kevin was dead on arrival at the hospital. They register a death differently, that may be why you missed him.'

'No, they don't. I was on the calls-car shift for six months. I went around the hospitals every night, twice sometimes. They register a death on arrival in the same book as casualty admissions.'

Knox's face didn't move, but as he looked at her his eyes softened in amusement. This is how big we are, he was saying; we can make a man disappear. I could make you disappear.

He was expecting her to shout at him, to meet his play and issue impotent threats, but Knox was as hardened as Donaldson and her threats would be just as flaccid. Instead, she made the one move he wouldn't have an answer to: she covered her face and pretended to cry, muttering about poor Kevin under her breath. She was only acting, and when her face was good and wet she looked up at Garrett, who blinked twice, for her the equivalent of an emotional flurry.

Knox had a stale smile stapled to his face. He rubbed the table top with his fingertips, trying to worry off a small stain.

Paddy took a shaky draw on her cigarette. 'McBree. He killed them both.'

Knox shook his head. 'No.'

'How can you possibly know he didn't?'

'Nothing links the two deaths. One's a shooting, one's a stroke, one's indoors, one's outdoors, neither man was involved in politics.'

'Why would Kevin leave out a line of cocaine to inhale when he'd swallowed enough to make him have a stroke and vomit? It's like finding a glass of whisky next to someone who died from drinking vodka, for fucksake.'

Knox stood up calmly and made for the door. The interview was over, though she couldn't see what he'd got out of it. She stood up too. 'You're refusing point blank to look at McBree?'

He stood, rolled his head back and turned to face her.

'They spent the night before Hewitt's death at the casino. A lot of strange people visit casinos. We're interviewing several of the people who were there that night.'

'But not McBree?'

'You will get the wrong end of the stick and keep chewing, won't you?'

She meant to give a cavalier laugh but it sounded like a hysterical sob. 'You're concerned that I may be slandering the IRA?'

'We're concerned that you may be spreading fear and alarm, Meehan.'

Paddy stubbed her cigarette out on the table, picked up her bag and brushed past Knox at the door. Outside, the two officers turned as she opened it, looking back into the room for guidance. Someone gave them a nod to let her go and she pushed through them.

She didn't want to wait for the lift and found the door to the stairs, jogging down three flights without drawing a breath. She stopped when she felt sure they weren't coming after her, leaned her back against the wall and let herself cry properly.

Her feelings for Terry were complicated. He'd frightened her and chased her and she knew deep down that her life would be easier now that he wasn't around. But Kevin Hatcher – Kevin was just a nice man.

22

Notes from a Texan

I

Blythswood Square was a short, steep street away from the police headquarters and Paddy found herself heading up that way, trying to think of a justification for going into Fitzpatrick's office and orchestrating a fight with him. She steamed up the hill, her face still puffed and red from crying. At the top she caught her breath, realized she was looking for someone timid to have a fight with. She couldn't go back to the *News* offices or Bunty would banjax her into writing about Callum. She found a seat on the square, looking back down the hill to a line of squad cars.

She could write a news piece about Kevin dying and phone it in. Writing things up always made her feel detached and calm. But the editors wouldn't take it without certain bald facts: she didn't know which hospital to name-check or even what he died of.

Kevin was dead, Terry was dead and the Strathclyde Police Force weren't showing a flicker of interest in the fact that McBree had to be involved.

She took out a cigarette and lit it, her throat closing over in disgust as she tried to breathe in. She persevered. The nicotine made her feel detached, calmer, fed. She sat back on the wooden bench, the heat from the slats soaking into her back, thinking about Father Andrew making a big point of shaking her hand after mass every Sunday and Mary Ann crying at the kitchen table.

Sickened, she threw the cigarette to the kerb.

II

The mousy receptionist rolled her finger around her necklace, half strangling herself with her pearls, as Paddy leaned on her desk, messing up the tidily sorted pencils laid out in a neat row by the phone.

'He's just very, very busy, you see.' She glanced at the door to Fitzpatrick's office.

'Listen to me,' said Paddy. 'I want you to go in there and tell him if he doesn't see me now I'm going to report him to the Law Society.'

III

She was too old for sitting on stairs in buildings, but today she didn't care about dignity or who she was supposed to be. The doors to the offices down and upstairs were open into the stairwell for ventilation on a hot day. The muffled clack of electric typewriters and distant chat wafted up to her and the soft brown folder sat on her knees. Her name was written in his handwriting, carefully scrawled in capitals, big and clear enough to be read by any stranger.

She stroked it. A small grease spot had blossomed on the front, on a low corner. Fitzpatrick had said Terry gave it to him a year ago, to keep in the safe, when he had just come back to Glasgow, before he went to New York, before any of this had happened, probably before he had even become good friends with Kevin again.

She opened it.

239

The covering letter from Terry was written in his shorthand. She sighed. Everyone started out using the same textbook shorthand but over a lifetime it became a private language, virtually indecipherable to anyone else. Paddy could hardly read her own any more. She peered at the sheet carefully. It was perfectly legible: Terry must have gone back to the book to write it.

P,
Notes here for you. Materials and stuff a friend gave me re your favourite person. Came to me through complex route, cost a lot of Marlboro and vodka.
   Now you can do him justice.

She thought it was signed 'Texan' but a second look told her he had slipped out of shorthand and marked the end T with a cross for a kiss.

Behind it, in a tidy pile of old papers, was a bill for two tickets on a commercial flight from Berlin Tempelhof in 1965. On a grey typewritten sheet behind that, a bill of lading acknowledging the receipt of prisoner 2108 by the British Embassy in West Berlin in the same year. In among yellowed press reports about the Patrick Meehan murder trial he had put a photocopy of the minutes of a meeting between the detective chief inspector in charge of Meehan's investigation and a source called Hamish, whose name always appeared in inverted commas. It was vague, referring to actions commenced re PM and continued, threats to national security, details of Muscovite facilities where PM was held and reports written by PM. She understood every abbreviation, recognized each date and location. She knew what it all meant.

It must have taken Terry years to gather the evidence for her and God only knew which shadowy figures he'd bribed them from. For nearly three decades Patrick Meehan had been insisting that he was the victim of a conspiracy by the security services, that at their behest the Strathclyde Police had fabricated evidence against him for the murder, but not a shred of supporting evidence ever came her way. Now she had it.

She had told Terry what the story meant to her, how she had followed Meehan's progress through the courts since she was eight years old, from before she really knew what a court was, how she became a journalist because of him, because a journalist led the campaign to have him released and won. She had always thought him some small parallel of her own wicked self.

It was the most thoughtful thing anyone had ever done for her.

Paddy shut the folder, placed the flat of her hand on it, felt the grease from her palm being absorbed by the thick porous paper.

Tearfully, she lifted it to her face and kissed it.

IV

As she stood on the top step, blinking hard at the bright day, a small figure materialized on the pavement in front of her. Merki.

'Oh,' he grinned cheekily, 'I was just thinking about you.'

'What you doing here?'

He was wearing a brown shirt and matching tie, his top button undone to meet the heat of the day, the fat knot of tie squinted to one side. He looped his finger under it and yanked it to the other side. 'Just, you know, going about. Polis let you out then?'

They nodded at each other.

'The gun story: who's your source, Merki?'

'A good journalist protects his sources at all costs.'

She folded her arms. 'Strathclyde Police just pulled me in to warn me off saying it was the IRA.'

Merki thought about it for a moment. 'Doesn't mean it is the IRA, does it? They could be worried. A story like that could spread fear and alarm.' It was Knox's phrase, word for word.

'You're an idiot. They're playing you for an idiot. If you weren't an idiot you'd have kept your name off it.'

He snapped, 'What the hell would you know, Meehan? You're a columnist. "I like TV", that's the sort of shite you write. You wouldn't know news if it punched you right on the nose, anyway.'

'It was Knox, wasn't it?' But the name didn't register. 'Garrett?'

He flinched, stepped back and shook his head.

'What were you typing this morning, Merki?'

'Oh, that?' He smirked down the empty street. 'A fan letter. To you. I think you're brilliant.'

'And I think you're handsome.'

His mouth dropped open with hurt and surprise. He was a wee cross-eyed guy, his head was a funny shape, his body thick and his legs stringy. It wasn't a choice he'd made. She'd gone too far. She always went too far. She muttered, 'Sorry,' and shook her head. 'Been a heavy morning.'

He looked at her sideways. 'You're fat,' he said petulantly.

'I am. I'm fat, Merki, sorry.'

Still sullen, he nodded, as if her admission had redressed the balance. 'It's just your luck, innit?'

She could have pointed out that she was fat because she ate too much while he was born ugly, but didn't think it would help any. 'Going in to see the boy wonder up there?'

'Been. Went round the corner to get a sarnie for lunch

but my car's here.' He patted the notebook in his pocket. 'Got great stuff.'

They were competing for the story. Whatever he told her about an interview with Fitzpatrick, the opposite would be true and they both knew it. If he'd had longer to prepare he would have come back to the office and said he'd got nothing, just to work a double bluff.

'Well done,' she said and they smiled at each other.

He turned to the kerb and a small blue Nissan with a key scratch along the bonnet and a dent in the driver's door, fitting the key in and opening it. 'You seen the house he left ye yet?'

'Nut.'

'Want to come with me?'

She couldn't go back to the office, Pete was in school and if she spent time with Merki she might be able to work out what he had been writing this morning. 'Can I smoke in your car?'

'Aye.'

She shrugged. 'All right, then.'

23

Cottage

The drive didn't take long but it was harrowing. Bunches of dead flowers were propped up at several turnings, marking the sites of fatal crashes. Merki took it slow, pootling along at forty, hitting fifty on straight stretches. A queue of cars lined up behind him, drivers who were familiar with the route forming an angry tailgated convoy, trying to embarrass him into hurrying along. He remained calm, checking them in the mirror, pulling over as much as he could to let them overtake, meeting their displays of aggression with a gentle hand raised and admonishments to 'calm yourself down, pal'.

They turned a particularly sharp corner on the road and suddenly the soft hills of Ayrshire lay before them, carpeted in vibrant green grass, distant hills dotted with fat cows. The road broadened to two lanes and they were free to hang in the slow lane while a long line of irritable locals sped past, variously flicking their fingers at them or indicating that one of them had a cylindrical item attached to his head. Merki smiled calmly and waved back.

Merki wasn't giving anything away about the Terry article. She asked him how he knew about Eriskay House and he said that the secretary had told him about that and the folder and Wendy Hewitt, but she knew he wouldn't be telling her the truth, he was too professional. Fitzpatrick had probably told him. It might be a big fancy house, he said, hopeful for her. It sounded like it, didn't it? Eriskay House sounded grand.

She let herself imagine for a moment that it was a gorgeous colonnaded country pile, but the only houses she could envisage like that were in *Gone with the Wind* and a white plantation villa seemed unlikely, even in rich rural Ayrshire. She reminded herself not to get too attached to the house, whatever it was like. She had no real right to a family home when there was a member of the family still living. Terry shouldn't have left it to her. The folder was enough. Her hand crept into the bag and stroked a corner of it. Terry knew her better than almost anyone else. He had got to know her before she learned to lie, before she had defences.

The double lanes merged again into single file and the road began to snake dangerously between two hills.

Suddenly Merki said, 'There!' and swung the car to the left, leaving the fast road for a dirt track, overgrown with waist-high grass and wild bushes. Twenty feet on they came to a clearing and he stopped, switching the engine off. The grass was so deep he was afraid to go on, he said; they didn't want to get stuck.

Scarlett O'Hara wouldn't have asked a slave to live here. The house was a small highland cottage, single storey with deep small windows and a low front door with a heavy lintel. Brush and grass had grown so high along the walls that they looked as if they were shoring the building up. The roof was punched in on one side and a drainpipe hung down over the front. What really drew the eye, though, was the enormous crack running from the corner of the front door to the roof, edges mismatched, as if the entire building might snap in half like an Easter egg.

They got out. Paddy stood by the car, slightly stunned at the state of the place, while Merki stepped gingerly through the long grass and peered in the windows.

'There's a piano in there,' he said, looking back at her. 'Come and see.'

She wished she hadn't come. It was so depressing. A family house rotted from a decade of neglect. It would have been lovely once, though, and it wasn't that far from the city. Terry always had a car, he could have lived here as easily as anywhere else. It made no sense that he chose to live in grimy bedsitters when he had this house fifteen minutes away.

'Come and see.'

Merki watched her reaction as she peered in the window, observing her so closely she wondered if he was going to write about it. 'Fuck off,' she said and he turned away, urinal polite.

The window sill was half a foot deep. She wiped the frosting of dust from the glass and looked inside. Storm shutters were propped open and beyond it the room was small and low. A piano was listing slightly against the back wall, the floor sinking into the dirt below. Old cottages didn't have foundations – they were built straight into the soil, the weight of the walls keeping them upright – but it meant that damp took over if they weren't kept warm and this house hadn't been warm for a long time. The fitted carpet on the floor looked warped and a tidal mark cantered across the back wall at head height. The wallpaper was faded and sliding down the wall at the corner. Pink with a pattern of disembodied baskets of flowers.

Merki was at her shoulder. 'What do ye think?'

She stepped back and looked at him. 'Are you going to write about this?'

'Mibbi.' He'd have denied it if he was.

She looked at him, wondering. 'Merki, why are we here?'

He shrugged, looked away, shrugged again. 'Dunno. Background?'

He was up to something. Definitely. He was doing innocent but he'd kept checking his watch all the way up here and now a smug smile was tugging at the corner of his mouth. He didn't know about Kevin or he would have mentioned it. She remembered the McBree and Donaldson clippings in her bag, the dates on the front of them showing they had last been looked at months ago. Merki didn't know anything about McBree either. But then she hardly knew anything about him herself.

'Let's look round the side,' she said.

They waded through the damp grass in single file. At the back the land opened up into a long garden, now choked with a decade of neglect. Large trees hid the road but they could hear it, the cars and lorries speeding past. At the far end was the orchard where his parents had stood under a tree for a photograph. Green baby apples the size of cherries were just appearing on the trees but the trunks and some branches had been colonized by thick waxy ivy. She couldn't see the exact tree they had stood under but she was sure it was here. It must have been a lonely place for an only child to grow up.

The kitchen was bare and basic, the table covered in dust and mice droppings. A cardboard box sat on a dresser, rotting in the damp, ripped by mice making a home. There didn't seem to be a cooker. It was in the country and it wasn't council but it was modest. She had always assumed Terry came from money, but she suspected everyone of that because she didn't herself.

She stood back and saw that Merki was looking at another crack in the wall, this one beginning above the kitchen window.

'Let's go home.'

But Merki was reluctant. He stepped over to the back door and wiped the dirt from the keyhole. 'I can jimmy this. Want to go inside?'

'Nah.'

'No bother,' he said and got a ring of L-shaped metal sticks from his pocket.

'Merki, I can't be bothered, there's nothing to see in there but mice.'

He stopped, checked his watch, did some mental calculations and nodded. 'Aye, all right.'

Head down, he led the way back to the car.

She lit a cigarette when they were inside and offered him one but he declined. 'What are you checking your watch for all the time?'

He shrugged, flinging an arm over the back of the seat to reverse out to the mouth of the driveway, keeping to the tracks in the flattened grass they had made on the way in.

'Are you waiting for something to happen? Was someone supposed to meet us here?'

He stopped the car, looking out at the traffic speeding past on the road.

Just three feet away cars were going past so fast she couldn't make out the driver's faces. Behind them, coming from Glasgow, a lorry took the blind turn in the road and hurtled towards them, correcting his trajectory at the last minute and narrowly avoiding clipping Merki's boot.

'I want to go back that way but they won't . . .' He pulled the car forward to the edge of the tarmac. 'Just . . . go, I suppose.'

It was terrifying: Merki shot forward just as a Range Rover belted round the corner at sixty. His Nissan had no power and he couldn't speed up to get clear. The Range Rover was on top of them, brakes screeching, lights flashing in the rear-view.

It was at that moment that Paddy realized in a wash of horror why Terry Hewitt didn't live here: when he was seventeen years old his parents had died in a car crash and they had died on this road, somewhere, on a corner with dead flowers. He had told her about it when she was young, when she told him about Patrick Meehan and all her secret shame about the case. He heard her but she didn't take in what he was saying: her family didn't own a car and the crash seemed glamorous to her then, Jayne Mansfield-esque. She'd envied his freedom.

Merki raised his hand to the Range Rover and carried on, building his speed up to thirty-five. She'd dropped her cigarette on the floor but was too afraid to let go of the door handle and reach down to get it. They hit a straight stretch of road and the lumbering four-by-four pulled into a break in the oncoming traffic, honking furiously as it overtook them. Merki waved back. 'Thank you,' he said. 'Shit, we're going the wrong way though.'

'Don't you dare turn around in this road.'

'I'll just go on to the next roundabout then,' he said happily.

She picked up the cigarette from the dusty floor and took a long welcome draw. The traffic was building up behind them again, oncoming cars passing them in a blur, only to slow abruptly at a roundabout up ahead. A petrol station on the far side of the roundabout was full of haulage trucks.

'This is a nightmare road,' she said.

Merki glanced at his watch.

'What's with the watch, Merki?' He smiled so she gave his arm a light slap. 'And what do you keep smiling about?'

'My cousin's due a baby,' he shouted, annoyed for no real reason. He rubbed his arm where she'd touched him. 'Heard you got a bollocking from Bunty this morning anyway.'

'Oh, aye, he set the police on me. Did ye hear that too?'

He smiled. 'Did he get you arrested, did he? For visiting Callum Ogilvy, was it? He had me arrested the other day, drunk in charge of a stapler.'

They were journalists, they could lie to each other for hours at a time, but she really wanted to know. 'Come on, why are we here? Why the watch?'

He checked it again and smiled out of the windscreen, slowing for the roundabout up ahead. 'OK.' He sighed through his nostrils. 'Ogilvy's out.'

'Out of prison?'

'Aye. Released. Everyone and his auntie's going to get sent to Driver Sean's house to sit it out and I figured, you know, don't be there. They'll send someone else. If there's a story you're never going to get it sitting between the *Standard* and the *Record*, are ye? You were visiting him the other day, weren't ye? That's why Bunty was shouting at ye, eh? Eh?' He smiled, glancing at her, taking his eyes off the road.

'Pull into that petrol station. I need to make a call.'

'If you're phoning the office don't tell them I'm with ye, eh?'

'I'm not phoning the office,' she said, winding her window down and throwing the cigarette out, watching in the side mirror as it bounced behind them on the road and disappeared into the dark under the chassis of a coach.

Despite being next door to the toilets the phone box

still smelled of fresh urine. She punch-dialled the Ogilvys' number quickly, as if she could beat bacterial infection with speed.

They weren't answering the phone and she wasn't surprised. When the answer machine clicked on she spoke loudly, knowing kids would be screaming in the background. They were noisy at the best of times.

'Sean, it's Paddy, pick up the phone, I need to talk—'

The phone clicked and Elaine sighed into the receiver, turning away to tell one of the kids to be quiet.

'Elaine, the papers know Callum's out.'

Elaine sighed again, heavier this time, in a way that suggested she already knew that, thank you very much, and handed the receiver over to Sean.

'I guess you know then?'

'There's a bank of them outside the door. They've been taking pictures of the kids and the windows and the street and everything.'

'Can he stay indoors for a while? I'll bring ye in groceries if ye need them.'

'He's not here, Paddy, he's gone.'

'Gone where?'

'No idea. The STV van was the first to pull up, he saw it and slipped out the door, went round the back and we've never seen him since. That was half an hour ago. Could you drive around and have a look for him? He can't be far.'

It was the last thing she wanted to do. 'My car's in the lot at work, Bunty's looking for me, I've just been picked up by the police and – fuck – Hatcher's dead ...' But Sean Ogilvy had been a father to Pete when he was a baby. He and Elaine had babysat to let Paddy go to work sometimes, minded him when he was teething and let her sleep. The only valid excuse now would be if she herself was dead. Sean said nothing but she heard it all.

'OK. OK, OK.'

When she opened the car door Merki had turned on the radio and was happily singing along to 'Daydream Believer'.

'Get me the fuck back to Glasgow, Merki.'

24

A Tethered Balloon

I

Bright corridors smelling of disinfectant were lined with paintings and collages by various years, proof of work done and time filled. High-pitched singing came from the far end of the corridor but the children behind the door, in Pete's class, were very quiet. Paddy and the deputy head looked in through the window on the door. Four rows of tiny desks were pointing forward to Miss MacDonald, who was reading them a story. Pete sat in the very front row and Paddy watched him for a moment. He kept turning to his neighbour, a small girl with a patch over one lens of her pink glasses, then glancing at the teacher, remembering he wasn't to talk.

'Maybe we should get him out of there before he gets into trouble,' smiled Miss McGlaughlin, the deputy head, a stately woman with grey hair held in a butterfly clip.

She knocked once and opened the door. When the children saw it was her they stood up.

'Thank you, children,' said Miss McGlaughlin. 'Good morning.'

They chorused, 'Good Morning, Miss McGlaughlin,' at her and she spoke quietly to Miss MacDonald, telling her Paddy's lie, that Pete's granny was gravely ill and he was to leave with his mum right now. Miss MacDonald looked sceptical and whispered back, 'Is that your mum or Mr Burns's mum?'

Paddy could have slapped her. 'My mum.'

'I see.' Miss MacDonald turned to Miss McGlaughlin, who looked a little startled that she was quizzing a mother about a potential death in the family. 'It's just that the other day Miss Meehan was telling me Pete's dad might come to the school and try to take him out.' She looked back at Paddy, stopping short of calling her a liar. 'Because if he does come now, what should I tell him?'

Miss McGlaughlin watched her for an answer.

Paddy motioned to Pete to come to her. He stood up and walked over, self-conscious, looking around the adults as if he'd done something wrong. 'Pete's daddy will bring him to school tomorrow, if it's appropriate. Where's your coat, son?'

'Am I going to see my dad?'

'Where's your coat kept?'

He could tell that she was defying the teachers and his eye took on a gleeful glint. 'Cloakroom.'

''Mon.' She took his hand, remembered her manners and turned back to the teacher. 'Thank you, Miss MacDonald.'

She was in the corridor before the teachers could stop her, Pete giggly by her side.

He shouted down the corridor to the open classroom door. 'Bye ya!'

II

It was typical of his flamboyant style: the giant black Merc dwarfed the small, new-build house he lived in with Sandra, the second, but almost certainly not the last, Mrs George H. Burns.

The new estate was set on what had been a school sports ground. Making clever use of the small space, wavy roads led off around corners into shallow cul-de-sacs, calming traffic at the same time as giving the impression of not being absolutely tiny. None of the yellow-brick houses were exactly alike, but the differences were minimal and cosmetic, a garage to the left instead of the right, a small window on the stairwell, a window on a roof, just enough to give the impression of individuality without the architect having to go to the trouble of thinking of anything original. The cookie-cutter blandness made Paddy crave a ghetto.

Pete was delighted to have been whipped out of school. He liked going well enough, but it was his nature to enjoy unexpected turns of events: surprise days out, holidays changed at the last minute, onerous trips cancelled leaving empty hours to be filled with something else. He clutched his backpack and looked out of the taxi window as if he'd never been here before.

'I'm staying here? For how long?'

'I don't know, son, but that's only if it's OK with your daddy and even then it'll only be a couple of days.'

'My *Ghost Train* video's here. Dad lets me watch it all the time. Will I still be going to Granny Trisha's on Saturday though? Will I still get to play with BC on Saturday?'

The taxi pulled up outside the house. 'That's a long way off.'

'But, on Saturday, will I see BC?' He was excited, a little smile playing on his lips and his eyes wide and shining. 'Will I, but?'

'Aye, ye will.'

His mouth sprang open in a grin and she threw her arms around him, kissing him all over his face until he got bored and pushed her away.

They paid the driver and got out of the taxi, walking the

length of the short lawn, following the yellow slabs making up the path to the front door. Coming from an old West End flat to here made everything seem slightly too small: the doors narrow, the ceilings low, even the windows like miniature impressions of the real thing.

They rang the doorbell, and looked at the white plastic door. Pete traced his finger on the wood effect, finding the groove repeated note for note on the next panel.

'Is it from the same tree?'

'I think it's plastic with a wood pattern on it.'

He squinted at it. 'Plastic should look like plastic.'

'I think so too.'

Following a scuffle of feet in the hallway, Burns opened the door to them, dropped his shoulders and then remembered himself. He gave Pete a big showbiz smile.

'Hiya, wee man,' he said as Pete clutched his leg, then lifted him up to give him a hug. 'Why aren't you in school?'

Pete hung on to his dad's neck, squeezing tight before letting go and sliding to the ground. 'Mum came and brung me out.'

'Brought you out,' corrected Paddy.

He ran off down the hall to what looked like the kitchen.

'Well.' Burns looked her up and down. 'Now why would she do that?'

She looked like shit, she knew she did. Her black skirt was crumpled, her black silk shirt was missing a button at the bottom and she had big stupid orange trainers on. Burns had lost weight in the past few years; he was TV-thin now, so thin his head looked disproportionately big. Dub said he looked like a tethered balloon. Today Sandra had chosen a white T-shirt and white jeans for him, ironed so well they might have come straight from the packet. He had a tan too; they owned a sunbed. Paddy could imagine the house in the dwindling light of an evening, dark but for a tiny bedroom window glowing fluorescent blue.

In the kitchen Pete slid a video into a machine and she heard the opening strains of the *Ghost Train* theme.

Unexpectedly, Paddy covered her mouth with her hand, pressing the fingers hard into her cheeks, digging into the skin with her fingernails as tears welled up in her eyes. She turned away to the street to hide her face.

Burns watched her for a moment, hand idling on his hip. He leaned forward, took her wrist firmly and pulled her into the house, out of sight of the neighbours.

The front room had two white leather settees and a glass coffee table in it. In the small picture window Sandra had arranged yellow tulips in an ugly crystal vase. Burns put Paddy on one settee and sat himself down in the neighbour, calmly watching her cry, reaching forward once to pet her knee.

She took the cigarettes out of her handbag and looked for permission. He nodded and she lit up, trembling, her lungs resistant to the deep breath.

'What's happening?' asked Burns.

'Terry Hewitt was killed, you probably heard.'

'I did, aye.'

'I was named as next of kin. They made me ID the body on Saturday night.'

Burns thought back to Sunday. 'You never said.'

She nodded out to Pete in the kitchen. 'Well, anyway, I may be a bit freaked by that, and I know I'm overprotective, but Callum Ogilvy's out of prison and he's gone missing. I just don't want Pete in the house or alone in school. It doesn't feel safe.'

'What happened to Terry?'

'He was shot in the head.' She lifted her cigarette to her

mouth but couldn't face it and dropped her hand. 'D'you remember Kevin Hatcher?'

'No.'

'A photographer. He was working with Terry on a book.' She shook her head, bewildered now she thought about it. 'A bullshit book, a coffee-table thing. Nice pictures, nothing. Anyway, I was looking through his letter box—'

'How like you.'

She shut her burning eyes. 'Please, George.'

'I'm teasing. Just trying to get a rise out of you.' He touched her knee again, telling her to go on.

'Kevin was lying on the ground. He'd had a stroke, swallowed a lot of cocaine, which he wouldn't. Now he's dead, there's no trace of him arriving at any casualty department in the city, the police are warning me off and a bit of the book was missing.'

He stopped her. 'You're not making any sense.'

She tried to sort it out in her mind but gave up. 'I used to be fearless about these things. 'Member Kate Burnett? 'Member Callum Ogilvy? Back then I was scared but not like this, not shaken and shitting it and crying all the fucking time.' She took a puff of the cigarette and looked at the floor. A white carpet. What sort of idiot would choose a white carpet in a house with a child? She looked around for an ashtray but there was nothing in the room but the empty coffee table. 'Since Pete was born, it really matters if I die, you know?'

'Is that why you're smoking again?'

She managed a shaky smile.

He looked at her stubby cigarette. 'Can you think of anything less regal than Regal?'

They took three puffs to smoke, were favoured by women who went to bingo and rebelling teenagers because they were cheap. Feeling in her handbag, she found an old paper hankie. Burns watched her make a bowl shape out of the crumpled tissue, spit into it and touch it with the tip of her cigarette, letting it hiss itself to death.

'Seeing you spit into a dirty paper hankie makes me want you in the worst way.'

'Fuck you, Burns.'

He smiled. 'There's my brave girl. I'd get you an ashtray but then I'd be implicated. I'll get battered when Sandy smells it.'

'I doubt you get battered for anything much, George.'

He shook his head slowly. 'You don't know what goes on, Pad. See this room, this white, empty room? You could do operations in here.' He did a stage sigh she'd heard many times before. 'She has got ... *problems*.'

She nodded, trying not to smile. George Burns had been confiding that his relationship was in trouble since she first met him, seven women ago. It was a sore lesson, she'd fallen for it often, but over the years she had finally realized that what George wanted wasn't a big helpful chat to sort out his feelings; it often wasn't even mindless sex with her, really. What George Burns craved was to win over disapproving women. Temporary was an essential precondition of what he wanted. No single woman in the universe was enough for him. Although they laughed about him and he was a philandering arsehole, his craven need to be well thought of was still kind of adorable. She just hoped it wasn't genetic.

She crumpled the tissue into a ball and put it in her handbag, already smelling the rank stink and thinking of McBree's awful breath.

'Can I leave Pete with you, George? Until they pick Callum up, I don't want Pete staying where he could find him.'

'Well, I don't know what Sandy'll say but ... I suppose I could take him to work with me.'

'Could you?'

'I'll get one of the production girls to look after him.'

Sandra didn't work and Paddy knew she had a cleaning lady who came in three days a week. She allowed herself the luxury of a snide aside, since she'd had a shock. 'What does Sandra do all day?'

He looked out of the picture window. 'Shops for clothes. Takes them back. Shops for more clothes.'

She already had a guilty aftertaste in her mouth. 'Good,' she said, bringing the conversation to a close.

He slid towards her on the sofa and softened his voice, inclining his head towards hers. 'D'you ever think about us?'

It should have made her feel special, but she knew him too well to mistake it for lingering affection. He would do some variation on the move to whichever woman he was left alone with. She looked up wearily.

'George, give me a fucking break. I don't want to have a fight.'

He slid back to his seat, offended. 'Are you and Dub together?'

'Don't be ridiculous.'

Burns was as suspicious as a faithless man could be. He could never accept that most people made friends and kept them, met lovers and stayed with them. His world was in a perpetual state of tectonic shift and he wouldn't believe that it wasn't so for everyone else.

'So much for the Three Musketeers,' he said caustically.

She didn't have the energy to be angry. 'No one ever called us the Three Musketeers but you, and you're the one who let both of us down. You left me to move in with that bint Lorraine, and you got another manager when Dub told you to turn down the TV show. He was right, wasn't he?'

He chewed his tongue for a moment and shrugged. 'Suppose. Who's he handling now?'

'Loads of people,' she lied. Word got out that he advised you against it and the phone's never stopped ringing.'

'This new guy – he wants me to cash in on the TV show, tour the working men's clubs.'

'Don't do that.'

'I'm not going to.' He looked sheepish. 'But the money's good.'

The clubs were a graveyard. He'd never get back on the circuit again and that was where the radio and television executives went looking for talent to pin shows on.

'Don't do it,' Paddy told him. 'It's a dead end.'

'Would Dub talk to me, do you think?'

'You want him to manage you again?'

'Possibly.'

'I don't know. He's pretty hurt by what you did. If you'd left him and found a new manager that would have been one thing, but you did it behind his back.'

George dipped his chin and looked up at her, puppy-dog penitent, asking her to fix it. Paddy knew that Dub was signing on and the dole paid next to nothing. He represented a number of comics but none of them had half of George's talent. On stage Burns was the man every woman wanted to be with and every man wanted to drink with, but offstage his persona was a bit more problematic. He was unpopular and not just because the TV show was crap: he kept sleeping with people's wives just because he could and had a habit of launching into his act in the middle of a conversation, reducing the listener to a passive audience member, obliging them to laugh.

'You should talk to Dub, see what he says.'

'I never see him.'

'Phone him.'

'He's never in.'

It was a power play: Dub was in all the time but Burns wanted Dub to come to him.

'Are you troubled at all by the fact that your son and I came here in mortal danger and now we're discussing your career?'

He laughed at himself, the kindest side to him, and she sat forward. 'I'll say goodbye to Pete.'

But Burns could see she was still shaken. 'Sit for a minute, Pad.' He put his hand on her knee, leaving it there, and she was glad of the warmth.

Paddy could well imagine how much Pete would see of his father over the next few days, building up to the recording of the show on Thursday night, just as she could imagine the fury of some woman working her way up in TV who was expected to give up her proper job and be an impromptu nanny for George H. fucking Burns's spoiled kid. She didn't give a shit.

He squeezed her hand kindly. 'I'm proud of the wee man. You're doing a great job.'

In a moment of weakness she pecked a kiss at his fingers, the white leather sofa squeaking unattractively under her arse.

25

Better Buy a Gun

I

The taxi dropped her in the street, at the opposite end of the car park from the *News* building so she could get back to her car without being seen.

The car park was a dirty stretch of ground, not even flattened for the cars. It was concreted over near the building but here, on the far fringes, the ground was potholed and dusty. A city tenement had been pulled down here, a long time ago, whether because of a German bomb or general decay she didn't know. The pavement was the only part still standing, a ring fence around the empty space. Cars were clustered up near the front of the building, more now than there used to be. A cab rank had been set up at one end, near the road into town, because the paper's budget had been cut back dramatically and the first thing to go was the pool of cars with staff drivers idling by the front door.

She walked carefully along the pavement, moving at a normal pace, hoping not to be seen. Upstairs the early shift would still be on, the final few pages being set and finished. All it would take was for Bunty or the Monkey to glance out of the window and spot her and she'd be dragged upstairs again, made to write an article about a fictitious visit to Callum. They'd be desperate for any copy about him now.

His shoe size would command a front-page lead.

Level with her car, she left the pavement and crossed the dusty ground towards it. She had parked in the same spot this morning as she had been in the night before, when she left Mary Ann smoking fluently in the car. Mary Ann smoking, upset about a boyfriend. It jarred, not just because she was a nun, but because she was a child to them all. Not just a child of the Church but of all the Meehans, and it wasn't to her benefit but to theirs. She was a token of their childhood, a nostalgic reminder of how they were.

Both the Press Bar doors were open to the summer night and a warble of chat and the chink of glasses sounded warm and friendly. Paddy would have loved to be in there, trouble-free, gossiping and having a laugh among her own.

She smiled at the thought as she drew level with the car and stopped, her toes kicking up brown dust from the dry ground. The boot had been broken into, the entire lock drilled out, leaving a gaping black hole thick as a man's thumb in the carcass of the car.

Reaching forward, she put her finger into the hole and lifted the boot. It opened lightly, the spring mechanism taking the weight after her initial pull. A plastic bag with dry cleaning she had yet to hand in was there, one of Pete's footballs and a pair of his trainers were there, and a squashed box for apples that she had used to take some frozen shopping to her mother's was there too, but Terry's portfolio was gone. His photographs were gone; his notebook full of shorthand which he had tucked protectively into the spine was gone too.

A breeze picked up, swirling grainy dust around her bare ankles. She stared into the messy boot. It was the photographs they wanted, and she knew completely, whatever Knox or Aoife said, that it was McBree. She rummaged in her handbag. The photocopies were in there. They weren't very good, she didn't have a proper picture of the woman any more, but she did have a photo of McBree standing at the door of the car facing a fat man in a blue suit. This story could be huge.

She shut the boot and walked over to the *News* building, pulling open the fire exit door and jogging purposefully up the stairs.

11

Her entrance to the newsroom elicited a small cheer from those who could remember back to the morning's drama, but the look on Paddy's face killed the joy stone dead. The lights were on in Bunty's cubicle.

She knocked once and opened the door, to find Bunty and the Monkey relaxing at the far end of the table, eating poached salmon sandwiches and drinking half-pints of beer in Press Bar glasses. Bunty retracted his feet from the conference table when he saw it was her, rearranging his face to denote managerial fury.

She held a hand up and took a deep breath. 'I lied. I wasn't visiting Ogilvy, I didn't even meet him. I was waiting in the car while Sean went in, keeping an eye out for journalists.'

She waited for a moment, steeling herself against a gale of shouting, but none came. She carried on:

'There's a story, a much, much bigger story going on. It's a keynote story and I've come to you with it because I haven't got a fucking clue what to do.'

Intrigued, Bunty flicked his fingers, waving her forward, and nodded to the Monkey to leave them alone for a moment. Monkey took his sandwich and half-pint with him.

She sat down near him, feeling exhausted, her stomach aching. She told him about Kevin, about the bruises on his arm and chin and Aoife's theory about the methods of cocaine ingestion. Ask anyone, she said, about Kevin's drinking; he wasn't a man who would take drugs quietly and have a mishap. She told him about Kevin's disappearance in the ambulance, about the innocuous coffee-table book, about McBree and the portfolio, and her boot being broken into.

'Every single copy of that photograph has been taken. I've got some bad photocopies of it.' She pulled them out of her bag and unfolded them on the table.

Bunty glanced through them, chewing his sandwich, looking back at her to continue.

'Now,' she said nervously, 'the really interesting thing about this is Knox.'

Bunty looked sceptical. She'd raised Knox with him before and he stymied her plan to do an investigation into him.

'This is real, though, listen: Knox pulled me in for questioning this morning. They made me wait and then in saunters Knox and tells me to stay off McBree: Kevin wasn't killed by anybody, the IRA had nothing to do with this, I should go home and let the whole thing drop.'

Bunty swallowed his mouthful, took a sip of beer and looked up at her. 'Maybe you should.'

She was shocked. He was a good editor, a good journalist and any idiot could tell there was a story here. 'I cannot believe you're saying that.'

Bunty took another bite of his sandwich, folding the crusts into his mouth. He leaned back in his chair, lifting his feet up on to the table, making her wait for him to finish his mouthful before he answered her. He swallowed, reached forward for his glass and took a sip of beer. He rolled his tongue along the line of front teeth, top and bottom.

'Get a fucking move on,' she said.

'Don't you ever wonder,' he said quietly, 'why Knox is out of bounds?'

She didn't answer. She hadn't wondered that actually. She often wondered why she couldn't catch him, wondered what he did to frighten so many people into keeping quiet about him, but she had never been aware that he was being kept from her.

'*Is* he out of bounds?'

Bunty cradled the back of his head with his hands, sucked a morsel from his front teeth and nodded once.

'Says who? British Intelligence?'

Bunty raised an eyebrow.

Paddy shook her head at the table: it was so obvious now. Consecutive editors had turned the Knox story back, no one outside the police knew a thing about his activities and she couldn't find a policeman with a bad word to say, and they had a bad word about everyone. It was a sure sign that he was being kept clean. And then Kevin's admission to hospital being wiped off whichever record while they fixed the body just so, the deserted office and Knox's arrogant assurances about what was and wasn't the case.

She'd interviewed Patrick Meehan many times about his brushes with British Intelligence and what always struck her was how commonplace it all sounded. A room set aside in a police station. Stone-faced men with Oxbridge accents and just the right coat from the right tailor's, unimaginative and protectionist, unashamed of their agenda. They called them spooks but they sounded like irritable bank managers. Knox had that commonplace look. She remembered him in Babbity's, recalled him sliding around at a hundred press functions.

'If,' Bunty paused dramatically, '*if* you can get anything on him, which I doubt, I'll go with it.'

'You'll publish it?'

He sucked his teeth again, enjoying himself. 'Yes.'

Any senior editor who OK'd a story that threatened national security could get sacked by the proprietor, or worse.

'Bunty, you could get the bullet for it.'

'I could get the bullet anyway. They could sack me tomorrow for not selling enough advertising.'

She leaned forward. 'What do you think? Why are Intelligence protecting McBree?'

He thought for a moment, slowly brushing breadcrumbs from his shirtfront. 'It's one of two things: either McBree's still loyal to his cause but is working with them. He could be a bridge, helping negotiations in Northern Ireland. Or else, and if this is the case you better buy a gun: they've got something on him and McBree's a double agent.'

He looked her in the eye and they both drew breath.

'Fucking hell.'

Bunty nodded slowly. 'Quite so: *fucking* hell.'

Traipsing downstairs to her car, she thought about McBree working for the British government. He wouldn't just be spying for them, telling them what was going on inside the Republican movement in Northern Ireland. He'd be too valuable an asset to use so lightly. If McBree was working for the government they'd be getting him to mould and shape decisions in their favour. And if he was working for them he'd kill to stop anyone finding out. He'd have to. If his own side found out he'd be a dead man.

She walked over to the car and looked back at the bright door of the bar, saw McGrade smiling benignly as he poured a pint, heard the chat and a drunkard's laugh. A man passed inside and she thought for a moment it was someone she knew a long time ago, a union official who got a kicking the night her first boss, Farquarson, was sacked. But that was a long time ago in another garden.

III

She knew before she reached the door that something bad had happened. The light was wrong, it was too bright in the close and warm air was filtering down from up above, from her house, her open door. The wood around the lock had been shattered from a rough kick and the door hung open into the hallway.

She ran up the final steps and found the hall in a mess. The boxes of Dub's records had been tipped over, some of them stamped on maliciously, the broken bits kicked around the floor. Terry's trunk had been opened and upended, the binbags of his papers emptied. In the living room the mess was even worse. The bookcases had been ransacked, cushions ripped off the settee and chair and the screen of the telly was kicked in.

'Hey, you.' Dub came out of the kitchen. 'I've been trying to get hold of you all day.'

Paddy threw her hands up, shocked into silence.

'I know. The police came and looked around, made some notes but I can't really tell what was taken. They didn't nick anything, just broke stuff. Left the records, the radio, didn't even take the telly – look, just kicked it in. My watch was in the bathroom, they didn't even take that.'

She brushed past him into her bedroom. Her underwear was all over the place, the sheets on her bed had been dragged on to the floor and a dark wet stain was drying in the middle of her mattress.

'Piss. Consider yourself lucky, they said, some of them do a shit. They get excited and it loosens their bowels.'

She slumped in the doorway, staring at the mess.

'Aren't you going to say anything?' She didn't so Dub stroked her hair awkwardly. They were rarely affectionate to each other when the lights were on. His hand found a rhythm, some way between boyfriend intimacy and supportive friend.

She looked up at him. 'What did they say?'

'The police? Neds. They asked the neighbours and one of them saw a wee guy in a tracksuit heading down the stairs.'

'A black tracksuit?'

He was surprised that she knew. 'Yeah. Black tracksuit.'

She took hold of his arm. 'You need to come with me. It's not safe here.'

'I'm not scared of a vandal.'

'He's more than that. He's a lot more than that. Get your coat.'

They pulled the door over to make it look secure, fitting the splintered wood back in around the useless lock.

Dub looked at it. 'Paddy, that won't fool anyone who wants to steal something.'

'They don't want to steal anything,' she said. 'They're trying to scare me.'

IV

A tin of white paint had been thrown over the windows of the Shammy since she had been there last, probably by a Loyalist. A rudimentary effort had been made to wash it off, smearing the white over the shopfront, mixing it with the street dust already gathered on the walls, making it look like a slightly dirty protest. Irish flags hung in the high-up windows.

She turned the engine off and Dub looked at her.

'You're not going in there?'

'Wait here,' she said, getting out of the car.

He was on the pavement next to her. 'Don't go in. Those places are mental.'

But she shook his hand off. 'I've been in before.'

She left him standing in a quandary by the car, watching after her, afraid to let her go but worried about leaving the car unguarded in such a rough area.

She pushed the black-painted doors open and walked into a wall of smoke and chat. There were hardly any women, but it looked no rougher than the Press Bar in the olden days. The clothes were cheaper, the chat less conversational, just drunk men slurring at each other. Music was playing in the background, a high tinny Irish tune played on pipes, an old song about the green of the home-land and Brits shooting at children.

She glared along the line-up at the bar, checking each of the leathers, but didn't see Donaldson. The barman recognized her though, half watching her as he wiped the bar with a stained cloth. She looked around the tables tucked to the side of the door. Red-faced men looked up at her from a crowd grouped around an ashtray. Two of them had taken their jackets off and wore Celtic tops. She didn't recognize any of the faces.

Their eyes were gathering on her back and she pushed through the crowd to the dimly lit booths. Behind her someone whooped at the sight of an angry woman: 'Some-one's getting a thick ear tonight, bhoy.'

Six plump men were squashed into the booth but he was standing by, a hanger-on, no more than that, a heel-sniffer. His hands were in his pockets, his elbows locked tight with excitement at being in their company, pulling the tracksuit trousers out at the side, making a V of his legs.

He saw her and started. A parliament of heavies sat at the table, a thick smog of smoke hanging over their heads.

Their shot and half-pint glasses were filthy: an old man's habit to keep the same glass all night, build up a taste on it.

The leader of them looked up at her, taking the measure of the plump, furious woman standing at the side of his table. A flushed face, drink-sodden eyes, his fist so big that it obscured his half-pint glass. The other men looked to him to say something, set the tone.

'Wha'?' The effort of talking seemed to take it out of him.

Paddy pointed at the tracksuit. 'Who is this fucker?'

The men looked at the boy, bewildered, as if he'd just appeared at their side and they'd never seen him before. They looked back to their leader.

'Wha'?'

'This idjit, is he working for you?'

'Him?'

The men looked at the tracksuit, who smiled nervously back, tipping on to his toes, keen for someone, anyone, to acknowledge him. No one did.

They looked back at the leader and he shook his head slowly, signalling to the others that he didn't want to talk to her. A big man at the end of the table stood up, blocking her approach with his chest. She tried to step around him but he wrapped his hand around her arm, pulling her back. 'Naw.'

'Your boy's been following me for two days. He ripped my house apart. He followed me taking my son to school.' The memory of Pete made her angry enough to pull her arm away from him. 'My *son*.' She looked up at his face and spat at him, '*How dare you.*'

A fleck of saliva hit his cheek but he didn't flinch. This man wasn't fat. This man looked as if he had just left a maximum security prison, possibly through the wall. As she stood three inches from him, his chest looked as big as her bed. He glanced back to the drunkard boss, who flicked his wrist in the direction of the door.

The Mountain stepped between her legs and took hold of both arms, ready to wrestle her out of the bar. He was expecting Paddy to fight him but she went limp and he fumbled as she slid below his waist, letting go for a second, giving her an opportunity to duck around him and scream across the table, 'He threatened my son!'

The Mountain grabbed her around the waist, dragging her back from the table just as the tracksuit came forward and punched her in the stomach. It wasn't an expert punch. The flat of his knuckles didn't slam into her spine, but made a short jab up to the diaphragm, knocking the wind out of her, bruising her lungs, making her jackknife over the arm.

An uncomfortable quiet fell over the bar. The tinny music droned in the background, an upbeat tune with a jig rhythm. She opened her eyes as the Mountain spun her in a half-circle. The whole bar was watching them now, retreating, appalled.

The Mountain dragged her on her heels, not to the front door but out the back.

'What the fuck did ye do that for?' a Scottish voice asked.

Lifting her head for a second, she saw the tracksuit shrug.

They were going through a fire exit door, painted black with a bar handle, leading straight out to the dark and a dirt floor next to stinking bins. He lifted her over his own leg, dumping her but keeping hold. Rats scuttled away behind a wall and Paddy realized that she was utterly fucking done for.

The door slapped shut behind them, blocking out the music and the silence, leaving them alone. The Mountain pinched her face between his thumb and middle finger, cutting the inside of her cheek on the edge of her teeth, and held her up to look at him. He was very calm.

'You—'

Behind him the door opened again and Paddy shut her eyes, expecting the tracksuit with his sharp jab.

'Off. Inside. Move it.'

She opened her eyes. Donaldson.

The Mountain dropped her back on to her feet and turned. 'Oh,' he said, politely, 'awful sorry.' He looked down at her. 'Awful sorry. Are you OK?'

She nodded hard, hoping he'd go away. Donaldson flicked his thumb at the door and the Mountain stepped back into the bar, letting the door fall shut behind him.

Donaldson reached out and brushed her shoulder, making her jerk upright, flinch away from him.

He dropped his hand and stepped back, giving her space. As she breathed in deeply a sharp pain shot across her gut, making her feel as if she might vomit.

Donaldson stood calmly by, hands in his pockets, letting her gather herself together for a moment before turning back to the door. 'That was . . .' He looked perplexed. 'Well, that was . . . what it was.'

The bins behind him were stuffed full, overflowing with ripped black bags and bottles, newspapers and smell. Paddy rubbed her stomach. 'That wee shite in the tracksuit's working for you?'

Donaldson dropped his head and pinched his nose, his shoulders jerking.

'I don't see what's so fucking funny.' She sounded angry when he had just saved her. She shouldn't. He might step back in and send the big guy out again.

'Ah.' He held out his hand. 'Come on.'

'Come on *what*?'

'Come on, shake my hand. You're a wild woman.'

'My house is smashed up, he pissed on my bed. My friend died and I'm trying to find out what happened to him. Is that what happens to people who ask questions? I thought you nut jobs were all about justice for the working man and truth, for fucksake.'

He looked at her playfully. 'Well, girlie, that's a different story from the one you were telling me the other day. You sat across from me and said we were nothing but thugs who'd hijacked the history of the Fenian Brotherhood.'

'And that annoyed you enough to set that wee shit on me, did it?'

'That wee guy *is* a – what's this you call them, neds?' He savoured the unfamiliar word and fell serious. 'He hangs around the bar, trying to be part of something he doesn't understand. He hasn't any conviction, knows nothing about history. He's just angry. People tolerate him.'

'You know about history, do you?'

'I got a two one from Trinity.'

She looked up at him, not sure if he was telling the truth, but he seemed serious and rather impressed with himself, the way genuinely degree'd folk did. 'Well, no one with a degree ever did a bad turn, did they?'

He flashed a dutiful smile. 'The boy's a sympathizer for a cause he doesn't understand. Thinks making his first communion qualifies him as a Republican. He wasn't following anyone's orders; we wouldn't send him for cigarettes. He was here that day you phoned. He must have asked the barman who called and gone looking for you. He'd be trying to impress the boys. He's a hanger-on, nothing more.'

'The Celtic top was a clever disguise.'

Donaldson pinched his nose and laughed again, shaking his head to stop himself. 'I'm very sorry. We'll tell him to back off. I had no idea.'

She rubbed her stomach theatrically.

'Still got that photo, have you?'

She didn't answer him.

He swivelled on his heels, looked around the dark yard, looking at head height, looking for people. 'Ye want a safety tip? Get rid of the picture.'

'Yeah.' She was annoyed he hadn't asked her about her stomach. 'No one likes the McBree picture. I gathered that.'

He moved closer to her, sliding in, shoulder on. 'Meehan, Paddy, if I can call you that.' He was standing so close to her and his voice was so low she thought for a moment he was going to try and kiss her. 'That picture.' He shook his head and stopped, staring hard at the bins. He stepped away from her and raised a hand. 'This is my office, ye know. This bar, this filthy yard. This is where I do all my business. I got quite a thrill when you came to see me the other day. I don't know who told you I was the man to talk to, but they were wrong.' His face laughed but his eyes didn't. 'I used to be the man, but now . . .'

Donaldson was a bit pissed, she realized. It made him more animated than he had been the other day, loose, and it suited him.

'What are you doing in Scotland?'

'Oh, I'm out. They sent me away. I used to be the king of the Sweetie Bottle Bar. Drank with all of them, gave orders from there. If a woman was worried about her boy she'd come and see me, ask me . . .' He stopped, looked back at her, staring at her chest, taking that male, every-seven-seconds moment.

She circled her sore stomach with her hand, finding it helped. 'Sweetie Bottle Bar?'

His face warmed in remembrance of a better time, when he mattered. 'Ye know the Sweetie Bottle?'

'No, just . . . good name. I read about your son in the clippings. I'm sorry for your troubles.'

'Aye.' He didn't react. He must have heard it a hundred times.

They stared at each other across the gloom of the evening, both fat and out of shape, both sick thinking about their sons.

'What should I do with the picture?'

He answered quickly. 'Burn it.'

'Or one of you'll kill me?'

He shook his head slowly. 'Not us.'

'McBree came to my house. He threatened me. I was lucky. My son was out and someone else was there or I don't know what he'd have done.'

'But we don't kill journalists.'

'Ye bombed the Stock Exchange a month ago.'

'We gave fourteen different coded warnings half an hour before it went off.'

'Are you telling me McBree's working alone?'

He shrugged.

'Why won't the police touch him then?'

He looked surprised at that, gave her a warning look and glanced back at the door to the bar. 'Won't they?'

'I got warned off by a DCI, no less.'

Donaldson looked at the door, at her, at the ground, fitting bits of something together in his head, something that made him angry and upset. Whatever it was, he shook his head, glanced at the bar door and back to her. His eyes were wet.

'They won't listen to me.'

'Who?'

But he just shook his head again. His voice sounded strained when he spoke. 'You know, Miss Meehan, if I was a journalist with a death wish I'd be asking who that other fella in the photograph was.' He nodded at the door. 'McBree'll know that you came here. He'll see it as a provocation, wonder what you're telling me. Someone could be on the phone to him right now. He hears everything.'

He turned away, took a deep breath, blinked his sadness away and pushed the door open, walking back into the light and the noise. The door banged shut behind him.

She stood in the dark, rank yard, heard a bus rumble past beyond the wall, a dog bark a long way away and thought about what he'd said for a moment. McBree was acting alone because he had something to hide and whatever his secret was, Kevin had captured it in the photograph. The fat man in the suit.

Her lung was still aching but she felt freshly fired up as she scouted the yard for a back way out, but the wall around the yard was solid and the gate was locked.

She had to knock on the fire exit and wait for the Mountain to come and let her back in. The tracksuit was gone and Donaldson was back at the bar, ignoring her as the Mountain escorted her to the main door, apologizing over and over, barely audible through the wall of catcalls and whistles from the other men.

26

Get Down, Mutley

I

Dub waited in the car, listening patiently to a comedy show on the radio, saying he didn't mind.

Paddy checked her notes again, read the door numbers on the gates opposite and turned back, certain that this was number eight. Dub always said that house envy was the one sure symptom of middle age. The sight of it made her mouth water.

It was everything she would have wanted Eriskay House to be: in the city, gloriously well kept and absolutely massive. A trellis arch from the street was hung with roses, the flowers faded and dropping on to the pavement, littering the path to the house.

The asymmetric facade had Arts and Crafts decoration on every finial and doorknob, small, perfect details that spoke of class and taste, oak leaves and acorns worked into the carving on the architraves, faces easing out of the stones, a lizard frozen mid-scamper across the door frame. To the right of the building was a glass conservatory, leaves of lush plants pressed hard against the greening windows. She paused to look in through the glass and saw trays of seedlings and flowering potted plants on a bench.

The doorbell was ceramic and chimed a time-worn gong

into the hallway. She waited, looking back out into the street to see Dub alone in the car, laughing.

Suddenly the door was opened by a young girl with blonde hair pulled up in a ponytail, her face fresh and welcoming, making Paddy feel shabby and fat and old.

'Paddy Meehan?'

'Hi.'

'Come in, come in.' She almost giggled with delight as Paddy shuffled in. 'Mum's still working, believe it or not.'

A square stairwell filled the hallway, carved in warm red wood, Gothic details elaborate enough for a church pew, with coats hung irreverently on delicate finials. A spindly jardinière held a chunky black Bakelite phone. The stone floor was littered with welly boots, sandals, leashes and mauled tennis balls. It smelled of dog.

The girl led her through a passageway to the left of the door, a narrow servants' corridor that ran between the rooms, into a back office covered in papers and poster-sized book covers. French windows gave on to a garden and a golden Labrador was dozing outside in the early evening sunshine, tail dreamily batting the ground.

Joan Forsyth stood up to meet her. She was a mannish version of the pretty girl, in her forties but still vigorous. She was dressed in a white tailored shirt with the collar standing up in the manner of rugby players. Her hair was carefully unkempt, thick and blonde with traces of white around the temples. She wore expensively cut green slacks with a thin yellow check through them.

'Hello.' She leaned on top of her desk with one hand and took Paddy's hand with the other, pumped firmly once and let go. 'Do sit down.'

She let Paddy settle, flashing her another smile and offering tea.

'Oh, lovely, thanks.'

'Darjeeling?'

'Fine.'

'Tippy.' She addressed her daughter. 'Pot of Darj and two cups, please.'

Tippy twitched her head at Paddy, mock sulk. 'She's using you as an excuse to boss me, you know.'

Paddy pretended to give a shit. 'Sorry.'

'Never mind,' Tippy said prettily and turned on her heels, disappearing back through the dark corridor.

'So, you're Paddy Meehan?'

The Labrador was awake, nuzzling at the door, but Joan Forsyth ignored it.

'I am, yeah. I hope you don't mind me coming to see you but I wanted to ask about Terry Hewitt's book.'

'Right,' she nodded and waited for Paddy to continue.

'You knew Terry personally?'

'I knew Amy, his mother. We were at school together in Perthshire. He came to me with a book proposal and I thought it sounded good, the pictures were great so, yes, I said yes.' She seemed a little defensive.

'But you didn't really know Terry that well?'

'No.' She sounded very sharp. 'I knew his mother.'

Paddy waited, listening to the dog whine at the door, snuffling hard at the joist.

'*Get away, Mutley.*'

The dog gave a whine and backed off. Paddy was almost afraid to speak again in case Joan shouted at her. 'I see,' she said quietly. 'I just went out to Eriskay House, you know? Where they lived?'

'Ayrshire?'

'Aye, Ayrshire. The road's very dangerous. Did they die there?'

'Yes. At the end of the driveway. A lorry took the corner at seventy and lost control. Lucky Terry wasn't in the car.

He should have been. He was in the house at the time. First on the scene.'

Paddy saw him then, with his shaved head and scars showing on his scalp, standing in the thick grass staring wide-eyed at the end of the driveway. He'd never told her that he'd been there, never even hinted at it. He was all of seventeen.

'Poor little thing,' Forsyth said absently. 'He was a lovely boy. She adored him.'

Paddy cleared her throat. 'Terry and I went out together, not long afterwards, when he first moved to the city.'

'I see,' she seemed to soften. 'You knew Terry?'

'Yeah, I knew him very well. He left me the house in his will.'

'Oh.' She leaned back in her chair. 'I thought you were writing an article about him or something.'

'Well, I kind of am.'

'Not that awful column? You insulted a very good friend of mine in that rag – you know, Margaret Hamilton, the newsreader? Said her hair was made from wood.'

Before Paddy could apologize Tippy clattered in with the tea on a wooden tray and a plate of digestive biscuits. Paddy thanked her as she unloaded the things on to the desk, trying to think of a new approach. But she was too tired to be subtle. She asked Tippy for milk in the tea, not lemon, bit off a mouthful of biscuit and waited until Tippy had retreated before coming clean.

'Look, I'm sorry about your friend, Misty's a bit scurrilous sometimes but this is important. The photographer, Kevin, he's been killed too.' Forsyth's jaw fell open. 'They had a photograph of a major player in the IRA in that book, in the background of one of the shots, and he's hanging about Glasgow. It can't be a coincidence. If it was about the picture, if someone wanted the book stopped, I need to know who could have seen it before it was published. Could you have shown it to anyone?'

'No!' Joan thought hard and her eyes opened wide in surprise. 'No! Kevin's dead?'

'Did you know Kevin?'

Forsyth looked wildly around the walls of her office. 'God, how awful. What a dreadful– God!'

'Who got to see the pictures from your side?'

'Well, I didn't show them to anyone, but everyone in the book got their own picture. Kevin was a news journalist, so he didn't know that much about the portraiture business. We had to send them all a copy with a release form to get consent to use their images.'

'Everyone in the book got a copy of their own photograph?'

'Sure.'

'But they only got their own photograph?'

'Yeah. God—'

'Who sent the photographs out to people?'

'Me.'

Joan didn't seem able to make the next logical leap so Paddy had to spell it out for her. 'Maybe we can trace the person who got that photograph. Do you have all the names and addresses somewhere?'

'Um – yes but I don't know who got what. We put a release form in each envelope, addressed them, then Terry came in with a small six-by-four of each portrait and put the right one in each before we sent them off.'

She still had the list of addresses though, a messy sheet of lined foolscap with Terry's handwritten list on it, thirty-four names and addresses. Over half of them were men's names. It shouldn't be too hard to find the black woman.

Paddy smiled at the jagged, childish scrawl. Like herself,

Terry was spoiled by the speed of shorthand and his letters tumbled messily over each other. She remembered a note she left on the noticeboard at work once, when she wanted to sell her old car. Someone drew a speech bubble, attaching it to the last letter on the page: 'Stop pushing at the back!' Journos doing interviews often wrote notes without looking at the page, keeping eye contact with an interviewee. Terry had forgotten to look at the page sometimes while he was copying the addresses and his writing escaped the lines, soaring upwards.

She folded the sheet and put it in her bag. 'Look, can I be a terrible bother and borrow your phone to make a quick call?'

Forsyth was still stunned about Kevin's death. She waved a hand vaguely over the phone on the desk but Paddy stood up. 'I'll use the one out in the hall, on my way out. I don't want to interrupt your work.'

'Sure, sure.' Joan stood up to shake Paddy's hand again. 'If you ever have an idea for a book come to me.' She looked her up and down. 'You're very marketable.'

Paddy wasn't altogether sure it was a compliment. 'Tell your friend I'm sorry for insulting her hair.'

'No.' She waved the offence away. 'She had it cut because of you, no bad thing.'

'And I'm sorry the book won't come out.'

'Are you joking?' Forsyth managed a weak smile. With a story like this attached to it, it bloody well will come out.'

Paddy remembered Kevin sitting in his living room on a quiet Sunday night, proudly showing her the portfolio, saying Terry had offended someone in the Lebanon and nothing would happen to him.

'Joan, I'd keep that really quiet for a while if I were you.'

Tippy was playing music upstairs somewhere, and Paddy was alone in the hall. She rang Burns.

Sandra picked up, putting on a breathy telephone voice and answering as 'the Burnses' residence'. Paddy kept her voice down and asked for Pete. Sandra leaned away from the phone and called 'Peter, Peter,' into the kitchen. Paddy could hear the theme to *Ghost Train* playing on the video in the background.

'All right, son? What are you doing?'

The sound of his voice made her relax, resting her forehead on the cool wall above the telephone table. He was monosyllabic, looking into the kitchen where the video was, but he sounded happy and said he'd been to a neighbour's kid's party and had a lot of Coke and crisps. His dad said Pete didn't need to have a bath tonight and he'd had toast for dinner.

'No veg?'

'Crisps are made from potatoes,' he said, quoting BC who compounded his fatness by being a smart-arse.

'Are you quite happy staying there tonight? Have you got a clean shirt for school?'

'Yes and yes,' he said, succinct because he wanted to get off the phone. 'The video . . .'

She made him promise to phone her at home and say good night before she let him go. She hung up and let herself out into the cool of the evening.

27

Enjoying the Slide

I

It was dark outside. Paddy and Dub had been everywhere they could think of, up to Springburn where Callum came from on the off-chance he'd managed to get a train and bus up there, back down the road for a scour of Rutherglen and the fields around it, following the bus routes from the main road nearby, to a local supermarket that opened late, into a couple of cafés that were brightly lit and a pub that stood out cheerily against the dark because of the red neon 'food' sign in the window. As Dub pointed out, Callum wasn't off looking for a good time, he was hiding. He would be hiding in a dark ditch somewhere, not going into the obvious places. Paddy knew one thing for sure: she didn't want to be the one to find him. He was scary enough with the lights on.

She told Dub about her conversation with Burns and how he wasn't feeding Pete properly.

'It's only one night, you'd think he could cook him something *once*.'

'Yeah,' said Dub. 'Maybe I'll phone him.'

'Let him phone you.'

They drove past Sean's street, stopping and peering down the road to see the hordes parked up outside the house.

Photographers stood in groups, their bags at their feet, fingering their cameras and looking bored. Journalists stood separately. She knew the scatter pattern well enough: clusters of the genial ones, gathering round to swap lies about their wages and expense accounts and all the coups they nearly had, the loners hanging about on the fringes, telling themselves lies and coming up with schemes to trounce the others to the story. A large television van was parked up on Sean's side of the road, a massively tall transmission aerial sticking out of the top. She could already imagine the complaints from the press journalists: the van would be in their view, spoil the pictures. But that was why it was there, to get the logo in any of the pictures that got published and show that STV were on the scene too.

Dub suggested they get fish suppers and park to eat them and she realized how hungry she was. She hadn't had any lunch, just the biscuit at the publisher's house. No wonder she felt so ropey.

Rutherglen was her old stamping ground. When she dated Sean they often went to the Burnside café to pick up fish suppers for his mum and brothers. It faced on to a dark, hilly park full of old trees and they used to hand in the order and then go across and snog behind a tree for ten minutes while the man cooked their food.

She parked across the road and Dub said he'd get them if she waited in the car, so she asked for a battered haggis supper with lots of vinegar and a can of juice. He mugged a sad face at her. 'No veg?'

'Batter is made from veg.'

The café was empty. Paddy watched through the car window as the bored proprietor shucked chips into plastic trays, wrapping them expertly in white and brown paper, picking the haggis from a display shelf sitting above the fryers. That meant the haggis had been fried earlier in the evening. That meant it would be dried out. She was cursing to herself, imagining the rubbery casing around the meat, when she looked over to the park and saw something move behind a tree. A head, a big head, the right height for Callum as well.

Paddy looked at Dub, a long strip of cool buying her nice chips to share after a hard day of misery and grim. She chewed her tongue hard and looked back out into the park. It would be getting cold soon: the heat from the day was leaving the earth and there wasn't any cloud cover. Fuck him, she thought, fuck him. He's a creep and I've had a hard day, but her hand found the door handle and she got out into the street, hoping he'd see her and run for it. She stepped out of the street light into the shadow of the trees and cleared her throat.

'Is that you?'

Whoever it was slipped back behind the tree.

''Cause if it is you, Sean's very worried and we're out looking for you.' She looked back at Dub handing a fiver over the counter, the parcels tucked neatly into a flimsy blue plastic bag hanging from his hand.

'We're getting chips.'

Her heart sank as Callum peered skittishly around the trunk of the tree. He must be hungry. For the sake of Sean she waved him over to her. 'Come on.'

'I can't go back. They're all over the place.'

'OK, get in the car and we'll eat the chips and think of something.'

Dub was surprised to find Paddy getting into the car with a bulky young stranger but he managed to defer his curiosity until they were inside. They could tell Callum had been crying. He had managed to get dirt on his face and there were clean tracks where the tears had fallen, smeared where he had wiped them away. She looked at him in the dark and remembered the terrified wee boy in a hospital bed ten years ago.

She introduced Dub to him, him to Dub and they opened the chips. The haggis supper was too big for her anyway so she halved it with him and Dub donated a third of his fish, giving Callum his can of Irn-Bru. Callum thanked them through a mouthful of sausage, cramming chips into his mouth, explaining that he'd only had a cheese sandwich and he was starving. The chips were sweet and salted to perfection and they sank into the easy camaraderie of hungry people enjoying a good meal.

Dub finished first, gave a satisfied sigh, wiped the grease from his mouth with a paper napkin and looked at Callum, still eating on the back seat.

'What are we going to do with you, my friend?'

'We can't take him to ours,' she said.

'How no?' Callum was sitting in her warm car, his mouth was full of her dinner and neon orange juice and he still sounded as if he'd been slighted.

'Because journalists were coming to our door looking for you before you even got out, and someone smashed the door in and pissed on our beds today. You want to sleep on that?'

Callum wasn't sure whether to believe her but he looked to Dub and he confirmed it with a wrinkled nose. 'We were lucky, though. I mean, they didn't shit on them.' The way he said it was so ridiculous that Paddy started laughing and couldn't stop: it sounded as if the guy had given them the option of one or the other. She laughed and looked at Callum, who was frowning at Dub until he caught Paddy's eye and started laughing too, like a sad child out of practice, opening his mouth wide and pumping laughs out of his face. Dub was used to being laughed at. He had been a comic for a long time before he became a manager and he took it as a compliment, smiling and nodding at them, saying 'it's true' every so often. It reminded Paddy of her father. One of Con's loveliest traits had been his willingness to be the butt of jokes; he let the children laugh at him when he was silly, smiled when other men ridiculed him.

When the hilarity had died down Dub turned to Callum, eyeing him as if he was measuring him up for a new suit. 'Where are we going to keep this guy safe, then?'

Paddy looked back at Callum. He already looked nicer, softer and less wary of her. 'Uff, I don't know. Can't take him to the Ogilvys', or ours.'

'What about my mum and dad's?'

Dub managed comedians for a living. The closest he had ever come to real danger was defusing an ego. His parents were indulgent but Paddy didn't think they would appreciate him arriving with a famous murderer looking for a bed. And they only had two bedrooms, which meant that Paddy and Dub would be dumping him and leaving again. Callum was pleased by the suggestion though, possibly because it made him sound trustworthy.

'They are quite elderly,' Paddy said reluctantly, 'a bit stuck in their ways, Callum. I don't know if you'd like it there.'

'I like family units,' he said hopefully.

His face looked calmer now he wasn't hungry, traces of the laughter still showed in his eyes and as he leaned forward to answer them he held on to his shins, bending eagerly forward like a child discussing his Christmas present.

'Well, they've only got one room anyway and I think we should stick together. What about a hotel?'

'Nah.' Dub was certain. 'The papers've all got reception paid off to tip them about anyone interesting.'

He was right.

'And we can't go to one of my clients because they're all publicity-hungry wankers and they'll drop the dime.'

'"Drop the dime"?' mimicked Paddy, and she and Callum laughed again, less because it was funny than because they had enjoyed it so much the first time.

'OK.' She started the engine. 'We'll go back to ours, pick up some stuff and go on to a place I know. We'll get the sleeping bags, unless someone's shat in them.'

They drove back across the Kingston Bridge, a high concrete arch over the river. The city lay spread out below them, bright and thrilling, and Callum sat, awestruck, with his face to the window, wondering at the lights.

A high white moon hung above the city and Paddy had the sense of skidding across ice to her doom, pausing to enjoy the slide.

II

She left the lights off in the hall, put the bits of wood that completed the front door on the floor and went into the dark kitchen to call Sean. The answerphone caught the call so she told it she and Dub had found the package in question outside the supper shop, and were going to look after it for a while. See you tomorrow at the cathedral.

She crept into Pete's room. He would need clean shirts for school, fresh underwear; there wasn't that much at his dad's house. He only ever stayed there for a night or so.

She held the neatly folded bundle of clothes and looked around Pete's room. Dub made Pete's bed every morning, plumped the pillows and pulled the duvet tight across the bed until it was a smooth marshmallow. The bed was still made; the whale mobile that hung from the ceiling spun slowly in the stirred air; his toys were all in order. Nothing was moved in here, the tracksuited ned hadn't been in here. He must have come to the door and balked at smashing up a child's bedroom. It gave her hope. She went into, her own room, looked at the stain on the stripped bed, smelled the caustic tang of piss and then remembered that he'd been at Pete's school gates. There were no boundaries.

Frightened by the thought, she gathered black clothes for herself and Dub for tomorrow, pulled two tightly rolled sleeping bags down from the top of her wardrobe, remembering buying them in the scout shop with Pete when he and BC decided to sleep in Trisha's garden for BC's birthday. They'd come in after an hour because it was cold.

She got Dub's funeral coat out of his cupboard. Her neat black coat was still in the plastic wrap from the dry cleaner's and she folded it over her arm for Terry's memorial service tomorrow. From the hall cupboard she brought out a torch and the round bowl of an old tin barbecue.

Laden, she stood in the hallway and looked back at the records scattered on the floor, at Terry's silver trunk sitting on its lid, at the general mayhem he had caused to her perfect little house, and the feeling she got was how angry the ned was, how angry and frightened.

III

The road was quieter than it had been during the day but still some drivers careered around corners as if they were meeting a dare. On long stretches of dark road pin-prick lights would appear behind them, filling the mirror a few minutes later, blinding her until she slowed to the side and let them pass.

Dub put the radio on to a pop station and Callum seemed to go into a trance, gazing out of the window at the moonlit countryside without seeing, his eyes steady during the whole course of a song. He didn't speak unless he was spoken to, she noticed, and it made her feel sorry for him. One day they might talk to each other, a long time in the future, and he might tell her what had happened to him in prison.

She couldn't quite remember where the turning for the house was so she slowed when she saw familiar hills, irritating a small car on the road behind her. The driver hooted at her to hurry up and Callum turned and looked out of the window. He said it was a really old guy who could hardly see over the steering wheel and he and Dub laughed at her for being so cautious.

She saw the turning up ahead, indicated carefully and took it, the impatient pensioner behind giving her a farewell-and-fuck-you toot on his horn as he passed behind them, making them all smile. When his lights had disappeared all they had to see by were their own headlights. The grass on the driveway had been flattened by Merki's car but in the dark it seemed deeper and more impenetrable.

She drove on as far as she dared, realizing once they got out that she was much further into the drive than Merki had gone. In the harsh moonlight the cottage was forlorn and ramshackle. They could almost smell the damp from outside.

Dub and Callum were unenthusiastic but she'd stopped at a garage and bought some bread and butter, some cans of juice, firelighters and smoke-free coal and promised them a fire when they got inside. Back at the house she'd had the idea that they might be able to use the old barbecue as a grate but it seemed a bit stupid now.

They carried the stuff around the back and Dub tried the kitchen door. It was locked so he used a penknife to pick around the lock and the wood crumbled away easily. Chipping at it, he managed to expose the lock and push it out of its nest. He swung the door open.

The sweet-sour smell of mildew hung in the air and a

frantic scuttling marked the exit of a brood of mice into the other room. Callum didn't mind but Dub looked around distastefully at the buckled lino floor and the mouse droppings on the worktop. He was quite meticulous in their house, wouldn't use the bath unless it had been cleaned and was always throwing things out of the fridge because they had reached their sell-by date.

The room was empty of personal effects, but otherwise it looked as if someone had just walked out. Ten years of grey dust encrusted the elaborate Victorian cast-iron range in the inglenook, the oven doors all firmly shut, lids down on the cook plates. The black stovepipe at the back had collapsed and slouched crazily against the inside of the chimney. She had seen the pine dresser through the window during the day but not the feet swollen and rotting with moisture. A Formica table was pushed back against a wall, a matching chair on either side, backs to the wall. The sink under the window was basic, a white ceramic Belfast box with a shelf on the right-hand side, serving as a draining board. The cottage looked as if the family had spent their savings a generation ago, and this was the dwindled remains of a poorly managed natural advantage.

Dub stood stiffly by the door, his eyes flickering around the room, finding a thousand things to complain about but saying nothing. Callum asked his permission to go and look in the front room, which they both thought was weird but neither of them said so.

'Sure,' said Dub and Callum went off through the door, stepping carefully over the wobbly floor. He shouted back to them that it was darker in there, the mice were in the skirting, he could see a baby mouse. Dub shuddered.

She put the barbecue on top of the range, put four fire-starter bricks in the bottom and coals on the top, touching a match to the greasy bit of white peeking out of the coals. Orange light filled the room, highlighting all its shortcomings, and Dub made a frightened face.

Paddy smiled at him. 'If you can't handle it we can sleep in the car.'

'Nope. I'm fine. It's fine.'

She wanted to touch him again. Callum was in the other room so she slid over to him. 'There's only two sleeping bags. We'll have to share. Is that OK?'

He looked around the floor. 'But where?'

No part of the floor was any cleaner than anywhere else. She suggested seeing if they could find a broom and he liked that.

They found Callum in the front room, lifting the lid on the sloping piano. He tried a key but found it dead, tried the next and the next and the next until a faint twang came from inside the piano's belly.

Seen from the inside, the room was a good size. There was no fireplace but a fat pot-bellied stove sat at an angle in the corner. One of its thin legs had sunk into the carpet, ripping a hole and pulling the chimney pipe from its shoring in the wall behind.

Dub held back at the door to the kitchen. 'Smells revolting in here.'

Paddy wanted to point out that it was pretty though, the windows were nice, and then she wondered why she was trying to sell it to him. It didn't matter if he liked it or not. They were only staying a night.

The other rooms were in no better state. A rudimentary bathroom had a blue plastic toilet with a horribly stained dry bowl. The window was broken and leaves had gathered on the floor and in the bath, mulching through the years. Ragged spider webs coated the break in the window.

Two bedrooms, both small, one with a fireplace and a dead bird in the grate. There was no broom.

It was a relief to get back to the civilized kitchen, where the smell of damp was tempered by the warmth of the barbecue fire.

Dub said he didn't think he would be able to sleep at all in here because it was so dirty. Callum took the cardboard box down from the dresser, shook it to make sure nothing was hiding in there, flattened it, and used the edge to brush part of the floor clean for Dub's head.

Paddy watched him, bent double in the flickering light, scratching at the floor to clear a space for someone he barely knew, enjoying the roughness of everything, adapting to his new life and not at all bitter, and she found herself thinking that if Pete had lived through what Callum had and was like this on the other side, she'd be quite proud of him.

Dub thanked him.

Callum unfurled the sleeping bags and sat down in his, zipping it up to his neck, expertly rolling his jumper into a small cylinder to make a pillow. He lay down with his hands behind his head, shut his eyes and became still almost immediately.

Dub and Paddy sat up, drinking a can of juice in silence to let Callum sleep, passing it back and forth. Paddy lit a cigarette and Dub gave her a look that suggested she was adding to the smell in the kitchen.

'I like them,' she whispered.

Callum's leg stirred in the dark. He wasn't asleep at all. She looked over and saw that he was smiling in the dark. He'd misheard her. He thought she'd said, 'I like him.' And she was glad.

Fully clothed, they stood up and tried to negotiate two people in one sleeping bag. They unzipped it and laid it out on the floor, putting the opening in the space Callum had cleared for them. Paddy lay down, Dub lay next to her and they had to cling to each other to do the zip up.

She looked up at the warm orange light rippling across the ceiling, felt Dub's heart racing beneath her hand and fell asleep smiling.

28

The Darkness in Suburbia

Martin McBree looked back up to the dark windows of Paddy's flat in Lansdowne Crescent. It hadn't been hard to get the door open, it was only propped shut and when he got in he realized why: ransacked, the beds pissed on. No one was coming back here tonight. She was lost to him.

Back in the car, he lit a cigarette and started the engine. There was nothing for it but to go to option two. The nasty option. He had a grandson that age.

He pulled out of the crescent and made his way to the broad Great Western Road. It was three in the morning and very quiet. Taxis and the odd night bus sped along the straight road, making use of the clear stretch ahead of them.

He parked carefully in the street, reversing neatly into a space between two cars, nudging tentatively backwards and forwards until he was equidistant between the two. The first rule of a lightning strike: attract no attention.

He opened the car door and threw his cigarette end into the street, stepping out after it, the toe of his shoe crushing the scarlet tip against the tarmac. A double-decker night bus sailed past him, speeding down the incline of the hill. In the cold white cabin light the lone passenger's pasty face looked drained and ill, staring blindly out into the dark, seeing nothing but his own reflection in the glass.

McBree hated Glasgow. He hated the plump women with their rasping accents, the aggressive undertone of the men in bars, the chatty shopkeepers who asked personal questions. New York wasn't like that. In New York they told you about themselves, the women were handsome, the accent exotic and mellifluous. He smiled at the thought of New York, recalled the warm evenings and the smell of car fumes mingling with street food, being able to drink in bars without a soul raising the subject of politics.

In New York he changed how he dressed. Val asked him about it when he came home, said he looked cheap in his print shirts and loafers. She hated change. If she had her way they'd take the kids and go and live in the parish house with the gnarly old priests, but Martin had seen another life out there, a life devoid of the Church or the struggle, where a man could just be.

He smiled as he stepped on to the pavement. New York. Everything was brighter then and it wasn't even very long ago. Over the cusp of the hill came an old man in a deer-stalker hat and overcoat, dragging an elderly King Charles spaniel out for a stroll in the middle of the night. Incontinent dog or insomniac owner. Martin sank his hands into his pockets, keeping his head down, pretending to feel for house keys as he walked past the old man.

'Come on,' the old man muttered, attentive to his charge. He looked up to McBree, keen to engage with the only other soul in the street at that hour, but McBree kept his head down, frowning, preoccupied, a man on his way home. He strode on to the entrance to the estate.

In keeping with his training, he kept his eyes on the road in front of him, not glancing around. People who belong in a place don't swivel their heads like lost tourists. In a familiar environment no one looks around. People walk blindly, thinking; most let their faces drop into a half-scowl.

The road surface changed at the mouth of the estate, from the patched tarmac on the old main road to yellow brick, set in a hound's-tooth pattern, with matching slab pavements and an orange lip of bricks separating them. It was a new estate. The bricks had not yet had the time to settle into the ground and become irregular, no corners jagging upwards to trip the toe or wobbly slabs with secret puddles underneath to splash the shin. It was pristine.

He allowed himself an orientating glance upward. The map of the shallow streets was pretty clear but it was always possible to follow a pavement to the wrong corner, especially when it all looked the same. The houses were small and regular, expensive still because they were in a posh area but unremarkable none the less. The cars parked in the driveway showed the real income: big foreign cars, a sports car, all sitting next to freshly laid lawns living out their first summer. By next year the care of the owners would tell. The lawns wouldn't be uniform then; some would flourish, others would die back to dandelions and alopecia patches.

The roads were ablaze. Yellow street lights were dotted along the yellow pavement, their bulbs new, placed so that each pool of brightness formed a Venn-diagram overlap with the next. The houses had porch lights that remained on even when all the lights in the house were off. It was three in the morning and the place was bright as day.

A problem with new estates, and he had come across this before in Poleglass, was that they had no dark back alleys to skirt through and wait in. Here the houses had small rear gardens backing on to other small gardens, and nothing between them but a wooden fence. The back wasn't an option.

He came up to the house and saw a shiny black Merc

sitting in the driveway, glinting under the porch light. All the windows were dark.

Without looking up or slowing his stride, McBree scanned the house. No alarm box blinking a warning. Front door, plastic, big window into front room, curtains open, garage on the other side. Second floor, small window, bathroom or bedroom, big window master bedroom. New developers liked to squeeze en suites into cupboards in these things, just for the spec in the estate agent's window, so a good bit of the second floor would be taken up with that room. There was a second bedroom though, he knew that. The guy wouldn't have a Merc in the driveway and make his kid sleep on the floor when he came for a visit.

A TV comedian. McBree had watched the show last week, to see the face, weigh the guy in. Not funny but the guy seemed angry and looked tall, six foot one or so, unless everyone else in the show was very small. It was hard to guess. Ex-policeman. It would be a pleasure.

Without a dip in his stride he walked down the driveway and cut off to the side of the house, round the corner where the empty bins were. He stopped. A deep velvet blackness enveloped him. He let his face relax and pulled his latex gloves on. He looked up at the side wall of the house next door. No lights on, and only one small window on each house, high up, the neighbours' netted, the target clear but dark. He stepped back against the dividing fence and looked more carefully. Clear but even in the darkness he could see the outline of bottles neatly regimented, shoulders to the glass. Main bathroom. The small window at the front was the second bedroom.

A high slatted fence ran between the properties and there was a gate into the back yard, locked with an old-fashioned black bolt lock. He fingered it and smiled. It wouldn't have kept a chicken out.

Reaching into his pocket, he felt for his old skeleton key, the cold, firm shank sitting comfortably in his hand. It was a while since he'd used it. Most locks were more complex now. He spat on the bit, rubbing the saliva over the teeth to silence the entry into the lock, and tried it. The lock sprang back with a loud, unaccustomed crunch. McBree stood perfectly still for a moment, listening for movement. Nothing. He spat silently on to his fingertips and rubbed the exposed hinges on the gate, trying it tentatively at first until he was sure it made nothing louder than a mild creak. Pausing only to pull his balaclava on, he adjusted the eye holes and slid through the gate into the garden.

A patch of grass surrounded by the high fence, a glass conservatory, shallow, leading into a kitchen. A television on standby sat on a table, the lone red eye lighting the floor in front of it. The place looked tidy, no clothes or newspapers left on the floor or counter tops, which was good: it was unlikely there would be any debris lying around to trip over. Not like the photographer's house. Shit everywhere. Val would have had a fit if she'd seen that. She liked the house perfect. It was her one sphere of control. Her mother had been the same.

The back door was plastic like the front but windowed, a long mottled strip of glass in a PVC frame. He looked at the lock, standing close in so that his shadow would blend in with the line of the house if anyone looked. It was complicated, a bolt and a Yale, a lot of work.

He turned back to the conservatory. A ground-level glass panel could be cut and slipped out of the frame easily enough and he would fit in sideways. He paused, half listening for noise inside and out, but really savouring the moment. These quiet times, when his mind was fully occupied with an immediate problem, when his hot breath gathered as droplets of moisture inside his mask, he was content.

He wanted a cigarette. He always wanted a cigarette. Sometimes while he was actually smoking he craved a cigarette.

He took the penknife from his pocket, checked carefully with his finger that the blade was exposed and spat a long line of saliva down the glass. He'd left saliva at a scene before but he was the most common blood group and the police would be steered away from him even if they spotted it. The blade scratched quietly down then across, and he pushed with his fingertips, starting when one edge of the glass snapped and the muffled crack echoed across the lawn. No movement.

Taking hold of the edge, he pulled first one section out, then the next and the last. Just wide enough. He squared his shoulders to the hole and wriggled in easily, landing on the cold floor like a snake shedding its skin.

He stood up, looked around, padded silently through the kitchen to the hallway – carpeted, better. He turned the locks on the front door, snibbing them so that both would be ready for a quick exit, and watched the door in case it fell open. Fine.

Upstairs, padding the steep carpeted steps, moss green, to the landing. Stop. Breathing behind one door, the master bedroom, a man snoring in a light regular whistle. The bathroom to the side, where the window looked over the alley. The door to the second bedroom straight ahead.

Stop.

Nausea. Confused images. His own grandson sleeping over on New Year's Eve, nuzzled up to Val on the settee, his cheek resting on her thigh, and McBree creeping through the dark of a house to harm him.

Bullshit.

He stepped forward, aware of the brush of his sole on the fibres of the carpet, the rubber of his gloves catching on the landing banister as he trailed his fingers. He was facing the boy's bedroom door, could sense the living presence on the other side. He did a quick mental rehearsal: open the door, step in, find the torso, knife into left side, straight for the heart. He had a point to make. Every drop of blood, every gut-churning task – they were all necessary. But McBree's heart weighed like a stone in his chest. The justifications weren't working tonight. A child. A healthy child. Asleep, trusting the world to mind him.

He remembered his O level Shakespeare. Macbeth. Losing it. 'I am in blood stepped in so far that returning were as tedious as going over.' Something like that. Go. Just go.

His fight hand circled the handle of the blade. His left took hold of the door handle, his wrist moving awkwardly, pressed it down, releasing the catch.

'What are you doing here?'

McBree spun on his heel. He hadn't even heard footsteps, hadn't heard a door open, no padding feet or steadying hand brush a wall. A woman, good-looking, blonde hair pillow-blustered, eyes heavy with sleep, standing in the doorway to the master bedroom in a long white nightie, the ties at the neck lying open, exposing the curve of her breasts. He lunged with the knife but she fell back into the room and he only nicked her skin, carving a wide crescent on her left breast. She fell to the floor, scrambling backwards on all fours like a spider, blood gushing, panting and whimpering at the same time.

The man snoring in the bed sat up very suddenly, threw the duvet off and got to his feet, staggering sideways, facing the wrong way. He was six foot two, three maybe, and broad, much bigger than McBree.

McBree's combat-hardened mind gave him two options: kill them all, stage-lit like a break-in, or run.

The man stumbled to where he had begun as the woman rolled her head back to let out a ripe, ear-splitting scream.

McBree bolted down the stairs, threw open the door, and was gone.

29

Very Terry

I

It felt like the first day of school. Everyone was wearing black and looking neat and scrubbed. Men she hadn't seen looking clean in years were standing around in groups, hair smeared flat, dressed in whatever formal clothing they could find, chatting on the forecourt of the cathedral.

There was Merki and Keck and Bunty and his Monkey. All of the *Standard* guys were there, none of whom could possibly have known Terry more than in passing. McGrade, the manager from the Press Bar, was there, together with his tiny, bearded sidekick, which meant the bar was shut for the first time in living memory. Sean was standing with the drivers and gave her a wink and turned away.

McVie had called everyone in the business and they had all come because it was about more than Terry Hewitt: it was a celebration of who they were. Terry would have loved it.

Paddy's eyes prickled. Tipping her head back to stop her mascara running, she looked up at the Gothic spires of the cathedral and the green Necropolis hill beyond, Victorian death monuments choked with ivy. She was getting Pete withdrawals, a tightening in her stomach because she hadn't spoken to him before he went to school, didn't know what he'd eaten or if he'd slept at all. She'd call Burns after the ceremony and ask Sandra what he'd had. At least she knew how to make toast.

Glasgow Cathedral dated largely from the end of the thirteenth century. It was saved from destruction during the Reformation when a gang of the city's tradesmen armed themselves and fought off a mob of treasure-seekers in a pitched battle. The squat building was blackened during the Industrial Revolution and sat at the top of the High Street like a fat toad draped in a mourning mantilla.

McVie was greeting mourners like a maitre d', working the crowd, certain that the *Mail on Sunday* would be mentioned in all the coverage. He spotted Paddy and Dub coming towards him, did a spot check of her clothes and saw she was dressed smartly.

'You're up first then,' he said. 'Set the right tone.'

'But I haven't got anything prepared.'

He saw the panic in her eyes. 'Just do it off the cuff. Since when could you not talk? Did you see Merki's exclusive?'

'Where did he get that from?'

It was a rhetorical question but McVie looked irritated. 'The fuck should I know?' He slipped away to talk to someone else.

A hand landed hard on her shoulder and she turned to see Billy, her first-ever driver, standing behind her, grinning. Billy had beefed up in the intervening years. He had left the *News* after a firebomb attack on her car, using the payout to buy a burger van so he could continue working nights. His hands were badly scarred, the skin smooth and watered; the little finger of one hand had been removed after a graft didn't take. He'd had long hair then but it was shaved now, tight into the wood, like Terry's when she first knew him. His wife, Agnes, was at his side, as warm as a tank. She looked away as they greeted each other with kisses and slaps to the arm.

'And is this your young man?' asked Billy of Dub.

'Oh no, this is Dub McKenzie. D'ye not remember Dub?'

Billy said he didn't, so they told him about Dub's time as a copy boy at the *News*, gave dates and outlined a couple of stories: Dub getting caught hiding in a café when he was supposed to be death-knocking a widow, Dub stapling prawns to the underside of an editor's desk before he left. Billy still didn't remember but pretended to and that did well enough.

Paddy and Dub moved away.

'Why are we a secret?' asked Paddy under her breath.

'I can't remember,' said Dub, pretending he hadn't seen Keck waving to him. 'Let's body-swerve that tit for a start. Will Callum be all right out there on his own, do you think?'

They had left him back at the cottage with three cans of juice and a loaf of bread, promising to come back later or send Sean. He was happy to stay there, said he had never been to the countryside and wanted to know what all the trees were.

'Not gossiping, dears? Naughty, naughty.' It was Farquarson, Paddy's first-ever boss, the last editor any of them had known who stood up to the board for them. Paddy had hero-worshipped Farquarson, who'd taken an interest in her, given her writing assignments when she wasn't due them. He had aged badly since she last saw him. He was wearing a trilby hat but she could still see that his hair had thinned. His ears were long, drooping, the skin loose where they were attached to his skull, and his face was livered and jowly.

He pointed at Paddy, couldn't locate her name and then it occurred to him. 'Monihan!'

Paddy grinned at him. 'Meehan, you mad old bastard.'

McVie was persuading everyone inside and nipped her elbow, muttering, 'You're next to me at the front.' Then he turned to greet Farquarson. 'You look a hundred years old.'

McVie didn't like Farquarson. He had languished on night shift under him and only got out of it by convincing a grieving mother to let him document her son's death from a heroin overdose.

She was worried that McVie was picking on a faded old man but Farquarson answered, 'And I hear you're a nancy now.'

Insults met and meted, everyone settled into the company and headed towards the chapel doors.

A big chauffeur-driven car pulled up suddenly at the kerb. They watched as the driver leaped out and ran round the car to open the door. Out stepped Random Damage, the short, overbearing editor who had turned the *News* from a dull-as-dust broadsheet into a tabloid success. He was dressed in a beautifully cut grey suit and was carrying a small black box. Paddy realized it was a portable telephone. Why Damage would need a telephone at a memorial service was obvious to anyone who knew him: he was obsessed with image and wanted the world to know he had a portable telephone. Second out of the car was his slim, six-foot-tall wife, who straightened her black velvet overcoat and stood, willowy, at his side. Paddy heard that he had left the press to run his wife's chain of luxury hotels.

'Is that a walkie-talkie?' asked Farquarson.

Damage held it up. 'Portable telephone.'

McVie looked sullen. 'Not that portable, though, is it?'

'Can you only phone other portable telephones with it?' asked Paddy.

Damage laughed at her. 'No. You can telephone any other phone. Soon they'll have faxes on them as well. That's the new thing.'

'And you'll have to lug tons of paper around,' said McVie, jealous and not making a good job of hiding it.

Paddy reached out. 'Can I have a go? I need to make a two-minute call.'

'Be my guest.'

'Fucking hurry up,' said McVie.

Paddy dialled Burns's number.

'Hello?' Burns sounded a long way away. The line crackled and spat.

'Oh, hi, George.' She was shouting, her voice lost in the big open space, so she turned away from the crowd of people and shouted into the street. 'Just wondered if Pete got away to school OK?'

Burns was quiet.

A fist tightened around Paddy's heart. 'What?'

'Paddy, Pete—'

'What? Is he ill? Is he there?'

'He's here, he's fine but the house is full of policemen. We got broken into last night. Sandra went to the loo at three in the morning and found a guy on the landing heading into Pete's bedroom with a knife.'

'Fuck!'

'Wearing a balaclava. He cut Sandra's tit open and ran away but he was definitely headed for Pete.'

'I'm coming now.'

'No, look, the house is full of CID and they're taking us to the station so they can tape our interviews. Come later. Come and get us at Pitt Street.'

'How's Pete?'

'I'll put you on.' Burns opened a door and called Pete.

Her son's tinny voice came on, distorted, sounding far away and electronic. 'Mum? We got burgled! A man came in in the night and tried to steal Sandra's jewellery.' Paddy fought back choking tears, kicking at the ground, nodding. 'Gosh. That's mad. Are you OK?'

'It's exciting. He broke a window and climbed in.'

'I need that back now.' Damage was standing next to her, holding his hand out to the phone, deliberately ignoring the tears in her eyes and her evident panic.

'Son, Dad's going to take you to the police station, won't that be something?'

'I can see where he used to work. He knows *everybody*.'

'Come on,' shouted McVie, waving her over.

Damage had circled her and was in her face. 'The battery'll run out. Give it to me.'

'I'll come and see you this afternoon, darlin', OK?'

'Mum, a man said he's going to show me the *cells*.'

'Meehan, give it.' Damage lunged forward to grab the phone but she clung on.

'I love you, son.'

But Pete had hung up.

Damage was saying something about the battery life. McVie came over and took her elbow, dragging her towards the church.

McBree had come for Pete, with a knife. She felt very cold, her breathing deepened, every muscle in her body was loading itself with oxygen, ready to coil and spring. She felt as if she could outstare the sun.

McVie dragged her into the cathedral. The internal walls were as black and forbidding as the facade of the church but it opened up to an arched oak ceiling and tall needled windows, jewelled with blue and red glass. McVie had gone to a lot of trouble. Big bouquets of lilies and white chrysanthemums, strung with red and blue ribbons, were hanging on both sides of the aisle with a giant wreath in white, red and blue sitting at the base of the altar. They were the colours of Ayr United, Terry's football team.

Feeling nothing but cold blind anger, Paddy followed McVie into the front pew. Ben, his precious, queeny boyfriend, was waiting for them. McVie would never admit to Ben, but here he was in plain sight, standing at the front of the massed mob of the Glasgow journalistic mafia. In a show of support, Paddy leaned over and kissed Ben's proffered cheek, settling back in the pew and realizing that her lips were coated in face powder.

A minister came in and everyone stood up. The organ struck up a short tune, drowning out the sound of the singing, which was very ragged and rambling. A minister talked for a bit about life and death and why it was a shame, but not really, because of Jesus, and then, without warning, he stepped aside and looked at McVie, who looked at Paddy. Ben looked at Paddy. Everyone in the church looked at Paddy.

She wanted to drop her head back and scream but instead stepped out into the aisle, began to genuflect and then remembered it was a Protestant cathedral, getting a laugh when she bolted upright again.

She didn't even know where to stand, but the minister held his hand out and guided her up the winding staircase to the pulpit.

The wooden platform groaned beneath her feet as she looked out at the expectant faces. Shug Grant, Keck, JT, Merki, McVie, a hundred and fifty men, some arseholes, some good souls, most both depending on the occasion.

She leaned into the microphone.

'Terry Hewitt was a friend of mine.' The words echoed around the hollow church.

It felt strange to say his name, to think of anything but Pete. He was safe at the moment and this was for Terry. Terry. Terry who wasn't at all who she'd thought he was. He was an ordinary man who'd done his best with a lot of bad luck. But she'd made him into a paragon and then hated him for not living up to it. She couldn't talk about that Terry, the real Terry, who came from a small home and belonged nowhere. She started again.

'Terry Hewitt was my hero. I was a copy boy at the *Daily News* and he was a junior reporter. He had a leather jacket.' That got another laugh. 'He lived alone.' If anyone didn't already know she came from a big Catholic family the aborted genuflection had told them, and they laughed at that too. 'I didn't know then why he lived alone, just that his parents had died in a car crash. He told me but you don't really hear those things when you're young. They died thirty yards from the house and Terry was the first on the scene. He was seventeen.' The pathos of the moment overwhelmed her. She paused, swallowing hard, getting a grip. 'We spent a lot of time together when we were starting out. Well, most of you know,' she looked up again, 'we went out together. But all we talked about was our work, what we wanted to do in our work, and Terry was going to change the world.'

She looked down and saw Shug Grant whispering to the man next to him. They both sniggered and avoided looking at her. A sexual slur about her, not thinking about Terry or who he was or what he meant his life to be, just there because everyone else was, and there would be drink afterwards.

'Some of us are here because we loved Terry. Some of us are here because our editors said we could get the morning off.' A nervous titter rolled around the church. They could see she was looking stern, staring down at Shug. She was famous for losing her temper and going beyond what was appropriate, and they could see that she was angry. 'But I'm here because of what Terry represented to me. He worked on a bigger scale than most of us here. He went to war zones, conflict zones, did hard reporting on a world stage.'

Paddy could sense the atmosphere plummeting. She knew she should tell a funny story, make herself popular by lightening the mood, but all she could see was Terry as a young man standing at the end of his parents' driveway, looking into the fireball engulfing their car. And Pete, asleep in a bed she had never seen, with a bad man outside the door and herself miles away.

The security forces would blanket the whole episode with rumours and dripfeeds to hungry journos like Merki. McBree would come for Pete again and next time he'd hurt her son, to hurt her. The best she could do, what Terry would have done, was draw the fire to herself. She began to weep but her voice remained steady.

'Terry was killed over a book he was writing, executed on a dark road late at night, shot in the back of the head. The official word is he was mugged. If you believe that, if this audience believes that, then journalism is dead. He was killed by a man called Martin McBree, a high-ranking Republican. Don't let anyone tell you differently.' A ripple of consternation feathered the crowd awake. Merki sat up and attempted a casual laugh but no one looked at him.

Paddy's voice weakened. She leaned into the microphone to be heard. 'Terry would have stood here and said that. He made me proud to be a hack. He was the best of us.'

She stepped away from the lectern, crying, ashamed that it wasn't really for Terry, and walked back to her seat to a hesitant round of applause.

A guy in a khaki jacket got up from the pew behind, carrying copious notes, and took her place.

McVie leaned over to her, talking out of the side of his mouth. 'What the fuck was all that about? Cheer us all up, why don't you.'

She elbowed him gently in the ribs.

'No,' he whispered, handing her his handkerchief. 'It was good. Really good. Very Terry.'

The khaki man had come from London to speak. His accent was posh and public school, which immediately made everyone hate him. He claimed to be a great friend of Terry's. Referring back to Paddy's speech, he implicated himself on a grander world stage, which compounded the audience's prejudices. Then he told a couple of stories about Terry and himself at significant world events, in Gaza, then in Lebanon, the point of which seemed to be that he was there, and filed his copy before Terry, who had trouble getting things down on paper. He made a horrible allusion to Terry having sex with a fat woman whose children were waiting in the next room. He slunk off to a silence an audience at the Glasgow Empire would have thought harsh.

Two or three other local journalists tried their hand, one to talk about Terry's capacity for drink, another to tell a story about them investigating corruption at a greyhound track and trying to get a urine sample from a dog, which went down well.

Last up was McVie. He slid past Paddy and took his time getting up there, pausing to rest a hand on either side of the lectern and look down his nose at the crowd, letting them know he was in charge.

It was an after-dinner speech but no worse for that. He made some sweeping statements about the nature of journalism, told three perfect stories about quips Terry had made, none of them hugely funny, but they were well delivered and stormed with the audience, who were ripe for a laugh.

He finished on a rousing note: sales were dropping across the board, Terry Hewitt might well be remembered as the last of a dying breed. No one had funding for foreign journalists now and papers were in danger of turning into nothing but daily bingo games and holiday giveaways. It was up to them to make sure that didn't happen through their dedication and commitment. Then he invited everyone back to McGrade's for a toast.

Paddy wondered how commitment could trump a lack of funding but no one else seemed to. The crowd rose for him, applauding him for organizing the event and bringing his boyfriend as much as for his call to arms.

McVie got back to his seat. The organ struck a note and the cathedral emptied as suddenly as a toilet flushing.

But Paddy, McVie and Ben lingered, looking at the Ayr United wreath at the base of the altar.

When the clatter of feet behind them died down Paddy whispered to McVie, 'How can dedication stop the decline?'

McVie sighed and looked down at his legs as they stretched out in front of him, flexing his ankles. 'It can't,' he said. 'Nothing can.'

II

Paddy knew that if she went roaring over to Pitt Street and demanded to see Pete before his tour of the cells he'd know something scary was happening, that the man in his father's house had been there for him, not for Sandra's jewellery. So she and Dub went to the Press Bar.

McVie had put three hundred quid behind the bar and ordered McGrade to line up whisky shots all along it, just to start the drinking off on a nice, mental note. Most of the attendees were Protestant and had never been to a wake. They didn't understand that the idea was to drink until the misery evaporated and tell stories about the dead person, remember them as a companion, celebrate their life. All they knew was the tradition was Irish so they'd better get hammered and fight each other. And so they did.

By the time Paddy nudged the car into a far corner of the full *Daily News* car park the noise from the bar was deafening and the crowd had spilled out into the street. She stood next to Dub, looking at the shabby brown-tiled exterior, at the men smoking on the step outside and the general hubbub and decided, fuck it, they'd go and wait in the lobby at Pitt Street until a decent amount of time had passed. At least they'd be near Pete then. Paddy was pulling out of the dusty car park when she saw the khaki man crossing the road in front of her, heading towards the bar.

She wound down her window and shouted over to him but he didn't hear her, just kept his head down and sidled through the crowd at the door.

Dub nudged her. 'Go on after him. I'll park.'

'Sure?'

'Go on. I'll park the car and wait.'

The khaki man was at the bar when she got in, the only person there with no one to talk to, standing uncertainly with a whisky shot in his hand as the choppy crowd drank their way to gale force. She kept her head down and made for him.

'Hello,' she said, refusing a whisky from McGrade.

'Oh, hello.' He gave her a look as if she'd interrupted something terribly important. 'You were the first speaker, weren't you? Very good. Moving. Great speakers, the Scots.'

'Thanks. So you knew Terry in Lebanon?'

'Yeah, yeah.' He saw that she wanted him to elaborate but misunderstood and gave her a potted history of his own career, sipping at his whisky shot as if it was sherry. He was terribly clever, seemed to be the gist of it, cleverer than other people. He named a couple of other Middle Eastern correspondents, big national names, and told her why they were wrong and foolish.

'But to get back to Terry. What was he doing there?'

Terry had been sent to Lebanon by the national editor when the usual guy's wife was having a baby. But he hated it, said it was impossible to write up a Lebanese bus timetable without having a first in history. Khaki Man paused there, nodding a heavy prompt that suggested he did have a first in history, if only she would ask.

She pulled a sheet of paper out of her pocket and unfolded it carefully on the bar. The toner was crumbling at the folds but McBree's face was still recognizable. Did you ever meet this guy?'

'Martin McBree? Yes, he was in the Lebanon, everyone knows that.'

'Did Terry ever meet him?'

'Sure. Everyone did. We all did. He was at a dinner organized by a Reuters agency man from Hong Kong. *Samkeh harrah*. Very good.'

'Sammy Hurrah, is that the guy's name?'

He smirked. 'No. It's a Lebanese dish.'

'Was Terry at the dinner too?'

'Did he and McBree have a fight or anything?'

'No.'

Khaki's absolute certainty that there was never once a jostle at a urinal or an argument over a bowl of peanuts on a bar was getting on Paddy's nerves. 'How can you be sure?'

'McBree was much more interested in established Middle Eastern correspondents. He talked to me for over half an hour. Was very interested in my analysis of the Camp Wars. Terry really struggled to understand the interests of the different factions out there, he couldn't—'

'For fucksake, I'm not asking whether Terry was more important than you, I'm asking if he ever fought with McBree.'

Khaki sipped at his whisky again, an insult to a host in Scotland. He rolled the microscopic portion around the back of his throat before swallowing and his mouth stayed puckered when he spoke. 'Young lady, you'll find politeness and a pleasant manner will get you further—'

She was spluttering angry, 'Oh, shut up, you utter cock.'

McGrade grinned at her from behind the bar. He reached over, handing her a brimming whisky shot and she downed it in one, slammed the glass on the bar and gave Khaki Man a parting piece of advice.

'You keep talking like an arsehole and you'll leave this bar with a sore face.'

She heard later that he flew back to London with a splint on his nose and an arm in plaster.

30

Slip of the Knife

I

The Pitt Street reception area was busy. Police officers, uniformed and plain-clothed, bustled by, all with the same military-precision haircut and shoulders-back bearing. They greeted each other, waited for the lift, disappeared through doors behind reception or took the stairs, never pausing to consider Paddy and Dub, both in funeral clothes, both scruffy and frightened, waiting anxiously on the black leatherette chairs, sweating with the desire to see their boy.

The receptionist was a young man this time, officious and cold, anticipating their annoyance by deadening his eye every time they asked when the questioning would be over, when would they be able to see Pete. Burns was still being questioned. Pete and Sandra had been taken for a tour of one of the stations nearby but Paddy and Dub needed Burns's say-so before the police could let them see him.

Paddy sat back, twitchy and sickened, thinking that it was a good thing really: she might have been an agent for McBree, they were keeping her boy safe.

Resting her head on the back of the chair, staring up at the stained polystyrene ceiling tiles, she tried to clear her mind. It had been a declaration of war. She had named McBree at the memorial service and some of the journalists who had been there would pick up on it. She'd given them his name, they'd make calls, he'd hear about it. He had the prints and the negatives but Knox would have told him that she had been brandishing photocopies. He had to come for her now. If he didn't get the last few copies the IRA would kill him for his betrayal.

What she couldn't understand was why McBree had turned. He was a lifelong Republican, it was his devotion and his career. He was a hero. It must have been his whole identity. The clippings said a bomb had gone off near his family home while he was in New York, she remembered. He'd left his wife and family to deal with the consequences of his commitment to a cause, while at the same time he took money and protection from the enemy. She didn't know what the security services had over him but it must have been compelling. Blackmail was usually about sex or money.

McBree and Paddy came from the same background. She knew that with rigid moral laws all it took was a stumble on the path, a slip of the knife, unrepented, to put a person on the outside for ever, looking in on their families and friends. Paddy herself had stumbled and slipped, scrabbling back but never quite making it. She'd spent most of her childhood on the outside looking in on that warm place. Eventually, when she was older, she had let herself career down the mountainside. It was a lonely journey, but when she came to the bottom she had found her own people in the newsroom, among friends like Dub.

She looked up at him. Dub was leaning on his knees, his back tense, head dropped forward and a big bony hand on his neck. She nudged him with her knee and he sat up and looked at her.

'This is taking fucking ages,' he said.

'He's safe.'

Not comforted, he shrugged a little and looked round at three policemen waiting at the lift doors. They were all out of uniform but tall and clipped. One wore a green wax coat, the other two suit jackets over slacks. Dub leaned back to mutter to her, 'Ye wonder how they ever manage to go undercover, don't ye? They look so polis-y you could cash them in.'

A bad suit stopped at the corner of her eye, pale blue, slightly crumpled skirt. Paddy turned to find the police-woman who'd interviewed her for Knox standing just inside the doors, looking at her, wary. Paddy nodded. 'Garrett.'

Garrett nodded back, hesitated and came over. 'Why are you here?'

Her abruptness made Dub snort indignantly but Paddy quite liked it about her. 'Waiting,' she said, copying Garrett's style. 'My son was attacked by McBree.' Garrett's eyes widened. 'He was staying at his daddy's and someone broke in and was interrupted trying to get into his bedroom with a knife.'

Garrett's eyes jerked up to a higher floor and back. 'ID parade?'

'Had a balaclava on. They haven't picked him up. Even if they had a photograph of him leaning over Pete with a knife between his teeth they wouldn't pick him up, would they?'

Garrett bit her bottom lip, her face as emotionless as Paddy remembered. 'Balaclava? So it might not be him?'

Paddy smiled miserably, shook her head and turned away.

Garrett persevered. 'There is a chance it might not be him.'

Paddy looked back at her. 'My son is five years old. He hasn't had time to make many enemies.' She looked away again. 'You're not going to help me, so fuck off.'

But Garrett lingered. Eventually she spoke, dropping her voice to a breathy growl: 'Fax it.'

Paddy looked up with renewed interest. She touched her fingertips to her handbag, showing she understood. Garrett nodded and walked past her, taking the stairs at a jog, her head down, ashamed.

'What was that last bit about?' asked Dub.

Paddy scratched her cheek as her eyes skirted the floor, thinking. 'Nothing,' she said. 'Nothing.'

A fax. It was less of a plan than a slap on the wrist afterwards. McBree'd come for her and the best move she could come up with was that she should be alone so no one else got hurt.

The receptionist called out for Mr McKenzie, telephone. Dub took the lobby floor in two enormous loping steps and grabbed the receiver from him. He smiled and turned back to her.

'Hello, wee man.'

II

They were led up one flight of stairs by a skinny young policeman with a lisp. He took them along a noisy corridor, through a set of doors marked 'interview rooms' and into a side room with more black chairs, an instant coffee machine and a dead plant.

He left them there, flicking his hand vaguely to the machine, telling them to help themselves if they had fifty pence.

A door opened out in the corridor. Paddy and Dub stood up, expecting Pete, but Burns peered in at them, looking like shit warmed up. He was flanked by a tall man in rolled-up shirt sleeves.

'That's her,' Burns said. 'She's his mum.'

Pete had been having a lovely time. He told them who he had met and where the cells were and how they smelled of pee with bleach in it, like the time Cabrini took her nappy off and weed in the cupboard and Mrs Ogilvy scrubbed it but made it worse. Like that. And he'd had a cake with raisins in it.

Paddy didn't want to alarm him with a terrified burst of tearful affection. She gave him a hug but didn't cling or cry, and let go so that Dub could say hello, but she couldn't get her hand to leave him. She cupped his head, held his shoulder, tried to take his hand, which he didn't like, even when they were crossing roads. He wriggled his fingers free but she couldn't bear not to touch him and contented herself with resting her hand on the back of his shoulder.

A woman officer had been assigned to look after him. She kept putting her hands between her knees and bending down to patronize him, but Pete ignored her, caught up in the excitement of being in a police station with real-life actual policemen.

Burns took a seat across from them, tried the coffee machine and lost his money. He had blue circles under his eyes and kept blinking slowly, telling them he'd had three hours' sleep and felt sick. Sandra couldn't bear the thought of going home. She had checked into a hotel. The most expensive in the city, Paddy noted, where the pop stars stayed when they came by on tour.

After a while Pete calmed down and sat on the floor playing with some leaflets about joining the police. Burns sagged in his chair and Dub leaned over and slapped his knee.

'Shouldn't you be recording that piece-of-shit show tonight?'

Burns looked up, eyes reddened and flashed him a filthy look.

Dub misunderstood. 'OK, OK, "that show". Better? Shouldn't you be recording it tonight?'

Burns blinked hard at the floor. 'Cancelled.'

'Hmm.' Dub tried not to smile. 'Rough.'

Burns sprang to life, sliding over to Dub's side and telling him that his manager had gone ahead and arranged a tour of the clubs without waiting for Burns to confirm and now half the gigs were sold out and his name was up everywhere.

Dub frowned at him. 'But you haven't signed the contract?'

'No, but I'll be letting everyone down if I don't do them.'

'Do you know what sort of backhander your manager's getting? Above the ten per cent?'

'Backhander?'

'If he's pushing it this hard he'll be getting a good few thou in cash, ten or twenty, you can guarantee.'

The thought hadn't occurred to Burns and he was furious. 'I'm only getting fifty-five gross.'

Dub reached forward with his foot and tucked it under Pete's leg, lifting it and rocking him, making him smile at the pamphlets. 'Flat rate? He didn't offer you a percentage of the door?'

Paddy watched them talking, looked at Pete reading and smiling, saw the patronizing WPC sitting across with her knees clamped together, head tilted at a saccharine angle as she watched Pete.

She looked at the back of Pete's head, at the perfect black whirl of hair at his crown. McBree didn't want Pete. He wanted her.

She took out her cigarettes, lighting one, sliding away from Pete when Dub gave her a warning look. She sat on the edge of the long row of chairs, looking back at them, inhaling bitter courage.

As inevitable as daffodils, McBree would come for her. He was trained, brutal and desperate. It was unwinnable.

A strange calm came over her as she looked at the little family group. If she died, the mortgage would be paid off by the insurance. Dub would keep Pete – he did most of the childcare anyway – and Burns would chip in when it suited him. And if all that broke down her mother would take him and his dream of living with BC full time would be realized.

Ash dropped from her cigarette on to the industrial-grey carpet and she rubbed it in with the tip of her shoe. Unwinnable.

IV

They were released into the baby-killing world with assurances from the police that it was a random incident, that they would do all they could, that it was probably some nut who had become obsessed with Burns because he/she had seen him on telly. Goodbye and good luck.

Useless, lazy bastards was the gist of Burns's rant on the pavement outside, as if it was only happening to him, as if Paddy wasn't standing in a shit storm waving out.

They stood in the afternoon sunshine in Pitt Street, Pete pulling at Paddy's arm as Burns related the traumas of the morning. More officers than necessary had tumbled into his house, all eager to have a look round; the incompetent forensics that failed to find as much as a fingerprint; it had taken thirty minutes to get an ambulance for Sandra, and then she had to get a taxi from the hospital over to the station to subject herself to questioning. They gave her a valium tablet at the casualty department and she wasn't used to it.

He suddenly turned his anger on Paddy. 'So what do we do now?'

'Well,' her hand was on Pete's shoulder and she felt very calm, 'you go to Sandra. Hide out for a bit. Stay in your hotel room. It'll all be settled in a couple of days.'

Burns glanced at Pete, censoring himself. 'What about the burglar?'

'That'll be sorted out.' She looked away, sudden self-pitying tears nipping her eyes. Afternoon buses floated past the end of the road. A cyclist zipped down the hill, red hair fluttering out behind her. People walked, friends in twos and threes, contented, enjoying the warm weather, looking for lunch before they had to head back to work.

'I'll sort it out.'

31

Phone Calls from Home

I

Pete had only ever been in Paddy's office once before, when he was one and a half, teething molars and refusing to sleep unless it was light. Her mother was at some dead friend's rosary with Caroline and BC and she'd had no option but to take him with her. It was late at night, at that quietest moment in the twenty-four-hour culture of the place, when she took Pete in to pick up a folder and some telephone messages from her pigeonhole. She hoped he would fall asleep in the car but he didn't; expected him to cry in the office but he didn't do that either. He sat on her hip, watching everything, smiling for everyone and pointing everywhere, shouting a string of consonants at a desk and dribbling on her shoulder.

The night came back to her as she pushed in through the double doors. She would love to hold Pete like that again, wrap her arms around him and have him reciprocate. She was his world then and he was still hers now.

The few journalists who hadn't stayed at Terry's party downstairs or passed out or gone home were at the desks, burrowing away. Only the secretaries sat up at the sight of the little boy standing in the door looking around with honest interest.

Two of them came over and made a fuss, told Paddy that he looked like her and asked Dub if he was the daddy. Pete smiled up at him until Dub said kind of, aye. Pete punched Dub's thigh, narrowly missing his balls, insisting that he wasn't his daddy, his daddy was his daddy, but smiling all the same.

Paddy led them over to a desk on the fringes of News with a big space behind it for Pete to play in, found him some paper and pencils and asked him to do some drawings of the police station with Dub while she worked.

She laid out the photocopies and Joan Forsyth's list of names and addresses in front of her. It was long but she crossed off all the men and called international enquiries to get telephone numbers for all the other addresses. The operator would only give her three at a time so she kept having to phone back until she had the full fourteen. Then she called again, because she was in the swing of it, and got three Irish numbers as well. None of the names on Forsyth's list sounded African or even West Indian so she began at the top of the list.

Two no answers and one reply, a man, said that the woman she was looking for, Fransy, was at 'woyk'. Call later.

'I'm trying to trace someone, it's quite urgent. I hope you don't mind me asking but is Fransy black?'

The man stalled. 'Who is this?'

'The woman I'm looking for is black. Is she black?'

'No, but I am.'

A yappy dog began to bark in the background.

'Right? But she's white?'

The dog gave a sudden yowl and the speaker came back on the phone. 'The fuck are you getting at?'

He sounded ready for a fight so she thanked him and hung up.

Two more calls and two more answers, both of whom

were offended when she asked them about the colour of their skin. Evidently, the question meant something over there that it didn't mean over here.

'Hello?'

'Can I speak to Karen, please?'

'Speaking.' Her voice was a sexy Southern-belle drawl. She sounded as if she was lying down, or at least walking around looking super in nice underwear.

'Karen, I wonder if you can help me. You had your photo taken this summer by a photographer—'

'Kevin? Sure, I have the form here, right in front of me. Sorry.' She didn't sound sorry. 'I'll sign and send it back.'

'Well, the thing is—'

'How is Kevin anyway? Is he coming back? Do you know Terence?'

Paddy touched her funeral skirt, thought about telling her and then realized it was far too long a story to go into. 'Fine. See, the thing is we don't know which photo is yours. I've offended a lot of people this morning by asking this, but are you black?'

Karen laughed. 'Well, sweetheart, I'm not surprised they were offended. It's a *issue* over here.'

'Right. But are you?'

'As a midnight river.'

They smiled at each other down the phone. 'Lovely,' said Paddy.

'I am that,' said Karen and let out a frank, dirty cackle that made Paddy want to meet her.

'You've got your hair in braids with yellow through them?'

'No,' she said sharply. 'Not any more.'

'But you did when the photo was taken?'

'Yeah. That was last year. No one does that any more.'

Odd clunks in the background and the sound of the

receiver being pinched between her shoulder and chin made Paddy think she was fixing breakfast.

'Karen, I'm sorry to be the one to tell you this ... Kevin died, that's why I'm chasing up his notes for him.'

Karen gave out a sad 'oh', like the final breath from a deflating balloon.

'Yeah, he, well, he was killed by somebody.'

'Tssh. They're animals.' She didn't sound very concerned.

'Yeah. But you got the photograph?'

'Yeah.' Voice suddenly high, a little defensive, Paddy thought. 'I didn't really look at it, just saw my own face. Listen, could you leave me out of it? I do *not* look good in that picture. That's kind of why I didn't send the form back, you know, that old hairdo and all. Very unstylish now. They'll be laughing about me from here to Union Square.' She laughed with her tongue clamped between her teeth, an obligation laugh. Now that she was talking Paddy could hear the phoniness in her US accent, the way it slid up and down the west coast, the occasional flat vowels creeping in to match Paddy's own Scottish accent.

'Karen, Terry's dead too.'

Down the line, metal clunked against metal. She heard a hiss and 'plouf as the gas was lit.

'I see ... Really?' She paused as if Paddy was talking and then replied, 'Great, baby, so you can leave me out of it?'

Karen wasn't alone. She was putting on a show for someone. Paddy flattened the close-up of McBree and the car, touching the corner of Karen's face that she had included in the enlargement. 'The book won't come out now, Karen. You're quite safe.'

'Well, that's great ... Yeah, I'm making coffee.' She laughed again, for a long time. The sound of her voice seemed to pivot away from the receiver and back, as if she was watching someone moving. Suddenly they were alone.

'Listen, you see that picture doesn't come out, right? I'll get my fucking arse felt if it does.'

Flat Glasgow Southside accent, undisguised.

'Karen, I've known both Kevin and Terry since I was eighteen. I need to know why.' She looked at the photocopy of McBree, at the fat man turned away from the camera, a hand on the driver's door handle. 'Who's the suit?'

Karen drew a breath, muttered, 'In the bathroom now.'

'Who is he?'

'British.'

English people were English. Scottish people were Scottish. The only people who called themselves British worked for the military or the government and he was too fat to be a soldier.

'I, um,' Karen was whispering, sounding tearful, 'I *liked* my picture. I'm sorry.'

Paddy found herself listening to a flat dial tone. A small hand landed on the soft inside of her elbow.

'Mum, I'm hungry.'

II

Dub remembered where the canteen was. They no longer made hot food but the room was furnished with fizzy drink and food vending machines, selling all the crap adults tried to keep children away from. Paddy asked him to pick the least appalling thing and promised Pete a proper meal when they went to his granny's.

They walked up the stairs and Paddy went back into the office, considering her next move.

Back at the desk she put her notes, the photocopy and the list into an internal mail envelope with a note to Bunty, asking him to get Merki to write it up. She found some small satisfaction in the thought that Merki would have to contradict himself in print. She jotted notes on the meaning of the picture, and slid the clippings envelope in with it, folded the envelope shut, opened the wire butterfly clips, put her name on the front as the sender and slipped it in Bunty's pigeonhole.

She kept thinking about her dad. Couldn't shove him to the back of her mind the way she usually did, but his company felt comfortable today, as if he was supporting her elbow, helping her.

She needed to be alone when McBree came. Eriskay House was blighted by death already but Callum was there, eating dry bread, enjoying the countryside. She could get Dub to drive out with her and make him come back to the city with Callum. She could tell him she was meeting a contact from British Security, top secret, ask him to come out and get her the next day. If Dub promised to stay with Pete and her mother and she made sure McBree knew where she was, they should be safe enough.

She had one last thing to do, though. She could do it on the way out to Ayr. Garrett's suggestion. She smiled when she thought about the taciturn police officer. Decent woman.

32

Marty

An unfamiliar van was parked outside Trisha's house, a rusted burgundy van with painted back windows and empty food wrappers on the dashboard. Paddy had never seen it before but knew exactly what it signified.

She bolted for the front door and fitted her key, Dub and Pete hurrying after her. As soon as she saw the light from the living room she knew that the television was on and the lights off. Her brothers, Marty and Gerry, were home from London.

They looked up at her from the settee, side by side, cups of tea and the trail of biscuit crumbs on the arms. Marty slipped his eyes back to the television but Gerry tried a smile, sensitive enough to be a little shamefaced about his sudden appearance.

'All right?'

She didn't answer him.

Marty had changed his style since he moved to London. He had grown his hair long and was dressed in a threadbare checked shirt, jeans and scuffed Converse trainers. Gerry had stuck to a plain T-shirt and jeans, clothes his mother could have bought for him in a charity shop.

'Not pleased to see us?' Marty kept his eyes on the television screen.

'I know why you're here.'

Pete squeezed past her legs and threw himself at his uncles. They caught him, making a fuss of him without smiling. Gerry let Pete slide down his legs and yanked him back on to the settee by an arm and a leg.

'Mum phoned ye about her?'

Marty answered for both of them. 'Aye.'

'It's more complicated than you think. You both know what Mary Ann's like. She can't talk about things, describe things.'

'Is she pregnant?'

'No,' said Paddy sharply, worried about Pete picking up on the conversation. 'Just, you don't know what's going on.'

Pete pulled himself free. 'Where's BC?'

'Visiting his dad,' said Gerry. 'He'll be back soon.'

Dub sat down in an armchair that their father had always used, nodding his hellos. The boys had known him for ever and didn't question his presence, just nodded back, glancing at the television again to break off contact.

A sudden clack of plates from the kitchen announced Trisha's presence.

'You two keep Pete in here,' Paddy ordered her brothers and stepped into the kitchen.

Standing facing the door as she came in, beyond a table set with five places, Trisha glared at her, bitter as a mafia widow.

'Mum—'

'You didn't tell me.'

'Mum—'

Trisha had raised five children, her husband had been unemployed for five years before he died, had a breakdown that no one ever acknowledged and died a terrible death, but Paddy had never heard her shout as savagely as she did now. '*You didn't tell me.*'

Shocked by the violence of her own voice, Trisha clutched the back of a chair to steady herself. The Church was the only certainty left to her.

'Sit down, Mum.' Paddy took her arm and backed her into a seat, pushing her up against the table to trap her. The teapot was underneath the tea cosy, still warm enough if a little stewed. Paddy poured out a cup and put milk in it, setting it in front of her mother, taking a seat next to her and ordering her to drink.

Holding the cup with two hands, Trisha lifted it to her mouth, gurning at the strong tea but taking another sip anyway.

'She only told me two days ago,' said Paddy. 'When did you hear? Mary Ann was here two days ago, wasn't she? Did she tell you then? Because if she did you've known longer than me and I should be shouting at you.' Her mother looked out into the living room again. 'So you called them and told them to come home. For what? To batter Father Andrew? Why?'

'Because of what he did to her.' Trisha's face contorted with shame and pain.

'He didn't rape her, Mum. She's in love with him.'

'In love?' Trisha slammed the cup down on the table. 'In *love*? What would you know about that? Love isn't taking a shine to someone you've met once or twice, it's living together year after year, getting through bad times, caring for each other, nursing each other.' She was rocking back and forth in the chair, missing Con, her softer self.

In the living room someone turned up the television to keep the sound of the conversation from Pete.

Paddy couldn't bring herself to mention her father

directly. It would hurt too much. 'Mary Ann's grown up. She knows her own mind.'

'She knows nothing about life.'

Paddy took her hand and Trisha melted towards her. 'You're kidding yourself. She's seen more than you or me or both of us. She works in a soup kitchen and she's been beaten up more than once. She might not know anything about our world but she knows a lot of stuff we don't.'

Trisha looked deep into her bitter tea. 'He's a man of the Church. A priest. How could he?'

'And you think she's passive in this? Because she's a woman?'

Trisha yanked her hand away and showed Paddy her palm. 'Don't you bring your women's lib into this.'

'For fucksake, Mum, Mary Ann isn't a child. We're none of us children any more. Women can instigate relationships. It's not like the old days. We're not all sitting against the wall waiting to get danced.'

Trisha looked despairingly at her cup. Her white roots were showing and her back was bowed. She looked old and spent.

'Mum, she's nearly thirty. She's a woman.'

Trisha turned on her. 'I supposed you're pleased. You never wanted her to take her final vows, did you? You never take communion, never go to confession.'

But Paddy wasn't going to act sorry. She had been hiding her lack of faith since she was seven. For a long time she genuinely believed that everyone in the family would get marked down on the Final Day because of her, that she herself was damned to hell by a God she didn't like or respect. It was a terrible load and she'd been carrying it alone. 'I don't get religion,' she said defiantly. 'But I love Mary Ann and I want her to be happy. Battering her boyfriend won't make her happy. I hope she gets married and has fifty children. She'd be a brilliant mum.'

The possibility that there would be a time beyond this moment, that Mary Ann might marry and give her grandchildren, hadn't occurred to Trisha. She sipped her tea and thought, catching her breath to speak but stopping.

Paddy could see it all unravelling: Trisha would send the boys to see Father Andrew. They were so protective of Mary Ann she knew it would get physical as soon as he opened the door. The housekeeper would call the police and the boys'd be up on a charge. The story would get out, everyone would be ruined and Trisha's shame would be compounded.

'Being happy isn't all there is to life,' Trisha said eventually. 'There's doing the right thing and duties and honour.'

'Is it honourable to lie and pretend she has a vocation if she doesn't? Because she'll do that to please you. Mum ...' Paddy started crying before she even spoke his name, 'Dad wouldn't want this.'

Trisha's head dropped forward. Con's name had been unspoken since they emptied his clothes from the cupboard.

They sat together, clasping hands until their fingers turned white, crying silently while the ghost of Con flitted cheerfully around the kitchen, making tea, emptying bins, arranging chairs for visitors, showing off lucky finds from his aimless walks.

Finally, Paddy licked the wet from her lip, forced a breath into her chest and spoke. 'My gentle wee daddy wouldn't want this.'

II

Sitting on her old bed, looking across at Marty perched on Mary Ann's, Paddy realized that she couldn't remember seeing her brother in this room when they all lived at home. He and Gerry had their own bedroom, their own hangouts, their own secrets. Neither of the boys was a talker. Since they moved to London they phoned her mother once a week to tell her they weren't dead and lie about their chapel attendance, but that was as intense as the interaction got.

Marty was wary when she caught his eye in the gloomy living room and nodded him out to the hall, led him up the steep carpet-padded stairs, to sit under the bare light bulb on the two narrow single beds with balding chenille bedspreads. His knees stayed together, steadying hands on either side of his thighs, looking around at the unfamiliar walls and the half-pulled curtains.

They hadn't liked each other much when they shared a house and it felt strange that she should be about to ask so much of him.

'What is it?' he said, forcing himself to look at her. 'Is Mum ill?'

'No.' She took a deep breath, wanted a cigarette but couldn't smoke because Pete would be sleeping here tonight. 'I have to ask you and Gerry a massive favour.'

That caught Marty's attention. 'Money?' He gave a half-smile.

'No. Look, I'm involved in something heavy. Two of my friends have died—'

'Have you got Aids?'

She felt a familiar heat on the back of her neck. 'Marty, shut up and listen, will ye?'

Marty stood up. The beds were low and he seemed very tall; his black hair fell over one eye as he leaned towards her. 'You always fucking do this.'

She was supposed to ask him what, what did she always do, and then they'd slide into the deep track marks of their well-worn argument: she was a bossy self-important cow,

339

he was a bully, she was fat, he was stupid, yeah, well, fuck you then and fuck you too.

'Someone tried to kill Pete last night. A man, an Irish Republican I've been writing about, broke into Burns's house and tried to stab Pete because he couldn't find me. It was a warning. It's me he wants.'

Marty dropped back down to sit on the bed, staring at her. It was the traces of fear in his eyes that made her see it: he looked so much like Con it was all she could do to stop herself from crying again. 'I need you to watch over Pete.'

He took her hands in his, easing her thumbs out and baring his wee sister's palms.

'Why? Where are you going?'

She took another deep breath. 'I have to go and meet him.'

The words hung heavily in the air between them as Paddy looked out of the window at the tree nodding in the summer breeze at the end of the garden.

'Can't I come with you?'

'I need you to watch over Pete.'

When they first moved in, her father thought the tree was a bush and left it. She'd found out recently that it was a sycamore. Every summer it grew taller and more lush until now it dominated the whole garden, the only feature that rose above a rusting washing machine peeking like a commando over the tips of the tall grass. No one had ever liked that tree but Paddy. She loved it for daring to be beautiful in an ugly place.

Marty pressed her palms together, warming them in the circle of his own hands.

'Can't you call the police?'

'The police are protecting him. He's killed two people already and they warned me off investigating him.'

'Call the papers?'

'The two guys he killed *were* the papers.'

Marty looked terrified. 'Me and Gerry could hide in the van and—'

'No.'

'We could get a gun—'

'No. We're not that kind of people. He's after me and whoever is with me, Marty. He's been doing this for twenty years ... Please trust me. I could spend an hour explaining and I'll still have to go by myself.'

He was holding her hands tight now, his head almost in her lap. He whispered, 'Will you leave Pete here?'

She nodded at the window.

'Will he come for Pete tonight?'

'Not if I go to meet him.'

She looked back at her brother. He was stroking her hands and crying, face red, chin quivering, and now he really looked like her daddy. Con cried a lot at the end. Spontaneous outbursts of limitless sadness.

'We, um ...' Marty broke off to sniff. 'We'll take turns staying up. We've got baseball bats in the van and we'll keep knives by the settee. If you do meet him—' He shut his eyes and curled over his knees, tensing his back into a tight curve. 'We'll move home and mind Pete.'

She pulled her thumbs free and cupped Marty's hands in hers, lifted them, holding them to her cheek.

Slowly, he rocked forward until their heads were pressed tight together.

He pressed so hard he numbed her scalp.

33

From a Mile under Water

She called Pitt Street and asked for Knox. The receptionist put her through to a secretary. DCI Knox wasn't in right now but she wondered if she could take a message?

'It's really him I need to speak to,' Paddy told her. 'It's quite urgent.'

'Well, I'm very sorry but he won't be back in again tonight.'

Paddy couldn't go and wait in the cottage on her own all night if McBree didn't know where she was. He'd come after Pete and find him in the house with her mother and brothers. It would be a massacre.

'It's about Martin McBree, I have some—'

'Just a moment.'

She heard two soft-tone beeps and Knox picked up.

'This is Paddy Meehan. I've got McBree's pictures, the last few copies. I want to hand them over.'

He thought for a moment. 'That's nothing to do with me,' he said.

'Tonight. Eriskay House, off the Ayr Road. There's a small sign for the house, shortly before the Troon petrol station on the roundabout.'

'Why are you telling me?' He sounded so casual and self-assured it made her furious.

'Knox, I *will get* around to you.'

'Will you?' He was smiling.

'I know about you.' She had nothing on him, but the more threatened he felt the more likely he was to call McBree immediately.

'Miss Meehan—'

She hung up on him. Knox moved in that murky area between criminality, and government-licensed corruption. He would have his finger in a hundred scams and couldn't know which of them she was alluding to.

She stood in the hall, felt the familiar breeze at her ankles from the gap under the front door, the murmur of the television in the living room, looked at the tread on the stair carpet, unchanged throughout her entire life. She began to tremble.

II

The twenty-four-hour shop was a five-minute detour from the motorway, on the lip of the West End. It sold munchie food, catering to hungry drunks on their way home from clubs in the town and hash-smoking students who ventured out in the night in search of nourishment. As a back-up source of income it had diversified, offering a hundred other services: handwritten adverts for rooms to let, a bulky photocopier near the back, magazine subscriptions and, behind the counter, under the cigarettes, a fax machine.

'Nah, ye can't send it yourself. Give me the number and I'll send it for ye.'

The sleepy young woman had bleached hair that seemed to be melting at the tips. Paddy wondered at the wisdom of entrusting her with her revenge. 'It's quite important. Can

I come round and make sure you do it right?'

The shop assistant sighed as if she'd been asked to clean her room. 'I can't let people around the counter. Yes or no. Hurry up.'

The machine was small but looked new.

'OK.'

The girl pulled out a cover sheet from under the counter. 'Fill it out.'

Paddy used a pencil:

Number of pages including this one: two.
From: blank
To: blank.
Subject. Martin McBree's meeting with British security agent in New York, 1989.

She stacked the photocopy of McBree under the cover sheet and handed it over with the list of Irish phone numbers she had got from directory enquiries that afternoon. 'These three numbers.'

The girl took them, turned her back and fitted the picture face down into the feeder. She looked at the numbers. 'Which one first?'

'Sinn Fein Offices. Then the *Irish Republican News*. Then the Sweetie Bottle Bar.'

'All in Northern Ireland?'

'Yeah. The area codes are all there.'

The blonde punched the numbers in lazily, sensing that Paddy was anxious and in a hurry, so taking her time. Eventually the machine swallowed the sheet and spat it back out, gave off a whirring-beeped burp and a short slip of paper slid out of the underside.

'And I'll take a couple of Snickers bars as well.'

Paddy checked the transmission report as she waited for her change. It was number perfect. It would take some time, she felt sure, for the word to get out, be checked and double-checked and finally for someone to believe Martin McBree was working with the security services. But one day he'd get a knife in his neck and he'd know it was because of her.

He was coming to get her and, she realized, she didn't even have a pocket knife

The shop assistant held out the change to her, looking at her hand and noting the tremble in her fingers.

'Sorry,' said Paddy, 'do you sell kitchen scissors?'

III

She stood by her Volvo, cramming the second Snickers bar into her dry mouth, hardly tasting it on the way down but aware of the stringy caramel sticking in her throat. She looked at her hands, at her chocolate-coated fingertips. She was too full even to lick them clean and they were still shaking.

She rapped on the window and Dub rolled it down. 'Could you drive, Dub? I wouldn't mind just looking out of the window.'

They got back on to the motorway, took the bridge across the river and followed the signs for Ayr. Before long the lanes narrowed, then converged and they were in a drag race with the late commuters who had missed the rush hour and were desperate to get home.

Dub wasn't used to driving. The dark, the sweeps and turns through the hills and the aggressive locals made him lean forward in his seat, hanging over the steering wheel, neck craned, cursing under his breath every time a car or a van shot past him. When they reached a broad stretch to the south of the city he relaxed a fraction and sat back.

'Now,' he said, 'this meeting: you're just going to hand over the photos to the McBree guy? Are you sure you'll be all right out here on your own?'

'Yeah.' She drew on her cigarette, keeping her hand close to her face so he couldn't see her shaking. 'He won't approach if there's anyone there.'

An articulated lorry overtook them at an alarming speed, clearing the side of the car by less than a foot, the canvas straps whip-cracking at Dub's window. He panicked and hit the brakes hard, slowing down to thirty, panting and leaning over the wheel again until he'd calmed himself down. His eye kept flickering to the darkness in the rear-view mirror as if he expected another assault. 'The crying at the house, what was all of that about?'

'Mum called the boys up to come and batter Mary Ann's boyfriend and I said Dad wouldn't want that.'

'Quite right, neither he would.'

Outside the window the gentle hills of Ayrshire rolled softly away to a darkening sky. I may not come back this way, she thought. I may never come back.

She looked at Dub, memorizing his face. She could think about him when the time came. Not Pete, because she'd sob and struggle and lose it, but if it came to it, if McBree got her, in her final moments she could think about Dub and smile. She'd remember walking home with him late at night, eating sticky pasta in the flat, the warm toasting smell of him ironing behind her while she watched TV and his hand finding hers under the duvet in the dark night. They should have gone on holidays. They should have dated each other.

Like bubbles rising from a mile under water, the words found her lips: 'I love you.'

Dub slowed down to twenty-five again and looked sternly out at the road. 'I don't think this is the time or the place ...'

She smiled at his discomfort. 'Yeah, yeah.'

'We talked about this before.'

'Yeah, your fat arse, Dub McKenzie.'

He turned his head but was afraid to take his eyes off the road. 'Meehan, it was you who said we shouldn't try to pin it down, not me.'

'Shut up and drive. You wanker.' She grinned out of the side window. 'And I do love you. I don't even love you as a friend, I'm in love with ye. I think everything you do is brilliant. So ye can shove that up your arse. Fucking proddy twat.'

When she glanced back he was smiling at the road, sucking his cheeks to stop his face splitting in half.

'Happy now?' she said seriously. 'You've trapped me with your wiles and sexual trickery.'

Chewing his lip, he slapped her leg with the back of his hand.

Paddy threw her hands up in mock exasperation. 'And now the violence.'

IV

Their headlights left the road and sliced, waist-high, through the dark around the cottage. They could see that Callum had been busy.

The sturdy grass pressing up against the facade had been flattened, roughly cut away under the windows and the door. An orange-rusted rotary-action lawn mower stood indignantly upright in front of the house.

Dub parked and Paddy got out, looking around for Callum. She felt Dub behind her and his fingertips found hers, squeezed them and then retreated. 'He's round the back,' he said and walked off.

Paddy took a step and the tip of the kitchen scissors needled her thigh. They weren't very sharp.

She felt a front of cool air sliding up the hill from the sea, heard the bushes whisper beyond the orchard wall and the old house groan at the weight of its history. The crack across the front looked deeper in the dark. She followed Dub's shadow.

The lawn mower's last act had been to chew the grass off around the side of the house. Callum had cleared a path along the side wall, down to moss-covered paving slabs underneath. The thick spongy surface was waterlogged and her trainers squelched as she stepped across them.

They found Callum sitting on the ground by the kitchen door, his back to the wall, looking out and enjoying the sunset. He was eating dry white bread, squashing slices into hard dough and biting chunks off. 'It's so quiet here, I heard you two a mile away.'

'You've been busy enough,' said Dub.

Callum smiled and stood up. 'I'm going to live in the country one day. Come on in.'

Though the light was failing outside, they could see that he had cleared the whole kitchen floor, found some cleanish water in the water tank on the far side of the house and used a bucket with a hole in it to drag it into the house. He'd managed to wipe the thick layer of dust off the worktop and the range, but he didn't have a mop so the floor looked not so much cleaner as dirty in a different way.

Dub was at a loss. 'Lovely.'

Glassy-eyed with pride, Callum grinned and swept an arm around the filthy kitchen. 'But this didn't take half as long as the other job did.'

He planted his hands on his hips and waited for them to ask. Paddy didn't have time for this. She needed to get him the fuck out before McBree turned up.

Dub obliged. 'What other job?'

Gleefully, Callum made them stand by the back wall, clearing a space on the floor. 'Ye can sit down if you like.'

'Callum, I need you to go with Dub. You can stay at his mum and dad's tonight. I have to meet someone here.'

'Two minutes.'

He disappeared into the front room. Dub looked at Paddy and smiled the warmest smile she had ever seen. She took his hand, dropping it abruptly when Callum reappeared holding cardboard flattened like a pizza box, carrying it carefully in front of him, holding the lid down.

Callum looked coyly at Dub. 'I did this for you. So you can sleep.' He lifted the lid.

Paddy was expecting a drawing, pressed flowers, something creative and asinine. But Callum hadn't made a drawing.

Dub slid along the wall, rolling his shoulder to the doorway, half muttering 'fuck' before staggering outside. They could hear him vomiting.

Paddy sat down.

Sitting in the base of the box were nine dead mice, their slender bodies lined up neatly. The fleshy pink pads on their feet looked too tender to have carried them through rough wall cavities and fields. Paddy could see soft brown hair on their bellies, and, from the low-down swelling, that one of them was pregnant. Their front paws were curled tightly up at their chests. Above the neck their heads were bloody tattered smears.

Callum looked sadly at the door. 'I battered them with a brick. But it wasn't for a laugh, I did it for him.' He dropped the lid and slumped to the floor.

Paddy couldn't look away from the box. She could still see their feet, the skin on their toes, translucent as an embryo's. She hugged her knees to her chest.

Callum slid along the floor to her side, his shoulder tight to hers. 'Are you crying?' He looked at her closely. 'You're not crying about the mice.'

It wasn't a question so she didn't answer him.

She rubbed her face roughly. 'Look, Callum, son, you need to go with Dub, go back to the city. It's not safe here anymore.'

'Are journalists coming? Aren't you coming?'

'I have to meet someone here.'

'Who?'

'A man.'

'A journalist?'

'No, a man. It's not about you, it's about another thing.'

'What other thing?'

'Nothing to do with you, just another thing.'

They looked at each other and she saw a spark of recognition in his eyes. 'It's not safe here. Who's it not safe for?'

She shook her head, looking at her hands. 'You need to go.'

He nodded as if he understood perfectly and wrapped his arms around his knees, mirroring her pose. 'Can I come back here after? I could be happy here. If I had a radio and food, I'd be happy here. I could look after it, sort a wee garden out for myself.'

Her eyes welled again. 'Sweetheart, you won't want to come back here.'

He stared at her rudely for a long time, watching her cry. Embarrassed, she fumbled her cigarettes out of her pocket. Callum took them gently from her hand, opened the packet, and handed her one. He lit a match for her, but her whole body was trembling and she couldn't dock the tip to the flame. Callum held the end of her cigarette steady so that she could light it.

He sat back, very calm, muttering so quietly she had to

tease the words apart in her mind to make sense of them. 'Gotaknife?'

She shook her head. 'Scissors.'

'No gun?'

'No.'

'Plan?'

She inhaled and took Callum's big hand in hers. 'Son, you're young. Go home and have a life. It's time for you to have a life. Live in the country. Meet a girl. You're handsome, did you know that?'

Callum blushed.

'You're a nice young man, well-meaning, good-looking. You're an Ogilvy. Have a family, go to chapel, that's what Ogilvys do. You like families?'

He nodded eagerly.

'That's what Ogilvys do.'

'You're my family.'

'I'm not your family, Callum. I'm close to your family but I'm not your family.'

He sounded sulky when he answered, 'Aye, ye are.'

Dub leaned back in the door, pasty-skinned and wet-eyed, afraid to cross the threshold of the kitchen. 'Callum,' he gestured outside, ''mon. Let's go.'

'I only did it for you,' Callum said to him.

'I know, pal, that was nice of ye. I'm a bit soft. Come on. Paddy needs to be alone here. Someone's coming to meet her. He won't come if we're here. Pad, I'll be back at ten in the morning to pick you up.'

'Take care on the road,' she said, keeping it light.

He left. They could see him through the side window as he stepped carefully across the moss on the paving stones by the house.

Callum stood up suddenly, staring down at Paddy sitting

balled up on the floor, his voice was shaking. 'Ye call me son. Ye look after me. Ye are my family.'

Paddy'd known Callum since he was eight years old, had been to his father's funeral and fought for him before she ever liked him.

'Son,' she said, her voice a growl, 'you're right. We are family.'

v

She went to wave them off. Dub backed nervously out of the driveway to the lip of the road, Callum guiding him through the grass with waves and warning slaps on the bonnet.

Out on the road, cars were speeding past at irregular intervals, more frequent on the opposite side of the road. Callum climbed into the passenger seat. Paddy could see Dub's head flicking back and forth, worried about how to get across. Finally, Dub revved the engine, jolted forward and hit the road going the wrong way. He sped off in the direction of Ayr. They'd have to turn at the roundabout.

The noise of the road died as she walked around to the back of the house. A low sun was setting over the lush green hills, the horizon baby-girl pink. It would be a long night.

She stood at the kitchen doorway, holding the frame to steady herself, and thought of her father. It was resisting death that made it painful. Con should have embraced it. She'd never thought about it before but his resistance was the ultimate act of defiance. She didn't recognize it at the time, mistook it for fear because she'd never seen him resist anything before, but it took real guts to cling to life when the odds meant you'd die.

It was too dark inside, so she lifted one of the spindly-legged kitchen chairs and took it out, setting it against the back wall, on the spot where they had found Callum. She arranged her funeral coat around herself to keep warm, took the useless scissors out of her pocket and sat them on her lap.

Then she lit another cigarette, leaned her head back against the crumbling wall, and waited for the sun to go down.

34

Don't Get Out of the Car

I

A car was approaching them from behind, coming out of the dark. Dub slowed to let it pass but it lingered behind them, wary of straying on to the midline of the road until they were out of the hills.

Callum looked at Dub, hunched over the wheel. He didn't look as friendly as he did when Paddy was with them. His jaw was tight and his eyes narrower. His breathing was fast.

'This fucking road,' he mumbled, glancing nervously in the mirror.

He seemed angry and Callum was afraid that Dub hated him because of the mice. He thought back to Paddy at the cottage, worried, crying and not saying why, wanting him to leave. She said it wasn't safe.

The car behind slid out to the side, peering around them, and slipped back, gathering speed, headlights growing in the mirror, shining a rectangle of blinding light into Dub's eyes, before pulling out into the road and passing them in a flash.

'*STOP!*' yelped Callum, making Dub's hands jump so the car swerved towards the grass verge.

'Fuck!' shouted Dub. 'Don't scream like that, this is hard enough.'

Frightened at the level of anger in his voice, Callum moderated his voice: 'Stop the car.'

But Dub wasn't listening. He wasn't looking at him, he was watching the road, checking the mirror every few seconds, holding the wheel so tight his arms were pulling his body forward in a rigid curve. He slowed on the approach to the roundabout, the lights of the petrol station glistening in the dark.

Callum tried to explain. 'I need you to stop the car. I need to go back. She said it's not safe.'

Dub didn't answer but pulled the car across the round-about and veered left into the petrol station, blinking hard at the brightness and carrying on until they were around the side of the building, right round at the back, in the dark again. He slowed to a stop.

Callum was sweating. 'This isn't right. She's not safe.' The words rattled around the inside of the car. The silence afterwards was suffocating.

Dub's voice was barely a whisper. 'She said she loved me. I don't know how to handle myself. I'm not a violent man.'

Callum wanted Dub to think well of him, not because he could give him a good report or parole, just he liked the gentle way he had about him and how scared he was of the mice. 'But I am,' he said quietly. 'I am violent. I know how to handle myself. She's on her own up there and she's my family and I'm going back.'

Callum wouldn't have thought someone as wet as Dub had it in him but his cheeks flushed a furious red and he leaned across the gearstick to press his face into Callum's: 'You fucking listen to me: *you are a child*.' He was pointing in Callum's chest, poking his finger as if he wanted to stab him. 'Sean Ogilvy didn't take you to live with his family so you could get involved in rubbish like this, d'ye hear me? Paddy didn't drive all the way up the fucking coast and take shit at her work so you could be a heavy for her. *You are a child.*'

'But I know how to—'

Dub leaned into his face, eyes bulging, as angry as Haversham. 'If this guy does turn up and you batter lumps out of him, how fucking fast do you think they'll whip you back into jail? You've been out for under a week, the world and his dog are looking for you, we're all busting a gut to protect you. D'you think I'm going to let you wander up the hill to have a fight?'

'But she's my family,' he said weakly.

Dub sat back, eyes still wide. 'You're not her dad, you're not her brother, so what are you?'

Callum shrugged.

Dub made a little circle with his finger. 'In this family, in our family, you're a child. And in this family, in our family, the big ones look after the wee ones.' He opened the car door and took a step out of the car. 'If you get out of this car I will never speak to you again.'

'You'll need a weapon,' said Callum.

Dub looked back at him. 'I'm going to the petrol station. To get a knife.'

He shut the door behind him and walked off around the corner to the shop.

Alone in the car, Callum blinked burning eyes. He thought he was a nuisance to them, a problem. It hadn't occurred to him until Dub said it: they were protecting him. He was their child. He hadn't been a child since the dark night and the baby. They weren't hiding him, they weren't tolerating him. They were looking after him.

When Dub came back round the side of the station Callum groaned. He was carrying a red plastic petrol can.

He opened the driver's door and looked in, and repeated his warning: 'I will never speak to you again.'

Callum shook his head. 'Ye can't use a can of petrol on him. It's soft, ye can't hit with it and don't try to set fire to him because you'll get her too. You'll set yourself on fire, probably.'

Dub looked uncertain for a moment. 'Well, what then?'

'Get a brick. Hit him there . . .' Callum fingered the top of his head, where he knew the skull was weak.

Dub looked at him, softer this time. 'Promise me you won't get out of the car, Callum.'

'OK,' he whispered. 'I'll stay.'

II

The grass had been cut short all the way through the field. Long stripes ran up the hill and back again, marks of a mechanical mower, scything the grass to no more than an inch high.

Dub had to keep to the ditch at the far side from the road to avoid being seen by passing cars. It should have been easy to follow: a trickle of water had carved a gentle cleft in the soft rich land for him to run along, keeping low. But the farmer had used the burn as a line for fencing, four wires topped with razor tips, the stakes deep in the black soil, and he had to go slowly or risk sliding down the side and cutting himself. He didn't know how much time he had.

The can in his right hand swung heavily, the petrol sloshing against the sides, following the rhythm of his walk.

Water in the burn trickled melodically, high-pitched and playful, jarring with the dark night and the fat seagulls cawing overhead. His ankles were taking the strain of hurrying along an incline. He stumbled on loose ground once or twice, always stopping to check he hadn't hurt himself, and then carrying on. He couldn't see the house yet but knew it was there, at the top of the hill, beyond the clump of bushes and trees.

Reaching the edge of the short grass, he came to a fence into another field and climbed carefully over. The ground was looser here, strong grass that was razor sharp at the tips. He ran in a crouch, skirting the summit, his hand sweating around the plastic handle of the petrol can, making it slippery. He arrived at a tumbledown wall, two foot high, made of old stones, the mortar weather-worn and crumbling. He raised his eyes.

He had reached the old wall around the garden of the cottage.

And there at the far end, the flare of a match, an warm orange target in the dark. She was there, sitting in a chair, in the dark, quite alone.

He let his eyes adjust to the thin light. He could make out her face in the glow of the cigarette. She was smiling.

He watched her as he squatted on his haunches and sat the petrol can on the uneven ground. Listening, alert to any noise he might make, he unscrewed the plastic lid, working his fingers slowly until it was quite loose. He lifted it off and sat it on the ground.

And then he waited.

35

Into the Bad Fire

I

Paddy was on her third cigarette. It was quiet here and she didn't like it. She could hear the grass waving in the wind, the scurrying of tiny feet back in the house, mice or rats, survivors of Callum's killing spree. They seemed to have got into the roof and she was afraid they might drop down on her head, so she moved her chair out from the wall a bit.

She had been trying to think some momentous last thought, a great all-encompassing conclusion about the nature of existence, but her attention was drawn back by the mundane: she felt queasy after eating the Snickers bars, she was tired, she needed a pee. She might be here all night. For all she knew, Knox couldn't get hold of McBree. She could be sitting here alone for ten hours.

She looked up at the dark sky. A thick band of navy blue rain was moving in from the sea, chasing seagulls inland. The distant landscape was becoming indistinct, melting into the dark. She tried not to think about Pete or her mother or Terry Hewitt, just to smell the crisp evening air and feel the nicotine pulsing softly through her, pushing the weariness away and making her skin tingle, but her thoughts kept flipping back to her house and her son and all the deeds left undone, all the kindnesses unrepaid. If she had been at home she would have wandered into the office and filled her mind by doing some work.

She smiled to herself. *IRA in Pay of British. Brits Pay IRA. Terror Boss Works for Us.* She jumbled the headlines around; none of them worked all that well but she had fun doing it. Then she started on the article, imagining what Merki would make of the materials she had left him. *Terror boss.* They'd use that for sure.

Very slowly she became aware of a low droning engine on the road. At first it sounded like any other car slowing as it broached the sharp turn, but it didn't speed up when it was past the danger spot. The wheels left the tarmac, began a tentative slide into the driveway, became a muffled crunch over grass.

Long shafts of white light glared around the side of the cottage, bleaching the grass blue. And then they cut out.

Paddy dropped her cigarette, opening the scissors, trying to find a way of holding them that wouldn't mean pressing her fingers to the blade. She stood up stiffly, turning to the mossy path round the side of the house, expecting McBree to appear.

A soft breeze blew the hair from her face. Silence. He wasn't coming round the side. He was going to creep up on her.

She felt horribly dismayed. It would have been less frightening if he had walked round to face her, spoke to her first, but McBree was planning to leap out of the dark and startle her like an old spinster. The thought that her last words on earth might be an undignified whoop of surprise was too humiliating.

She turned her back to the wall, took a step sideways and was swallowed by the darkness of the house.

The floor objected to every trespassing footfall so they both stood still, Paddy in the kitchen, hanging on to the cold metal of the range, feeling the greasy dust beneath her fingers and the cut of the scissors as she held them tight. He was near the front of the house, in one of the bedrooms or the bathroom, off to the left somewhere. She could hear his feet crunching on something, leaves or glass. The sound travelled through the warped walls, bouncing and distorting.

A floorboard groaned as he took a step and corrected himself. Cloth brushed a wall. He was hanging on to the wall because the floorboards would be better attached there. Smart. Following his lead, she slid around the room, taking careful steps, tiptoeing silently along the edge of the room, past the back door, around to the side of the dresser where it was dark. He would come in here, look around from the door, searching at head height. So she crouched, keeping her feet exactly where they had landed, twisting her knees to keep in the shadows.

She heard a breath, a nasal exhalation, coming from the living-room doorway. A congested smoker's breath. And then McBree spoke, not whispering, just in a normal voice. As if he was asking for a paper.

'Well, you called me here.'

He was right. She slid up the crumbling wall to stand. He stepped around and looked at her, flashed a smile as if they were friends of old.

'Come out here,' he said, sounding kind.

But she didn't. 'Do you know who lived here?'

He gestured for her to come over.

Again, she stayed where she was. 'Terry Hewitt grew up here.'

There was no flicker of recognition. 'It's like a lot of the old houses at home.'

''S a bad road out there, isn't it?'

'Bad, aye. Blind turn out there.' McBree looked around the room, as if there was anything to see in the inky dark. He reached into his pocket and took something out. She didn't realize it was a packet of cigarettes until he lit one. He held them out to her, trying to goad her out of her corner.

She ignored the offer. 'Terry's parents died on that driveway. He was seventeen. Only child. First on the scene.'

'Aye.' He lifted his cigarette to his face, inhaling greedily, the glow casting a vibrant red over his glasses, masking his eyes. 'My parents' chip shop got bombed. That's how they died. Ripped limb from limb, my daddy was.'

'Are you an only child?'

'God, no.' He looked at her pointedly. 'There's hundreds of us.'

'Did they get the bombers?'

'Who? The police?' He chuckled. 'No, never got them. Knew them but never bothered arresting them.'

'And now you're working for the people who let your parents' killers walk.'

McBree gave a small start, then laughed at her and twirled a finger at his ear. 'You messing with my head, are ye?'

'How can ye? What have they got over you? Are ye gay, or a gambler or something?'

He laughed again, less certainly this time. '"You're very young for your age. Things are more straightforward when you're young.'

'Have they got pictures of ye doing something nasty? Torn loyalties: betray the cause or be known as a gay boy? Or did you just forget what side ye were on?'

'What *side I* was on?' His voice was high and as he looked at her she could see the hate building behind his eyes, the loathing that would justify the attack. 'Like there's two sides in the world and you get to pick one, *you stupid bitch.*'

'There's more than two?'

He sneered. 'Whose side are you on, ye fat, ignorant cow, your mother's or your wean's?' His glance slid suddenly to the side and she knew instantly that he regretted saying it. He lifted his cigarette to his mouth, sucked smoke deep, deep into his lungs, the red tip flaring against his troubled face.

'It's your kid?' she said softly. 'They've got something on one of your kids?'

McBree held his breath, exhaled thick smoke and looked back at her. 'Ye've got the pictures?'

'I read about Donaldson's boy being murdered in prison. Did they have something on your kid? Were they going to send him to prison?'

Eyes downcast, he held his hand towards her. 'Just give us the fucking pictures.'

'And you such a big man, they'd try to kill him for sure. You're doing all this for him. You'd kill Terry and Kevin and my five-year-old son to protect him?'

He dropped his hand, looked at the ceiling, composed himself. When he looked back at her he was smiling. 'Will I come over there and get them from ye?'

She put the scissors in her pocket carefully, took the photocopies out, balling them in her fists and throwing them over to his feet.

He smiled wryly. 'Is that your wee hidey-hole over there, wee mousey?' He bent down, scooped up the balled photocopies and stood up again in a flash. He was more agile than he looked. He watched her as he pulled the paper straight, glanced at it and took his lighter out.

'Now . . .' He touched his lighter to the edge of the sheet, holding on to the top corner while the flames took hold and then let go, watching the flickering paper float to the floor. 'Well, I for one feel much better.'

She didn't see him coming. Didn't see him drop his cigarette or take a step – just, very suddenly, he was across the room with one hand on her neck and the other on her wrist, pinning her against the wall, pressing her head into the crumbling plaster. He had seen the scissors in her hand. The fist around her neck tightened, squeezing the breath from her, making her tongue swell, lifting her off her feet.

Paddy swung her foot at his balls but missed, waved her free hand at his face and managed to knock his glasses off, but he didn't flinch. He just pressed tighter and tighter until her eyes felt too big for her head, until her ears began to scream a high-pitched tone and then he let her go.

Too stunned to go for the scissors, she stood, the very tip of her nose touching his, looking into his eyes wide with shock.

McBree dropped to his knees, bending forward, pressing his face into her groin like a man pleading for mercy. She raised her hands away from him, remembered her scissors and fumbled to get them out of her coat pocket as McBree swayed first one way, then the next, and fell on to his side.

Callum Ogilvy was standing behind him, panting, holding a brick.

Behind him, framed in the kitchen door, furious and carrying a red petrol can, stood Dub. *I told you to wait in the fucking car!* he shouted.

Paddy, Dub and Callum sat close together along the wall, numbed, watching the man die. McBree's right hand had landed on his chest but the left hand was thrown out to the side, palm open to the ceiling, like a singer reaching the crescendo. On the top of his head, facing the three of them, was a gash of bloody skin, a ragged split. Warm blood was still oozing lazily out of it, the puddle black in the dark of the kitchen, a slow-moving slick of ink that glistened silver as it split into tributaries on the uneven floor, making lakes of dips, looking for the sea.

The left hand was near to them, sitting in a diamond of the morning light coming through the window. Paddy could see a strip of soft white skin under his heavy wedding ring. His face looked strange without his glasses, naked, vulnerable. His eyes were smaller than she'd supposed, his lashes short and curled.

'We bury him in the garden,' said Callum.

Paddy was perturbed by his attitude. 'He's not dead.'

'You shouldn't be here,' said Dub.

They sat in silence for a moment. Callum took a breath and spoke again. 'We burn the place down with him in it. They come here and find the food and one sleeping bag. We leave a lighter near him and a packet of fags and they'll think he was a jakey who was living rough and set fire to himself with a fag. The problem is the car out the front ... We could drive it back, lose it in the city.'

Paddy and Dub looked at him. He was very calm, as if he had been born for this moment.

'Callum,' said Paddy, 'the man is not yet dead. What part of that don't you get? He's not dead, he's alive.'

Callum sighed. 'OK, call an ambulance then.'

She tutted, cutting him off, but Callum persisted. 'If he

lives will he kill you? Will he come back and get you and hurt Peter?'

'Maybe.' She thought about it. 'Probably.'

'Grow up, then.'

'You should be in the fucking car,' said Dub, as if that helped anything.

Paddy covered her face with her hands. 'God, I'm fucking starving. How could anybody get hungry at a time like this?'

'Adrenalin,' said Callum, calmly watching a bloody rivulet creep across the floor towards him. 'You get a big whoosh of it and then it passes and makes you hungry.' He saw them looking at him curiously. 'Anger management course. Prison.'

Paddy looked down at the crumbled heap on the floor. 'Maybe he'll bleed to death?'

Callum wrinkled his nose at her. 'What if he doesn't?'

Dub stood up and looked down at Callum. 'The thing that really bothers me about this, I mean really fucking does my head in, is that you shouldn't be here. Whatever happens, you shouldn't be here, seeing this.'

'He's right,' said Paddy, standing up, keeping her eyes on McBree's wound, repulsed but afraid to take her eyes off him in case he leaped suddenly to his feet and came at her. 'You should go back to the car.'

Callum got up, wiped the dust from his bum. 'You're trying to protect me but you're too late.' He gestured down at the half-dead man. 'This is what I understand. You two, you don't understand this. You're sitting watching him, hoping he'll die, but we *need to do something*.'

He had a point but Paddy stepped between him and McBree's body. '*I* need to do something.'

His eyes were imploring. 'Let me do it. I know what I'm doing. You don't.'

Paddy hesitated. 'I want you to go back to the car with Dub. Most people, Callum, most of us come from a comfortable home, we grow up and then we see things like this. It's going to be harder for you. You'll have to do it backwards.'

'I'm not leaving you here, you don't have a clue—'

'You WILL go to the car with Dub.' It was her warning-mother voice again. It had worked on the sports guys, it worked on Pete but Callum had spent his whole life being shouted at. She could see him smiling a little, swithering. He suppressed a grin and dipped his eyes, glanced at Dub's feet.

'I'll go back to the car.'

IV

She lit a cigarette and looked down at McBree's head. The wound had stopped bleeding, the pool of blood no longer slithering across the floor but still. She kept her eyes on his face as she skirted his feet, stepping towards his left arm. She should feel for a pulse, see if he was alive or dead, but she didn't want to touch him, couldn't bring herself to bend over him, afraid he'd sit up suddenly and grab her, pull her down, throttle her again.

She stood over him and thought about Callum's unnatural calmness. He had been here before, stood in front of a person and made a decision to take their life. She imagined herself having to face this as a ten-year-old child. The man that made Callum kill the baby had been raping him. She imagined that threat hanging over her as she looked at McBree. She knew suddenly that if she'd been a frightened ten-year-old like Callum, she would have hurt the baby to save herself too.

Playing for time, she thought again of checking for a

367

pulse but it didn't matter whether he was still alive. She couldn't exactly call an ambulance. She was waiting, she realized, for the decision to be made for her.

Outside, a lorry rumbled past on the road, birds began to call. The sun rose, the wind rustled the tops of the trees.

Quite suddenly she thought of her father lying in his hospital bed, the skin on his sunken face dry and thin as ricepaper, clinging furiously to life.

She stepped forward to McBree, felt in his jacket pocket, fumbling past his cigarettes and a tissue to the car keys. Moving quickly, she picked up the spare sleeping bag, and skipped over to the petrol can. She lifted it carefully, trying not to get any on her hands or clothes, and gently spilled it on the floor around him, crouching as she worked her way around the body, circling it with the greasy fluid. The packet of coal left over from the barbecue was on the range and she stacked it under the table for kindling, throwing the firestarter bricks on top.

She stood and looked at the scene for anything out of place. The house was quiet, the calm morning filtered through the dirty windows, the smell of damp cut by the sharp tang of petrol. An animal hunger scratched at the lining of her stomach.

She stepped outside into the morning and lit a match, heart hammering in her chest as she reached into the kitchen. Her thumb left her index finger and the match dropped through space, flaming red and blue, spinning. She felt the muffled 'whooph' pat her eardrum as the flame caught and a glittering carpet of flames rolled out across the bloody floor.

She was watching the firestarter bricks under the table burst into merry little lives of their own when a movement in the corner of her eye caught her attention: flames tickled around McBree's left hand as the square fingers unfurled, graceful, flowering open to the ceiling, appealing for mercy.

Horrified, Paddy lurched forward to the door. She grabbed the handle and slammed it shut.

36

Son

It happened again. The pasta shards were clinging to each other, stuck in inseparable lumps that the sauce couldn't infiltrate. Pete saw her disappointment and looked into the pot. 'I like it like that.'

'It's not supposed to be sticky though. I've done it wrong again.'

'No, but I like it like that.'

He was trying to make her feel better and it wasn't his job.

'It'll taste lovely anyway,' she said, sounding more cheerful than she felt, 'because you made it.'

'Yeah.' He nodded, climbing down from the kitchen chair. 'I'm good at that.'

Across the kitchen Mary Ann caught her eye and smiled at Pete's casual confidence. She looked neat and small, never taking up any more space than she needed to. She still lived like a nun: still got up before clubbers went to bed to begin her morning round of prayers. The bedroom looked even more spartan than it had when Dub slept in there. She laid her prayer books and rosaries out on a chair, owned three dresses and a jumper, some changes of underwear but no make-up or favourite shampoos or books or records, none of the flummery of a normal life.

'Auntie Mary,' said Pete, sitting down next to her at the table, 'you and me, we'll grate the cheese.'

Paddy looked a warning over at him and he giggled. 'I'm not to use the grater,' he explained, 'in case I cut myself. You do it and I'll order ye about.'

Mary-Ann glanced at the clock. 'Is it not a bit early?'

'Naw, go ahead,' said Paddy. 'We'll be eating any minute.'

As she spoke she heard the key in the door and Pete leaped to his feet, bolting out to the hallway, and then he froze, standing framed in the doorway, staring at the front door.

'Hiya,' he said absently.

'Hiya.' The voice was deep and shy compared to Pete's.

'Right, wee man?' Dub appeared, scooping Pete up and swinging him about a bit, dropping him to his feet and giving a mock stagger at the weight of him. 'This is your cousin Callum.'

'Hiya,' said Pete again.

'Hiya.' Callum looked nervously around the hall until he spotted Paddy in the kitchen.

She blinked slowly and her smile widened. 'All right, son?'

Callum smiled back. He was.

THE END